BACK IN FUNERAL BLACK

The Chronicles of Henry Mack

By Amy Hopkins

BACK IN FUNERAL BLACK

ISBN 978-0-6489761-5-8

Cover design by Kelley York at Sleepy Fox Studios

Published by Amy Hopkins 2023
Publishing services provided by Salem Shaw 2023

In loving memory of Howard James Sinnott, beloved father, avid supporter, endless jokester.
I miss you so much.

Author's Note

Writing a book is never an easy or a simple task, but it has never been harder than in the last two years. I know I'm not the only one who still bears the weight of what has passed, but I hope for all of you, that weight is slowly lifting. I hope the skies are clearing, the flowers are showing their tiny buds, and that in some tiny way, hope flares once again.

I cannot begin this story without first thanking those who helped create it.

Danuta, dear friend, constant carrot-dangler, and terribly helpful editor and story consultant. Without you, this book would have emerged some months earlier – although it would not have been this book, but an inferior version. Thank you for pushing me to become a better writer, and for the people you've brought to me in this journey.

To the Women of Outstanding Promise – you know who you are. I love you all, and thank you.

To Rascals and Dear Hearts, for getting me through a rotten year and introducing me to a wonderful community of friends. For helping me rediscover the unfettered joy of reading for fun. For the clockwork octpi, the badly made cakes, the badly fried eggs, and company while jailed for sleep crimes. ILY.

Thea, my editor, word-finder, comma-herder. I can't tell you how much I appreciate not only your technical knowledge but your kind words and support.

Kelley, who has been endlessly patient with my drawn-out schedule. She'd made three covers for this series already, so readers, it's thanks to her that you will definitely, 100% be seeing more of Henry! She has brought him to life in a way that bettered my expectations and makes me so excited to share the final products with you, readers. Thanks for your patience, and for the forty-nine-million times you have helped me log into my portal.

Speaking of readers, some of the first to put eyes on Henry and the gang were instrumental in making sure it's a story worth reading, and one that truly represents my vision. Chris, Leslie, Ron, Elisabeth, Anne, Ella, KT, Susan, Michael, Stace, and anyone I may have missed. You guys gifted me your time and effort, for which I am most grateful.

Not for Henry, but Suzanne, all the thanks in the world for helping me get Talented to print at long last. You reminded me why I do this.

And finally, but most importantly, to you. To all the people reading this book, whether you've been with me on this journey since my very first books in 2016, or if you pick this up on sale one day having never heard of me. Thank you. Thank you for being a reader, for supporting authors, for helping people like me do what we love. It's for you guys that we do it, and it's you guys that make it entirely worth doing.

Chapters

Chapter One

Having a zombie for a sister might seem like a bad thing, but it can have its upsides, too. Especially if she's got a particular talent for scaring the willies out of people.

It was two in the morning, freezing cold, and black as pitch beyond the weak glowf the streetlight above my head. It cast a circle of light on the newly laid road, glinting off the purple gloss of my '71 Dodge Demon, and highlighting the steam that clouded around my face with each breath.

I normally avoided jobs called in at such unsavoury times of the morning, but this one was different; I was in the pursuit of stolen goods. And not just any stolen goods — no, the woman I had sent my sister to visit had, we believed, come into the possession of a very magical and potentially dangerous stolen item. I had been tasked to retrieve it by Fergus, a purveyor of such things and a very dear friend.

The details I had were scant. I knew it was an item of great power, stolen by someone with connections to organised crime. It had then — somehow — ended up at the address Fergus had given me a day earlier. He stressed that the new owner of the item probably hadn't stolen it, and very likely had no idea what it was.

Which made two of us. Rather than confront the woman and ask if she had come across a book, or possibly a candle, perhaps a pebble or even a big stick; and rather than risk tipping anyone off that we knew about the theft, I had decided to obtain it in a more creative manner. Put simply, we would scare it out of her… and get paid in the process.

A quick glance at my phone said it was six degrees out. Bollocks. I shivered in my leather jacket and snorted sceptically — it was cold as the devil's balls out here and if it wasn't freezing, it could only be a few degrees off. "Come on, Ollie." I stamped my feet, wishing I had brought my heavier trench coat. "How bloody long does it take to scare a lass?"

A scream echoed, distant but clear in the quiet estate. It cut through the night, high-pitched and feminine, laced with the panic of one in true distress. A twinge of guilt needled my conscience, but I continued to wait, reassuring myself that the woman wasn't actually in any danger. *Not long now. She just has to call it in.*

Another minute passed and I checked my phone again, tweaking the volume to make sure I hadn't accidentally put it on mute. The screamer let out another one, then a third. I can't deny I was starting to worry about that. "Stop faffing about, Ollie." More steam clouded around my words as I muttered them. "Let the lady get her phone before she falls over and dies of fright."

I checked over my shoulder to make sure no one was loitering around. A bad habit, that. A man shouldn't be talking to himself out loud, it's not good for his image. Not that mine could drop much further. There was a rip in my jeans from my last adventure, and my jacket — beloved though it was — had a smear of mud on the sleeve. It wasn't the kind of thing that bothered me, but Ollie would pitch a fit if she noticed. Just as I was contemplating how to clean it off, my phone finally rang.

I clicked the green button and silenced the AC/DC song blaring out of the wee speaker and lifted it to my ear. "Aye, this is Henry MacDonald, Catch and Dispatch officer code 691-912. What can I do you for?"

"Mr MacDonald, we have an incident in the Coatbridge area. Are you free to attend?" The voice on the other end — someone in the emergency dispatch office — was an older woman with a brisk, no-nonsense tone.

"Heather! Back on the phones, I see. I missed you, love."

"As much as I love your natter, Mack, need I remind you these calls are recorded?"

I chuckled. Heather was one of the best at her job, and she wouldn't let me forget it. "Coatbridge, was it? Why, I just happen to be in the area with nothing else to do. What have we got?"

"One intruder of Otherworldly origins, small build, inside a residential building. A woman is trapped inside. This one is a code red, MacDonald."

"Aye, sounds bad." I hummed a note of sympathy, still leaning on the car. "I'm already on my way."

"You'll need the address," Heather noted dryly. She rattled it off, then asked to connect me to the caller.

"Go ahead." I waited while the line went silent, clicked a couple of times, then buzzed back to life.

"Is someone there? Oh, god, don't tell me you're gone."

"No, ma'am, I'm here. My name is Henry. I'll be right to you in a jiffy so don't fret. Now, what seems to be the situation."

"There's a — God I'm losing my mind and I don't know what —"

I cut short the woman's panic. "I take it by your current anxiety you are having a wee issue with one of the previously deceased?"

"Yes. Yes, that's what it is. Help me! Oh god. Oh, God, it's coming closer!"

"I'll be right there, ma'am, just hold on a wee bit longer." I pushed myself off the car and opened the door to haul out my staff. It was about what you would expect of a Scottish wizard — six foot tall, made of ancient, polished wood and topped with an amber stone caught in a twisted net of wires. I gripped it in one hand, my other holding the phone to one ear, and hip-checked the door closed. Now set, I sauntered down the empty street. "Can you get to your kitchen, ma'am?"

"My kitchen?" The caller's voice was shallow over the sound of running feet. A door slammed. "I... I think so. Why? What's in my kitchen?"

"Well, unless you're on one of those awful low-sodium diets, I imagine you'll find a bit of salt, aye?"

"Yes, I have salt."

My staff tapped the ground as I walked. I passed three houses in various stages of construction, and another that seemed finished, but vacant. The next house still held the feel of a new build, but a crooked curtain and a soft glow from an upstairs window revealed the new owners had moved in.

"Right. Now, what I want you to do is get that salt and pour it in a circle. You want it big enough to step in. Can you do that for me?"

"I'll try." A door squeaked open and clicked shut, softly this time. "It's too dark. I can't see!" The voice bordered on hysteria now and another flutter of guilt began to tickle my jaded soul.

"You have a phone in your hand, aye?" I prodded.

"I — yes!" Her voice became muffled, and I guessed she was using the screen glow to find her way around rather than the torch on the back. I could hear the quick slap of bare feet on hard floor before she spoke again. "I've got the salt!"

"Are you spreading it around? Once the circle is closed, just hop on in."

"It's done." She took a wavering breath. "I'm safe now?"

I stifled a chuckle. Bloody fools. They'd believe anything you'd tell 'em if you say it in the right voice. "Safe enough. I'll be there in a jiffy, love. Just sit tight and old Henry Mack will be right along to save your a — uh, your skin." I held the button down on the side of my phone to turn it off and slid it safely away in my pocket.

In fact, I was there. I strode up to the bland, white door of the bland, beige house in the bland, cookie-cutter suburb, and I rang the doorbell. "Henry MacDonald at your service. Could all persons who are recently deceased please stand back and stay out of trouble while I let myself in."

I pushed against the door. It was locked. I thought about asking my wee dead sister to let me in, but I thought that might be bit of a stretch. Instead, I resigned myself to the inevitable.

"Nothing for it," I muttered under my breath.

All around me, remnants of power lurked in the shadows, left there by fae creatures, old spirits, and ancient beings who had channelled the magic from the Otherworld into ours. Every footprint, every spoken word, every movement made by something from there left a tiny scatter of magic behind, waiting to be scooped up by one such as myself and crafted into a tool. I harnessed what lay around me, sketched a symbol in the air with my finger, and pressed my other hand against the lock.

It sprang open with a click and for a moment, I thought it might have just unlocked instead of —

Pop. The tiny explosion inside the locking mechanism sent a wee screw flying out and a few splinters of wood bulged over the handle. "Bloody hell. I never get that stupid spell right."

I used the tip of my staff to push the door all the way open, then reached for the light switch nearby. It wasn't hard to find. Never is, in a building like this. The estate was typical of new developers, full of identical houses with no personality.

Nothing happened when I flicked the switch. "Good girl." Ollie had flipped the safety to keep my magic from overloading the circuit-boards. Not that I *intended* to do that. Accidents happen, though.

They seem to happen to me quite a bit, actually. A spell with too much juice, or one that darts sideways just as I throw it. I pushed the thought aside. I knew why my magic was lopsided but there wasn't a damn thing I could do about it.

"My name is Henry MacDonald, and I work with the nice folk over at the police station. If any beings of dubious life status are in the building, I must insist you come forward and surrender yourself to me now." Formalities complete, I crept in past the broken door and peered up the stairs. *Silence.* I veered to the right, towards what I guessed was the living room. It was cloaked in shadows, but I could make out the furniture — or the lack of. All this lass seemed to own were boxes. "Where are you, you wee shite? Come out to play with old Henry."

A scuffling sound drew me back to the stairs. "What the bloody hell are you doing up there?" I darted up as softly as I could, my footsteps muffled by the thick carpet.

Ugh. Carpeted stairs. My worst bloody nightmare, that.

Another sound, this time like a strangled gasp, led me forward. I took a moment to check the room at the top. Empty, except for a mattress leaning against a wall with the disassembled bed in pieces beside it, more boxes, and a giant pile of clothes in a heap. Not a stolen relic in sight, unless the ancients had begun imbuing petrochemicals with magic that had survived the process of being manufactured into pleather skirts.

I backed out onto the landing. Half a dozen paintings had been stacked against the balustrade and I stopped for a quick gander. Nothing interesting, just those generic prints of hairy cows and pretty beaches that you get for a few bob at the local discount shop. Clearly, the owner of the house had about as much taste as the boring executives who designed the outside.

I checked the second bedroom. Just a desk and a chair and... you guessed it, more boxes. The tiny bathroom wasn't big enough to hide a penny, let alone a person. Bedroom number three was bare as a baby's arse. Just the main bedroom to go. I took myself a deep breath and pushed the door open.

"Ollie?" I whispered. The room was empty. "Where in the Otherworld are you?"

This was getting tedious. I stomped into the room and peeked in the tiny ensuite. It was even smaller than the other bathroom. Confused, I took myself back out to the landing and stood at the top of the stairs, listening carefully.

Not carefully enough. Two small hands grabbed the back of my jacket and gave it an almighty shove, and I tumbled down the stairs.

"Och! You bastard shite-goblin!" I yelled, trying to get my feet back under me. Easier said than done — one foot was stuck between the spindles of the balustrade. I yanked it free, ignoring the sudden pain in my ankle joint, and clambered up. "I'll get you for that, you festering lump o' dead flesh. I'll set the bloody red caps onto you, and I'll shove your howlin' face down the lavvie when I catch you!"

My rage overtook my ability to speak as I thundered up the stairs. My sister, the zombie, loitered at the end of the landing. She stared at me with dead eyes and a cheeky grin. Her dark hair was lank and greasy, thanks to a concoction of oils and dye, and a smudge of makeup accentuated the dark circles beneath her eyes. She was a child and only came up to my chest, but she had the strength of a water horse and the speed of an angry demon. Though her presence here was a ploy, she wasn't going to make this easy for me.

I darted forward, a spell already on my lips. Too late. Ollie sprang over the side and landed on the bottom step, just like a cat jumping off the mantle after it's pushed over all your kick knacks and pretties.

Blowing out a long breath, I took off after her. "I don't like to bloody run, you know!" I called down.

Not that Ollie cared. She waited until I was close enough to see her stick a mouldy tongue out, then ducked around the corner. I dashed after her, only to go sprawling on my face when I tripped on the pasty, white foot jutting out in front of me.

"Fecking little..." I reminded myself this was no time for words, except for the ones that would put a bloody end to the shenanigans. This time, I drew my sigils *before* I ran after the cheeky little gobshite.

My hands glowed with magic channelled from the spirits of the Otherworld. They shone bright enough to light the room. Instead of running, I stepped carefully, looking out for traps and surprises. There were none, until the woman in the kitchen let out another ear-splitting shriek.

"She's in here!"

Now, I ran, almost tripping on a chair in the dining room as I bolted for the kitchen, the zombie, and the poor victim. Though I can't say my ears wouldn't have appreciated the 'poor victim' shutting her blow hole for just a moment.

My victim cowered in one corner, Ollie looming over her. Well, as much as someone half your height can loom, anyway. I used a glowing finger to draw a circle in the air, and the magic lit it up like the neon sign outside the local watering hole. I added sigils to the circle and they hung in the air, glowing images suspended in a ring of light.

When she saw what I was doing, Ollie let out a dramatic screech. She launched herself at me, her jagged, torn fingernails reaching for my throat. With a flourish, I finished the spell and pulled the circle of light toward her.

She fell into it and the circle shrank, tightening around her and pinning her arms to her sides. She let out a wail of frustration and gnashed her teeth, which were, I have to admit, pretty damn clean for someone who's been dead for twenty years.

"Shut your pie hole, you rotting corpse." I nodded at the woman trembling in the corner. Thankfully, she had stopped screaming. "See what you did? You've gone and scared this poor lassie."

Ollie growled and then roared at me, making a show of her struggles. I slowed my breathing and muttered another spell. Silence fell. Not because my sister wasn't trying to gargle obscenities at me, but because I'd cloaked her in a spell that muffled the noise.

"Well, looks like that's taken care of." I brushed my hands together and grinned at the lass in the salt circle.

She was short, blonde, and white as a sheet of fancy three-ply bog roll. Noticing my scrutiny, the woman smoothed down the front of her fluffy, hot-pink dressing gown, as if it might make her look a wee bit more respectable. She did not, however, address the frizz of hair matted to one side of her head, and there was nothing she could have done about the streaks of half-cleaned mascara that lined the left side of her face.

Pretending I hadn't noticed her dishevelled appearance, I stuck my hand out. "I suppose I should introduce myself. I'm Henry Augustus MacDonald. You can call me Mack."

Despite her fear, the woman's eyes narrowed. "You and everyone else in Glasgow."

That pulled me up short for a moment. "Well, that's true," I admitted. There were, after all, more 'MacSomethings' in the Glaswegian phone book than there were anything else. "But only *one* Mack is descended from the one and only Black Donald."

It was a startling revelation. At least, it should have been. "Oh, off with you." She rolled her eyes. "You're not descended from the bloody devil, you tosser."

"I am too!" I pointed at my catch for proof. "And I just took down an angry spectre in your kitchen, thank you very much. Do you think any old MacDonald could do that?"

"I suppose not." She quietened, perhaps realising that if I had taken a spectre down, I could probably let it back up again, too. "My name is Claire." She paused, then offered a tentative hand. "Claire McAdams."

"Lovely to meet you, Claire. Now, do you care to tell me why you're getting visits from the previously deceased?"

She waited, then threw her hands up. "You think I know? I've never even seen a zombie before. Hell, I knew people were banging on about ghosts lately but zombies? It's like a bad fecking horror movie!"

"Technically, this one is a ghost," I lied. "It's just a little firmer than most on account of its age. Definitely a ghost, though."

Claire looked unconvinced but kept any arguments quiet. Not that it really mattered — Depending on the strength of the ghost or spectre, some of them were pretty bloody corporeal and could easily be confused with a reanimated body.

"So, you've had no dealings with shady individuals lately?" I asked. Claire shook her head. "You've not got a teenager somewhere who's been snorting huff and playing around with arcane rituals?"

That got her attention. She stood straighter and wrapped her fluffy gown a little tighter across her front. "A teenager? How bloody old do you think I am?"

"It was just a question, love."

"Well, I don't have kids. My boyfriend hasn't moved in yet, either. It's just me."

"If it's not something you've done, maybe it's something you've got." I paused, waiting for her brain to click over before prompting her a little harder. "Any new antiques? Old coins, funny stone, mouldy statues..." I waited, hoping I wouldn't have to jump to plan B. Mostly because there wasn't a plan B... "No paintings?"

Her eyes widened. "Yes! Marcus gave me a musty old tapestry. He said it'd look nice hung in the loo. It's ugly as a dog's arse, if you ask me." Her hand went to her chest. "Are you saying that thing could have led this..." She gestured at the trussed-up corpse on her kitchen floor. "This *thing* to my house?"

"Anything is possible." I shrugged, downplaying my excitement. "How about I take a wee look at it?"

"It's in my bedroom." She looked me up and down, no doubt taking in the mess on my jacket and the rips in my jeans. "You can wait for me down here."

I couldn't resist giving her a cheeky wink, which she ignored completely. While Claire trotted upstairs, I cocked a grin at Ollie. My silencing spell was still in effect, which made the hard glare and mouthed obscenities somewhat comical.

"Aye, you keep flapping your lips, love. We'll have you out of here in no time, then you can give me a piece of your mind."

"Can they talk?" Claire's question startled me. I hadn't heard her come downstairs. "That one only growled at me. I don't think it knows how to speak."

"Some of them," I explained, pointedly turning my back on the subject of discussion. "They can't hold a proper conversation, though. Spectres are mostly a bunch of primal emotions covered in goop. This one couldn't think her way out of a paper bag, really."

I looked back at a thud. The "spectre" — who could hear what we were saying perfectly well, had smacked her head on the wall beside her. The resulting noise was unaffected by my silencing spell. "Enough of that, you. Behave, or I'll string you up and give you a wash before I officially dispatch you." At Claire's confusion, I explained that the fleshier spirits hated all aspects of personal hygiene. "Their stench is awful to us, but they think they smell like roses."

Thud. Thud, thud.

"Right." Claire finally tore her eyes away from the undead child on her floor and held out a hand. In it she clutched a bit of cloth, rolled up into a wrinkled tube.

I took her offering and unrolled the fabric to examine the tapestry. It depicted a woman, old and haggard, brandishing a staff much like mine in one hand, and stirring a giant cauldron with the other. Her one red eye stood vibrantly against the blue-grey of her face and despite the muted tones of her grey dress and the brown plaid over her shoulders, the colours didn't seem to have faded at all. Three stylised birds stretched their wings out in the sky above her.

At least, that's what it looked like to the average, non-magical person. To me, it glowed. Not with the amber sparks of magic that drifted about me, but a swirling, ethereal green that dipped through the weaves of the cloth, pulsing with life. As I watched, the shifting light touched the hag's eye, turning it my way for a brief moment.

"Aye, this is your culprit. Do you know who this is, lass?" Claire hesitated, then shook her head. Good, because I was only taking a stab in the dark myself. "That's the Cailleach Bheur. Goddess, or witch, depending on who you listen to." I released the bottom edge, and the tapestry sprang back into a rolled cylinder. "It's her power that creates life, you know. There's a wee bit of magic in the piece that must be calling to them. Best you lock it up tight if you want to keep it, because this won't be your last visitor seeking it out."

"What?" Claire snatched away the hand she had reflexively held out to take the item back. "You mean... more of those monsters might come after it?"

"You said a man named Marcus gave it to you?" I probed, stuffing the cloth in my pocket.

Claire's face hardened. "He's my boyfriend. Or he was, the bloody wank. Fancy him getting his hands on something like that!"

"Do you know where he got it?" I asked.

She immediately clammed up. "No. Didn't ask."

"You could ask him now. How about we give *the bloody wank* a quick call?" I was pushing my luck, but I really wanted to know if Marcus, whoever he fecking was, knew he'd inadvertently stolen a bit of old magic.

Claire swallowed, clearly uncomfortable with my questions. "He's away... on a business trip. It's been a few days since he was last in touch."

I wondered if his 'business' was with the fine and upstanding Glaswegian police force, or more in the form of a board meeting with some deep-sea aquatic life.

"Well, no bother." Fergus could chase that loose end up. I grinned widely and stooped to pick up my writhing prize. I threw the wriggling zombie over my shoulder, being careful to keep her teeth away from my ears. "I'll make sure to dispose of this when I dispatch your wee friend here. Many thanks for your cooperation and please don't hesitate to call emergency again if you experience any future interruptions to your daily schedule by malignant spectres, malicious spirits, or manky spooks."

I'm not sure why Claire looked even less impressed with the idea of calling me again someday. Oh, well. My job here was done and I had a warm, dry bed waiting for me at home. And an ear chewing — possibly in the literal sense of the phrase.

I took my leave, giving Claire a cheery wave as I left.

Chapter Two

Once back at my car, I dropped my package unceremoniously on the ground. With a quick, one-handed gesture, I removed the spell keeping her silent.

" — to our great-great-grandfather himself, I'll bite your face off in your sleep and stitch your eyelids shut. And then, I'll —" Suddenly realising she was talking out loud, Olivia Mack, my sister, a member of the exclusive club of the previously deceased, clamped her mouth shut. She darted a glance around the quiet streets and, seeing she was in no danger of drawing attention, she started up again. "You called me *stupid*! Who helped you with your catch and dispatch qualification? Who filled the bloody paperwork out on your behalf, because your fecking handwriting looks like a drunk spider wiped its arse on the paper and you can't even remember your own bloody address half the bloody time?"

"Oi." I hushed her with a raised hand, then released the magical rope that pinned her arms. "Language, please. You're twelve!"

"Go suck a sacrificial goat." She flipped me the bird. "I might have been twelve when I died, but that was twenty years ago, arsehole. I'm the same fecking age you are."

"Aye? Then stop acting like a cranky bairn." I smiled widely to show her I was just joshing around, but she launched forward and tried to bite a chunk out of my arm. "Ach! You wee shite. Behave yourself, Ollie, or I'll tie you up again."

She scowled, but thought better of trying to attack me again. When she settled, her eyes flicked to my bulging pocket. "You checked it, right? It's definitely what Fergus sent us for?"

"Aye."

Ollie glared at me for a moment, then threw her hands up in frustration. "It's like talking to a lump of coal! Are you going to tell me why Fergus wanted that scrap of cloth so badly?"

"You weren't listening? I explained it all to Claire. Well, I was mostly guessing but it's the best I've got."

She gaped. "You *idiot*. Fergus sent you to fetch a bit of dangerous, ancient magic and you didn't ask a single bloody question?" Ollie heaved a sigh. "Of course you didn't."

Without responding to the implication that I was possibly not the smartest spell caster in Glasgow, I pulled out the fabric I had taken from Claire McAdams. The cold streetlight above did little to highlight the pattern, so I closed my eyes and drew upon the power of the spirit world. I funnelled it into one hand, then out of my palm in the form of a warm, glowing light. For once, it lit up just how I intended — no scorched eyeballs, no flickering shadows.

"Show off," Ollie muttered.

I didn't pull her up on that one. Twenty years, and the pain of losing her own magic upon her death hadn't faded one bit. Sure, Ollie could be a vicious wee brat, but she was my sister and I loved her dearly. Not to mention her condition was, in a roundabout way, my fault. I was, after all, the one who raised her from the dead.

"It has to be her." I traced the pattern of the tapestry with one hand. "Right?"

"They don't tend to tapestry pinstripe wallpaper, Henry." Ollie's tone was dry, but curiosity won out over her obstinate nonchalance. She leaned forward for a better look. "I don't know. That could be any old lady, really."

"An old lady stirring a pot," I pointed out. "Who, in the history of magic in Scotland, looks like a one-eyed hag and stirs a big old pot?"

It was a rhetorical question, but Ollie answered it with a defeated sigh. "The Cailleach Bheur. She who built the mountains and brings the winter." As her mind started ticking over the new information, one of her hands started tapping the fingers against her palm. It was a tic she'd had since childhood.

"And her eternal cauldron." I tucked the fabric back into my pocket as a few light drops of rain splashed my hand. The wet probably wouldn't hurt it. If it was true magic, it would be robust enough to weather a bit of... well, weather. Still, I had never seen anything quite like this before and it wouldn't hurt to be careful.

Magical relics tended to be scrolls, stone tablets, pretty gems, or jewellery. Occasionally, it came in the form of a big stick, like my staff, or some fossilised snail vomit. But a bit of lady's needlework? Not impossible, but surprising nonetheless. Luckily, I knew just the man to take it to. Doubly lucky, he also happened to be the man who had paid me to retrieve it.

"If her boyfriend isn't dead, he will be when she finds him," I commented as I slid into the driver's seat of the Demon. After switching off my phone — I didn't want any more emergency call outs tonight — I tossed it on the seat beside me. "She looked right pissed when she realised it was his fault she woke up with a spectre in her bed."

"She didn't make it that far." Ollie sat in the back seat, positioned so she could see me in the rear-view mirror. As she spoke she wriggled out of her tattered dress, then folded it neatly beside her. Under it, she wore her usual clothes – a t-shirt and tights, both carefully chosen for their soft fabric and smooth seams. She ducked down and then resurfaced, scrubbing at her face with a cloth. "Gods, Mack, I thought I'd never get out of that scratchy, horrible dress. Does the woman never get tired? She finally came up to start getting ready for bed, but I mustn't have given her enough time before I flipped the breakers."

As I pulled off the shoulder of the road and started the journey home, I recalled the smudged eye make-up Claire had sported.

"That's why she looked like a crooked panda?"

"Aye." Ollie recounted what had happened in my absence. "She was on her way downstairs to check why the power went out when she spotted me. I may or may not have been hanging from one of the upstairs curtain rods." She grinned proudly. "Thought of that one myself, I did."

"You used the upper level to get in?" I asked. It was Ollie's usual mode of leaving or entering a building without being seen. Zombies, you see, are incredibly strong and — contrary to what those silly computer games and tv shows will have you believe — they're also really bloody fast. A quick one or two-story jump was nothing to my sister.

"Aye," she confirmed. "People are so dumb. Just leaving windows and balconies open for any old jobber to walk in."

"Most jobbers would need a ladder," I pointed out. "That makes noise and calls attention."

"Fair. Anyway, she hollered a bit, then ran downstairs. I got there first, of course. She's not very bright, Mack. Don't people watch horror movies anymore?"

"Ollie," I said, my patience wearing thin. "You're getting distracted."

"Oh, right. Sorry. So, I chased her upstairs and she locked herself in the bathroom. Without her phone. I had to let her get to it, so I climbed back out the bedroom window and knocked on the one in the loo. Mack, she screamed so loud she almost scared *me*! And I'm fecking dead!" Laughter bubbled out of her, and I couldn't help but chuckle too. The image of a terrified Claire and an equally startled zombie looming over her lavatory would have been a sight indeed.

Ollie explained that once Claire had escaped the tiny bathroom, found her phone, and called for help, she had simply herded the woman around in circles until I arrived.

"Do you think she knew what it was, Mack?" Ollie asked.

It took me a moment to catch up to Ollie's change of subject. Sometimes it was like she'd already had half the conversation in her head and only said the last part out loud. "You mean the trinket we were sent for?" Remembering Claire's blank look when I asked her about magical items, I shook my head. "She didn't seem to. I think Fergus was right, it just got caught up in a bigger theft of boring shite like televisions and laptops. There's no proof, of course, so we need to be careful."

She chewed her lip, then quickly stopped when she realised. It wouldn't be the first chunk of flesh she had accidentally nibbled off, but she did try to keep herself in one piece. "I think you're right. Did you see all those boxes of stuff in her house?"

"Aye. The lass must have only just moved in."

"They weren't just moving boxes, Mack. Did you pay *any* attention?"

I had no idea what she was getting at. "No. Boxes are boxes, aren't they?"

Ollie snorted. "How many books and dinner plates can you pack in a box for a flat screen tv, Mack?"

"Oh." Perhaps I had been paying less attention than I thought.

"She had three brand new tv's, a new laptop, two new Gucci watches and four pairs of air pods." She shook her head again. "She's only got two ears, Mack. I checked!"

"It's a nice house," I said. "Maybe she's just got expensive tastes?"

"It's a nice house, aye, but not that nice." Ollie clicked her tongue, but its partially decomposed nature turned it into more of a slurping sound. "That's the sort of stuff you see in million-quid gaff, not a cookie cutter house in an estate like that one. I bet it was all stolen, Mack, every bit of it."

"Aye. It does seem likely, now you point it all out like that." And it made me feel a bit better for scaring the woman. "That's more or less what Fergus said, anyway." The next turn took me onto the motorway. This close to dawn, cars zipped by often enough to make me nervous. "Keep your head down, aye? Sun's nearly up and I don't want to get done for carting around an unsecured body. Did you know the fine for that is two hundred and fifty quid?"

"Of course I bloody know," Ollie protested. Still, she flopped over on the back seat and sprawled out comfortably. "I'm the one who helped you study for that test, remember?"

"Aye, how could I forget?" I let the sarcasm drip from my voice. "You've reminded me twice already tonight, and another three times earlier this week."

"And I'll keep reminding you as long as you keep asking stupid questions like that, you numpty." She sighed. "I can't wait to get home. A nice soft, pillow, warm, fluffy blanket and —"

Her words were cut off by the peep of a police sirens.

"Ahh, shite." They were behind me, so I knew they hadn't seen Ollie yet. If they did, it could make things very awkward.

"Mack... Did you fix that taillight I told you about two weeks ago?" She didn't wait for my answer. "I swear to Black Donald himself, you're as useless as tits on a bull!"

"In the boot with you, child." I pulled off the road slowly, angling my mirror so I could see the patrol car that pulled up behind me.

Ollie yanked down the folding seat and scrambled through into the boot. Before pulling it back up, she muttered, "Call me a bloody child again and I'll —"

This time, I cut her off myself. "Child! Boot, *now*!"

The seat slammed into place, and I thanked the old gods that I had installed it nine months ago. Transporting Ollie in the boot was uncomfortable for her but letting her sit in the car was risky for me. This gave us the best of both worlds. I killed the Demon's engine and pasted the most innocent smile I could muster onto my handsome face.

"Good morning to you, Officer," I beamed.

"Good morning, sir." The officer — Quinn, according to his name tag — was black, with short shaven hair that showed a propensity for curls, even though it was barely long enough to qualify as hair. He was clean, probably good looking, and professional. It wasn't until he spoke again that I realised how out of place his broad Australian accent was. "Were you aware that your back taillight is out? The one on the left."

"It is?" Shock laced my voice and I mentally awarded myself a BAFTA for my convincing performance. "I apologise, Officer

Quinn. I had no idea!"

Quinn just lifted an eyebrow. "Right."

Clearly, he needed a little more convincing. "After all, it's not like I can see my taillights while I'm driving, now, is it?" Something thudded and the officer glanced towards the back of my car.

"What was that?" he asked.

"What was what?" I shrugged, looking about. "I didn't hear anything, officer. But about that ticket — do you think, seeing as I really didn't know about the light, you could maybe let me off, just this once?"

Another thud. This time, followed by the crack of broken plastic. *I swear to every god of the underworld, you little gobshite, I'm going to strangle you back to death when we get home.* "Officer Quinn, I don't suppose we could wrap this up? Happy to take any ticket you might need to write, but I really do need to be going."

Bang, bang, bang. The car shuddered under the force of the small hands beating at the closed boot.

Officer Quinn drew back and pulled out his ASP. He flicked it and it expanded to its full length. "Oi, Martin!" Quinn yelled for his partner who was still in the police car, oblivious to Officer Quinn's sudden distress.

Seeing the ASP and the look of worry on his colleague's face, Officer Martin jumped out of the car to join his partner, extending his own weapon as a precaution. He wore the more familiar pasty-faced ruddiness of a native Scot, with a heavyset build and a large mole hanging from the side of his nose.

Not only did promising to pass on any beating that might occur onto my wee sister seem to be in poor taste, it wouldn't work. That bloody zombie strength meant she was awfully resistant to a good thwack. Instead, I muttered a vow to put the spell of silencing back on her head and leave it there for a week. Not being able to sass me would drive her bonkers.

"Out of the vehicle, sir." Quinn barked the order, his authority clear. "On the ground, face down, hands behind your head."

I took a slow breath and put my hands on the dash. "All right, all right. Seems there's been a wee misunderstanding here, boys."

"Get. Out. Of. Your. Car." Quinn pointed at the ground to emphasise his words.

I clambered out just in time for a few fat drops of rain to land on my head. The downpour we had escaped near Claire McAdam's house had followed us. Bloody great.

I followed the instructions I was given, carefully exiting my car and dropping to my knees. I lowered myself to lie on the damp ground and linked my fingers behind the back of my head. Meanwhile, the thumping from inside the boot of the Demon started up again.

"I really wouldn't open that if I were you," I said.

"One more word outta you and you'll be spittin' teeth for a week." Quinn stood over me, his weapon at the ready. "Martin, pop the boot."

For a moment I debated using brute, magical force to escape my rather unfortunate situation rather than trying to explain my way out. Then I decided that if I were arrested and held in a cell for a few days, leaving Ollie to rot in the car — or worse, face off against a professional dispatch team — it would probably serve her right. And, fighting back might get me out of spending the night in jail, but would only cause me bigger problems down the track.

So, I pressed my face into the cold, muddy grass by the motorway and waited.

I heard the boot click open. "Uhh, Dave?"

"Yeah, Jim?" My guard shuffled back, unwilling to step too far away from me, despite — or maybe because of — the sudden concern in his partner's voice. The sudden switch to first names surely didn't bode well for me.

"Dave, there's a dead body in here." His voice dropped. "What do we do?"

"Ahh, shit." Officer Quinn let out the kind of long-suffering sigh that only a copper facing an absolute mountain of paperwork could utter. "Call it in."

"I left my radio in the car." Officer Martin's voice was small. I guessed he was new on the job.

Quinn cursed again. "Then go and bloody get it!"

"Wait!" The last thing I needed was more police involvement. "She's not dead." I risked tipping my head up to give Martin a pleading look. It wouldn't work on Quinn, but perhaps this young lad might take pity on a pair of puppy dog eyes.

He screwed up his face, scepticism written on every freckled inch. "Looks pretty dead." He leaned his face back over the car and sniffed. "Smells pretty dead, too."

"Aye, but —"

"What do you mean, it *smells* dead?" Quinn snapped. "Did you check for a pulse? Sweet Jesus, Jim, if a vic dies in our care because you were too squeamish to check for a —"

"FECKING SHITE!" Jim jumped back, the blood dropping from his face quicker than a virgin's pants in front of a naked lass. "It moved. Dave, the body feckin' moved!"

"Stop stuffing around, Jim. It's either dead, or —" A limp hand flopped over the side, bloodless skin and jagged nails highlighted by the early morning sun. Four fingers waggled in a cheeky wave. "Oh."

"I tried to tell you." Craning my neck around to glare at Quinn, I waited for him to let me up. "She's not dead. Not anymore."

Officer Quinn wasn't going to back down lightly. "Officer Martin, is it secured?" he called.

"What?" Martin had backed away from the car and stood like he expected an entire football team to rush him at any moment.

"The gho — the previously deceased." Quinn groaned. "For crying out loud, watch the suspect, will you?" He strode over to the car and gingerly leaned inside. He reared back when Ollie shot up to a sitting position, growling.

Quinn swung his ASP and whimpered when it met her hand with all the force of a pencil hitting a brick wall. Ollie grabbed the weapon and yanked it out of his hand.

"Do you think I could maybe get up, now?" I asked Officer Martin.

"What?" The poor boy looked like he was about to wet himself. "No! Y-you're a suspect."

"Aye, but I'm the only damn one here with any chance of stopping that there ghostie from stringing your partner up by his baws, and then coming straight for you."

"Shite." Martin made no move to stop me, so I stood, careful not to startle him. He tore his eyes away from the scene unfolding in front of him — Quinn stumbling back, Ollie jumping to a crouch — long enough to meet mine. "Met'll have my arse for this."

"At least you'll still have one," I reassured him. I strode toward the car, conjured my light, and barked a command. I'd tell you what it was, but I don't remember it, probably because I'd just made it up on the spot.

It did the trick, though. Ollie went rigid and flopped back down, looking for all the world like a lifeless doll. I stormed over and slammed the boot closed.

"Section two-point-four of the responsible application of catch and dispatch requires the previously deceased be properly secured." Quinn pushed forward so that he was toe-to-toe with me. "That's a breach of your C&D permit, assuming you even *have* one. At a bare minimum, you're looking at a two-hundred and fifty pound fine and a suspended —"

"She *was* secured," I growled. "In the bloody boot of my bloody car!"

"And how the bloody hell were we supposed to know that?" Quinn's hot breath washed over my face as he yelled.

"I *told* you not to open it!" I threw out a hand, pointing to my car. "My permit is displayed as per regulation five-one-six. The boot of my car is warded to shite, making it an acceptable restraint as per regulation nine-oh-two. *You* disobeyed a direct request from a qualified, permitted C&D operative. *You* compromised the safe storage of a live PD. You want to take me in? I *dare* you. I canna wait to tell your superiors about your monumental screw up here, and ask what the hell kind of training they've given their officers on the appropriate procedures regarding catch and dispatch operational matters."

Quinn stepped back and cleared his throat. "That wouldn't be a bad idea, actually."

"What?" His sudden change of tack almost gave me whiplash.

Quinn shrugged. "The only training they gave us was a bunch

of useless PowerPoint presentations. That's half an hour of my life I'll never get back. I've never even *seen* a catch and dispatch permit, let alone an actual member of the previously deceased. I didn't think they were so... meaty. They send us out here with no preparation, bugger all information and nothing but a pointy bloody stick to defend ourselves with!" He finished his explosive rant and wilted a little. He stuck out a hand. "You have my most sincere apologies, Mister MacDonald. We regular cops appreciate what men like you do to keep the streets and graveyards of Glasgow safe."

I shook his hand, then quirked a cheeky grin. "Do you want to have a proper look?"

His eyes widened. "Really?"

"Aye!" I gestured Officer Martin over as well. I spoke loudly enough that Ollie would hear and play along. "Gentlemen, in the interests of educating the officers of the law, here is one previously deceased, apprehended at approximately five a.m. this morning after a short tussle inside the house of an innocent woman."

"Wait!" Martin yelped. "Won't she come after us? I don't want to lose me baws." He hunched a little as if trying to pre-emptively protect the precious package.

"I used a spell to immobilise the PD — that's shorthand for 'previously deceased', by the way. Much easier to use in the field." I added the last for Officer Martin, who waited until he thought I had looked away before snatching out his notebook and jotting that down.

I popped the boot open. Inside, Ollie stared up with bloodshot eyes. She rolled them dramatically but kept the rest of her body perfectly still.

"Now, the thing to remember when dealing with spectres, spirits and haunts is that they come in several variations. This here is a spectre, the strongest of the lot owing to the age of the soul." Thankfully, Ollie had chosen authentic mid-nineteenth century garb for her little appearance today, giving credence to my explanation. "Spirits are younger, usually tied to the location of their life or their death. They haven't levelled up to gain complete freedom yet. They have facial features and clothes, but they're a little more transparent."

"And haunts?" Martin asked, scribbling furiously as I spoke.

"The weakest. Usually moaning in attics or giving the grandkids the odd shiver, pushing about old photographs, that kind of thing."

"Why don't they lose power as they age?" Quinn asked.

I shrugged. "They do, initially. Haunts are fuelled by pettiness, or sometimes just concern for their loved ones. Once they see everyone is fine — or in the former case, take their frustration out — they fade to nothing. If, however, they have a *real* reason to survive, they stick around and mop up the residue left by other supernatural entities. There's a tipping point, see. If they can sustain their existence beyond those first few years, they can grow in strength rather than dwindle."

"How do we fight them?" Quinn had all the good questions and I flicked him an appraising look.

"You don't. At least, not by hitting it with a stick. They're bloody strong, and bloody fast. You can't take them on without a trained professional who can fight on their level. Trying to do so could turn fatal." Despite the inconvenience the two officers had caused to my day, they certainly didn't deserve to die. And they would, if they ever tried to hit a real spectre with a piddling wee stick like Officer Quinn had attempted earlier.

"If you see one, the best course of action is to freeze. Stay as still as you possibly can." I eyeballed the two men, who hung off every word that dropped off my lips. "They aren't very clever, but they're malicious bastards. Their instinct is to tear apart anything that moves. Their eyesight is poor and their hearing worse, so if you can manage to not run screaming, you actually have a pretty good chance of survival."

"Fat bloody chance of convincing a terrified crowd not to wail like banshees and start a stampede if they were faced with one of these," Quinn said ruefully.

"Aye." I knew we were both thinking of the same incident.

The previous year, three spectres had somehow found themselves in the middle of an impromptu football match in one of the villages. They had ripped through the players in moments, then gone on to attack the small crowd of spectators. It was just lucky the match had occurred at three in the morning — as matches often do when you're rip-roaring drunk — and there were no children attending. The small handful of people who had survived were those who had fainted from the sheer terror, or been scared stiff in the literal sense, unable to move, and therefore safe.

The three spectres had then wandered off into the nearby forest where they were later apprehended by a crack team of idiot catch and dispatch operatives. Some of those died too. Like I said, bunch of fecking idiots.

The absolute ineptitude of these so-called experts was what eventually led me to getting my own official licence in catch and dispatch. Sure, I broke half the damn rules in the stupid manual they gave me, but I was still alive.

"Look, the best thing you can do if you run into a situation like that is to get a halfway competent dispatcher on the scene as fast as you can." I nodded at Quinn. "Do what you can to keep them calm, but don't bloody risk yourself, matey."

Quinn lifted his chin proudly. "It's our job to protect people. No matter the cost."

"Aye." I couldn't help but admire his idiotic stubbornness. "You might even make a decent catcher yourself, if you're so inclined."

Quinn gave a self-conscious chuckle. "Nah. I don't have the balls."

"What about me?" Martin piped up. "Do you think I could train up and be a crack catcher?"

Quinn and I both burst into laughter at the same time. "You want to go catchin' cracks, you go do it on your own time, lad," Quinn told him. "Like I have to."

Realising what he'd said, Martin tried to hurriedly backtrack. Then, realising his superior officer might get offended if he protested too stridently, he gave up. He stomped back to the police car, cheeks flaming red. Meanwhile, I appraised the young copper in front of me with new eyes for a moment, before deciding he was just a bit too young for my tastes. That, and my last three relationships had ended in unmitigated disaster. It tended to happen when your taste runs to vampire queens and homicidal kelpies.

"Bloody hell," I said to Quinn. "If you've survived in Glasgow as a cop who's foreign, black *and* gay, you'll have the PD's running from you after a few weeks of solid training." I flicked a card from my sleeve. "But if you ever decide to go for it, promise me you won't do it through the tossers at the catch and dispatch headquarters. That bunch of useless fools couldn't catch a spook inside a locked box in the middle of the Kirk."

"It's true, then?" Quinn asked, his curiosity piqued. "You can ward them off with crosses and prayer?"

"Don't be daft," I said. "What's a wee couple of sticks going to do against a mindless killing machine? The only reason they go limp inside a proper church or a mosque is because they're cut off from the power they draw from. Religion isn't a weapon, just a stifling of power."

"The ability to take away one's power is a weapon in itself though," Quinn pointed out.

"Aye." I personally had no beef with the church, or any of the other newfangled religions the Romans dragged over here with them. As long as they stayed out of my business, I stayed out of theirs. Unless, of course, it meant a free feed and good booze. I'd convert to any religion for that.

Quinn examined my card, then carefully tucked it in his pocket. "I'll keep it in mind."

He turned to head back to the car where the young Officer Martin waited. A quick burst of static from the radio buzzed as Quinn opened the door, quickly muffled as he pulled it with a thud.

I closed the boot, jumped back in the driver's seat, and felt the soothing rumble of the Demon's engine when I turned the key. Go home, light the fire, and take a day-long nap, I told myself. The very thought of warmth and comfort weighed my eyelids down.

My moment of peace was interrupted by a knock on the window. Fine, I'll admit it — I nearly shat myself in fright. Seeing the look of concern on Quinn's face didn't help my nerves to settle.

I wound down the window. “Something wrong?” I asked.

“You might say that.” All traces of joviality had vanished. He wore the face of a police officer set to do a very particular type of job. My heart thudded. I had seen that face once before, when I was twelve.

“I’m sorry, mate. The S.O.P.D. had your name flagged in the system, they’ve been trying to get in touch all morning.” Quinn’s eyes darted away as he looked for the words that would deliver the blow. “It’s about Augustus McDonald.”

My stomach dropped and bounced nastily somewhere in the vicinity of the street below. “What about my Granda?”

Chapter Three

Officers David Quinn and Jim Martin drove behind me at a sedate pace, right up until I turned into the long driveway of my grandfather's estate. I had to give them props for that — Granda lived out in Coytland, a fair drive from Claire McAdams' house in Coatbridge. Though I wondered if maybe their instructions to track me down, and very politely request my presence at Granda's farmhouse had included a directive to make sure my hairy arse actually made it there without any detours first, I reassured myself that Officer Quinn was a top bloke and likely just looking out for my wellbeing.

My wellbeing was just fine. So the old bastard was dead. It wasn't like I'd miss him, even though he more or less raised me after my parents passed. I felt no grief, just a deep, numbing confusion that almost led me right past the all too familiar rusted letterbox and rutted gravel driveway that led to Granda's.

Claire's gaff may have been a damn sight bigger than my own one bedder in Glasgow proper, but it was nothing compared to the nine-bedroom farmhouse my Granda lived in. It wasn't just the house. A sizable annex, an old outbuilding, and some stables that had at some point been converted for Granda to use for his rituals and research made it look like a wee castle, if a little muddier. To get there involved a long meandering trek down a poorly maintained driveway. In bad weather — which, being Scotland, occurred three-hundred and sixty-four and a half days of the year — there was a risk of getting bogged, blocked by a herd of cows, or charged by a cranky old fart on a Clydesdale. With news of Granda's death, at least I didn't have to worry about that last one. I hoped.

Quinn gave me a bolstering toot of the horn as they cruised past. I watched them go in the side mirror, which is how I almost ran Detective Chief Inspector Annie Fife over. She darted out of the way, slipping in the mud and falling on her arse. She clambered back to her feet carefully, flicking big gobs of wet clay off her fingers. She used the back of one hand to wipe a small clod off her cheek and brush some damp red hair off her face. The lock of hair did not cooperate, instead springing back up into a curly frizz.

"Watch it, jobber!" she yelled. Then, she looked closer. "Ah, feck. Sorry, Mack."

"It's fine, Annie." I pulled up alongside her and wound the window down. She leaned in and I wondered again how such a tiny, wee lass could be so damned intimidating if she wanted to. Thankfully, this was not one of those times. "What's the Ice Cream Van doing here, anyway?"

"I'll bloody Ice Cream Van you." She hated my nickname for the Scottish Otherworld and Paranormal Enforcement Division, or, ScoOPED if you string it all together. Just because some uptight wanker in the department dropped a bunch of initials and made the official acronym S.O.P.D. to keep it from being at the arse end of every joke in the force, didn't mean I was going to treat it any more seriously than it deserved. Her usual scathing tone was softened with sympathy, though. "You okay, Mate?"

"I'm fine." Swallowing hard to dislodge a sudden lump, I shook my head. "Don't fuss at me, Fife. You know we never got along."

She raised a sceptical eyebrow. "He was your Granda, Mack. You can't fool —"

"Unless you're up there with bottles of whisky chanting a

dirge, you're here on official business," I insisted. "What's going on? Something got him. Something not human."

"He's on our list, Mack. A practitioner of notable strength, with numerous connections. Even if he fell off a bloody ladder, we'd be here." Annie tipped her head my way. "And we'll do the same for you one day, when you finally piss someone off enough that they remove your smart mouth from the rest of you by way of decapitation."

"Annie..." There was no doubt she was dodging my question.

Annie sighed and bit her lip. "It was technically a heart problem," she said with absolutely no confidence at all.

"What kind of heart problem?" I asked.

"The kind where it stops beating. Probably because it was on the wrong side of his ribcage." She winced at the harsh delivery of the news, but there was no kind way to drop news like that.

"Fecking hell." I closed my eyes and rested my head on the headrest of my seat. "Was it quick?"

"I hope so." She shrugged. "Without knowing exactly what happened, it's hard to say."

"I need to see." I grabbed my door handle but Annie put her hand against it.

"No, you don't. The coroner already has the body down at the S.O.P.D. lab." Annie's lips pressed together and she shook her head. "It was bad, Henry."

Her use of my first name threw me a little, but I wasn't giving in this easily. I unlatched the door and pushed it open a few inches. She didn't budge. "I can handle it, Annie. You know me. Tough as old boot leather."

"And a person of interest in this case." Annie shoved the door back, hard. "As much as I trust you, Mack, there are rules I have to follow."

"What?" I spat the word loaded with every bit of offence her comment deserved. "You really think I'm going around ripping hearts out of chests. And my own Granda? Come on, Annie. You know me better than that."

"You said it yourself, the two of you were on the outs." She folded her arms. "I know you fought with him before you moved out, and that you've barely seen him since."

"Bollocks. I may have had my problems with the old goat, but he was family. You know more than anyone how little I have left of that."

Annie softened. "I know. Look, Mack... I don't think you did it. I'd stake my job on it, in fact. But I can't let you in there. You *know* that."

"Then why in the hells did you ask me to come?" Anger bristled and I clamped down on it. Anger was dangerous. It made people do stupid things, messy things. Things they'd regret later.

Annie looked at me again, her usually sparkling green eyes now dark and sad. "When we couldn't get in touch, I got worried. I just wanted to see for myself that you're okay."

I couldn't argue with that, but I still managed a grumbled oath about meddling police officers.

Annie reached through the window and patted my arm. "We'll get them, Mack. Whoever did this, we'll get them. And you can be damned sure I won't let you screw up this crime scene and have the bastard off on a technicality."

"Who's to say that would be a bad thing," I muttered. Granda and I hadn't talked for a long time. We had our problems, sure. But if I could just get my hands around the neck of the bastard that killed him... "When you find out who did it, just slip me a name. I'll get you out of a whole lot of paperwork."

"Mack." Annie stared me down. "You're not going down that path. I won't let you." I carefully released my white knuckled grip on my steering wheel. Annie waited until my hands dropped to my lap before nodding. "Good lad."

I snorted. "I'm not a bloody two-year-old, lass."

"Then act like the grown up you claim to be." Annie stepped back from the car. "You look like you've been up all night. Go home, get some sleep. Aye? I'll come and see you at some point. Officially, first, but I'll make sure to check on you as a friend, too."

I stared ahead, my gaze stony.

Annie sighed. "You need your friends, Mack. Don't push us

away. Not now."

She was probably right, but I wasn't ready. Not yet. I just wanted to go home and wallow in my misery. "Maybe later."

"I'll hold you to it." Annie smiled gently. "Off home with you. We've got things covered here."

My eyes narrowed. No one in the ice cream van knew any magic. You couldn't actually believe in fairies and demons and still pass the psychological tests required to get into the elite arm of the police force that deals with such things. Bloody ridiculous if you ask me.

Instead, they hire consultants on a per-case basis. I had done my share of that. It's how I met Annie Fife, in fact. However, my opinion of most of the other consultants they used wasn't particularly high.

"Who's on it?"

Annie darted a glance away and her cheeks, already ruddy from the cold, flushed redder. "It's covered, Mack."

"Feck off, Annie." My heart dropped to my boots. "Not him."

"God, Mack, you're such a prick." Annie leaned closer and lowered her voice. "You know he's perfectly qualified."

"Qualified?" I choked out a laugh. "Rat-bait couldn't manage a locating spell to find his own baws. And that's not just because he doesn't bloody have any."

"Mack!" Fire flashed in Annie's eyes. "Don't call him that. I don't know what your problem is with Alan, but —"

"My *problem* is that he doesn't know what he's doing, to the point where he's a fecking danger to the public."

"My higher ups have never had an issue with him, Mack." There was an edge to Annie's words, a warning to back off... but any force it might have had was offset by the very words she used. The higher ups had never had an issue — but *she* had, I was sure of it.

"You know I'm right, don't you?" I hissed a breath through my teeth. "Annie, he's missing stuff. How many cases have you had that ran cold because he's as useful as a knitted condom?"

Annie smothered a smile. "Look, I don't have a choice in the matter. Believe me, I'd put you on this if I could, Mack. I'm not going to lie to you; I think this is shaping up to be a bad one." She held up her hands, wrists touching. "But my hands are tied."

I slammed a hand on my steering wheel in frustration. "Dammit, Annie!"

"Go home, Mack." The fight had gone out of her, and she gave a tired wave back down the driveway. "Go home and sleep. I'll call you as soon as we're done here. All right?"

Without answering I yanked the gear stick into reverse. Turning away to look behind me, I pushed the accelerator, leaving Annie looking after me. I didn't look back, so I don't know if she watched until I was out of sight. I hoped not. Whatever she thought I was, she was wrong.

Chapter Four

At some point during the journey home, Ollie climbed out of the boot. She huddled in the back seat, forehead pressed against the cold glass, left hand twitching open and closed in a silent clap. Her face was blank, expressionless. It didn't fool me – Ollie only shut down like that when she was in deep distress.

At any other time, I might have said something about her riding in the back seat during the day. Ollie might be better preserved than the average b-grade movie zombie, but she was still clearly dead. For once, though, there was something more important than the secrecy we had abided by for so many years.

We made it home without complications. I parked at the back of our flats, in a narrow alley that people rarely used, thanks to the overwhelming stench of rotten cabbage and dead fish. I had cultured it enough that it only needed the occasional top up of aged seafood and discarded fruit to maintain. Ollie threw open her door and burst out of the car. She crouched, then jumped into the air. The flat thud of her landing on the second-floor balcony was now so familiar that I didn't even look up to check she had made it safely.

By the time I let myself into our tiny flat, Ollie had curled herself into a ball in the corner of the kitchen, silent and still. I didn't approach her directly, worried she might lash out or flee. It had always been like that. Ollie, so strong and brave and kind, would close off to the world when she was upset, unable to tolerate the attention of those who loved her. As much as I loved her, it had taken me a long time to realise that the best way to show I cared was to accept that, instead of fighting against it.

Without speaking or looking at her, I walked into the kitchen to make a pot of tea. I stood near her, but not too close. After I put the kettle on to boil, dumped a scoop of leaves into the pot, and poured myself a wee shot of whisky to sip while I waited, Ollie sniffled.

She stared up at me through blank-faced tears. "Don't coddle me, Mack."

"Who said I was coddling anyone?" I grabbed another shot glass and poured a second drink. "Just making a nice cup of tea."

"Bollocks." Ollie stood and snatched the whisky from my outstretched hand. "You never heat the water on the stove top, you're too damn lazy. You always use magic."

I spread my arms. "You got me. Black Donald forbid I take the time to comfort my wee sister in her time of loss."

"I don't need your comfort." Her words were belied by the sleeve that scrubbed at her nose. "I need to know what we're going to do next."

"Next?" It hadn't occurred to me. "Well, I suppose we'll need a solicitor to —"

"We don't need a solicitor to avenge his death, Mack!"

"Avenge his death?" There was more chance of me kissing Black Donald's arse than letting my sister chase down someone with the power to take out Augustus MacDonald. He was old, true, but when you're in a profession like ours, you never really lose your skills. "Ollie, we're not going to do that."

The shot glass, now empty, missed my temple by less than a finger width, and only because I'd already started for the hissing kettle when she threw it.

"I knew you'd say that, you big, stupid arsehole."

"Easy, Oll. I know you're upset." This time I was prepared as Ollie shot across the kitchen. I managed to dodge to one side, but not before she grabbed the whisky bottle. She held it aloft, a furious glare pinning me down. "Come on, lass. Not the whisky?"

Apparently, yes, the whisky. She threw it and the bottle shattered on the wall behind my head. "*I'm* upset, Mack. Me. Just me. Why the bloody hell aren't *you*?" The second glass lived up to its name as it shot past me with enough force to leave a gaping hole in the flimsy plasterboard. "He was *your* Granda too."

"Aye, a Granda who treated me like the bloody devil himself." I regretted the words as soon as they were out, but it was too late. Ollie flew at me, hammering my chest with her fists, heaving sobs as she pummelled me. My quickly sketched protective sigil should have dampened her strikes enough that I could barely feel them, but like so many of my spells, it didn't quite work. "Dammit, Ollie! You're hurting me."

She jerked back. "Just say it, Mack. Say you hated him."

"I didn't hate him!" Fury, pain and grief welled up, eager for an outlet. "I didn't hate him, Ollie, but I couldn't forgive what he said."

"He had reasons!" Ollie screamed. "You threw a bloody tantrum like a child, just because he didn't agree with what you did."

"*Bullshit*." I slammed my hand against the kitchen counter. "He was selfish, Ollie. He only cared about his reputation, about what people would think if they knew his precious grandson had raised the dead."

"He was worried about me, Mack. He knew I'd never have a normal life, that no matter how you tried to justify it, I would end up rotting away in some room somewhere, too afraid to leave in case some bloody catcher saw me."

"And *are* you?" I growled, almost daring her to say it. "Are you rotting away in hiding, or are you alive, here, with your brother and another chance at living?"

She snatched the bait like a starving vampire next to a bleeding man. "I can't go out! I'm thirty-two and I'm stuck in the body of a twelve-year-old. I'll *never* grow up, never get a boyfriend or a job or a house of my own, and I can *never* do magic again! Do you think about any of *that* before you yanked me out of my grave?"

"I was twelve!" I bellowed. "Twelve, Ollie. And in one day I lost my Ma and Da, and I lost you. You weren't just my sister, you were a part of me. A part of me that I couldn't live without was gone and I could either use the only bloody spell I was any good at and try and heal the death out of you, or I could join you on the other side. I was ready to do it, too. I figured out how and everything. But I chose life instead, for both of us, and fuck you if you think I chose wrong."

Ollie stared, frozen with shock. "Mack —"

Snatching my jacket from where I'd dropped it on the way in, I stormed towards the door.

That was the problem with anger. It bubbles up and it spews out, and with it comes all the things you've been hiding for a lifetime, things you never intended to let see the light of day.

Chapter Five

When I turned up at The Wicked Stag twelve hours later, I looked like I hadn't slept in two days, smelled like I hadn't washed for three, and felt like I had just gone hand to hand with an angry zombie.

On all points... well. It was bloody lucky that Jack Mackintosh had low standards for his musicians, and that his patrons liked my music enough not to complain about the stink. At least, not in front of me.

Jack had owned the bar for longer than I had been alive. To be honest, I didn't know how far back his legacy went. He once made a reference to Granda's younger days, though Jack didn't look a spit over sixty-five himself. Deep creases lined his weathered face, and his tawny colouring contrasted with the crisp white of his hair. It was clipped short over his head, though his beard was left to run wild, curling around his face and trailing down to a few wisps ending somewhere below his belt.

"Henry Mack, I'm not going to ask why you look like you do." Jack poured a double shot of something blue and smoking. He slid it across the bar to land in my hand. "But I *am* going to ask why you're nearly an hour late for your set, and why the hell you're standing here instead of up there." He waved a hand at the empty stage.

"Had to go home and get my car." I didn't mention that it was because I'd spent the day trudging around East Kilbride, trying to wear off my anger by embedding it in ruts in the footpath. I tossed back the bitter drink and screwed up my face as a ripple of goosebumps washed over me. "What's this shite?"

"Something to wake you up." Jack shrugged. "If nothing else, it's touched up the bags under your eyes, you bloody hobo."

"Thanks." Rather than a stock standard liquor, the brew was one of Jack's special potions. I could feel it working almost immediately, infusing my bones with gentle energy, and sapping away the tiredness that had settled around me like a suffocating blanket.

"Get your arse up there, boy, before I tan it myself." Jack's mouth twisted into a crooked smile. "'Course, the crowd would like that just as much. Spilling the blood of a descendant of Old Black would give them a night to remember, be sure of that."

"I'm going now, Jack." Grabbing the guitar at my feet, I headed for the stage, gratefully noting that Jack — or one of his employees — had set up my equipment for me already. "I'll make it up to you, promise."

I muscled past a small group of women clustered by the bar, scooting away quickly when one tried to plant her hand on my rump. She looked up and bared pointed teeth in what I hoped was supposed to be a smile. Perfect lipstick lined her mouth, the deep red poking at the part of my brain that knew what danger looked like.

"I heard talk of blood." She shook out her platinum hair and for a moment, I was mesmerised. Despite the gloomy underground lights, it shone like the sun beamed down on her — not that it ever would. Vampires, or baobhan sith to give them their true name, lurked in the shadows of the night and preyed on weak, lustful men.

I may be a lot of things, but I'm not weak. "Find your own dinner, lass. I'm just here to play." I lifted my guitar and edged past them. The sisters let me pass, leaning their heads together and giggling.

"Bloody vampires." I didn't bother to keep my voice low. The women knew they wouldn't get fed here, Jack's rules around that were tight. No fae deals, no human meals, and especially, no steals. A visiting leprechaun had tried to break his last rule, once, and the story says his agonised squeals could be heard all the way from his Irish homeland.

Not that I put a lot of stock into the stories. Half of them were false, and the other half lies. There were nuggets of truth, yes. Like, you should never make a deal with a fairy unless you're right desperate, and that the fastest way to piss off a brownie was to give it clothes. But for the most part, it was best to take them with a pinch of salt.

Before playing, it was my habit to take a moment to watch the crowd. Apart from the blood suckers, I spotted three boadachan sabhaill, or wee old barn men. They were the most frequent patrons of the Stag, stopping by to get goosed on Jack's best Drambuie, and probably the best behaved.

Closer to the stage, a gorgeous woman with damp hair batted her eyes at me and blew a kiss. She was a ceasg, or mermaid. Bloody good-looking wenches, but they'll drown you as soon as date you. The ceasg ignored the trio of kelpies staring at her from across the room. Jack would have to send one of the barmaids over to mop the drool up after they left.

Otherwise, it seemed there were few people of note in the crowd tonight. I spotted three fuath, but they knew better than to cause mischief here, and a half-dozen grey-skinned glaistig.

At the fringes, lurked a scatter of humans. They would all have connections with the Otherworld somehow, or they wouldn't have known about the Stag. Hidden by magic, and locked to those without an invitation, the Wicked Stag was one of the few safe places for us creatures of legend to mingle with our own, even if 'our own' might be more dangerous than your average Glaswegian pub fight.

My fingers danced over the strings of my guitar and I closed my eyes, seeking the tune. It came to me quickly, trickling out through my fingers almost of its own accord. My breathing slowed. The chatter in the room softened as the attention turned my way, but I paid that no heed. In that moment, my head, my heart, and my soul were with the music.

I took a breath and began to sing.

In the depths of the winter did we set sail, just out of sight of land,
When out of the waves a beauty sprang, with a tot and a knife in hand.
Deep do the waves of the ocean roll, cold do the rough winds blow.
We started the journey on top of the world, but soon we'll lie below.
She'll take us all below.

I crooned the words, my eyes locked on the ceasg as I sang. A slender eyebrow raised, perhaps because I had taken some liberties with the words to the old ballad, but the smile that touched her lips suggested she didn't mind so much. After all, the old folk song was written long before Henry Mack came along and had probably existed in a thousand other versions over the centuries.

The first that she took was the captain, a man who knew no fear;
He said, "Though I know my wife won't mourn, I hope she'll shed a tear."
Then three times 'round went our gallant ship, and three times 'round went she,
Three times 'round went our gallant ship, and she sank to the bottom of the sea.

The ceasg nodded in appreciation as I launched into the song's chorus. As my voice trailed off, my fingers plucked faster, a moody, complicated melody that matched the story of the sailor who gave his life to a ceasg, leaving his wife and family to mourn him.

I played for four hours, taking a quick stop for a bowl of

Jack's stew, otherwise breaking only for the occasional sip of water between songs. After a day like I'd had, my mouth craved whisky, but I knew I'd be under the table by my second drink. Not from the liquor mind you. I was just *really* bloody tired.

About three quarters of the way through my second set, I saw Jack staring at me. He wore a look of forlorn sadness and pity. Though he glanced away when he saw me looking, I knew the look was meant for me. I tripped over the next words of my song but saved the performance thanks to the bone-deep memories my hands had of playing it so many times before. I quickly caught myself and continued, and the watching crowd seemed none the wiser.

The short, silent exchange with Jack pulled me out of the reverie I usually sank into when playing a set. Music was the magic of my soul, a meditation unlike any that involved awkward leg positions and nauseating visualisation exercises. Tonight, I had been interrupted and though I was able to sink back into the state where my words and strumming required no conscious concentration, my mind still buzzed with questions.

Someone had told Jack about Granda, I'd bet my night's booking fee on it. But who, and how had they known? *If you have to ask that, you're a fool, Henry Mack.* I shrugged away the self-criticism. Jack knew every creature from the Otherworld that frequented Glasgow, and some of them had mysterious ways of knowing things they shouldn't. I hadn't seen anyone approach the bar while I played, though. If Jack had already known when I came in, he'd have said something.

My thoughts didn't take long to loop back to Ollie. I had barely said two words to her when I dashed up to the flat for my car keys. I saw the questions and recriminations burning on her tongue, but she had kept them to herself, probably because I was already running late. She knew my schedule better than I did and often pushed me out the door for a booking that had slipped my mind.

I considered staying at the bar until sunup. Ollie might have given up waiting for me by then, and I would be able to sneak in and catch a short kip before sneaking back out again. Of course, I was so bloody tired that I might end up snoring my way through the wee hours with my face planted firmly on Jack's bar. I knew from experience that was a fast way to end up in the gutter at dawn. Then again, a night sleeping rough seemed like a fair trade for avoiding Ollie's anguish for one more day.

The final few notes drifted away from the strings of my guitar. A smattering of applause pulled me back to the present. I stood, gave a short bow, and set my instrument down. Ignoring the trio of barn men who clamoured for one more song, I made my way to the bar.

Before I could get there, a pretty, young bean sith sashayed in front of me as she tucked something into the top of her dress. Her ginger hair was long enough that the tips brushed the backs of her thighs, just below the edge of her skin-tight green dress. Which was not to say her hair was long so much as that her dress was very, very short.

"Favour for a song, wizard?" Her lips turned up in a cheeky smile.

Snorting, I edged around her. "Do I look like an eejit?"

She giggled, a throaty sound that made my feet tingle. "Ye look like a man that needs a favour."

"I..." I could think of a few favours this lass could grant me. In my mind, I ran my hand up her naked legs, pushed her dress — I shook my head, channelling a wee bit of magic to clear it.

Her magic was subtle, but effective. Once I had engaged my sight and pushed her fae witchery away, I immediately found her less attractive. Not that she wasn't gorgeous, mind you — but now she was just 'pretty girl' gorgeous, not 'magically powered, irresistible seductress' gorgeous.

"Not tonight, then?" She tinkled her hand in a wave and turned her body, though her head angled back so that she was still looking at me.

I studiously kept my eyes on her face, not the assets she was cleverly displaying. "Not tonight, lass." Not ever, I silently amended. It wouldn't do to say that aloud. Bean sith exuded the kind of pride and vanity only the younger women of the fairy race could. One day, perhaps in a year or perhaps in a hundred, she would age into a haggard old woman; but until then, she would remain youthful and gorgeous, and she bloody well knew it.

Jack saved me. He muscled his way past the fairy and grabbed my arm. "Mack," he chastised. "Why didn't you tell me about your Granda? You could have had the night off."

I shrugged. "Not like it would have changed anything. And who would have played?"

Jack shook his head. "I could have called Frankie."

"Frankie?" I barked a laugh. "That broad has a voice like a rusty hinge. Do me a favour and if I ever don't show, just shove the microphone next to the receiver and let it squeal before you replace me with Frankie."

"Mack, you're deflecting. Come on. Up to the bar with you, and I'll pour us his favourite."

I dutifully followed Jack, though every cell in my body shouted in protest. I would have one drink, say something nice about the old goat to his friend, and then I would leave.

Seven shots of top shelf whisky later, I was leaned over the bar, telling Jack about the time I had swapped out Granda's best frog-stone for a marble. He then attempted to use it in a demonstration that was meant to teach me how to harness a form-taking spirit. Instead, it had ended in a pungent eruption of burnt hogweed seed.

Jack cackled and slapped his hand on the counter before pouring another shot. I raised a wary eyebrow at it. "Jack, what the feck are you feeding me now? It's purple!"

"Aye." Jack gave a knowing nod. "But you're about to fall off your stool, Henry. You need a wee bit o' sobering up before you go home to your wee siùir."

"My sister can look after her bloody self." I shoved the potion away. "I'm no' goin' home tonight."

Jack scowled. "You two fighting again?"

"Fightin'? Nah. She's just bein' a wee bampot over..." I couldn't say it out loud.

Jack had no such reluctance. "Over the tragic loss of her Granda who raised her? The loss her bràthair should be helping her cope with?"

"Don't you feckin' Gaelic me, you dobber." I snatched up the bottle we had been drinking from earlier and put the mouth to my lips. In one long pull, I emptied it. "And before you —" I swayed. My feet tried to catch me but somehow, they had gone numb. As I stumbled to my knees, I managed a lopsided glare towards Jack. "You prick. You spiked mah drink?"

And then, I passed out.

When I came too, Jack was leaning over me in the back seat of the Devil. The tiny glass bottle in his hand was empty and a foul taste lined my mouth.

"Ach!" I lurched forwards and spat on the ground. When I looked up, I saw we had parked in my usual spot behind the block of flats. "You fecking shite, Jack!"

"You need to take better care of her, Mack." Jack shoved me back into the car. His grip was strong — stronger than mine, certainly.

"She's no child, Jack, she can take care of her own self."

"I mean it!" The old man pushed his face closer, and I saw into his eyes. Not the icy blue of an ageing bartender, but a whirling, sparkling vortex of frozen water and fae magic.

"What are you?" The words slipped out, whispered in muddled awe.

Jack sniffed, then released my shirt. "Bit o' this, bit o' that." He shrugged. "Don't quite know myself, actually. But sometimes I *see* things, Henry. Usually just wee, silly things. Sometimes it's big things, like your face when you heard your Granda had died. It came over me while you were playing."

"What did you see about Ollie?" I growled. Whatever squabble we might be having, if Ollie was in danger, I would spit hellfire and throw brimstone to keep her safe.

"A storm is coming, Mack." Jack rubbed his face. "More than a storm. A period of dark and unrest, the like of which your generation has never known, and your wee sister is standing right at the centre of it all."

"Ollie?"

"Aye." Jack sighed. "She'll either save us from the tempest, or she'll be the one to call it. Maybe both. It's too early to tell."

"Well, that's just great." I reached for the doorframe and awkwardly climbed out of the car. "Hold on a moment. Ollie can't call a storm — she's got no magic."

"I saw what I saw, Mack."

"Then… there's a way." The muddled cogs of my brain ground to life. "A way to bring her back properly. Jack, this is what I've been looking for since she died!"

"You ever heard the phrase be careful what you wish for?" Jack held up a hand to halt my angry retort. "I know, lad. I'd give my own life for your wee sister, and you know it. But you have to be careful, for her sake as much as everyone else."

"How, Jack?" I was ready to drop to my knees and beg. "How do I do it?"

"I wish I knew." Jack shook his head. "Sorry, friend."

"Don't be. If there's a way, I'll find it." Something warm spread through my chest, tingling my fingers and toes. *Hope.* It had been so long since I had felt it that I almost didn't recognise it.

I wasn't unfamiliar with the Sight, but it was usually given in trade with something seelie (or unseelie if you were especially brave) or it was a skill inherited from a parent or ancestor who was not-quite-human. Jack's words suggested he was of the second variety. It didn't lower my opinion of him one bit, but damned if I wouldn't use what information he could give me if it would help my sister.

"Aye, Mack, there's a way." Jack leaned against the brick wall and I joined him. He pulled out a small cigar and held it up. "Light?"

I obliged him by sketching a quick sigil and holding my finger against the tip. When it started to smoulder, I pulled away.

Jack sucked at it deeply then blew a cloud of smoke into the night air. "Do they know what happened to him?"

He could only be talking about Granda. "Well, it wasn't natural causes, that's for damn sure. Unless you count a violent attack from some kind of unseelie creature 'natural'?"

"Must've been a nasty shite to get the upper hand on old

Auggie. Who've the S.O.P.D. got on the case?"

"Alan Bloody Rat-fecker."

Jack groaned. "Rattray, huh. That gobshite couldn't consult his way into a hoor with a pocket full of bawbees."

I groaned. "Donald's arse, Jack. They're called sex workers now. And they're worth a mite more than a pocket of sixpence these days. How bloody old are you?"

He puffed at the cigar again. "I'm not that old. Or if I am, I don't feel it. You're right, though, it's too damn expensive to get laid these days." He waggled his eyebrows. "Unless you've finally taken that detective lass to your bed?"

I socked him in the arm. "Mind your bloody manners talking about my friends, arsehole. If Ollie heard you talking about a lass like that, she'd have your baws for breakfast."

"Aye, that she would." As if the thought made him uncomfortable, he reached down and adjusted himself. "Mack, I think it's all connected."

"What? Your baws? I bloody hope they're not rolling loose around in there."

"I meant your Granda and your sister, ye daft knob."

That pulled me up short. "What would make you think that?"

He chewed on the question for a bit before giving a non-committal shrug. "Just a feeling. No, more 'n that. It's the *taslaich*. It's like that deep ache in your bones when it's going to rain, or that bad feeling you get just before your phone rings with bad news." His eyes slid my way. "You know that one, don't you, boy."

"Aye." In my case, it had been three sleepless hours. I had gone to the birthday party of a classmate and spent the night. A nightmare woke me, a terrible dream of my sister screaming and calling my name. When I jolted awake, I tried to tell myself that's all it was — a bad dream. But the glowing red numbers on his alarm clock that said twelve minutes past four were etched into my brain. Johnny's Mam had come in just after sunup, picking her way past sleeping boys to beckon me out into the hall. When she passed me the phone, the news would change my life forever.

It was two more days before I learned I had woken at the exact time the coroner's report said my sister died.

"What's the link, then?" I asked. "Why would someone go after my family, wait fifteen years, then take out an old man who was near ready to kick the bucket anyway?"

I didn't really expect an answer. Even the Brahan seer himself often didn't know what form his prophecies would take, and he was said to be one of the best. Jack confirmed my hunch by stubbing his cigar on the wall and bidding me farewell. "I've told ye what I could, Henry Mack, and if I hear anything else, I'll tell ye that too. Watch yourself, lad. You know where to find me if you need me."

"Thanks." I waved the surly bartender off and steeled myself to face my sister.

Chapter Six

Lacking Ollie's acrobatic skills, I headed around to the front of the building. Water pooled in the gutter, rippling as I stomped through it. I'd have walked up on the footpath, but at some point after Jack left, I realised I was almost too tired to stand, let alone navigate the narrow path between the building and the road.

The streetlights flickered, then went out. I froze, skin prickling with awareness. Without waiting to see if something lurked in the shadows, I cast a spell of self-protection. Magic hung thick in the air around me, a result of the many spells I had cast in my flat or on my way to and from my car. I sucked it in, feeling my bones saturate. A few murmured words and some sigils etched in the air was all it took to create a hard layer over my skin.

Just as my fingers swiped the final glowing line, something hit me from behind. It sent me tumbling forward into the road, hands out to stop my fall. My skin didn't graze, so I knew I had finished the spell in time, I rolled forward, using the momentum to bring me back to my feet.

It was too bloody dark, I couldn't see. Another sigil lit the alley and I staggered in a circle, looking for my attacker. Just as my eyes slid past a slice of deep shadow, I thrust my hand out, a spell already on my lips. The creature that launched from the darkness squealed when I snatched it, sparks flying as flesh met fae.

In the split second I held it, I recognised it. Bright green eyes and ginger hair, with a scrap of vibrant cloth around her body; but now, the bean sith's teeth were curved and sharp, her skin too pale and her body tight with sinew instead of softness and curves.

Her leg snapped up and her foot connected with my arm. It didn't hurt, but the force knocked away my grip on her throat. The bean sith hadn't stopped spinning, but I didn't realise that until her foot returned, this time aimed at my jaw. The impact scrambled my brains and I reeled back. The spell I had cast would seal my skin from damage, but the inside bits could still get shaken.

The bean sith shot forward, hands outstretched. She threw me back on the ground, landing on my chest like a perched bird, her hands around my throat.

"Where is it?" Her voice was a violent hiss, and for a disjointed moment, I wondered if Peter Jackson had employed a bean sith for the part of Gollum.

Her grip tightened, cutting off my air. My mouth opened, gaping like a fish as I struggled for breath.

"Where?" She pushed her face against mine, impatient.

I slapped a flailing hand against her head. She turned and I pointed at my mouth.

"Oh." Her grip loosened and I sucked in a strained breath. Leaning in again, so close I could feel the chill of her skin radiating against mine, she repeated her request. "Where is it?"

"It's... it's in..." Instead of an answer, I yelled, startling her. The diversion worked — she hadn't noticed the quick twitch of my fingers. The ground swelled like a breaking wave, then erupted into a narrow wall between us, forcing us apart. I heard the bean sith curse behind it, but I didn't stop and wait for her to react. My next spell pulled the wall, curling it around me like a shield even as I drew my light closer, nestling it just above my head to illuminate the cocoon I huddled in. A third spell softened the barrier, creating a texture like wet cornflour.

A moment later, the gelatinous wall bulged inward. A thin, viscous layer stretched over the bean sith's fingers then split open as one hand emerged. She used it to leverage her body through. Her teeth snapped furiously and I pressed back to avoid her bite. As I did, I flicked a finger through the air.

It scratched through one of the runes I had used in my third spell. The circle of glowing forms puffed out, the soggy walls hardened again, and the bean sith screamed, an ear-splitting wail that I felt to my bones. She struggled and writhed but was unable to escape her concrete prison.

"Tell me." She whipped her head up, eyes burning with fury. "Tell me where it is."

"I haven't got a bloody clue what you're talking about, lass. Where's *what*?"

That made her pause. "He said you would have it." She stretched as far as she could, closed her eyes, and sniffed. "I smell it on you, human."

"Settle down with the accusations of humanity, wench." I thumbed my chest proudly. "I have the blood of —"

"Black Donald?" The bean sith burst out laughing. "I've seen more o' the devil in the cloth he wipes his arse upon."

"I'm a direct descendant," I protested. It was not usually a hill I would die on, but nobody insults my lineage.

"A thousand times descended does not a Donald make." She calmed, flashing me a toothy smile. "How about you let me go, Henry Mack? Together we could make a child with real magic, a power to rival the devil himself."

"No, thanks." I kept my voice bland. "But I would appreciate it if you would tell me what in the name of my many-times-great Granda you're on about, lass."

She snarled, dropping the brief attempt at politeness. "I had a deal, mortal. I will die before I see it left unkept."

"Aye, that you will." It was all the answer I was going to get, that was clear. I scratched out both spells I had left hanging, then snatched at a scrap of white tucked into the top of the bean sith's dress. The heavy walls around me receded, pulling back towards the road and taking a very unhappy fairy with it. Her screams echoed for a few moments after she was sucked under the bitumen, but I didn't worry about that too much. Humans would not be able to hear it, and any sith that might, would be reluctant to engage in the kind of business that would elicit such a pained cry.

I dusted off my hands and knees, grimacing when I realised I had torn right through my jeans when I fell. "That's a bother." I beckoned my light and guided it to drift above me so I could examine the bit of paper I had stolen off my attacker.

The top line had an address scratched out, but I recognised it. It was Fergus's shop. I didn't for a moment believe Fergus was the one who sent her, so he must have been the first stop on her mission to find whatever she was looking for.

The second address was also scratched off. That one gave me chills — I had been there only a day before. Claire McAdam's house. *She's after the tapestry.*

Then, in heavy, thick print and underlined four times, read

Catch and Dispatch, Henry Mac-Something. Big stick, bushy beard, bit of a smart arse but easy on the eyes.

Clearly, that last bit was about me. Claire must have told her who had come for it. Hopefully she had lived through the ordeal. I made a mental note to check on her once morning finally arrived but changed my mind after flicking a quick glance at my watch — it was only three. I didn't want to leave the poor woman for another five hours, so I made a quick phone call.

Annie answered on the second ring, her voice still muddled from sleep. "Fife."

"Annie, my love, I have a wee favour to beg of you."

"It's three in the morning, arsehole. This better be good, or *really* fecking bad."

"Well, I hope it's neither... but can you ask one of your blokes to pop over to Coatbridge? There's a lass out there who may have had an interaction with one of the… uhh, less friendly citizens of Glasgow."

Annie didn't answer right away, but I heard movement. "Address?" All trace of sleepiness had vanished and the terse, efficient detective I knew had replaced her.

I rattled off Claire's address. "The location should be safe," I added. "The visitor in question has… gone underground. She won't be causing any more problems."

"You'll need to write a full report, Mack."

"Not a damn chance." I ignored Annie's protest. "You can either lodge it as an anonymous tip or spend the rest of your career chasing paperwork that will never be found."

"I hate you, Mack." Annie sighed. "But thanks for calling it in. I'll let you know if we find anything."

"I knew you would, love." I tapped the phone screen to end the call and slipped it back in my pocket.

Before I left the scene of the bean sith's untimely death, I took one last look around. Upstairs in the flats, the lights were out in all the windows except Ollie's. Hopefully my neighbours were all tucked up safe, oblivious to the commotion I had caused down below. The alley itself was quiet and the road was reassembled — I had even fixed a couple of potholes in the process. Despite my struggles with precise outcomes when I wanted them, I did do a bang-up job when I was casting by the seat of my pants.

Proud of my impeccable crime scene cleaning skills, I rounded the corner, then let out a sharp curse when I almost tripped on a man cowering against the front wall of my building. He lifted wide eyes as I stumbled over him, and I cursed again.

"Officer Quinn? What the fecking hell are you doing here?"

Quinn stammered a nonsensical answer, then pulled a card out of his pocket and offered it up to me. It was mine. I vaguely remembered giving it to him during the traffic stop, but I hadn't expected him to use it, much less turn up at my door without calling first.

"You saw the bean sith, then?" I asked. Stupid question, I know. Sometimes I can't help myself.

"She got sucked under the road." He pressed his lips together before asking, "Is she... dead?"

"If she's not, she's certainly not having a good time." I held my hand out and he lifted his. I grasped his forearm and pulled him to his feet. "Let's get you upstairs for a hot toddy and a lie down."

He stood up but resisted my tug towards the building's entrance. "You *killed* her. Now you expect to have a drink and forget about it?"

"If you didn't happen to notice, the wee hag tried to kill me first." I let his arm drop, crossing mine in front of me. "Look, you can call it in if you like. Then we'll have a big old investigation, which will find me not guilty by way of insufficient evidence presented by a clearly unhinged officer in need of psychiatric treatment. They won't find a body, they won't believe the floor up and ate a young lassie, and they won't believe your local catch and dispatcher — who, I might add, has a *flawless* record — is bounding about throwing impossible spells at a crabbit fairy."

Quinn stared at me, his mouth open just enough to make him look like a right bampit, then wilted like a dying bluebell. "Shit."

"Aye, you're in some all right." I waited a moment for him to decide what to do. When he gave no sign of what little intelligence he had returning, I turned my back on him.

"Wait!" He trotted after me, catching up just in time to slip through the door behind me. "Uhh... I'll take that drink if you're still offering."

"There's a good lad. We'll see if it's true that the only man that can drink like a Scot is an Aussie." I pointed him in the direction of the stairs and waved him up. "I'm on the second floor."

He took the stairs at a fast clip, leaving me to lag behind. By the time I reached the top, he was leaned casually in the doorway, watching me huff and pant on shaky legs. "You right there, Mister MacDonald?"

I snorted. "Don't you give me that 'Mister' shite. It's Mack, short and sweet."

"Sorry, sir."

I stomped past him. "That's no bloody better." I snatched my keys out, jammed them in the door, and pushed it open. "If you can't follow simple directions, we are not going to get along."

"Mack. What —" Ollie stood in the kitchen, frozen, staring at the strange man who had walked in.

"Sorry, miss, I'm Constable — AHH!" Quinn had followed me in. He jumped back in fright, smacking into the door frame behind him. That in turn startled him further and he shot forward again as though it had grabbed his baws from behind. He swung around, fists up and ready to defend himself from the horrible spectacle before him. Still panting from the shock, he leaned forward, squinting at Ollie a moment before his eyes widened. "Wait a minute. I know you!"

"Sit down, Constable." I shoved him aside and shut the door firmly. The back was painted with sigils, a silence spell that made sure my flat was the quietest in Glasgow despite the paper-thin walls between me and my neighbours. "Ollie, meet Police Constable David Quinn."

She stared, mute.

"It's ok, love. He's not gonna rat us out."

She nodded, swallowed hard, and spoke. "Is this the constable who almost arrested you for getting around with a wee body stashed in your car, and tried to hit me with a stick?" She tipped her head to one side innocently. "You have to be careful, Mack, or you'll get yourself in trouble one day."

I sighed. There had been a fifty-fifty chance that Ollie would freeze up and be too shy to even speak. Sadly, this was not one of those times, and I knew the cheek would only get worse from here on. "And this, PC Quinn, is my gobshite of a sister."

Constable Quinn stared at me, his brain slowly working through the second conundrum he had walked into. "You're... consorting with the dead? Mr MacDonald, that is *highly* illegal."

"Aye." I hung my head in a semblance of shame, then looked up. "But so is watching a gratuitous murder-by-sinkhole and proceeding to join the perpetrator for a pint in his flat, instead of immediately reporting it to your higher ups." Spreading my hands and giving him a cheeky wink, I added, "If you won't tell, neither will I."

Quinn gasped, his outrage warring with bewilderment at how neatly I had trapped him. "But... but..."

"Get your bum out the window, Mack." Ollie walked over to Quinn and offered her hand. "That means stop talking pish, for the foreign language speakers amongst us."

"He knows what it means, Ollie," I protested. "He's Australian, not Russian. He can speak proper English, you know!"

"How do *you* know he knows what it means?" Ollie replied primly. "I didn't, until you bloody explained it to me. Devil forbid people say what they mean instead of making up stupid phrases that make no sense." She turned a beatific smile on Quinn, who drew back warily. "Don't mind my numpty of a brother. It's okay, I'm not going to bite you."

Her lifeless eyes, blue lips and receding gums made the effect closer to horrifying than comforting, but somehow, it worked. Quinn squatted down to her level and reached out a shaky hand. Ollie grabbed it and gave it a firm shake. Then, she rounded on me.

"Mack, you're a bloody fool. What are you thinking, scaring the poor lad like that? He's barely more than a bairn, and you drop him in a room with a zombie? You could have warned him first!"

"He seemed to deal with the bean sith just fine." I neglected to add that 'just fine' was a bit ambitious. "Besides, look at him. He's a strapping young lad with a sharp mind and a gift for keeping his head on straight. He'll be right as rain in a jiffy."

To my disappointment, Quinn was indeed fine. He sucked in a deep breath and finally returned Ollie's horror-movie grin. "Sorry. I'll admit, I wasn't expecting..." He waved a hand at Ollie, then gestured vaguely downstairs. "Any of this, really."

"It's all right, love." Ollie sat on the lounge and patted the spot next to her. "Sit yourself down and Mack will get you a drink. I'll explain it all to you once you've had a drink to settle your nerves, aye?"

Ollie seemed to have a settling effect on Quinn, so I did as she asked and poured him a half measure of whisky. He downed it quickly, then held the glass out for another.

"Oh." Ollie patted his knee. "You're a bit of a drinker, then?"

"Not usually," Quinn admitted. "I think tonight calls for it, though. After what I saw downstairs..." He shuddered.

"Oh, right." Ollie dragged her attention away from her new friend and turned to me. "What by the black hairy balls of Old Donald himself were you doing fighting a bean sith, Mack? I bet you tried to seduce her. You should know better, they're dangerous!"

"I did no such bloody thing!" I rummaged through the cupboard, but Quinn had the last clean shot glass. I eyed the whisky, glanced at Quinn, then slugged from the bottle. "Ollie, she came after me. She was looking for something and I think I know what it was."

"That bit of knitting we stole from the desperate housewife?" Ollie guessed. "Aye, I heard you call Annie. No word back yet?"

I shook my head. "Feck. I should have checked on Fergus. She had his address too."

"Fergus?" Ollie giggled. "Come on, Mack. Fergus could take on three sithchean with his arm tied behind his back." She quickly explained to Quinn that Fergus only had one of them, so that was a feat bigger than it seemed. "He'd smash that wench's face into a portal to the Otherworld, then close it so she loses her head. And he wouldn't break a sweat doing it, either."

"What's a shit-yun?" Quinn's attempt at pronouncing the old Gaelic word was almost passable. "Are they like the banshee?"

"It's bean sith," Ollie corrected him. Though, the only difference really was the slight emphasis on it being two words, with slightly more emphasis on the second instead of the first. "A bean sith is a type of sithche. That's shee-chee for those who aren't native."

Quinn listened to her lecture with narrowed eyes. "And the shit-yun?"

"Shee-chun," I said. "Sithchean is just the plural for sithche."

"A bean sith is just a young fairy women. Gille sith are the lads, bean nighe are the old washer women... there are dozens, but really, they're all just fairies to the uneducated. And only a bloody idiot would make a deal with one." Ollie snatched the whisky out of my hands to pour Quinn another drink. "Unless you're very clever with your wording, most times it backfires and you end up owing some soul-eating fae monster your soul for the rest of eternity. Or scooping up kelpie poop, which is probably worse. Have you seen how much kelpies eat?"

"Uhh... no?" Quinn sipped his second whisky slower. I could see the gears turning in his brain — less in a frantic panic now, and more sorting through the questions he was too scared to ask. "Kelpies are real, then?"

Ollie's jaw dropped. She swung her head towards me, eyes wide. "What the bloody hell are they teaching the bairns these days? 'Are kelpies real'. Pah! Say that in the wrong part of Glasgow and you'll end up dragged to a watery death in the closest gutter." She slumped back on the couch with a glower, muttering *'are kelpies real'* between long strings of curses.

"They taught us about spectres," Quinn offered. "But they didn't say that zom..." He cleared his throat. "That there were also..."

I saved him from earning another scathing lecture from the zombie he was so desperately trying to reference. "Ollie is different. When she was raised, the ritual was one of healing." I chose my words carefully, not quite ready to admit I was the one who had cast said spell. "Her soul is more or less intact, it's just her physical form that presents like a zombie."

Quinn narrowed his eyes. "That whole time we had you pulled over, it was all an act? She was never going to eat our... faces?" He pressed his knees together anyway.

"I never would!" Ollie exclaimed. "I don't eat people! I eat chocolate and ice cream and whisky, you big dobber."

Of all Quinn had learned that evening, there was one thing he apparently couldn't abide. "Whisky? Mack, you're letting a child drink whisky?"

"Am not a fecking child, you fool. I'm thirty-two, same as my brother — just smarter, better looking and a wee bit shorter than he is."

"Technically you're two days younger than I am," I pointed out.

Ollie rolled her eyes. "And how do you figure that? We were born on the same day, stupid."

"You were dead for two days." I shrugged. "I've lived two more days than you have, so I'm two days older."

"My body was decomposing those two days, not stuck in a bloody TARDIS. That counts as ageing, so I'm still older."

"How much older?" Quinn asked, and I could have bloody slapped him.

"Forty-two minutes and twenty-four seconds," Ollie said proudly. "Because my idiot brother got lost on the way out. That's practically a lifetime of experience. By the time he shot out of our mother's —"

"Ollie!" I snapped. "You are *not* talking about our dead mother's minge to a complete stranger!" Even before my sister had spent two decades locked away from the world, her grasp on what was socially acceptable had been dubious at best.

"I'll have to agree with your brother on that one." Quinn gulped down the rest of his drink. He took it a little better this time, with just a slight watering of the eyes and a quickly stifled cough. "So, Mack, how'd you learn about all this stuff, anyway?"

"Magic, you mean? Family tradition. Ollie and I were apprenticed to our Granda. Da trained with his Granda. Mam dabbled a wee bit but it was mostly the kind of stuff girls learn in high school, not the serious study that her old man made us do."

"You're off your head, Henry Mack," Ollie scoffed. "Hedge witchery forms the entire basis of what we know today. Do you really think men invented the nine herbs charm? Or discovered the way to bless cotton thread to ward from fairy spells? You sexist prick."

"I was just having a dig, Ollie. I know Mam was one of the most powerful witches in Scotland. Remember that time a horny old bull tried to charge me? Mam wound him up in a binding spell, flipped him on his arse and turned him into the gentlest old soul you've ever met."

Ollie laughed at the memory. "I remember old Kirby next door yelling the house down when he found out the bull wasn't fertile anymore. That poor vet must've been beside himself!"

"What's the matter, Quinn?" I held out the bottle in case Quinn's long face was due to his empty glass.

"Oh, nothing. I guess you have to be born into it, eh?"

That gave me pause. "Magic? I thought you were here to train for C&D?"

Quinn gave a non-committal shrug, looking embarrassed he had even broached the subject.

"Don't be daft. Anyone can learn magic." Ollie screwed up her face. "All you need is an open mind and a bit of fairy in your blood."

Quinn snorted as he glanced down at the dark skin of his arms. "Believe it or not, Mum was one of your lot. Freckles and all. She wasn't a witch, though, I'm sure of it."

"You? Scottish?" I leaned closer, searching his dark face for any indication that he was taking the piss.

"Only half," Quinn clarified. "Mum ran off to Australia when she was nineteen, fell in love with my old man a year later. When she died, I came to live with Aunty Nora."

"What about your Da?" Ollie asked.

"Oh, he's still alive. He lives in Cairns — well, he lives a few clicks off the coast of Cairns. Marine biologist. I can't even tell you the irony of a man who spends every waking moment on the water having a son who pukes if he even sees a wave. We get along fine apart from that." He shrugged, resigned. "But I'm damn sure he's not magic, either. And Aunty Nora... well, she's mad as a hatter and spends her days off with the fairies, but that's only in the metaphorical sense, you know?"

Before I could tell him that attempting to learn magic – even if possible – was a *terrible* idea, Ollie jumped in. "If you want to learn a bit of magic, it's in you. You're older than most, but that just means you might have to dig a bit to find it."

"So... Do you think you could teach me?" Blow me if the bastard wasn't looking at my sister when he asked.

Ollie, to her credit, bounced his request to me. "What do you think, Mack? Are you ready to take on your own apprentice?"

I stared at Quinn. He had baws, I'd give him that. He hadn't run away from the bean sith even if he'd cowered around the corner — which meant he also wasn't a complete fool. He wasn't Scottish, so that was a mark against him, but he could hold his drink, and wouldn't embarrass me if I took him to Jack's.

"Not a damn chance." I slugged another mouthful of whisky.

"Come on, Mack. Why not?" Ollie leaned over to wrap an arm around Quinn's shoulder. "Look at the precious wee thing. He's *dying* to learn."

"Is it possible to keep the dying out of it?" Quinn asked.

"And he's got a *fantastic* sense of humour."

"Nope. It's not going to happen, Ollie. I don't know the first thing about teaching magic — Granda was shite at it and I've got as much patience as him, and only half the brain."

"Bullshit." Ollie dropped her arm from Quinn and shot to her feet. "I won't have you talk about yourself like that, Mack. You're clever, and you're bloody good at what you do. Just because you forget things sometimes..."

"Aye," I said. "And cock up my spells, blow things up every now and then, and have forgotten every mundane detail in every tedious tome Granda made us read as kids. Including the section in the manual titled How Not to Kill Your Fecking Apprentice."

Ollie folded her arms. "That wasn't a section in the book, Mack."

"But you canna disagree, can you?"

Ollie pursed her lips. "No. But I can add one very important thing... you have *me*. I haven't forgotten anything. I even kept all my study notes, they're safe and sound under my bed."

That didn't surprise me one bit. Ollie was a hoarder, but a very organised one. "How does that help?" I asked. "You can't reach the spirits because you're one step away from being one yourself. How can you teach the lad?"

"I can't. But *we* can." Ollie came over to kneel beside my chair. She reached a hand up and rested it on mine, looking up into my eyes. I thought she was, anyway. It could be hard to tell with her pupils all clouded over like that. "Together. Mack, *please*. I really think we should do this. For his sake, and for yours."

"And for yours, too?" I guessed Ollie was so eager to take young Quinn on because he was the first new person she had met in a long time. Bringing him into our little family might give her a new friend.

"If you want to think so." A smile tugged at one corner of her lip. "I do like the lad."

Quinn opened his mouth, head tipped to one side in confusion, then thought better of what he was about to say. Probably a good thing, if it was anything about a twelve-year-old dead girl calling him a 'lad'.

"Fine." I let out a strained breath. "I'll take him on. But only on a trial basis. If it doesn't work out, I'll wipe his memory and leave him in the street."

"You can do that?" Quinn asked. He seemed more excited than worried, making me immediately regret my words.

"We're not the Men in Black, Quinn." Ollie giggled. "He can't really do it."

"Now you've strong armed me into that, can we wrap this up, please?" I waved the whisky bottle. "It's been a bloody long night and all this yammering is making me tired."

"You might have agreed, but Constable Quinn hasn't." Ollie turned to the officer in question. "What do you say, Quinny boy? Are you up for a lifetime of magic, monsters and mischief?"

"I... guess?" He laughed, but it held a nervous edge to it. "Why not. Sign me up."

"Good man." I grinned widely, hedging on one last chance to change his mind. "All we'll need is a quick contract, a vial of your blood, and a small but lively sacrifice."

Quinn swallowed. "Sa — sacrifice?"

"You're a fecking prick, Henry Mack." Ollie patted Quinn's arm and to his credit, he didn't flinch at her touch. "You just have to say a few words and sign a simple contract. With ink, not blood. Well, maybe a wee bit of blood, but not enough to hurt."

"Oh." Quinn swallowed, but didn't rescind his acceptance.

"Are you sure about this, lad?" I asked. "I'll do my best not to let it interfere with your work, but there might come a day when you have to choose between two paths."

Quinn shrugged. "I signed up to be a copper to be part of something, you know? Something important. I thought the uniform would come with something... bigger. I don't mind the work, but lately I've wondered if it's worth it. I mean, driving the streets and doing mountains of paperwork, just for a few broken taillights? Nah. I want to get out and make a real difference. Save lives, keep people safe."

"Well, then, I guess I'm going to be the fool who teaches you just how to do that." I frowned as my tired brain sluggishly traipsed over my mental calendar. "Come back tomorrow. No hiding around the corner this time — If I get walloped by something on my way in the door, I expect you to get off your arse and help me fight it off."

Quinn straightened. "Aye, sir."

"And don't worry — I'll teach you proper Scots at the same time as I show you how to fight off a galloping kelpie with naught but two fingers of brandy, a pinch of ash and a shotgun."

"Mack, you don't own a gun. And if you did, a shotgun would take a kelpie down without a problem. Why do you need the other things?" Ollie asked.

"That's for the after party, lass." With a grin, I ushered Quinn out. "Right lad, what time does your shift finish?" I agreed to meet him at six, and promptly shut the door after him.

"Are you sure you know what you're signing up for, Mack?" Ollie asked, coming over to look up at me with piercing eyes.

"You're the one who bloody talked me into it, Ollie." I shook my head. "Don't tell me you're having doubts now."

"For someone who barely understands his own power, has no idea how to train a novice, and can't stay sober for more than a day? I'm sure you'll have no trouble." She laughed gently, then rested her head on my chest and gave me a hug. "I'm glad you're doing it. You need to stop living for the dead, Mack, and make some more friends with heartbeats."

I wrapped my arms around her, hoping she couldn't feel the suddenly painful thump of my heart. "You're not dead, lass. Not really. You're just... metabolically challenged."

Rather than protest, she just snuggled in closer. "I love you, Henry."

"I love you too, Ollie."

Chapter Seven

Fife leaned on the thin metal table between us, her usually friendly expression now carefully blank. "For the record, please state your name, sir."

"Henry Augustus MacDonald, though most people know me as —" I stopped as Fife's eyes flicked pointedly to the two way mirror adorning the wall of the interrogation room. "As Mack." I gave her a winning smile to convey that I had not for a moment intended to finish my introduction with, "As the best-looking Glaswegian wizard that money could buy."

"State your address please, Mr. MacDonald."

I rattled it off, followed by my date of birth when she asked. "And my underpants are blue," I added with a wink.

Fife ignored my display of wit, instead moving onto the subject in question. "Mr. MacDonald, can you account for your whereabouts on the morning of November Seventeenth, between the hours of three and six?"

"Aye, I can." I made a show of wrinkling my face in thought. "That was a Wednesday? In the wee hours.... Let's see..."

"It was yesterday, Mr. MacDonald. Not four months ago." Fife tapped her notebook impatiently.

"I was working." Tipping my head toward the mirror, I raised my voice. "That's what we competent Catch and Dispatch professionals, do, you know. Work? Catching and Dispatching. Not hanging off the coattails of —"

"Mr. MacDonald." Fife interrupted my jibes at the consultant on the other side of the wall — at least I hoped Rattray was lurking back there, or I would look like a right fool. "Where, exactly, were you working?"

I pulled out my phone and read Claire McAdam's address off the text message I had sent Fife earlier. Her lashes dropped, hiding her flash of recognition to anyone who wouldn't know to look for it. When she looked up again, her face was carefully smooth. "And the job?"

"One Claire McAdam called into the emergency line at approximately four-oh-five a.m., to report a previously deceased had entered her home and attempted to alter Ms. McAdam's status to currently deceased."

Fife cleared her throat. Right, no funny business. It was her arse on the line in this investigation, and I didn't want her taken off Granda's case. She was the best and I bloody well knew it.

"Sorry. The P.D. had entered through an upstairs window. Emergency transferred her call to me, and I gave her instructions on creating a barrier of sodium chloride to keep her safe until my arrival."

"Which was when?" Fife scribbled furiously as I talked, making note of everything I said despite the conversation being recorded.

"Approximately twelve minutes later," I answered.

This time, Fife didn't hide her surprise as well. "Twelve minutes?"

"Give or take." I cursed inwardly, but there was nothing for it. I couldn't lie, the phone call was a matter of public record. "Lucky for Ms. McAdam, I was already in the area." I held my breath and said a silent prayer that Fife wouldn't ask what the hell I was doing loitering about the streets at four in the morning, all the way across town from my own flat.

"So, you entered the caller's home between approximately four-fifteen and four-twenty." Fife's eyes didn't meet mine and I guessed she would be asking me more questions later. "Correct?"

"Aye." I gave a brief rundown of the actions I had taken to secure the nasty, terrifying spectral intruder, leaving out a few minor details like the tapestry I had taken from the lass. The last thing I needed was for Fife to request it for evidence or examination. It may not be directly related to Granda's case, but the Ice-Cream Van had powers outside the scope of the rest of the police and had the right to confiscate any magical gear they came across.

"And what time did you leave?" Fife asked.

"Not long before sunup. You can corroborate that with Constables David Quinn and..." I groped for the name of the other officer who had been with Quinn when they stopped me. "Barry Martin, I think his name was. They pulled me over on my way home, for a broken taillight I was not aware of at the time and have since had fixed." I made a mental note to fix the bloody thing post-haste.

"They were the officers who followed you to Coylton?" Fife confirmed.

"Aye. All the way from Coatbridge." I placed my hands flat on the steel tabletop. "As you can see, Detective Chief Inspector, I simply could not have had anything to do with Granda's death. I was an hour away."

"You lived with him for a few years, didn't you, Mack?" Fife dropped the mask of indifference and leaned forward a little. "After your parents died."

"Aye." I looked around for a distraction but in the sterile room I found none. "For a time."

"You were... what, ten years old?" Fife prodded.

It wasn't a topic we had ever discussed. After the first few cases I had consulted on, Fife had taken me under her wing a little. She was the sort to call a lad and make sure he'd been eating right, that he behaved himself at the football, to always send a card on Birthdays and Christmas. But most of our time together was either spent knee deep in the eviscerated guts of some poor victim or knocking back drinks with the team to celebrate catching the bastard that did it.

"I was twelve." My glare was stoney, but she didn't flinch. *All right then, you want to do this, we'll do it.* "He took me in after the brutal murder of my entire family. He was the only person I had left. He was crotchety old goat, and I was a teenage boy who knew it all. You can imagine the arguments we had. Ollie says she was always afraid we'd wake the dead, we yelled so bloody loud."

"Ollie — your sister?" Fife's lips pressed together.

Realising my mistake, I quickly tried to cover it. "Aye. When she was alive, she said that."

"These arguments — they ever get out of hand?" Fife asked.

I snorted. "You mean did I try to blow his insides to the outside? No. We just saw the world differently. I moved out as soon as I was old enough, but I didn't hate him."

"That's why you sent him money every month?" Fife had, as usual, done her homework.

"Aye. When I lived there, I saw the bills pile up. Only Black Donald himself knows how the old codger held onto the house as long as he did, but as soon as I got myself a job, I started sending him a bit every month. I couldn't stand the thought of him losing the house Mam grew up in, or him having to live on the street." I suppressed a shudder. "Or worse, moving in with me."

"Did he have any enemies?"

The quick change of direction threw me for a beat, and I chewed on the question before answering. "Nah. As much as he pissed me off, he kept to himself. The only person he ever crossed words with was old Natty next door, but she died a year or two ago." I chose not to mention that their dispute ended in Natty hexing Granda's cows to produce nought but sour milk after he summoned a fuath in her pond to eat all her fish. Much to his disgust, the fuath then proceeded to wreak havoc in Granda's herb garden, leaving Natty's livestock to thrive.

I supposed they must have made it up with each other eventually. Ollie had snuck off to old Natty's send off and she'd seen Granda there, front and centre, eyes wet with unshed tears. At least, that's what Ollie thought they were. My guess was that the old bastard had just tired himself out putting a curse on her coffin.

"Mack, your grandfather was one of the most proficient buidsichean in Glasgow. We know he was involved in... well, in things we don't even understand." Fife gestured impotently and I guessed she was referring to the S.O.P.D. as a whole. "Please. We want to catch this guy."

"Annie, he was involved in petty squabbles over cows and eggs, and the occasional kelpie-tipping expedition." I shrugged, leaning back in the flimsy chair. "Aye, he was strong in the craft. It didn't mean he was interesting. The older he got, the less he gave a damn about the outside world."

Annie pursed her lips. Her glare hardened and I shifted uncomfortably in my seat. I could tell it wasn't the answer she wanted, and I had a sudden, uneasy feeling that instead of the easy conversation-ender I had intended, I had instead dug myself a deep hole only to have my shovel snap at the bottom.

"You said you went to live with him when your parents died. That must have been a hard time for both of you."

I hadn't expected Fife to round back and poke at that old wound. Still, it made me flinch. My top lip lifted, baring a flash of white teeth. If Rattray had seen the short break in my composure, he wouldn't let me live it down easily. That thought, along with the knowledge that Annie Fife's eyes were examining my every reaction, was enough to pull my startled grief back into submission.

"Aye. Right mess, it was." I tapped my fingers on the metal table, aiming for bored nonchalance.

Fife raised a sceptical eyebrow. "You lost your sister, too?"

"Aye. Wee Olivia. We were twins, you know." Ollie was, at least, safer ground. She might be dead, but I didn't need to grieve for her.

"What happened to them?" Fife seemed honestly curious, which baffled me.

"Come on, lass." I laughed, a nervous bark that echoed in the sparse room. "You've read the reports, don't tell me you haven't. Are you trying to trip me up?"

She blinked. "Trip you? No, Mack... you were twelve. I don't have the clearance to read their file, that's all."

That stumped me. "You really don't know?"

Fife shook her head, the motion smooth. She was good at this — unbothered, blank faced, not hard and closed off, just waiting for me to give her a dribble of information I hadn't intended to. Well, sadly for her, I didn't have anything that would help her.

"It was a gas leak. Just a stupid, senseless accident." I relaxed back into my seat, careful to show how little I cared. "I was at a birthday party. Came home to find your lot swarming around the house, Granda sitting on the footpath. Never seen a man more broken." Something caught in my throat. Probably dust, going by the sting in my eyes that accompanied it. I cleared my voice before continuing. "The coppers said it was a faulty pipe. They didn't suffer — Ollie didn't even know it was coming."

Fife showed her first real reaction. Brows knitted together, she made a small noise with her teeth. "That makes no sense." Her eyes met mine. "Why would an accidental death be —"

The interrogation room door flew open, banging loudly on the wall. Rattray stepped in, his tiny eyes glittering over a triumphant grin. "I knew it!" He pointed at me, sneering. "I knew you were hiding something." He stalked towards me, his thin frame filled with piss and vinegar, held in by papery skin covered in broken capillaries. The wart on his nose bulged between the deep grooves of his screwed-up face and his cracked lips twisted into a smirk.

Not for the first time in my life, I thanked whatever spirits had ensured I had not been born into the narrow-minded, hateful life of Alan Rattray.

"What?" Fife and I both spoke at the same time, but where I had asked a question, properly bewildered by his sudden entrance, Fife's was an exclamation of outrage.

Eager to see her continue, I kept my mouth shut.

"How dare you interrupt an interview?" Fife spat. "I swear to god, Rattray, if you don't have a bloody good reason for barging in here, I'll have your —"

"He's whistling the deid." Rattray seemed to think this was not only possible, but some kind of point scored against my existence.

"I'm what, now?" I flashed him a grin, all the brighter for the fear bubbling in my gut. *There's no chance he knows about Ollie, surely?*

My easy manner took a pinch of wind from his sails, but only for a moment. "You've been talkin' to the ghost of your sister, haven't you? I knew your magic was unsanitary. You're an abomination, MacDonald."

"Och, settle down Rattray." A chuckle of relief bubbled up — he didn't know about Ollie, he was just flinging spaghetti at a wall to see what might stick. "I'm no' drawing sigils on the walls with a wet jobby. And I'm not talking to ghosts, either, apart from a few harsh words as I shuffle them off to the afterlife. You know, *while I do my fecking job.*"

"Liar." Rattray stabbed a finger down on the table in front of me. It bent backwards, far enough to make my stomach turn a wee bit. "You said Olivia MacDonald didn't know her death was coming. You spoke to her!"

"You think I'm running around talking to ghosts? Bloody hell, Rattray, did you learn magic off the back of a cereal box?" I directed my explanation to Fife, rather than pander to the idiot beside me. "I spoke to the coroner that dressed her for the funeral. He told me she passed in her sleep. He said she just drifted off and never woke up."

This time I didn't hide the sudden misting of my eyes.

Fife saw it. Her lips tightened as she turned to the man who had intruded upon her sacred space. "Do you have a reason to be in here, Alan? A legitimate one, I mean."

His eyes flicked towards the detective, then back to me. "Using your magic to speak with your grandfather is forbidden. You're a suspect in his death, and any intimidation of a witness would be —"

"Intimidation." I snorted. "Of a dead man? Oh, sorry, the *ghost* of a dead man. What are you going to do, Rat-bait, take out a restraining order?"

"If I have to!" Rattray pushed his face into mine. "I'll be there when you fall, MacDonald, you see if I'm not. You and your spells, and your secrets, and your illicit dealings with the unseelie court." He leaned closer, blowing a hot breath through his nose that washed over me like a fetid breeze over a beach full of rotting fish.

"Good luck taking this through the legal system, you wank." I shook my head and chuckled, as much to disperse the stench of his breath as to show him how little I cared. "Even if you had a shred of evidence I was involved — which you don't, because I'm not — they'll laugh you out of the building and strip your licence if you go in front of a judge and request a protective order against a fecking ghost."

"Why I oughtta..." Rattray's threat seemed to either be something he wouldn't say in front of Detective Fife, or something he hadn't thought of yet. I realised it was the second a moment too late. He drew back, eyes glittering dangerously, then lunged forward and tackled me. "No one laughs at Alan Rattray!"

The chair skidded under the desk and I hit the linoleum floor with force, Rattray flailing on top of me like an eel in a bucket of vinegar. I kicked away the chair that tangled my legs and rolled, using my shoulder to shove him off, and sprang to a crouch. I summoned a thread of power as I raised my finger to sketch a sigil — well, I tried. Though I could see the sparkling residue of old magic in the room, it did not heed my call.

"No magic here, devil-spawn." Rattray, sprawled on his back on the floor, laughed at my surprise. "I warded the whole damn room just for you. Not so useless now, am I?" He threw an arm out and a fist struck my cheekbone.

Hot pain flared and my vision went red. I roared and raised my hands, meaning to throttle the man, only to be jerked back by my collar.

"No you bloody don't." Fife's voice was hard and her grip harder. "Not in my interview room."

I gargled out a half-hearted protest through my strangled throat. "But he —"

"You're damn right he did, but I'll be the one to deal with him."

My shirt loosened, but not enough that I was fooled into thinking I was free. Instead of struggling towards Rattray, I leaned back and plonked down on my arse. "Fair enough. He's your chihuahua."

Rattray spluttered, almost tripping over in his apoplectic fury as he tried to stand. "You're going down, MacDonald. If we see even a dribble of magic out of your hands, I'll assume you're trying to intimidate our victim. I'll have you arrested and locked up until you're so old you can't remember your own name." He pursed his lips and nodded, satisfied with his threat. "Tell him, Fife."

"Rattray, get the hell out of my interview room."

Rattray gaped at her. "You have no idea what he's —"

Fife simply lifted an arm, finger outstretched and pointed towards the door. Her consultant gave an angry snort and stormed away, grabbing the door to pull it shut behind him with quite a bit more force than strictly necessary. Instead of slamming closed, it bounced open, struck the wall again — this time leaving a wee hole in the plaster — and drifted to a stop halfway between open and shut. Rattray flushed red. He stomped back to yank the door hard again, this time keeping hold of the handle until it was secure.

Fife calmly walked over, opened it again, and bellowed outside. "Charlie? Escort that piece of shite consultant off the premises, and don't let him back until you've spoken to me directly."

I had to restrain myself from giving her a round of applause.

"I apologise for that, Mack." Despite her words, Fife didn't seem overly sorry.

"Dinna fash, Detective. It was worth it to see that spectacular exit he made." I cocked my head, realising for the first time that the frustrated disrespect burning in her eyes had been there since Rattray burst into the room. "Why do you keep him around, anyway?"

"We're not exactly spoiled for choice." Fife shrugged one shoulder and sat back in her seat with a sigh. "You and Rattray are the only two consultants we have on the books, now. Steven quit after that bloody vampire gave him a Glasgow kiss."

Getting smacked in the face by the supernaturally tough skull of a vampire was no laughing matter. Steven's cheekbone had shattered like a fine china teacup, landing him in hospital for reconstructive surgery and some trauma counselling. Being the kind soul that I am, I took him three whole bottles of Scotch and a sad posy of flowers I grabbed from Asda for half price — probably because they were halfway to dead. Steve, who didn't drink on account of being a Muslim, kindly insisted on letting me keep the 'fecking useless gift' but made sure to show his appreciation by calling me a 'selfish prick with a face like a trod on jobby'.

"Steve wasn't cut out for it," I told Fife. "Too bloody fussy, he was."

Fife lifted an eyebrow but didn't comment on Steve's job suitability. "Regardless, I've got you and Rattray, and with you refusing to work holidays and weekends, we actually rely on him quite a bit. And now I'm going to have to throw him off this bloody case, and I can't ask you to help because it's a conflict of fecking interest. The feck am I supposed to do now, Mack?" She glared at me accusingly.

One corner of my mouth tilted up. "It just so happens I've taken on an apprentice."

"A what?" Fife looked less excited than I had anticipated.

"An apprentice." I gave her a quick rundown on Quinn, leaving out the bit where I had coaxed a good bit of Glasgow City Council's resources to participate in the brutal — though not unwarranted — murder of a bean sith.

"How long until he's useful?" Fife asked.

I took my opportunity, sensing I wouldn't get another one soon. "That depends on you. He's motorway patrol, and he needs to pay his bills, aye? I canna teach the lad if he's working all the bloody time."

"And you expect me to..." Fife left her question hanging, so I finished it for her.

"Put in to get him transferred, then let him off work with full pay to come and learn the art of kelpie-tipping with yours truly. He should be ready to go in less than a decade."

Fife rolled her eyes. "You bloody know that's not how it works." She tapped her foot, mouth working as she thought. "Fine. Leave it with me and I'll sort something out. Meanwhile, sit your arse back at the table, I've a few more questions for you if you don't mind."

I did as she asked but made a show of checking my watch.

“We’re almost done here, I promise.” Fife picked her notebook up from the floor. It had fallen when she broke up the scuffle between me and Ratface. “You said you don’t know of anyone who held a grudge against your grandfather. What about debts; did he owe money to anyone likely to come after him?”

“Unless the leccy people have changed their collection methods, no.”

Fife hesitated a beat. “I don’t think we’ll be adding Scottish Power to our suspect pool.”

“I’d be reading their reviews before making that determination, love.” I tapped the fingers of one hand on my knee, impatient to wrap the conversation up. Rattray had almost ferreted out my wee secret, and I was eager to get home and warn Ollie in case he came poking about.

“The last time you visited your grandfather was...?” Fife let the question hang, her pen hovering over paper, ready to scribble my answer down.

“Samhain. He was on the outs with the cait sith, so I went for a wee visit and snuck a big dish of milk on his back steps to smooth things over.”

Fife’s eyes met mine and I watched as she weighed scepticism against curiosity, and then balanced the equation with the knowledge that anything I said in the interview would need to be reported word for word, but presented in a way that left out anything untoward. And by untoward, I mean anything magical, supernatural, Otherworldy, or illegal.

Fife erred on the side of caution. “That was November. You’ve not been back at all since then?”

I shook my head, impatience forgotten as Fife slipped a hand into her pocket and dug something out. She tossed a sealed plastic bag on the table, making the set of keys inside clink loudly. I leaned over to look at them, careful not to touch. A miniature screwdriver, a bottle opener and a tarnished silver key with a pentagonal head were linked by a small chain to a battered plastic building block. Though the yellow brick was caked in something dry and brown, I recognised the set immediately.

"Hey!" I drew back in surprise. "That's mine! I guess I owe old Ratshite an apology, unless you pried them out of his thievin' hands."

Fife pressed her lips together a moment, thinking. "They were found at the crime scene, Mack."

"What?" I snorted. "You can't blame that on me. I never got them back, remember?"

In fact, the last time I had seen that key was just after Fife had tossed it into a baggy, then dropped it in an evidence box, promising to get it back to me as fast as she could. I had been at the S.O.P.D. facility to submit a statement about a particularly messy dispatch. And I, bampot that I am, had left my bloody keys in the Demon. When I finally returned to my beautiful car, the windows were open, the seats were soaked in a downpour, and an ugly scratch ran all the way down one side.

Of course, the CCTV cameras weren't installed in the new S.O.P.D. premises until the following week, so I was shite out of luck there. The keys had been retrieved the next morning where a canny young officer had spotted them in the gutter, and I had insisted Fife take the damage seriously.

That meant Fife had insisted on taking my key. She had bagged it for fingerprinting, meaning I was left to Uber my way around Glasgow until I could get a replacement. Which, in the end, I needed because the key taken for evidence was stolen from right under the noses of the department supposed to protect the citizens of Glasgow from petty crime.

Fife's red-faced apology had given me a solid month of ammunition to batter her with at the pub, but the keys were never found. She had even accused me of taking them myself, wiggling her fingers as if to insinuate I would use my magic to thieve them like a bloody criminal.

Of course, I would have done, if I'd thought of it.

"Mack, I know you said you never picked them up." Fife stared me down, daring me to tell her the truth. "But I need to hear it one more time."

"I swear on my life, Annie, the last time I saw those keys was on their way to evidence." I raised my hands, palms up. "To be honest, I'd forgotten all about them."

She nodded, satisfied with my plea of innocence. "Fair enough. I don't know what to say, Mack. I have no bloody idea where they've been all this time, and even less of a clue how they got to your Granda's." A thought occurred and she tilted her head with curiosity. "You don't think your Granda could have got a hold of them?"

"Not bloody likely. You know he avoids the establishment like the bloody plague." I emphasised the word the same way he always had. "And besides, I never told him they were lost."

I reached over to grab the keys, but Fife snatched them up again. "Sorry, Mack. They're to go back into evidence."

"Right. Try not to lose the bloody things this time, aye?"

"Bugger off. You know shite happens sometimes but we're not completely useless." Fife darted a glance at the tape recorder in the corner and clamped her mouth shut. It wasn't the done thing to slag off the police when you were not only one of their finest, but on record at that.

"It's fine, love. If we're done, I've got an appointment to get to."

Fife nodded and stood. "Thank you for your time today, Mr. MacDonald. You'll have to fill out a statement on your way out about the... uhh, incident earlier, but otherwise you're free to go."

"Report? Feck me, the gobshite really knows how to turn a day to pish, doesn't he?"

Fife's dry expression suggested I had best do what she said, then get my arse as far away as possible while she dealt with the cause of said paperwork. "Don't leave town, Mack. We'll be in touch."

Chapter Eight

Fergus cracked the back door to his shop open, angling his bushy-browed eyes across the damp and dingy parking lot. He eyed Quinn up and down, spat, then threw the door wide. Holding it open with the stump of his missing arm, he gestured for us to hurry inside before we were drenched.

Ollie scampered in first. I stood back, hunched against the rain, to let Quinn follow her. Fresh from his shift, the young officer had swapped his department-issued uniform for a sparkling white t-shirt and dark jeans. Not even the smattering of raindrops soiled the image. As someone who can't wear white for more than a minute without spilling something on it, I admit I was a little jealous.

"Who's that?" Fergus asked, jutting a bristly chin toward Quinn's back after he passed. "He stinks like establishment folk, he does."

"That's because he is." I ducked past Fergus, ignoring his scowl. "He's also my new apprentice. Or he will be, if I ever get a chance to scratch me arse and get him properly bonded."

"Henry Bloody Mack takin' a protégé? Never would'a seen

that comin'." Fergus pulled the door closed and shook like a dog, scattering droplets on the concrete floor. He scrubbed his left hand over the few stray hairs still attached to his scalp, flicking off the rain.

"You and me both." I waited for Fergus to click the latch in place, slide the deadbolt across, then heft a slab of timber and drop it across the two brackets on either side. "You expecting a battering ram to come flying through there?"

Fergus didn't give me a direct answer. "Things are afoot, Henry. Dark forces are on the move."

"Aye, they've been moving and shaking the last few thousand years, Fergus." I shook my head, unworried by his prophecies of doom.

Unlike Jack Mackintosh, Fergus didn't claim to have the sight. His predictions were, he said, based on observing the world and making logical deductions based on hard facts. Like the time he insisted the entire subway system would collapse during a Celtics game. His 'hard facts' were a sighting of three mice in a gutter, an odd-shaped shadow and a passer-by who left a pizza shop menu on a bus seat. His excuse for a fully-functioning subway system the following day? A five-legged lamb born the previous week, all the way out in Huntly.

My theory was that Fergus was playing the odds — if he spent every day of his prolonged existence predicting the end of the world, he might eventually get it right.

We picked our way through the storage area of Fergus's shop, past boxes teetering high enough to kill a man if they fell, and a line of dusty, headless mannequins. I sneezed twice. "I keep telling you old man, you need a bloody housemaid to give this place a proper scrub."

"Haud yer weesht, whipper snapper." Fergus smacked one of the teetering stacks, sending a cloud of dust into the air. "I've got more important things to be doin'."

"Like?" I blinked when Ollie pushed the far door open, the bright afternoon glare of the shop burning my already irritated eyes.

Fergus's shop was awfully like the cluttered mess he kept

hidden away from his customers, just more clutter and fewer boxes. Cheap supermarket stands sat beside antique bookshelves, both wedged between expensive glass display cases stacked with an astounding array of oddities and trinkets.

I ran my eye over the table in the middle. It changed every time I visited — today, it was cluttered with clocks, pocket watches, music boxes, and typewriters. I knew Fergus hid the best of his stock amongst the mess. His theory was that anything important would call to the buyer it was destined for, and that if some fool dropped a bag full of money on one of the pretty but useless knick knacks hidden behind the glass, they deserved what they got.

Quinn looked around the room, his eyes sparkling like a wean in a lolly shop. Ollie tugged his hand, and he trailed behind as she led him around, pointing out the skull of an old hermit cursed by a ceasg, and a small knife used by a hedge witch to cast the spell that would ensure her matrilineal line continued for all eternity. When she suddenly changed direction, dragging him past a tightly stacked bookshelf to look through a box of fossilised snails, Fergus sucked at his teeth and hummed approvingly.

"The lass has taken to him. She sees his potential."

"Potential to be a right pain in my arse," I grumbled.

Fergus subscribed to the old ways, believing a person destined for magic would show signs; random occurrences that, if interpreted by one experienced enough, would signify their aptitude for the craft. Much like his calculations for predicting future disaster, those signs and random occurrences made no bloody sense to anyone but him.

And anyway, I knew he was full of shite. Magic was a skill that was learned. With enough practice, any idiot could wield a spell. I was living proof of it.

"I canna say I envy him, learnin' with you." Fergus shot me a sideways glance. "Unless ye plan to let your wee sister do the work with him?"

Pushing away my irritation, I shook my head. "Ollie can't touch the Otherworld, not anymore. You know that."

"Aye, but she can still guide him." Fergus blew a puff of air through his nose. "She managed to teach you, and you had the potential of a stewed eel, didn't ye?"

I had spent enough years listening to Fergus's assertion that I should never have been able to learn magic, let alone follow in my Granda's steps to become a well-respected buidseach, that his jibes didn't bother me. "With the theory, at least."

Fergus wrinkled his mouth sourly. He didn't say the words aloud, but I could almost taste them. *Such a waste.* Yeah, well, it wasn't just her magic that was lost the day her life was taken, and damned if I would lament her lack of magic over her life, her freedom and her chance to lead a normal life.

"Laddie, come let me look at ye." Ignoring my glare, Fergus motioned Quinn to present himself to the old man. "What do ye know of magic?"

"Not much," Quinn admitted. "But I'd like to learn."

"Aye, that's a good start. Nothing worse than when a student comes in thinkin' he knows it all already." He peered into Quinn's eyes, sniffed his neck, then grabbed a wrist and lifted it to inspect Quinn's left armpit. "Aye, good stock. Let me guess, your Ma was a Scotswoman? Not yer Da, he was the one with the nice tan."

Quinn raised a bemused eyebrow. "You smelled that in my armpit?"

I figured it wouldn't hurt him to believe that, and Fergus certainly didn't admit I'd texted him the information before we arrived.

"Mack said that it didn't matter I'm only half Scots." Quinn tolerated his examination bravely but shook his head resolutely when Fergus told him to drop his breeks. "No chance, old man. My tweeds are staying put."

"Well, I suppose Mack is right enough. As long as ye don't barrack for the Rangers." Fergus screwed up his face at the thought of anyone pulling for a team other than his precious Celtics. "What's the first thing you want to know about it all? The one thing that burns into your brain at night, that keeps you awake 'til the wee hours, tossing and turning over it?"

Quinn gave me a questioning glance and waited for me to nod

before he answered. "It's probably a silly question... but how is all of this still a secret? The whole ghosts and spectres thing only came out a couple of years ago — back home they still have their head in the sand about it. Now I find out there's a whole world hidden in the shadows, waiting to kill us."

"We're not *all* homicidal monsters," Ollie protested. "Some of us just want to beat you up a wee bit."

"There are two types of people, lad." Fergus held up one finger. "The first? Dumb as a box of rocks. They'll believe anything ye tell 'em and because of that, all the rest think they're plonkers. Ye canna convince someone to listen to your stories of mermaids and magic horses if ye were tellin' 'em of aliens and moon conspiracies the day before."

"That makes sense, actually." Quinn sat with the idea a moment, digesting it. "But what about the rest? Surely if a sensible, well-respected person in the community says they saw a magic practitioner, people would take it more seriously. Not to mention, every man and his dog has a smart phone these days. Why aren't videos popping up all over the place?"

"Oh, there are films about. But there's also one of some penguins takin' flight, and that was put out by our very own BBC. Ye could summon up a herd of flying cows in front of their eyes and they would just ask ye where ye hid the film projector. That's why it's so hard to change the world, lad. Sometimes it's stubbornness, other times they're scared as a wean in a thunderstorm. They'd rather plug their ears and ignore it, than believe there's a whole world they just dinna see."

"No way." Quinn wore his scepticism openly. "People learn new stuff all the time."

"They only learn what they already believed." Fergus shrugged, seeming unphased by Quinn's rejection of the old man's philosophical ramblings. "No matter. Mack and I have work to do, lad. Off ye go, and don't touch anything that looks like it might be worth more'n fifty quid 'less ye can pay for it. Old Fergus doesn't have insurance."

"Yes, sir." Quinn ducked his head respectfully, then sidled off to join Ollie.

"Shall we get to it?" I asked.

Fergus nodded and moved over to his workbench, a long glass cabinet stuffed with taxidermy and a cluster of organs shoved into jars of murky liquid. I had seen it a thousand times and it still made my stomach squirm, but Fergus unrolled a sheet of brown paper over the top, thankfully obscuring the contents. Once he had weighed the corners down — three with stones shaped like arrows and one with an oversized glass eyeball that promptly rolled off the bench — I slipped a hand into my jacket. While Fergus squatted on the floor to look for the eye, I drew the tapestry out and unrolled it.

"Did ye have any trouble obtaining it?" Fergus popped up again, having given up on locating his eyeball. He dropped a handful of damp soil on the furled corner of paper.

I didn't ask where the hell he had found that. "Not initially. It was exactly where you said it would be. I don't think the lass had any idea what it was." I lifted my hand and let it hover over the fabric, fingers splayed. Channelling a tendril of spirit, I closed my eyes and let the magic emanating from the threads caress my hand. "Which begs the question... what is it?"

"Fecked if I know." Fergus busied himself with assembling a small stand that held a sheet of magnifying glass. He set it on the table and peered through. "Ye said initially. What's that supposed to mean?"

A quick glance confirmed Ollie and Quinn were out of earshot, huddled over a box of doorknobs. When I turned back to Fergus, I kept my voice low. "Someone jumped me later that night, after my set at the Stag. A bean sith. She knew about the tapestry, and she was adamant that she wasn't going to leave without it."

"What in the Otherworld would a jumped up fairy want with this?" Fergus frowned, and the slanted reflection in the glass twisted his face into a mean caricature.

"Not her," I clarified. "Whoever employed her services."

"A contracted sith isn't one to be shaken off," Fergus pointed out. "What'd ye do to her?"

"She ate bitumen. Or rather, the bitumen ate her." I shrugged, brushing away the slight guilt I felt over killing one of the sithche. Sure, I would have made the same choice again, but the fact remained that once a deal was made, the choice to step down was out of her hands. "Fergus, she had a scrap of paper tucked in her top. It had your address on it, and Claire McAdam's."

"That's a bother." Fergus opened his mouth to blow steam on the magnifier, then use his stumpy arm to wipe it clean. He finally broke his gaze from the artefact before him and looked up to meet my eyes. "Mack, I heard about Auggie. I'm so sorry."

"Granda had a good run," I said, looking away awkwardly. He and Fergus had been close. "The police are looking into it."

"Your wee bean sith might have been able to answer a few questions about it," he mused, his attention already drawn back to the tapestry.

My skin twitched like I had touched a live wire. "What? What's she got to do with Granda?" I waited, but the bastard had gone back to picking at the needlework. "Fecking hell, Fergus, if you know something you need to bloody tell me!"

"What? Oh, the sith. Well, the tapestry was for Auggie. He's the one who tracked it down to the current owner — some Canadian exporter — and had it shipped here. When everything went arse up, it was Auggie what managed to track down the syndicate who stole all the shit that came with it. I had me own people on it, but they came up empty." Fergus squinted at the glass. "Bloody fine work. It's older than I thought when ye plonked it down, but it's in impeccable condition."

"Shite on a biscuit, Fergus. You can't just drop that kind of news on me without warning." I rubbed my face, wondering how much I could — or should — share with Fife. Though I wanted her to catch Granda's killer, I didn't want to hand the tapestry over to her team. Especially after the cock up with my bloody car keys.

"Mack, this is going to take a lot longer than I thought it would. The pattern of this magic is old, much older than the piddling enchantments I usually work with." Fergus raised his head again. "Can ye leave it with me for a few days, lad? Auggie told me it was special, but not much more'n that. Only if ye want to, mind

— By rights it's yours if ye want to take it now."

"No bloody point having it if I don't even know what it is." Giggling from behind me drew my eyes back to my sister and her new friend. Quinn had a pair of old fashioned glasses perched on his face, and Ollie's cheek screwed up to hold a monocle in place. I turned back to Fergus. "Can you keep it safe if I leave it with you?"

"What do ye think this is, a bloody supermarket?" Fergus scoffed. "I run a tight ship, Mack. It won't leave me sight until you come back for it. I'll even keep an eye on it while I sleep."

"You'll have to find it first." I gestured at the floor in the direction the eyeball had rolled off.

"Aye," Fergus said with a chuckle. "Do ye need a hand getting' your lad set up to go?"

I nodded vigorously. "If you don't mind. I'm a bit skint on beginner level books, and I'll need some basic supplies for the entry level stuff." The two scallywags behind me fell quiet and I guessed they were listening in.

"Did ye tell him about the ritual sacrifice?" Fergus ducked his head and gave me a quick wink, his eyes twinkling.

They were definitely listening, then. "I didn't want to scare the lad away, Fergus. Still, I should give him a heads up, aye? All that blood and guts, and the screaming. Loud enough to shake a man to the bones, aye? Best not take him by surprise, because one wrong move during the ceremony..."

Fergus nodded seriously as he drew his thumb across his throat. "Aye. You don't want a repeat of what happened to the last one. Gods, that was a mess to clean up, and havin' to tell his poor, sweet —"

"Henry Augustus MacDonald." Ollie shot to her feet, hands on hips and an angry scowl on her face. "Don't you think for a second Davey would fall for your rubbish. He knows damn well you're takin' the piss, and he's not a bit scared."

Quinn didn't seem quite as convinced. His dark skin had gone a kind of grey colour and the whites of his eyes were showing. When he caught me watching him, he mustered an uneasy chuckle.

"Yeah. Sure. I knew you were joking." He smiled tightly before hiding his face in a dusty old book.

Maybe I'd have been convinced if he wasn't reading it upside down. "Since when is he Davey?" I asked Ollie.

"And what's wrong with it?" she demanded.

"Nothing!" I raised my hands defensively. "Nothing wrong with it at all."

"The lad will be fine, wean." Fergus wagged a finger at Ollie. "It does a boy good to have a bit of fright put in him. It prepares him for the nastier stuff he'll have to deal with, and ye canna say there won't be any of that, can ye?"

"There are better ways of going about it." Ollie flicked a bit of dust from her sleeve, then folded herself up to sit on the floor cross legged in front of a box of books. "Fergus, do you still have that old book of herbal remedies? The one with the green cover."

"Look on the crooked bookshelf behind the stuffed pigeon. Third shelf down, about halfway along, tucked behind the Faust and the third Potter book." Fergus answered without missing a beat and I wondered, not for the first time, if he had the location of every item in his shop memorised. If he did, it would be quite the feat considering it all moved on a regular basis. "Now, what does the lad need?"

I hesitated. "Honestly, I've no bloody idea. I've never taken on a student, and my own induction was a bit different to the usual." In fact, I didn't even remember having one. Raised by the fifth generation buidseach, magic had simply been a way of life, surrounding me for as long as I could remember.

"Yer Da never taught you about the rites? Lesson structures, learnin' plans, aptitude tests?" Fergus shook his head with a sigh. "Poor lad's going to have a rough time of it if his bloody master doesnae know his baws from his paws."

"Hands, baws." I held up my hands then pointed to my nethers. "See? It'll be fine, Fergus. How hard can it be?"

"Ye know what they say about last words bein' famous and all that." Fergus leaned around me to call over to Ollie. "Lassie? Promise me ye won't let yer brother blow up the city with his new pet, aye?"

"I'll keep him in check, Fergus." Ollie grinned and winked at me.

"Thanks for the vote of confidence, shite-goblin."

"Love you too, brother dear." Ollie blew me a kiss.

"Lassie, can ye trot on over to that set of green shelves? Aye, that one. Bottom shelf, six from the end. Aye, the black one next to the Book of Appin. Now, two shelves up and right in the middle, between the Shakespeare and the Maritime History of Papua New Guinea there should be one with a cracked leather spine. No, a wee bit to your left. Aye, perfect. Grab the orange one three over, too. Now, on that table over there, right about the middle, there's a wee satchel in the yellow — och, good lassie."

Ollie brought the pile of goods over, skipping on light feet. She deposited them on the counter, placing them carefully away from the tapestry, and ran back to check on Quinn.

The books were old and tattered. I picked up the first one and blew a coat of dust from the spine. The fabric cover was blank, so I cracked it open. The Idiot's Guide To Magick Apprenticing.

I gave Fergus a dry look. "Thanks."

The second book was a collection of basic cantrips and the third a book of Scottish legends. It mostly covered the basics — ceasg, kelpies, banshee and baobhan sith. All things I could have told Quinn about myself, but setting him some basic readings might free my time up for more important things. And, though I would never admit it, make sure that his knowledge wasn't lacking due to me having a memory like a goldfish swimming in a cask of rum.

"This is for the lad." Fergus unbuckled the satchel and pulled out a fat journal, some vials, a sewing kit and a feathered quill.

"Bloody hell, Fergus. You know you can take notes on a phone now? He doesn't need a twelve-hundred year old pen."

"Watch your mouth, lad. This was mine, once."

I opened the book and flicked through the empty pages. "Uh-huh. Sure. And I see you used it well."

Fergus slapped a hand on the book, closing it. "I never said I was a model student. Besides, do ye know how bloody hard it is to use this shite one-handed?"

"Then you and me have more in common than I thought." I slipped the contents back into the bag and strapped it closed again. "Thank you, Fergus."

"Will you need help with the official forms?" He didn't look up as he spoke, but his attempt to keep his tone casual didn't work.

I tried to keep my own voice even as I answered, knowing he only wanted to help. "I'm not a complete dafty, Fergus. I can read. Probably better than you."

"Never said you couldn't." Fergus rolled the tapestry up carefully. "But the Collective keeps bloody changing the website, and I swear by Beira's eye, those bloody questions get worse every year."

The prospect of navigating the complex website of the Collective, an organisation created to track and legislate the use of magic, was enough to make my guts plummet to my boots. And I couldn't really be mad at Fergus — I had a bad track record when it came to completing official documents. Which was probably why Fife had led me out of the SCOOP building and filled the statement out on my behalf when I left her earlier.

I had a secret weapon up my sleeve, though. "Come on, Ollie. We need to get home — you've got forms to fill out."

Her eyes brightened as much as a dead girl's could. "Canna wait!"

Outside, the last glow of dusk had faded to pitch. The rain hadn't stopped, but had gained a weight that suggested it could turn into a deluge at any moment. We hurried across the private carpark to the Demon, and this time I wasn't the only one casting nervous glances at the shadows.

"Quinn?" I called, voice casual.

"Aye, Henry?"

I flashed a wicked grin. "Drop."

Whether it was a fine-honed sense of self-preservation, or the barely-better-than-shite training the Glasgow police had put him through, Quinn threw himself down. Just in time, too, as a pikestaff stabbed the air where he had stood moments before.

Hands up, fingers moving despite the numbing cold, I spun off the fastest defensive shield I could manage. Before it was done, a small humanoid launched off the ground and tackled me, pike discarded on the ground. Thin fingers clutched at my neck and pierced the skin with sharp claws. The wee demon's red hat pressed against my face and the rotting stench of it made my stomach roil.

A heartbeat later, it jerked away. The soft skin of my neck stung as sharp nails raked across my tender human flesh, but it was a small price to pay for the satisfaction of seeing it slam into a brick wall with a bony crunch.

"Thanks, Ollie." My words were strangled, but Ollie gave me a nod of acknowledgement.

She dropped into a defensive crouch, hands raised and ready for the beastie's next attack. When it happened, it was too fast for me to see — one second it was a crumpled heap in a gutter, the next it was latched onto Ollie's hair, beating at her skull with a stone.

"Oi! Let my sister alone, you hackit little garden gnome!" Apparently, the wee prick didn't like being called ugly; or maybe it was gnome that riled him. It raised its big eyes to glare at me and the fiery hells burning in them sent me stumbling back a few paces. "Oh, shite."

Using the top of Ollie's head as a springboard, it jumped to me. I threw up a hand just in time to protect my stunning looks but squealed like a lass when the red cap snatched a handful of my hair and yanked it out of my head.

It crawled down the back of my neck, so I flung myself down, aiming to squash it on the ground. I slammed onto the wet road, winding myself badly and smacking my head on the ground in the process. The bastard red cap had already scampered away.

"Feck's sake, Mack." Ollie huffed a disappointed breath, then flung herself across the small allotment, bounced off a wall, then crash tackled the goblin. They scuffled and splashed and someone let out an inhuman yelp. Probably not Ollie, but I couldn't be sure.

"Quinn!" I yelled. When he looked up, I tossed my keys. They landed in a puddle by his face. "Back seat, brown bag, silver cross."

Quinn scampered toward the car and I darted over to help

Ollie. Not that she needed it — she had the wee goblin by the feet and seemed unconcerned about its mouth being attached to her arm.

"Lucky you don't bleed, lass."

"You're a useless knob, aren't you?" Ollie grunted, then grabbed the red cap's head, hooking two fingers up its nose for leverage. A quick motion yanked it up and pulled the long teeth out of her arm, leaving four neat holes behind. She stretched it out, feet in one hand, scalp in the other as it squirmed. "One wee goblin and you're on your back with your legs in the air like a —"

"Don't you dare finish that," I warned as Quinn trotted up with my crucifix. Even in the gloom it sparkled, giving me a flash of pride. It was custom made, a blend of silver and steel, and weighed about as much as you'd expect of a solid metal bar infused with the magic of the ancients. I plucked it out of his hands and held it out to Ollie. "Do you want to do the honours?"

Ollie grinned and turned to Quinn. "How about we give Davey a turn? He'll need to learn how to put a red cap down eventually. Why not start now?"

Chuckling at Quinn's terrified expression I passed the cross back to him. He gripped it hard and set his jaw. "What do I have to do?"

"Just press the cross onto its belly," Ollie said. "Och, no, not like that. The wee Jesus should face the other way." Ollie looked at me, exasperated.

Before she could hurl another insult to my intelligence, I jumped in to help Quinn. I flipped the cross around so it faced toward the red cap and showed Quinn how to grip it near the bottom so he wouldn't get his hands burnt off. "Now, lift up its little shirt and toss it on. Mind your eyes — they get a bit messy when they pop."

"Pop?" Quinn swallowed but did as he was told. Gripping the cross, he pressed it down onto white, bloated goblin flesh. When the red cap began to sizzle and steam, he pressed harder, though he had the sense to turn his face away just before the wee bastard exploded into a shower of blood and guts.

Now, red caps are angry little pricks, but at least they have the good grace to evaporate once you kill the bastards. Before Quinn could wipe the slop off his face, it dissipated to wherever goblin entrails go when they meet the light of day, leaving behind nothing but a crusty, malodorous hat and a long, shining tooth.

I picked the remnants up. "Here you go, your first trophies."

Quinn gingerly took the items, holding them at arm's length once the stink reached his nostrils. "What's that smell?" he choked out. Brown-tinged rain dribbled off the hat.

"It's their wee caps," Ollie explained. "They're actually white. They dip their hats in the blood of their kills, and gods forbid they wash the bloody things. They end up smelling like wet roadkill on a sunny —"

Ollie stopped at the look on Quinn's face, but it was too late. Dumping the spoils of his victory on the ground, he rushed to a corner and puked his guts up just as the back door to Fergus's shop opened.

He cackled in glee. "You right, lad? You're lookin' a bit peely-wally."

"Leave off, Fergus. It stinks like mank fish guts out here. You'd be feelin' ill too if you caught a whiff of this thing." Ollie used the toe of her shoe to flick the sodden hat away from where we stood. It landed near Fergus and he jumped away to avoid the splash hitting his feet.

Fergus snorted. "And how would ye know what it stinks like, lass? Last I checked, dead people canna smell a thing."

She scowled and stuck her tongue out at him in response. For all that she insisted she was an adult by virtue of the years she had spent on earth, sometimes she acted like a proper twelve year old.

"Did you know that little bastard was lying in wait for us?" I asked Fergus.

"Aye. Wanted to see how your lad would do. Bit weak in the guts, but he handled himself alright, despite the utter failure of his mentor to impart a single bit o' wisdom during his first trial." Fergus tottered over to Quinn once he had finished.

"No, thanks." Quinn eyed the stained, wrinkled hanky Fergus

held out to him. "I'm good."

"Smart lad," I said. "The Devil only knows where he got it. Fergus, I swear to the Cailleach herself, if you let us walk into a mess like that again without warning, I'll stuff your tailpipe with red cap hats and hide the rest in your curtain rods."

"No need to be mean." Fergus ambled back to the shop. "I knew Ollie would handle the little turd just fine." He paused to look back at me, the mirth drained from his face. "But watch your back, Henry Mack. Auggie's dead, then you said you were jumped by a glaistig. Now a red cap? Someone has it out for you and yours, mark my words."

"Just keep that bit of cloth safe, aye?"

"Ye know I will, Mack. Take care." Fergus disappeared back inside, and I heard the heavy barricade slide back into place. Devil knows how he lifted the bloody thing one-armed.

I turned to Ollie and Quinn. "Well, that was a bit of fun. Who else needs a swallie?"

Quinn glanced at Ollie, who said in a loud whisper, "It means a drink, Davey."

"Oh. Yeah. I could do with one."

"Bloody foreigner." I winked to show him I held no hard feelings over his poor grasp of our beautiful language. "Come on. Tonight, we drink. Tomorrow, we teach you how to speak Scots like a real man. Now give those bloody keys back, you're not driving my baby."

Chapter Nine

By the time we arrived at the flat, the skies had opened. I parked around back, tugged my jacket over my head, and grabbed the door handle. "You right to get up, Ollie?"

"No, Mack. I need you to hold my bloody hand and walk me there like a suckling wean."

"Be like that, then." I spoke without malice, knowing her ire had nothing to do with me for a change. Ollie hated the rain. It reminded her of all the sensations she no longer had — for her, there was no icy shiver from the dribbles running down your back, no stinging aroma as the first fat drops hit the bitumen. Once inside and dried off, her mood would likely perk up a bit. Especially now she had a new pet to take care of. Speaking of which... "Quinn, you ready?"

"I take it you're not the sort to keep a brolly in the car?" Quinn stared mournfully at the rippling drips that slid down his window.

"Don't be a pussy." I darted out of the car. "And don't forget to lock the door!"

"Haven't you ever heard of central locking?" Quinn popped the lock down and slammed the door. He jogged through the rain to catch up, hugging the wall of the building to take advantage of the thin slice of shelter it offered.

As I rounded the corner I opened my mouth to respond, but only a soft, "Oh, shite," came out. Leaning against the front door, her hair slightly frizzed from the damp, was no other than Annie Fife. Like Quinn, she had swapped her usual office attire for jeans and a t-shirt.

"Annie!" I forced a grin. "Nice to see you, pet. Is everything well?"

She pointedly looked over my shoulder, then gave a hum of approval. "Is that your new student, Mack? Not what I expected, but he'll do, I suppose."

"Thank you for your evaluation, Detective. I'm sure you know exactly what it takes to become a proficient student of the forbidden arts."

She eyed me up and down, taking in my torn jeans, scratched up face, and my half-soaked coat. "Not much, I assume. After all, you managed it." She flashed me a quick smile to take the sting out of her words. "And you never know — maybe the student will become the teacher and show you how to dress properly."

"David Quinn, meet Detective Chief Inspector Annie Fife, poster-child for the S.O.P.D. and general thorn in my side."

"Honour to meet you, DCI Fife." Quinn quickly held his hand out and Fife shook it bemusedly.

"Nice to meet you too, constable. Mack, do you have time for a wee chat?" Before I could foist her off with an excuse, she added, "That wasn't really a question."

"I don't suppose it's wee enough to have on my doorstep?" I guessed not, or she would have just texted me the information.

Fife shook her head. "Sorry. It's a doozy, this one."

"Then be my guest." I waved her ahead of me and she shoved the heavy door to the building open. I would just have to hope Ollie had the sense to stay hidden for a bit.

We made our way up the stairwell and to my flat. At the door, I coughed twice and dropped my keys with a jingling crash. "Oops, sorry about that Detective Fife."

Fife narrowed her eyes. Maybe I shouldn't have yelled quite so loud, but a wee bit of suspicion was better than my dead sister opening the door to an officer of the S.O.P.D.

Thankfully, the living room was empty when I swung the door open. I was less grateful to hear the shower running.

"Sorry Mack, I didn't realise you had a guest." Fife didn't look a bit sorry. Her eyes eagerly scoured the flat, probably looking for clues as to who I might be shacked up with.

"Aye," I said, hurrying towards the bathroom. "I'll just let her know you're here. Don't want a naked lady prancing about in front of two poli —"

I was too bloody slow. The bathroom door opened and Ollie stuck her head out. Her hair was wrapped in a towel and drips of water splotched over a clean blouse. Despite the billow of steam that escaped, there was no healthy glow on her face from the heat to offset the dark rings under her dead eyes, or her pale, lifeless lips. Even if there had been, there was no mistaking the opaque glassiness in her eyes. "Mack, the bloody taps are stuck again. I can't turn it off!"

"Stand back!" Fife had already grabbed my broom and held it out threateningly towards Ollie.

"Oh no you fecking don't." I darted between the two. "You even think about laying a hand on my sister and I'll start brawling you."

"Don't be a numpty, Mack," Ollie piped up. "She's holding a broom! She could hit me on the head with an iron crowbar and it wouldn't leave a dent. Now can you fix the taps, *please*?" Panic was beginning to well on her face.

"Allright love, just give me a —"

"Henry, you better give me a bloody good explanation right this second, or I'll shove this broom so far up your arse you'll be blowing splinters out your nose for the next month." To her credit, Fife didn't look a bit scared.

Quinn, on the other hand, looked as though his chief superintendent had just walked in on him with his baws on the photocopier.

“Mack? The *water*?” Ollie jerked her head imploringly in the direction of the bathroom.

“Fine, just promise me you won’t hurt anyone in the meantime.”

“I’m Olivia MacDonald.” Ollie pushed past me and held out a hand to Fife. “It’s so nice to finally meet you, Detective. Henry has told me so much about you.”

Faced with such politeness, Fife had no choice but to respond. She kept a white-knuckled grip on the broom with one hand, but held the other out cautiously.

I nodded and scurried away to escape the tension in the living room. I grabbed the wrench from the bathroom sink, left there for just such occasions, and gave the tap a few solid whacks. A couple of turns later, the shower head dribbled to a stop.

Before I strolled out of the bathroom like I wasn’t casually stepping into a war zone, I poked my head out the doorway. Fife’s hand was still in Ollie’s, and the detective was muttering some platitude to my sister. Her eyes, however, were aimed in my direction and spitting daggers.

When she spoke it was through gritted teeth. “I’m sorry I took such a shock on seeing you, Olivia. I don’t believe Henry ever mentioned you to me.”

“I did too!” I protested. “I talked about her for a solid five minutes in our interview today.”

“The one where you categorically denied, on record, having spoken to your sister since she died?” Fife dropped Ollie’s hand and swung the broomstick so that it pointed at me instead.

“Technically, if you recall, I denied speaking to her ghost. As you can see, Ollie isn’t a ghost. She’s a zombie. Sort of. But definitely *not* a ghost.” With a winning smile and a sudden burst of courage — or stupidity, I can never tell which is which — I strode forward and took the broom out of Fife’s hand. She held onto it for a moment, then let it go. “Look, Annie. You know that if anyone knew about her, they’d be after her with flaming torches and buckets of salt. I couldn’t let that happen. She’s my sister.”

“Do you have any idea how many laws you’ve broken?” Fife

snapped.

I shrugged. "Do you? As far as I can tell, I'm within the framework of catch and dispatch. I've taken control of the previously deceased entity and I've ensured any threats posed by it are eliminated. I may have neglected to file a few scraps of paperwork, but I haven't broken any laws that I know of."

Fife's mouth dropped open in shock. "Well, feck me. You might be right — don't think I won't check, though." She looked Ollie over. "You're sure she's not dangerous?"

"She can speak for herself, thank you detective." Ollie slowed her words down and over-enunciated them like she was speaking to an eejit. Then, with a cheerful smile, she added, "I'm at least twice as smart as my brother, and far nicer."

"You're... not quite a proper zombie, are you?" Fife took a step closer to Ollie. "Not like on the telly, I mean. You've still got your mental faculties. All of them, I assume?" She looked to me for confirmation, and I nodded. "What do you eat, then?"

Ollie lifted one shoulder in a shrug. "Sweets, mostly. I don't get hungry. Or tired or weak, nothing like that."

"She'll clean out your liquor cabinet in a day though," I muttered.

Ollie slapped my shoulder. "Hold your mouth, you big ugly shite."

Fife seemed more bothered by that than anything else she had seen. *Bloody coppers.* "Mack, tell me you're joking. She can't be more than thirteen."

"Detective Fife, I have already gone over this with your colleague. And half of bloody Glasgow, it feels like. Did you miss the part where we share a birth date?" Ollie asked.

Fife's brow furrowed. "Oh." She looked Ollie over, then sighed. "It's not like I can drag either one of you down to the station and have you charged, anyway."

"Ollie has the right of it, Fife. She's the same age as me. And as much as it pains my old heart to see the face of a wee angel swearing like a sailor, you do get used to it after a while."

"Now that's settled, Detective, to what do we owe the pleasure of your visit?" Assured that she was not about to be handcuffed and thrown in a cell for underage drinking or for being more dead than alive, Ollie flopped onto the couch comfortably.

"I'm here because there's a small problem regarding your brother's alibi for the morning of your grandfather's death." Ever the stoic, Fife had already gotten over her shock and slipped back into the brisk persona she wore on the job.

"Hold up, Fife. What did that scheming woman tell you? I was where I said I was, when I said I was there, and as far as Claire McAdam knows, I saved her damn life. Even if she tried to deny it, you've got the catch and dispatch call records to confirm it."

"It wasn't your whereabouts that are the issue, Mack. McAdam's whole house was wired with security cameras. The video evidence shows you were there, and that's more than enough to clear you for your grandfather's matter." Fife slipped her phone out of her pocket and tapped the screen a few times.

"Then what's the bloody problem?" I scowled at the bright screen Fife handed to me. I tapped the white triangle in the middle of the screen, and a video began to play. It was the front door to Claire's house, and showed my arrival early the previous morning. I watched myself enter the house and close the door behind me. "How long do I have to sit here watching a door before you tell me what the hell is going on, Fife?"

Fife leaned over and tilted the screen so she could see it. She dragged her finger along the progress bar at the bottom, passing over my departure at supersonic speed. The door brightened, then dimmed as it began to rain. Brightened again, then faded slowly as the sun set. A yellow light flicked on and a blurred figure vanished inside too quick for me to see. Fife cursed, pulling the video back a few minutes so I could watch. Quinn, curiosity getting the better of him, wandered over to stand behind me and peer over my shoulder.

The figure approached the door again, this time at normal speed. Or perhaps not. Though the playback had resumed its normal pace, the woman who slipped up to the door moved just a little too fast. She flicked her long blonde hair and it rippled down her back. She turned her head, face tilted just enough so that she looked directly at the camera. She smiled and ran her tongue over her pointed teeth before grasping the door handle and snapping it off. The woman reached out with a manicured finger and pushed open the door.

"Tell me I'm not the only one who saw that," Quinn said. "Her teeth, I mean. Did you see her teeth?"

"Aye, Davey. We saw it." Ollie glanced up at him. "You're not going to be sick again, are you?"

Fife's head jerked in my direction. "Do I want to know?"

"Only if you want to spend now until your retirement filling out paperwork," I shot back.

Fife considered it. "Do you have any idea just how much I let you get away with, Mack?"

"Too bloody much. By the same token, do you realise how often I risk life and limb to keep the citizens of Glasgow safe, sound, and blissfully unaware of the monsters that hide in the shadows?"

Fife directed my attention back to the tiny screen. A shadow, cast by the lights inside the house, flickered across the rectangle of light. Then, again. In a flurry of movement, Claire McAdam burst onto the screen, tumbling out of her doorway with wide eyes and a bloody scratch across her cheek. Before she could take more than two steps, a hand reached out and snatched her hair. Claire's head jerked back, exposing her pale throat. Her white flesh glistened in the misting rain.

The intruder stepped closer to her victim so they were both perfectly framed by the camera. Claire's chest heaved in panic, and when a hand gently caressed her throat, her mouth opened in a silent scream. One finger stretched out, and we watched the glistening red nail stretch and darken to form a sharp talon. It drew across bare flesh, leaving a dark and oozing line behind it. When the vampire — for only a vampire would take her victims in such a way — pressed her mouth against the wound to drink, her eyes lifted to the watching camera. As she drained the life of her prey, her gaze penetrated deep into my soul as if she were there before me.

Slowly, Claire's writhing protests stilled. She slumped, cradled in the arms of her killer. Finally sated, the vampire lifted her lips away. She smiled, her teeth still stained from her meal. Wiping away a trickle of blood that dripped down her chin with a ladylike finger, she tossed the body aside like an empty burger wrapper. For the grand finale, the woman crouched down, her body twisting and shrinking as it darkened. Moments later a glossy crow spread its wings and flapped off into the night.

"Mack?" Quinn's voice cracked and he cleared his throat. "Any chance of another drink?"

Not trusting myself to answer, I simply nodded and stood. After I grabbed the whisky from the kitchen, I waggled it at Fife. She gave a tired nod. "I'm supposed to be home resting," she explained. "As if anyone could sleep after seeing that."

"Detective, do you mind showing me that again?" Ollie asked. She took the phone Fife handed to her and frowned at the screen as she dragged her finger across the playback control. "And I'll have a double, please, Mack."

I poured four drinks, tucked the bottle under my arm, and clutched the glasses. Fife grabbed two and set them on the coffee table so I could unload them safely, but by the time I reached for my drink she was staring into an empty glass.

I nudged the bottle toward her. "I've seen some nasty shite in my time," I said as she refilled her drink. "I've even seen the odd person die. That was something else, though."

"I just don't understand." Fife rubbed her face. "Or... Maybe I do. They're monsters, I know that. But the vampires we met worked bloody hard to keep up an appearance of being civilised, law abiding people."

"Until you start arguing theology with them." It was, apparently, how Steve had ended up with his concussion.

"Mack, Fife's right, it doesn't make a lick of sense." Ollie absently took her drink and sipped it, her eyes still watching the tiny screen. "The baobhan sith are still in hiding from the regular world. They've only liaised with the S.O.P.D. so they could stay off the books, so to speak. Surely they wouldn't just walk on up to a house, kill the inhabitant and make a show of eating her on camera."

"That's how you say their name? That Agnes woman just called them "Ladies of the Night". Took her a while to convince us she wasn't just running a brothel." Fife said. She shotted the second drink and I raised an eyebrow. I knew she had the stomach for it, but it was odd to see her shaken like this.

"Baa'van shee." Ollie enunciated the words carefully for Fife and Quinn's benefit. "They're basically vampires." Ollie turned the phone to face me. The baobhan sith's frozen face stared into the security camera with unbridled arrogance. "Even if they decided to reveal themselves to the public, they wouldn't be stupid enough to do it like this. It's not their style."

"Wait, go back." Quinn rubbed a hand over his face. "Aren't vampires all about biting and bats?"

"We're not in Romania, Davey." Ollie seemed happy to give the lesson, so I sat back and stared into the swirling amber liquid in my hand. "Scottish vampires are sith, like the ceasg — they're mermaids — and kelpies and the like. They kill with their talons, like you saw, and they drink the blood of their victim. They're always women — total feminists, they are — they run in groups, and they can shapeshift into crows or wolves. The Glasgow baobhan sith are led by Agnes Ban-Righ. She's a canny one, and up until now she's been resolute in keeping the existence of the vampires and those they ally with under wraps."

"How many allies does she have, exactly?" Fife poured a third drink. "And more to the question, how bad have I screwed up by not asking in the first place?"

Ollie watched her curiously. "Detective, surely you don't think the creatures of the fae have been kept in check by the Scottish police all this time?"

"Not really," Fife admitted. "But I wanted to."

"The sith, the witches, the buidseach... all of them have a vested interest in staying under the radar." Ollie left herself off that list, I noted. "Agnes knows that, she wouldn't let one of her lassies off and screw it up for everyone."

"You wouldn't even know about the ghosts if that eejit Frank McGillie hadn't cocked up his summoning spell." I flinched under

Fife's glare. "Don't you look at me like that, I had nothing to do with it! McGillie got the bright idea to use a real, live ghost in his horror show all on his own. He didn't account for how hungry the dead bastard would get, faced with all those tasty teenage brains."

Fife paled at the memory. The haunted house ride had been a dying attraction at a travelling funfair. Despite the latex puppets and underpaid actors that were supplemented with a wee bit of magic, its run down façade and the real-life existence of genuinely scary things like taxes, plagues and Brexit, the haunted house just didn't hold the appeal that it did a few scant decades ago.

The Otherworld community had never admitted what Frank McGillie had traded for that spell, but the results would change the landscape of Scotland forever.

After breaking free from the spell binding it, the spectre had launched itself onto the three visitors to the attraction, tearing their heads off and scattering their entrails before turning its attention to the man who raised it. The spectre made short work of McGillie. The moaning bastard then made its way through the crowd at the fair, ignoring any and all attempts to bring it down. By the time the armed forces were involved, the spectre had killed two dozen people.

That was when we stepped in. And by we, I mean Granda. Ignoring the orders of his fellow buidseach, the pleas of the seelie court and the less-pleading and more-threatening demands of the unseelie court, he presented himself at the cordoned-off site, used a bit of magical deception to sneak his way in, and dispelled the curse that had raised the poor fellow from his nap.

Of course Granda, being the way he was, dinna realise every bit of it had been caught on camera. Within a week, it had gone viral. Not only that, a retired superintendent of Police Scotland had stepped forward and lambasted the powers that be for refusing to allocate resources to investigate such things. He leaked files on ghost sightings, loch ness monster attacks, and one account of a leprechaun swindling the residents of an old folks home out of their money. Utter tripe, that was — any idiot knows leprechauns are too stupid for a scheme like that.

"Agnes has styled herself Queen of Glasgow." I mulled over the problem at hand, talking out loud as I did. "She's always been clear about her stance — the sith should remain hidden from humans, at any cost."

"Any cost?" Fife raised an eyebrow.

"Aye. Annie, these aren't CEOs or politicians you're talking about. They are predators." I gestured at the now-blank phone screen. "They kill people every now and then — less since the collective began to take shape, and —"

"The Collective?" Fife's interjection held a brisk note of impatience and I made a note to myself to shut the hell up and stop giving her things to ask about.

"Aye." I sighed. "I shouldna' be telling you any of this, right?" Fife's lips thinned to a line, considering. Then she nodded. "The Collective is a group comprised of humans and sith, both friendly and not. There was talk of an alliance once the telephone came into common use, but they really lit a firecracker under it once the internet landed in the lap of every bairn in Scotland. Their job is to keep the Otherworlders out of the public eye. Keep them safe, right?"

Fife choked on her next Scotch. "*Safe*?"

"You spit out my liquor again and I'll cut you off," I admonished her. "And yes, safe. Bloody humans. When sharks and tigers eat people, we put them on a list and tell everyone not to hunt them. The sith are part of our world, part of our history. If they were known to humans, they'd be hunted down. Annie, it would be a genocide."

"So you just let them run around killing people?" Her white knuckled grip on the glass tightened.

I snatched the Scotch from the table before she could reach for it again. "Don't be a dafty. The baobhan sith hardly kill at all anymore. Do you know how many lads and lasses are desperate to act as their buffet? Nah, most feedings are consensual. They even have a selection of contract templates to sign, depending on your kink."

"Who would do that?" Quinn asked in dismay. "After what we

saw on that video. No one would agree to that."

"It's not *like* that," I explained. "Not normally. They use a bit of magic, soften them up, and have a wee nibble is all. The humans are well paid and they enjoy it. Bit like sugar mamas, the vamps, and the humans get all the effects of a good high without any of the pesky side effects like addiction or scabs. Every now and then they'll turn a lass, but every bit of it follows the informed consent guidelines."

"Claire McAdam didn't sign her life away, Mack. You can't convince me she chose to die like that."

"That's what worries me." I swigged from the bottle in my hands, ignoring Fife's look of disgust. "Either Agnes is declaring war against the humans and the rest of the collective, or she has a rogue player. Someone stupid enough to break her rules, someone with a death wish... or someone with enough power to think they'll survive her wrath."

"How do I speak with Agnes? She didn't exactly leave her email address the first time she made contact."

My jaw dropped. "Annie, no. You canna speak to the Vampire Queen. She's a complete witch! Not to mention, her ego is even bigger than yo — mine. Bigger than mine." I swallowed nervously, but Fife simply blinked. "And how the bloody hell are you not slurring yet? You've drunk half the bottle, love."

"I can hold my whisky."

Ollie helpfully piped up from beside Quinn. "Not everyone's a lightweight like you, Mack."

"Off with you, wench." I blew out a breath, dragging my mind back to the topic at hand. "Why did you show me that video? You know I was there. Since when does procedure let you share evidence with a suspect?"

"Mack, come on. You wouldn't have admitted to being there if you were guilty, and you sure as hell wouldn't have called me and asked one of my officers to go check on the girl." Fife frowned. "I need your help. I don't have anyone else to turn to."

"What about your wee rodent consultant?" It was too much to expect he had been taken off the books, even after his wee outburst at the station. Fife was too desperate.

"Rattray has scarpered. He was supposed to come in for a disciplinary and he never showed. Who else am I going to ask?"

I lifted one eyebrow. She wasn't doing a very good job of convincing me I was the first person on her list of people to turn to. "And you're sure I'm not a suspect?"

"You can if you want to be, I suppose. But you don't look that nice in red lippy and a dress. No offence." Fife sighed. "And let's be honest, even if you used a spell to brainwash that pointy-fingered bitch, or you summoned her up from some alternate dimension to do your bidding, what am I going to do about it? None of this exists, not officially. Even catch and dispatch are only supposed to know how to fling a bit of salt about." She put her glass down, finally, with a solid thump.

When her eyes met mine, rimmed with red and heavy with fatigue, I understood. Fife had finally come to the realisation that a lot of bad shite was out there. Big, nasty, dangerous shite that didn't play by the rules. And worse, she couldn't do a damn thing about it. After years of denying the possibility of magic, of creatures from our ancient myths and legends, Police Scotland had been dragged kicking and screaming into a reality where the dead could move... and they were still in resolute denial that anything else might exist.

"Look, Annie." I reached out a hand and carefully placed it on hers. She endured the gesture, but not happily. "I know it's a lot to take in. But you're not fighting this fight alone. It's not just monsters hiding in the shadows — there are a lot of good people there, too, people who work bloody hard to keep you lot safe from the things you don't understand."

"People and zombies," Ollie corrected. "One zombie. Me. I'm talking about myself."

Fife snorted a short laugh. "Well, I suppose the cat's out of the bag now. I'll just have to deal with it. It'd be easier with another drink, though."

I obliged, pouring her a generous couple of fingers before topping up Quinn's glass. Ollie watched the bottle drain and sighed. "You have that last bit, Mack."

"You sure?" I held it up, waving it at her. "There's enough for two wee swallies."

"I saw you put your disgusting lips on it, you pig," she reminded me. "And I know where they've been."

"I do have one question." Fife pursed her lips at me. "What were you doing at McAdam's house?"

"Answering a call. You have it on record."

"Aye, you got a call... and you arrived in about twenty seconds. Mack, you live half an hour away from Coatbridge."

"Oh. Right."

"And while we're at it," Fife continued, darting a suspicious glance at Ollie. "That call described the previously deceased as a young lass, brown hair, about one-hundred and forty centimetres. Not a single mention of it drifting through walls or anything, either."

"I can explain," I began, but she cut me off.

"In fact, you've had more than one callout for a previously deceased with that description. A description that, I might point out, holds a curious resemblance to your dead sister."

"I'm a hundred and forty-two, actually." Ollie smirked. "And I'm *very* good at scaring people."

Fife slumped. "Scammers. I've hitched my bloody wagon to a fraudster and his undead sister."

"We are not," I protested. "There's no scamming, Fife. We don't just dump a zombie in some person's house to take advantage of them. We're... we..." I scratched my beard, trying to decide what wording might best get me out of her bad books.

"We act as private operatives to secure articles of dubious provenance that pose significant risk to the general population." Ollie folded her hands in her lap and gave a prim smile. "Which is to say, we fetch bad magic stolen by stupid people, Detective. Stuff that will go kaboom in the wrong hands."

"Am I to believe your hands are the right ones?" Fife asked.

"Aye," Ollie said, holding hers up. "If mine are explosively amputated, I won't feel a thing. Promise!"

"So, what was the item Claire McAdam stole?"

"That's above your paygrade," I muttered.

Fife glowered. "I'll arrest you if I have to, Mack."

"Go ahead," I said. "See if you can get it to stick."

"By the black, hairy balls of the devil himself, Mack, stop flinging your dick about." Ollie shook her head. "McAdam didn't steal anything. Her boyfriend did. He was in on a big heist at the docks, along with the rest of his crew."

"Heist at the docks... you mean the one last month? You're telling me you had valid information on a criminal enterprise, and you kept it to yourself?" Fife didn't seem exactly buoyed by Ollie's explanation, so I jumped in.

"Fergus called in an anonymous tip," I assured her. "And it looks like they've already pinned him for it. But one of Fergus's sources — and I'm not telling you who, Fife, no matter how nicely you ask — managed to track down an item overseas that was of magical origin. The... uhh, person who brought it over thought it would be safer mixed in a delivery of more mundane goods."

"So... a magic practitioner of some description orders a potentially dangerous item. To prevent it getting in the wrong hands — presumably, hands that are also connected to magic — it's hidden in a shipment of new flat screens and counterfeit Gucci." Fife tapped one finger on her knee. "But that shipment is stolen by a criminal network and ends up in the hands of some mid-level gang member, who then passes it onto his girlfriend, Claire?"

I nodded. "Aye, that's my understanding of it."

"And you were sent in to retrieve it for this Fergus fellow." Fife took a moment to digest the information. "Does he have a last name?"

"Nope." Despite what Fife probably thought, I wasn't hedging. Fergus had never, as far as I knew, held a surname.

"What about the item?" Fife looked from me to Ollie. "What was it?"

I shrugged. "Don't know yet. I left it with Fergus to examine. He said he'll give it back to me in a few days."

Fife sat for another moment, eyes unfocused as she pondered. "Why back to you? Are you delivering it to the person who ordered it, or were you intercepting it to prevent them getting a hold of it?"

As bad as I was at keeping secrets, I had walked right into this one. There was no point hiding it from her, now I knew she wouldn't take the tapestry and dump it in the evidence locker. I made eye contact with Ollie, who nodded. "It would have gone back to the man who shipped it," I explained. "Except... he died. And being his only living descendant, it now belongs to me."

Instead of the furious explosion I expected, Fife slumped in her chair with a groan. "You're joking."

"Would I ever?" I winced as Fife's boot connected with my shin. "Fine. But I'm not. I didn't know until yesterday."

"Your grandfather was killed for this item?"

After a slight hesitation, I shrugged. "I have no information to confirm or deny that." Of course, the attacks by the bean sith and the red cap were probably related too, but I thought she had dealt with enough for now. No need to send the lass over the edge.

Fife chewed her lip, the first sign of indecisiveness I had seen from her. "Mack, what the hell am I supposed to do? I can't put any of this on paper. Magical items, vampire assassinations..."

"All you need to do is your job," I said. "You let us handle the rest."

"You said we'd let the police handle Granda's death, Mack." Ollie spoke quietly, but a sliver of hope ran through her words.

I clenched a fist, then relaxed it slowly. When I had told Ollie I was content to let handle the investigation into Granda's murder, I had been telling the truth. Well, more or less. Now, though, things were different. Some bastard wanted me to get involved, was practically daring me to stick my head in. Well, they were about to get their wish.

"Not anymore, Ollie. Not anymore."

Chapter Ten

Fife left sometime after two in the morning, dragging my new apprentice with her for reasons 'above my paygrade'. I watched out the front window as their Uber rolled off quietly into the night, fingers drumming a staccato beat on the kitchen benchtop.

"You're going to do something stupid." Ollie sighed, fingers tapping her palm. "And you're going to drag me into it too, aren't you?"

"Aye."

"Why'd you not mention it before the pretty detective lady left?"

I began hunting through my kitchen drawers. "Because she would insist on coming too. We can't risk that."

"I don't think you're giving her enough credit, Mack. She'll be fine!" Ollie tilted her head to one side. "If you're looking for the glass jars, they're in the top cupboard."

Throwing her a grateful glance, I yanked open the door she had pointed at. "It's not her I'm worried about. We'll be walking into a very volatile situation, Ollie. It would be nice to make it out without blowing anything up, for a change." Dumping a few jars on the bench, I turned my attention to the drawers.

"Third one down." Ollie waited for me to set the box of iron filings next to the jars. "Mack, this is a *terrible* idea."

"Sometimes, terrible ideas are all the ideas you've got." I stalked over to a cabinet and yanked the door open to grab a leather belt adorned with various loops and buckles.

"Well, you can't go now." Ollie walked over and slammed the cabinet closed, almost lopping off one of my fingers in the process. "You haven't slept properly in days. You know that makes your magic unstable... not to mention the rest of that shrivelled up brain inside your head."

"I'll take a cat nap before I leave."

"It's almost three." Ollie held the door closed until I dropped my hand away. "They'll be dead asleep by the time you get there. And you need more than a wee nap, you need proper rest, Henry. One wrong step and you won't be around to avenge Granda's death, protect me, *or* teach your new apprentice what he needs to keep himself from getting strung up by the toenails."

"Fine." I tossed the belt on the bench beside the iron and jars. "Tonight."

"Aren't you playing at Jack's tonight?"

Bollocks. Jack would have let me off, but the stipend for attending Claire's call hadn't come through yet. I needed the cash. "Like I said, tomorrow night." Crossing my arms, I wondered just how Ollie had gotten so effective at talking me down. "Tomorrow night, at sundown."

"Do you have a plan, or are we just walking in there with some snirlie jars and our fists raised?" She threw a mock punch that I easily ducked. Lucky, because even a mock punch from Ollie was enough to put a man on his arse.

"We need to make a strong entry, but we don't want to get Agnes offside. Not unless she refuses to help, anyway." My mind bounced from one scrap of information to the next. "She's vain, even more than most of her kind. If we can get into her chamber, be there when she rises, she *might* be put out just enough to give us what we need."

"What does vanity have to do with anything?"

"Well... some women don't like being seen without their hair done and a full face of makeup.

"You *really* expect the eight hundred year old queen of the Glaswegian baobhan sith to fall apart just because we saw her with coffin-hair and bags under her eyes?" Ollie snorted. "You're kidding yourself, Mack."

"We just need her a little off balance is all." I tried to grasp at the ideas buzzing past my consciousness. "Ahh, feck. Kelpies."

"Kelpies?" Ollie was used to my disjointed thoughts and knew they would coalesce into a plan eventually. That, or my brain would dissolve into mush and I would do something idiotic to compensate. The odds were about even.

"They'll be guarding the sleeping vampires."

Ollie groaned. "Seriously? I thought they were done with each other."

"The Vampire Queen and the King of the Kelpies kissed and made up a week or two ago, Jack said. Won't last, though."

"Why?"

"Agnes is still bangin' one of the selkies. You know what Achaius is like, the jealous prick. When he finds out, he'll flounce off back to his swamp again. If we didn't need Agnes's help, I'd be the little birdie that tells him."

"Ach, no, Mack. Think of the children! Remember last time they had a falling out? He threw a massive tanty, then ran through the main street, bare-arsed and dripping wet, playing Richard Marx on a twenty-year-old boom box. Agnes really knows how to pick them," Ollie sighed. "Right. So, we somehow make it past the homicidal horse-men and you stand there drooling over Agnes until she wakes up. Then what?"

"I don't drool, shite-goblin." I adjusted my shirt irritably. "After she sees we have the upper hand, we negotiate our swift departure. She won't be at full strength until an hour after sundown, give or take. She names the baobhan sith who killed Claire, we leave without plastering her bed hair all over the room — or worse, on social media. If we survive that —"

"Survive? Mack, we may as well take our own condiments for when they serve us up for dinner."

"Not like you to be such a pessimist," I chided. "Come on, Ollie. We've done stupider things."

"You've got me there." After a pause, she said, "Speaking of doing stupid things... we should take Davey."

That made me blink. "I didn't mean to insinuate we should be trying to set a personal record, Ollie. Quinn's so wet behind the ears he's dripping puddles on the floor like a fecking kelpie fresh out of its pond!"

"He needs to learn. And by tomorrow night, you'll have him all initiated, aye? That will confer some protection on him — which means he might even be useful." Ollie glanced at the jars. "You should teach him to make snirlie jars. Davey will be tickled pink to see you make those."

"You've taken a real shine to the lad, haven't you?"

Ollie grinned. "Aye. Mack, it's been so long since I've met someone new! Old Fergus and Jack are alright, but they're as old as the hills. Davey isn't much younger than us. I know you think I'm daft, but —"

"I do not." Softening, I pulled Ollie in for a cuddle. "I know you get lonely, lass."

She snuggled into me, letting the warmth of my body seep into her cold flesh. "Aye. It wouldn't be so bad if my brother wasn't such a wank."

I shoved her off with a laugh. "Shut yer weesht, lass. You should be right proud to have me for a brother! There's not a McDonald better looking than I am, or one with more charm."

"You talk some shite, Henry Mack." Stretching up on her tiptoes, Ollie planted a kiss on my cheek. "But of all the McDonald's in the world, I'm glad you're the one I got for a brother."

Chapter Eleven

I woke to the piercing shriek of my phone. Fumbling it to my face, I squinted until the bleary screen made sense to me.

"Bloody hell, Fife. Who calls a man at this ungodly hour?"

"At this... Mack, it's past midday, you lazy shite." Fife clicked her tongue in disapproval, then barked a muffled command at someone.

Past midday? Rain pounded on the window, hiding any hint of the sun, but the obnoxiously bright numbers on my bedside clock confirmed her unfortunate declaration.

"Don't you get all judgemental on me, lass." I yawned wide enough to crack my jaw. "And if you knew how bloody long it's been since I've had a wee bit of shut eye, you'd be tucking me back in right now."

"Don't you wish." Fife lowered her voice and the buzz of activity behind her faded away. "Look, there's been an incident and I'm going to need your help."

"Now?"

"Aye, now. Get your stinking baws out of bed and come do your job." Fife clicked her tongue again. "Feck's sake, Martin! If I have to tell you to put those feckin' booties on again, I'll rip your shoes off and shove them so far up your arse you'll be tying the laces through your left nostril. Yes, *every time*!"

"I take it I'm not the cause of your wonderful mood, then?"

"You will be if you start that shite up." Fife took a deep breath before she spoke again. "Sorry, Mack. It hasn't been the best of days. Rattray is still ducking my calls and this crime scene..."

"A bad one, then?" I threw the blanket off and shivered in the morning cold. Well, afternoon cold.

"Aye."

"You've got me until eight. Text me the address." I scanned the floor for the jeans I'd tossed there the night before. I found them under the bed, but a quick whiff suggested I find something a little cleaner. "You know I've got your back, love."

"I know. Thanks, Mack."

The phone went dead so I tossed it on the bed and went to look for some breeks. "Ollie?"

"Sleeping beauty is finally — Ahh, fecking hell, Mack!" Ollie slapped a hand over her eyes. "I don't want to see your hairy arse. Put some bloody clothes on, you prick."

"I would if I could find them." The living room, unlike my bedroom, was pristine. "Where are all my clothes?"

"Did you check the laundry?" Ollie slumped in exasperation, hand still firmly over her eyes. "When was the last time you did washing? Mack, we don't have a fecking house elf. If you want your clothes to be clean, you have to put them *in* the washer *and* turn it on."

"Aye, well if I wasn't so bloody busy —"

"Then you'd still have nothing clean and you know it." Ollie blocked my way to the laundry pile, arms crossed. "And don't you bloody dare suggest I do it for you. I already keep the rest of the flat free of your filth."

"I never would," I assured her. "I know it's my own stupid fault, and I don't have an excuse, really. But can you let me find some damn pants?"

Ollie begrudgingly stood aside, but when I made to dart back past with a wrinkled but mostly clean pair of jeans, she pointed at the pile of clothes I had pulled them from. "Not gonna do themselves, are they?"

I quickly grabbed the pile of dirty clothes, added a larger pile from my bedroom floor, stuffed them in the machine and started the load.

"I was going to let you put the pants on first, eejit." Ollie waited until she heard the clink of my belt buckle before taking a timid peek. Seeing I was decent, she threw her arms out. "You're such a bloody slob. I swear you're not normal. In fact, I'm pretty sure that if Granda had ever taken you to that shrink Mam had lined up, you'd have the reports to prove it."

"About as normal as memorising the entire '84 edition of the Guinness Book of records." In fact, I had a list as long as my arm of all the weird shite Ollie did as a kid — and still did now, come to think of it.

"Really." The hurt in her eyes bit me deeply.

I wilted. "Ach, I'm sorry. I rolled out of the wrong side of bed. I know I couldn't survive without you, Ollie. You do so much to keep things straight around here, the least I could do is clean up after myself and not be an arse about it."

"You're right about that." Ollie begrudgingly let me pull her into a hug. "Was I really that weird as kid?"

"Aye." I chuckled. "But it's not a bad thing. You were smart as a whip, and the cuddliest bairn Mam said she'd ever seen."

Ollie clutched me tighter at the mention of Mam. "Did she think I was weird?"

"She thought you were just like her." I pushed her back so I could look in her eyes. It had taken some time for me to get used to that after she died, but I'd done my best to never let it show. Ollie was the most important thing in the world to me, and I hated myself for hurting her feelings. "Remember the way Mam kept her pretties?"

A reluctant smile pulled at the corner of Ollie's lips. "All in a row."

"Aye, that's right. Just like you do. She was special, and maybe a few people thought she was a bit odd, but she was our Mam and we loved her for it. Just like I love you."

"Is there anything else she did that I do?" Ollie pressed her face back into my shirt.

"You both lost yourself in books. No pulling you out once your eyes hit a page of words. She was good with directions like you are — remember that time she took us all the way through London to that wee ice-cream shop? I figured she must have gone there all the time before we came along, but Da took her there one time. One time, Ollie, and she remembered it like the back of her hand."

"It's not that hard, really." Ollie tipped her head up just far enough to angle a sly glance my way.

"Cheeky shite, you know I don't have a head for it." I patted hers before disengaging from her clinging hug. "I have to go, pet. Fife needs me."

"I suppose I should be thankful you remembered pants at all." Ollie sighed and pushed me gently toward my bedroom. "Hurry up, I'll get your things."

I dressed quickly, mindful of Fife's mood and the knowledge that whatever she wanted me to take a look at, it likely involved a lot of blood. I wouldn't have said I had a weak stomach, but when Ollie asked if I'd like her to put some toast on before I left, I politely declined.

When I emerged, she gave me a critical once over. "Comb your hair or she'll never speak to you again."

She was right. When I ducked into the bathroom I was horrified to see that half of it was stuck in the air, while the other half was plastered flat on my face. I shoved a comb through it, which just made it fluffy, and compromised by splashing a bit of water on it.

"You know, there's something else you and Mam both did." This time, the comb worked. Well, more or less. I made a mental note to slip by the barber shop next chance I got, then I promptly forgot as I left the room. "Remember that time you were in the hospital with that manky chest thing?"

"The pneumonia? Or did the doctors say 'manky chest thing'

was the official diagnosis?" Ollie's eyes crinkled as she hid a grin.

"I'll let that one slide because I was a shite before," I warned. "Anyway, Mam was leaning over your bed and I caught her doing the hand thing you always do when you're angsty." I lifted my hand and curled the fingers over, flapping them in a soft, one-handed clap. "I asked Da if it was because she'd seen you do it so much, but he told me it was her thing first. Said she'd tried to stop it when we were born in case we picked up on her nerves."

"Oh." Ollie fell quiet, her face touched with sadness. "I wish she hadn't. It would have been nice to know it wasn't just me."

"Ach, I've gone and made you unhappy again, haven't I?"

Ollie summoned a tight grin. "Naw. Go on, go rescue your pretty detective, or she'll have your baws for showing up late."

"That she will!" I caught the keys Ollie tossed me, then my wallet.

She pointed to my big coat neatly hung beside the door — lucky, because it would have taken me forever to find the bloody thing — and waved me off. "Be careful, Mack."

"Always am."

The Demon started smoothly and I made it to Fife's location in a little less time than the speed limit should technically have allowed. I had to park across the street and down a few, though. Police cars and serious looking vans littered the narrow, paved street and packed the front lawns of the neighbouring houses. Between them, the neighbours themselves shuffled about trying to look as if they had a reason to be standing in the rain huddled under their macks and brollies, angling their curious glances so no one could accuse them of intruding on the horrible business down the street.

The red brick houses all held hints of the crumbling sameness one found in carefully planned out developments that had only begun to show their personality as they aged. New windows in one house, an extension on another, and hedges and trees in various states of overgrowth lent the suburb a feeling of comfort, like a well-worn shoe. It was nothing the like the sterile newness of Claire McAdam's street.

At a guess, I would have said the occupants were mostly lower to middle class. There were probably renters mixed with new families, and a few old folk that had long since paid off a house they had purchased brand new. This theory was borne out by the mix of spectators — a few women with babies of various sizes, one of them still in her dressing gown; two old men pretending to prune the same neatly trimmed dividing hedge; a young punk in black leathers and uncomfortable looking metal spikes through his ears and nose.

I kept my eyes forward, ignoring both the gawkers and the flutter of nerves in the pit of my stomach as I approached a cluster of uniformed officers. I didn't enjoy interacting with the police — nothing against them, you understand, it's just that I didn't like crowds and I didn't like questions, and this kind of job always leads to a lot of both.

The house in question was marked out by police tape, and a bevy of officers strategically positioned so that even the most persistent busybody would not get close enough to see what lay beyond. One of them approached as I lifted the flimsy barrier.

"I've got it, Mike." Fife's voice was a welcome beacon amongst the sea of unfamiliar faces. "Mack, this way."

Fife lead me up the short driveway, past the garage, and stopped at the front door. At least, a door had once been there, I was sure. The busted frame still bore a few holes where the hinges had been and the shattered remains of a feature window still sparkled on the stoop.

Fife grabbed my arm as I made to step inside, then jerked her chin at a small box on the edge of the path.

"Sorry," I mumbled. I plucked out two disposable booties and slipped them over my shoes. "Forgot."

"We'll have you trained up one day," Fife said with a long-suffering sigh. "But trust me, you don't want to go in there without them. In fact, I'd double up. Less damage to your shoes that way."

Grimacing, I took her advice and slipped a second pair of paper socks over the first. Fife's manner on the phone had worried me enough. Now, I wondered what I had gotten myself into.

"Let's get on with it, then." I took a breath and stepped inside.

A square bucket just inside the door held dripping coats, so I shed mine and added it to the pile. Then I donned my own protective gear: a red twine bracelet to protect from witch magic, strung with polished larch beads to ward off evil. A leather string hung around my neck, knotted between charms, the sort you'd see in a nice jewellery store. The charms themselves had little meaning, but the materials — silver, iron, steel — held protective properties I hoped would not be needed. Finally, I pulled my shirt over my nose to protect from the stench I knew to expect.

The tiny reception opened to a small kitchen, but Fife nudged me to the left. A sheet of plastic covered the doorway, and I pushed it aside, careful not to dislodge the small note scrawled in Fife's hand: **Put your fecking booties on!** "I take it I'm not the only forgetful one, then?"

Whatever she said in response sailed right past me as I tried to absorb the sight in front of me.

Blood. So much blood. The far wall dripped with it, oozing down towards the sodden carpet. Tiny red bubbles snapped and squelched around the edges of a pair of booties as the sole tech poked around with a camera. The bulk of the blood pooled around something long and soft. I swallowed. "That's no' good."

"Insightful, aren't you?" Fife replied. "You're looking a bit peely-wally, Mack. If you're going to puke, make sure you don't get it on my crime scene."

The brief exchange cleared my head enough to tear my gaze off what I was coming to believe was an arm. Most of one, anyway. Keeping my breaths short and shallow — you really don't want to suck in a big mouthful of that stench — I ran my eyes along the trail of blood splatter. Violent streaks tore across the walls like gaping wounds, cut patterns on the ceiling, swelled into fat globs threatened by the pull of gravity.

"I'm fine. Where's the rest of the... um..." I tipped my head at the dismembered limb.

"Study. We think one of the legs are in the bathtub — there are about a half dozen in there, so the numbers match what we've seen so far."

"There are three victims?" I asked, dread settling in my stomach like a lead weight.

Fife shook her head, eyes frozen. "They're all left feet."

Her face had fallen into a compassionless neutrality, her voice robotic, her movements mechanical. That was how she coped, losing herself in the process, the minutiae of procedures and reports that needed to be done.

Upstairs, someone laughed, a sharp, quickly stifled bark. Fife didn't flinch. She was used to that, too; the gallows humour and dark jokes that others relied on for their sanity when faced with the daily grind of living nightmares.

"What happened?" I asked.

Fife shrugged. "Best we can tell, they've been ripped apart. Heads, limbs, a couple of stray hands. All the torsos are badly mangled. None of the wound edges are consistent with cutting implements."

"What about puncture wounds? Bite marks, scratches, ligature marks... Anything like that?" Plucking up what little resolve I had left, I stepped around the sticky puddles on the floor and peeked around the door of the study.

A lifeless lump of torso rested on blood-blackened carpet. One foot lay on top as if carelessly dropped by whatever tore it from the rest of the person it had belonged to. The other arm sat askew on the desk chair, the limp hand dangling at an awkward angle. Dropping my shirt away from my face, I leaned in for a closer look.

"We've found no defensive wounds so far." Fife had picked her way over to me while I examined the body parts. "There was some odd residue, though, that I wanted your opinion on." She watched closely for my reaction. "Some kind of black, greasy substance."

"How can you tell?" So far, all the pieces I could see were saturated in blood.

Fife gestured for me to follow her. We returned to the reception room, made a left, and slipped past a few loitering techs into the living room. This time, the sight of body parts laying about like dirty clothes tossed on random furniture didn't bother me as much. The pure scale of the massacre had numbed my emotions.

The quiet house and subdued atmosphere was unlike anything I had experienced. Usually, an attack like this would occur in public, a loose spectre that had found a crowded public area. Then, my task was to save lives, to take down a monster while keeping the terrified, screaming targets around it safe from harm.

Fife pointed to another arm, this one still attached to a torso. The victim wore a white, long-sleeved shirt. I could tell it was white — or at least, it had been — because a portion of the sleeve was still fairly clean, except for a dark, greasy smudge at the cuff. Squatting down, I looked to Fife for assistance. She passed me a pen and I slid it under the cuff to lift the fabric and angle it toward the dim light of the window.

"How do you know the kid didn't just dip his sleeve in something before all this happened?" I asked, though my hunch was already forming.

Fife gestured around. "There are traces of it around. Doorways, floors, the kinds of places you'd expect to see it if it were left by a giant, rampaging monster forcing his way through the house. Like it had rolled in grease before it got here. It's hard to tell amongst all the blood, but it's there."

"It's not grease," I said. "Or not the kind you're thinking."

"Are you sure?" Fife stepped neatly over the limb so she could take a closer look without blocking the light. "Forensics have set aside extra samples for you, if you want them."

I nodded. Many spells involved burning various ingredients, so I was well familiar with the substance, if not the exact composition. "Aye. Something wet and green most likely, and mixed in a base, probably animal fats and ash. Mixtures like that are usually used in a summoning ritual and it often sticks to the beastie that comes through. If I can work out what it is, it might give us a clue what we're up against."

At least, I hoped it would. Summoning spells were rarely used by the average practitioner, and never for anything good. The quicker I figured out what — and who — had done this, the quicker I could track them down and stop anyone else getting hurt.

Closing my eyes a moment and taking the smallest breath I

could to centre my thoughts, I opened my sight. When my eyes flicked back open, the room swirled, thick with magical residue. The sparkling gold motes drifted from room to room, but didn't settle into any visible pattern that would suggest magic had been used on the premises. One thing caught my senses, though — a murky shadow beneath the brightness, something dank and fetid.

It was a dismal combination. Usually, death released a sparkle of power. A big massacre, or a violent one, could charge the air with emotion or leave a violent aura, but this? This saturation of power, loose and formless, discarded like the lives of those lost in this heinous crime? That could only be caused by something more than human, and the faint hint of rotten pond scum suggested one of the unseelie court.

With a sideways glance to check Fife's attention was elsewhere and a few sketched symbols, I channelled some of the raw magic into my staff. A buidseach didn't often stumble across this much power and to let it go to waste seemed even worse than stealing magic from a crime scene.

I took my time searching the rest of the house for clues but found little else. The occupant — a young lad renting off his parents, Fife told me — had hosted a party the previous night. There had been numerous noise complaints, first about the music, then the screaming. None of the neighbours had checked in, apparently assuming the young party-goers were drunk, high, or having some kind of gang-bang. That last had come from the elderly woman next door, who had phoned in the first, second, fourth, sixth and seventh complaints.

"What did she say about the lad himself?" The final upstairs room stunk, but not of blood. This was a room of emptiness, of mothballs and dust. I headed downstairs, Fife keeping pace with me easily.

Fife flicked through her notebook as she trotted downstairs. "I only questioned her briefly, she's undergoing a more thorough interview now. Said he was a bit of a troublemaker, probably dealing drugs, definitely having pre-marital sex. Had two lassies going at once, she thinks. Not a spit of evidence for any of it, mind you.

Apparently, she spent most of her days trying to convert him to the Kirk."

"Nothing about Satanism or blasphemy?" He may not have used magic, but if the lad had worshipped one of the more unpleasant spirits, it may have drawn its attention. A stretch, but it wasn't like I had any other leads.

Fife shook her head. "And she's one of those types, so she would have mentioned it if she'd seen anything like that. She happily admitted to digging through his rubbish to find evidence of the drugs. Any hint of un-Christian-like behaviour and she'd be all over it, calling him an evil devil worshipper."

"So if he was communing with dark spirits, she would have known." I shook my head. "This doesn't look good, Annie. There were no cameras? Phones, nothing that might have some video evidence on it?"

"All the electronics in a four-house radius shorted out when the screaming started. Even their phones. A lad two doors down said even his airpods are fried. It's like a tiny EMP went off and this house is at the bloody centre of it."

The uneasy suspicion wriggling in my gut morphed into a solid theory.

"You know what it is." Fife kept her voice down but one of the techs at the front door looked up when she said it.

"Nah. Sorry, love, this is a new one for me." I darted outside and took a deep breath, scouring my lungs clean with rain-soaked air.

"You're lying." Fife planted her hands on her hips. "Because if you seriously just spent twenty minutes in that house and came out with nothing, you're no more bloody use that Rattray."

"I didn't say I had nothing." I checked that no one was in earshot, then lifted a hand and prepared to count off fingers. "It wasn't a vampire, they don't leave blood. Definitely not a ceasg or kelpie, or there'd be water everywhere and the bodies would be gone. Well, most of them. Sometimes a ceasg will leave a few fingers behind."

Fife shuddered and rubbed her arms. "That's three of how

many possible entities?"

"Oh, thousands," I said, and grinned. "But I'll be able to pare down the list pretty quickly once I've got my wee assistant on the job."

"She's clearly the brains of the operation," Fife remarked dryly. "And clearly, I still have a lot to learn about what's out there."

I gave a theatrical sigh. "What do they teach you at spook school?"

"That people like you canna be trusted." Fife jabbed a finger in my chest for emphasis. "You done poking about?"

"Aye." There wasn't much else to see, and I itched to get back and see if my hunch would bear fruit.

Fife checked her watch. "It's only four, so you're out in plenty of time. What do you have on, a secret coven meeting or something?"

"A gig." I hesitated a moment. "You should come."

"Who are you going to see?"

"See?" I shook my head with a laugh. "Nah, lass, they're coming to see me. The famous Henry Mack, Scottish bard with a silver tongue."

"You're a musician." Fife looked more shocked than if I had just admitted to being a career criminal. "That's why you turn down so many consulting jobs?"

"Aye." I grinned. "Old Jack pays better than the Ice Cream Van, and besides, I might pick up some valuable intel. It's not just any pub, you see." I tapped the side of my nose with a knowing wink. "It's not easy to find, so you'll have to call me if you want to come."

Without waiting for her answer, I waved goodbye and vacated the crime scene as quickly as I could. Once in the safety and privacy of my car, I inhaled slowly through my nose, cracked the door open, and vomited in the gutter. It had taken everything I had not to let that loose in front of Fife. Not that she would judge me for it. I had seen her clean up after many a young officer who couldn't keep his stomach and respond with no more than a pat on the shoulder.

Still. I was Henry Mack, and I had a reputation to uphold.

With two hours before I had to be at Jack's, I decided to make a few stops on my way home. First, to see Fergus. He had determined that it was the thread used in the tapestry that held magic, not the pattern as a whole.

"As for what it does, that will take a little more time." Fergus frowned, his bushy brows sliding together so they formed a single crooked caterpillar across his wrinkled face. "I've had no trouble since ye left it here, lad. That concerns me more than anything."

"You think something big is coming?" As much as I tried to concentrate on our conversation, my eyes kept drifting across his counter, over to a wee plate stacked with tiny, sugar topped pastries.

Fergus either didn't notice, or deliberately ignored my interest in the delicacies. "I think maybe a bit of magical cotton wasn't the target at all."

"You think they're after me?" A big laugh bubbled up from my belly. "What the bloody hell have I done now, Fergus? Last time the Otherworld came after my arse, it was because a glaistig I shagged thought I was offering her breakfast when I asked how she liked her eggs in the morning. Try explaining *that* to an infertile race of beings who have no need to procreate."

"Who you been shacking up with, lad?"

"No one." I stifled a sigh. It had been a dry couple of months.

"Whether they're after you, your sister, your dug." He shrugged. "Who fecking knows."

"Well, it's not my dog. I don't have one."

"What?" Fergus seemed outraged at the prospect. "You've got a wee lass stuck in your flat all bloody day, and no dug for her to be lovin' on?"

"She'd love on it, alright. Right up until it tried to bury her leg." Something about the smell of overripe flesh sent dogs into a frenzy when they met Ollie. Dogs were great for hunting spectres and protecting from some of the worse denizens of the Otherworld — the S.O.P.D. had more than their fair share of the K9 units due to their enthusiasm for helping — but not so good for a wee lass pining for a furry friend.

"You're neglecting the girl, Mack."

"Aye. I'm sure she'd feel better if I took her home a sweetie, though, aye?" I gave the pastries another pointed glance. "And she may not be growing, but she's got quite the appetite these days."

Fergus scowled at me, scowled at the plate, and scowled at me again. "How do I know they'll make it back to her, eh? You're no' above a bit of thievery, Henry Mack. 'Specially when it comes to my cooking."

"I would never!" Of course, Fergus knew I bloody well would.

Still, he dug around in a cluttered drawer until he found a somewhat-clean hanky and folded a couple of pastries into it. "Did ye just come to check on me progress? If so, I'm sorry ye wasted a trip, lad."

"Actually, no." I turned and ran my eyes over the tightly packed shelves of the shop but gave up the attempt to find what I needed in about four and a half seconds. "I need a few books."

Fergus happily obliged my request. He trotted around plucking books off shelves as I explained what I had seen at Fife's crime scene.

"The carpets were dry — apart from the blood, anyway — so it wasn't a pond-dweller or sea creature. Nor a blood-drinker, unless they only had a wee appetite and a lot of pent-up frustration." I scratched my beard, pushing away the nagging feeling that I should just pack up my flat, my sister and my new apprentice and head for the hills. "Honestly, Fergus, I've never seen the like before. That worries me more than I'd like to admit."

"There's enough out there that ye haven't seen, lad. Though you're right that the signs are nae good." Fergus slapped a small stack on the counter beside me. "There, that should get ye started. Tell Ollie to give me a tinkle if she thinks of any others she needs."

"I'm no' asking for Ollie," I protested. "I plan to read them myself."

Fergus barked a laugh at that. "Then I'll see ye back in a year or two?"

"Haud yer weesht, old man." I snatched the books up and headed for the door.

"Wait!" Fergus dashed over to grab the pastries I had forgotten. "If ye lose one of my books, I'll hunt ye down and feed ye to Agnes, see if I don't."

Grinning, I took the wrapped parcel. "Agnes loves me too

much for that."

"Love isn't what that is, lad. She looks at you the way you look at my sweeties. Like ye want to stuff 'em in your mouth and swallow them down as quick as ye can."

"Same thing." My phone buzzed but I let it ring out. Once I was in the car, I pulled it out and cursed at the message. Ollie had sent seven text messages. I didn't bother to open them, instead tapping the screen to call her.

"Mack? Ye bloody bampot, where the hell are you?"

I glanced at Fergus's storefront. "Just grabbing some books for you to read. Bedtime stories of the horrifyingly factual type."

"You've got fifteen minutes to get your arse home, shower, eat and go!" Ollie waited a beat as I checked the time and let out a string of curses. "Aye, you lost track of time. Again. Hurry up, I'll get your stuff ready for you."

I'm not saying the tyres squealed a little when I left Fergus's shop, but I'm not saying they didn't, either.

Chapter Twelve

Clarissa, one of Jack's casual bar staff, greeted me at the back door with a pout. "Late again, MacDonald?" She flicked her dark hair back over one shoulder and glared up at me. At only five feet tall, it's hard to imagine such a tiny thing having the ability to intimidate a hulking, bearded wizard like myself.

I didn't have to imagine. Clarissa's ire bit into my soul, dredging up what small capacity I had to feel guilt at my tardiness. "Ease up, sweetheart. I made it in, didn't I?" I gave her my most charming grin.

Clarissa softened, though the effect was almost imperceptible. "You're lucky they like your pretty voice as much as they do, MacDonald. Otherwise Jack would have fired you long ago." She moved to one side just enough for me to squeeze past. "And you're welcome, by the way!" she called after me.

There were no consolatory drinks waiting for me tonight — the crowd at the bar was three deep at its thinnest and Jack was working like a maniac, flipping glasses and pouring layered shots and complex cocktails almost as fast as his patrons called their orders to him. Tansy and Michael worked alongside him, taking payment and serving up the basic orders of beer and liquor. Jack preferred it that way. His bartending skills had long since passed from skill to artform, and he used it to his advantage.

Clarissa had already resumed her place amongst the three. I watched a moment as Jack spun a bottle on one finger, then caught it, upside down, just long enough to top off a tall, purple drink and slide it across the bar. The bottle slammed on the bench next to it with out a drop spilled. As if sensing he had an audience, Jack turned to wink at me before grabbing three more glasses and plonking them down. Beside him, Tansy's dark ponytail bobbed up and down as she darted from side to side, tucking notes into the cash register, and either passing back change or sprinkling the coins into the tip jar. Michael ducked and weaved around her, tossing glasses to Clarissa to fill with beer and mead, artfully flicking a bottle of scotch in a quick twirl before dispensing a round of shots.

My mesmerised focus snapped away when my phone buzzed. I fished it out of my pocket on my way to the small stage.

When and where?

I grinned at Fife's message and fired her off some quick directions, making sure to tell her to mention my name at the door. Then, I fired of a brief addendum:

Dinna fash about the brute of a bouncer. He won't hurt you, he's just there for show.

The last thing Jack needed was for an officer of the S.O.P.D. to try arresting his doorman.

Be there in half.

That would give me time to settle into my set, and quell the burst of nerves that for some reason, seemed particularly violent tonight.

There would be no reverent silence this night. It was Saturday, and though the denizens of the Otherworld rarely took note of piddling things like weekdays or nine-to-fives, there were a striking number of regular humans with links to the magical side of Scotland. They were bankers and architects, artists and students, all with just enough seelie blood in them that they had eventually found their way to Jack's. Many of them would have a special talent. A man whose great-great-grandmother was a wise woman might be a proficient doctor, or the lass with broad shoulders and strong legs might be a champion swimmer, thanks to a wee bit of ceasg somewhere in her bloodline.

Some of those in the crowd, of course, were pure human. Or, as human as you can be after spending days-turned-decades in a seelie homestead, buried deep under the soil, heedless of the endless march of time in the mortal world. Those men and women had a strange look about them, lost and a little dazed, as if still wondering how they came to be.

As was usual on such a busy night, the actual seelie were few and far between. Those present were good at blending in. Two big, clumsy looking blokes in the corner were likely brownies, and the smatter of lasses with a grey hue visible at the edges of their thick makeup would be glaistigs. I recognised the lass with tight braids hiding her damp hair as a river spirit, and the pretty blonde in the corner licking the neck of her besotted boyfriend was a baobhan sith. Seeing her reminded me of my plans to visit her queen but I pushed the thought away. It wouldn't do to dwell on it — planning was all well and good for regular folk, but I much preferred to think on my feet, and trust in my own skills to get me out alive.

A cheer went up when I strummed my guitar. I'd brought the electric, knowing it would penetrate the noise of the crowd better than old Betsy.

"Play some Ed Sheeran!"

Despite flipping the bird to the lassie who yelled the request, I opened with a few covers to warm the crowd up. Then, I moved to old covers, sea shanties and folk songs I had tweaked over the years to be sung to a more modern tune. I acquiesced to the occasional request, from charting pop songs to remixed classics, including that bloody annoying song about the New Zealand provisioning ship that went viral when a Scotsman sung it to a dance beat. Utter pish, that one.

Not that I was jealous of some upstart making a few quid off an old song, or that not knowing what the bloody hell a 'shantytok' was made me feel older than the hills. It's just an annoying bloody song, is all.

I had just launched into Donald Where's Your Troosers when I realised it was no regular bar patron twirling about in the middle of the dance floor with another lass. It made my next choice of song easy. When I tore out the first few chords of Smooth Criminal, Fife tipped her head back in a rich laugh, before throwing a hand up and jumping with the crowd in time to the music. My shock at seeing Quinn appear next to her, hopping along like a seasoned club-goer, nearly made me skip a chord; thankfully my professionalism won out and I carried on without anybody noticing a thing.

Fife stayed on the dance floor for the rest of my set, only darting off to down the occasional drink offered to her by Quinn, who looked like a deer in the headlights whenever he approached the DCI. It was a look I had seen often. Fife was notorious for her ability to tear up a nightclub at the slightest prompting, and many of her younger colleagues found themselves utterly lost at how to react to their usually tight-laced superior officer.

Quinn would have to get over that quickly. If he was going to survive in the wild, he would need the confidence to assert his own authority, and demand certain things from the S.O.P.D.; not that Fife would ever say no to requests for crowd control, or backup, or anything sensible like that. However, she was less inclined to look the other way when I needed to light-finger a wee bit of evidence, or intimidate a witness to see which manner of unseelie beast he had been dealing with to access power he otherwise had no way of controlling.

And that train of thought yanked me back to the scene I had visited with Fife earlier. Someone, somewhere, had started a spell they thought they could control and it had gone terribly wrong. My bets were safely placed on some kind of summoning ritual, by some bampot that thought bringing a beastie over from the Otherworld was as simple as saying a few words, burning some weeds, and sending it off to do their bidding. For feck's sake, it's like some of them thought they were living in one of those tv shows where all you need to defeat a big, bad demon is supermodel-looks, a nice car and a few words scratched on a bit of paper.

Though, come to think of it… I'm no' so bad on the eyes, and I do drive a very nice vintage car…

I shook my head before my hands could get as distracted as my addled brain. My watch said I only had fifteen minutes to go, so I called out to the crowd for last requests. It was Quinn's voice that I picked out, shouting "Akka Dakka" in an accent so obnoxiously Australian, I couldn't say no. Besides, Back in Black was one of my favourite songs.

It was pushing three and the bar was still packed tight with a crowd who knew good music when they heard it. After that, and with a concerted effort to ignore the Sheeran fan who had begged for another of his songs every time I stopped for breath, I played some Guns n Roses, followed by a Bon Jovi song. It was a bit on the nose, but I finished off with Closing Time, to a few hollered protests and cries of disappointment.

After I wrapped up my set, Fife dragged Quinn over to the stage. Quinn held out a fresh beer and I took a relieved pull, half draining it before I took a breath.

"Devil's oath, Mack, you didn't tell me you could play like that!" Fife's eyes sparkled with delight.

"You never asked." I grinned and lifted my guitar strap over my shoulder with one hand. She helped me untangle it and I set it by the stage, safe in the knowledge that no one would dare steal from anyone at the Wicked Stag, lest they face the wrath of Jack Mackintosh and every unseelie creature this side of the Irish Sea.

We snagged a table, mostly by way of Michael, who ushered a trio of drunk hipsters out the door after they spilled an entire pitcher of honey mead over a lass who had just enough self-control not to curse them with the wee talisman she clutched with a white-knuckled grip.

After the lads were hauled out by their baws, Tansy sashayed over to us. "What'll it be tonight, Mack?"

“Ask Jack for a round of one of his specials,” I told her. That was the well-known code for ‘I’m showing off, so make it impressive.’ Before she could leave, I touched her arm and leaned close. “The lass who took a beer shower has a wee trinket that Jack may want to know about.”

Tansy gave a short nod and hurried off. Talismans like that weren’t explicitly banned, but you were an idiot if you even thought about waving it around like she had. It wasn’t unheard of for the bloody things to go off accidentally, and channelling that much fury while holding one was a recipe for disaster.

“Mate, you play a bloody good set.” Quinn shook his head in wonder. “How long have you been at it?”

“I first picked up a guitar to piss off my Granda.” I grinned. “He told me music was a waste of time, that I’d never make a career of it, and even if I could, my efforts would be better spent honing my magical skills.”

Tansy appeared with a tray of drinks, some kind of black syrup with flecks of glitter swirling about the bottom. “There you go, folks.” She caught my eye and glanced over my shoulder and I turned, just quick enough to see the lass with the talisman hand something over to old Jack with a surly frown.

“That must have pissed you off.” Fife stirred her drink and sniffed it dubiously.

“Aye.” I took a gulp of mine. It was sweet and fruity, and sent a tingling rush through my body that woke me up and washed away the fatigue and strain of playing such a long set. “It took me years to realise it was all a bloody setup. The more he pushed against it, the harder I practiced. Ollie eventually pointed out that the ‘gardener’ Granda hired wasn’t just shite at keeping plants alive, he was never pulled up for all the hours he skived off his work to teach me to play.”

“Canny old bastard.” Fife finally summoned the courage to sip her cocktail. “Oh. Wow. That’s not bad.”

Eyeing her for any adverse reaction, Quinn waited for Fife to take another swallow before taking a breath and gulping his down. “Hey, you’re right!” He closed his eyes, savouring it. They snapped back open a moment later. "Hold up, was there something in that?"

Fife narrowed her eyes at me. "I can feel it too. What's going on, MacDonald?"

"No need to get all threatening, love." I clicked my tongue before finishing my drink, making a point of sighing with satisfaction when I was done. "It's one of Jack's specials. There's a wee bit of something in it, don't ask me what. It's harmless, though."

"I wasn't threatening." Fife turned her frown towards her glass. "You're sure it's safe?"

"Just a bit of a pick me up. Nothing that'll show up in a test, and it's not going to impede your decision making, if that's what you're worried about."

"I don't know." Fife lifted her eyes to me. "Your decision making ability is pretty damn terrible, if you ask me."

"Are you basing that on the company I keep, or the fact that I keep agreeing to help you out on your cases?"

Fife snorted. "Both. Come on, I know the department pays half what you're worth and a third of what you'd get as a freelancer. And who the bloody hell would want to spend their day off with their supervisor?"

"You're not my supervisor," I protested. "You're my colleague. My partner in crime. Crime-solving. My partner in supernatural crime-solving."

"When we're on a case, I'm your damn boss and don't forget it, Henry Mack."

"Oh, so I'm not 'MacDonald' anymore? I guess that means you like me again." I flashed her a wide smile and waggled my eyebrows.

Fife laughed. "You're a cheeky shite, aren't you?"

"Aye, I am." Proudly thumping my chest, I winked at Quinn. "Don't worry, lad, I'll teach you the ways of wooing women to your side with style and sass."

Fife nearly spat her drink out at that. Her eyes met Quinn's and they both burst out laughing.

"What? I have style!"

The two only laughed harder. They didn't stop until I had given up and gone for another round of drinks. When I returned, they had both regained some semblance of control. The mood sobered further when Quinn told me Fife had more information about the massacre we had attended earlier that day.

"Aye," Fife confirmed. "Once the bodies — well, body parts — were cleaned up, the coroner sent over pictures of some unusual bruise patterning. I was hoping you'd take a wee look for me, Mack?"

"Aye, of course."

The images she pulled up on her phone were only a little less nauseating than seeing them in person. At least the flesh was now clean and pink, or in the case of two of the victims, light brown. Two of the images showed fresh contusions in the shape of a horseshoe. Another had what looked like an oversized bite mark on a dismembered arm.

Quinn sucked in a breath. "There goes my appetite for the next week." He pushed away his drink, then changed his mind and downed it in one go.

"Coroner says it's consistent with equine injuries. Big, though – like a Clydesdale, or a Shire maybe. Two kids were kicked, and another was bitten." Fife flicked back to the bruises. "None of them owned horses and their parents said they've had no contact with one, either."

"They're kids, Fife." I zoomed in on one of the images until it was blurry. Taking it out a bit, I looked for any tell-tale signs the coroner may have missed. "Kids are stupid. They probably snuck into a field for a toke and scared some poor pony. Hell, they might've been trying to steal it, for all we know."

"That's the official line we're going with," she admitted.

"Bullshit." Quinn sat back and folded his arms. "You can't seriously tell me that with all the shit you said was real, not one of them had feet like a horse. Animal myths are present in nearly every culture on earth, you're telling me Scotland is the exception?"

I shook my head. "I'm no' saying that at all, lad. Kelpies, water-horses and a few other beasties have hooves, though not all are horse-like. But I've ruled most of those out, already. And the sith, as a whole, aren't mass murderers. The repercussions for killing a human, especially in that manner, would be too great for them to even consider it. There are some less-sentient beings that might have a crack at it, but they'd leave signs of their own."

"One of the sith tried to kill you," Quinn pointed out.

"No, she made a deal with someone to get her thieving hands on something I had. Once that deal is made, she canna go back on it." I passed Fife her phone. "I just so happened to be willing to exchange a life in order to keep the trinket she was after."

Fife pressed her hands over her ears. "Stop. Stop, I don't want to hear it."

"Sorry, Annie. It was a clear cut case of self-defence, though." I shrugged. "From a fae perspective, the rules that protect humans don't apply to someone who has a fair chance of fighting back. She would have killed me to get what she wanted, so I did her in first."

"If I don't know, I can't judge you." Fife finally dropped her hands. "Or charge you. Look, I appreciate that you operate under different rules to the rest of us. But if our relationship is going to survive, you're going to have to keep some things to yourself, Mack."

I lifted an eyebrow and smirked. "We're in a relationship? Tell me more."

"Don't be that guy, MacDonald."

"Sorry, that was in poor taste." I stifled a yawn. "Did you get the forensic report back on the black stuff, yet?"

Fife shook her head. "I asked them to rush it. How about you, did you find anything?"

"Maybe. Ollie is doing the heavy lifting for me tonight. Literally — the stack of books I have her ploughing through weighs almost as much as she does."

"That doesn't sound fair." Quinn ducked his head, avoiding my glare. "I'm just saying, mate."

"You're right. I absolutely should be farming the work out to my new apprentice. After you get the tartan paint and the left-handed screwdrivers, you can come get a few of the books and read them yourself, aye?"

"I don't mind helping." Quinn shrugged, unbothered by the work I had proposed. "As long as it's not written in old Gaelic or anything."

"Well they didn't bloody write it in modern slang, now did they?" I waited for the dismay to cross his face before admitting a few volumes were in fairly legible English. "There's some Scots in there too, but it's not as dense. You'll figure it out."

"What can I do?" Fife didn't even hesitate. "Reading? Research? Come on, Mack, I've got to crack this thing."

"Not a damn chance. Annie, you just read me the riot act about keeping the scary shite out of your jurisdiction. Now you want to hop on in?"

She screwed up her face. "Don't be daft. Just because I read a bloody fairytale, doesn't mean I have to report it. And if I happen to send a book back with a few pages marked, who says it has anything to do with our case?"

"If you're going for plausible deniability, best not to half-ass it." I cracked my jaw on another yawn, then stood. "Quinn, come see me in the morning, aye? I'll give you a few books so you can brush up on your very imaginary, definitely not-real Scottish mythology."

Fife grabbed my arm. "I need you to keep quiet about the stupid shite you do, Mack. I might give you more rope than the rest of them, but I'm still an officer of the law. But if I know what I'm looking for when I work these cases, don't you think it'll be easier for all of us?"

"I do." I patted her hand. "But young David here is going to make it easy for you, by collating the information he gathers into an easy reference guide that will give you everything you need with a few taps on your phone."

"I am?" He didn't seem daunted by the prospect, in fact, the numpty almost looked excited. "How should I format it, spreadsheet or wiki?"

I shrugged. "I don't know what you need a wookie for, I was just going to get you to type it up and email it."

"Luddite." Fife nodded her head at Quinn. "I'll need something fairly innocuous, accessible on a mobile browser if you can."

"Will do, Detective Chief Inspector." Quinn ducked his head respectfully.

"Don't give me that bullshit, lad. We're off the clock and you're working for him, not me. Fife is fine. Or Annie, if you're feeling especially brave."

"Uhh, sure." Quinn pointedly avoided addressing her by either name. "Can I bum a ride, Mack?"

"Fine." I wasn't about to let him drive home anyway. He had the fuzzy headed glow of someone a few drinks in and Fife would have my baws if I let him behind a wheel. "What about you, love?"

"I can Uber." Fife tapped her phone screen to wake it up.

"Come on, it's not far out of my way."

She hesitated. "You're sure?"

"You won't solve the bloody case if you get mugged waiting for a ride. You'll be up to your armpits in paperwork for killing the poor sod."

"I wouldn't kill them. Just touch them up a bit. Knee to the baws, a Glasgow kiss, maybe a good stomping to make sure they stay down." Fife clenched one hand into a fist, examining it as if contemplating where she'd plant it on a theoretical attacker's face.

"If they're alive to give a statement, that has to go into the report, too." I watched her weigh up the options and felt a zing of relief when she gave in. The Wicked Stag was generally pretty safe, but without knowing exactly who had sent the bean sith and the redcap after me, I would feel better knowing Fife made it home in one piece.

Despite my worry, we made it to the Demon without issue. I dropped Quinn off first, leaving Fife in the car alone with me. I had only driven a few minutes when she realised the address I had plugged in wasn't hers. She cocked a question look my way.

"We're off to interrogate a person of interest," I told her. "Off the books. Aye?"

CHAPTER THIRTEEN

Luckily the weather had held during the short drive to the crime scene. A blustery wind whipped past, changing direction every other moment and stinging our faces with icy rain. After rummaging about the back seat for a moment, I emerged with a plastic baggy.

"We'll do it in the backyard," I told Fife.

"Do what, exactly?" She lifted the neon cordon over our heads.

Eyeing the slim strip of light peeking through the curtains next door, I chuckled. "Give the old hag next door a heart attack, if she's watching."

I waved Fife under the tiny awning and stood in the rain, waiting for just the right moment. My hand was around the dry, crumbling mess inside the bag.

It happened. The wind changed, and just for a moment, it drove against the rain, whipping it about. I threw the dry horse dung into the air.

"Ow!" The frail, haggard woman who tumbled to the ground glared up at me with baleful eyes. "Wee prick, what'd you do that for?"

"Sorry, my fine lady. I just needed to have a quick chat to one of your kind, in the hope that you could help me out with a bit of information." I dug in my pocket with my clean hand and offered up a second bag, this one packed with barley.

Her eyes lit up. "What kind of information do you seek, lad?"

"Something bad happened here earlier." I watched as her eyes narrowed. "I want to know what did it."

"I canna tell you that," she said. "What else?"

"Can you not tell me because you don't know what manner of beast killed those bairns?"

She stayed silent.

"You know what it was, then." I opened the bag and scooped up a sprinkle of barley. "I know you value your herds, my lady. And I know you need the grain to feed them. And these were innocents, children, struck down with a violence they should not have suffered. You want to tell me, don't you?"

"Aye." Steely-eyed and poised as though to run, she waited.

"Is this information a danger for you to hold?" I asked.

"Aye."

No sithche worth a pinch of salt would endanger their own for a pitiful handful of grain. Rather than slip it away, I tossed it to her. "Take it, then, and my apologies for interrupting your night."

The bag ruptured and grain poured through her hands, spilling onto the muddy ground. Heedless of the waste, she tipped her head to one side. "It was one of *your* lot what summoned it here." And she vanished.

On the way back to the car, Fife's first question was about the grains. "Why did she just leave them there?"

I grinned. "What spilled on the ground is empty shells. When the sith steal a thing, they don't take its physical forms, just its essence. She took what she needed from it, and her herd will thrive for a while because of it."

"And we got what, exactly, in return?" The question was genuine, I could see Fife's brain turning gears as she tried to decipher what little the fae hag had told us.

My own brain was scrambling to do the same in a less

methodical way. "It's big, it's bad, and it's something controlled by a human. That rules out most of the natives - You wouldn't get one of Agnes's kind bowing down to a mere human, and besides, they have free access to our world. It's not an answer, but it might help us narrow down the search."

"You didn't push her for more information when she said she was in danger." Frowning, she peeled off her jacket and shook it before folding herself into the front seat of the Demon. "Is that because you were worried for her safety, or because you knew she wouldn't give the information up regardless?"

"Both," I admitted. "If I had tried to strong arm her into giving me that tiny sliver of information she did, rather than letting her come to it freely, I'd have gotten squat and paid the price later. The sithche can be right bastards when they want. Still, I wouldn't put anyone in danger needlessly — human or otherwise." Before Fife could open her mouth, I added, "And for the record, I don't class self-defence as needless."

"I would never question that, Henry." Her quiet tone suggested there was a hell of a lot left she did question. Not one to let things lie, she spoke a moment later. "Mack… The S.O.P.D. thinks they have a handle on the supernatural. We don't have a fecking clue, do we?"

"Not even close, love. There are creatures and contracts and hierarchies that'd make your lot wet themselves if they found out about it. That's not to say the city isn't safe, Annie. For the most part, it is. You've got people like me making damn sure of it."

"Exactly how powerful are you?"

The question made me pause. "Compared to what?"

Fife shrugged. "An idiot with a machine gun. A pipe bomb. A nuclear weapon. I have *no idea* what the scale of your magic compares to, Mack."

"Well, I doubt I could level more than a city block," I admitted. When her face paled, I regretted my choice of words. "On my own, I could easily take down most of the threats you'd face one on one. With Ollie by my side, we could do a whole lot better than that. But we'd rarely need to — Annie, if the baobhan sith really were planning an uprising it would only take a few phone calls to shut it down. Like I said, there's a hierarchy."

"And you're near the top."

The laugh that escaped didn't last long under her withering glare. "Sorry. No, I'm not. I'm a lone operative, and I like it that way."

Fife settled back into her seat, seemingly satisfied with my answer. We travelled in a comfortable silence, her face lit by the soft glow of my GPS and the strobe of passing streetlights. We had been friends for some time, but I could feel the shift in the dynamic. A week ago, Fife saw me as a known quantity. A Catch and Dispatch agent, good at my job, bad at putting up with gobshites like Rattray. She knew I was a wee bit disorganised and forgetful, and she accommodated that with her text reminders and a shite load of patience.

Now? Now I was something more. I had connections she had long suspected but could no longer ignore, and knowledge she needed but also knew could compromise her work. My position as a simple contractor had morphed into something bigger, something she didn't yet understand.

She glanced over at me, perhaps reading my mind in the way she always seemed to. "We're good, Mack. You and me. Nothing has really changed."

"Are you so sure about that?"

"Aye. You're still a fecking numpty who can't find the keys in his hand most days." She paused a beat before adding, "I don't care if you outrank me in some secret wizardy way. I'm not the sort to give a shite about that."

"What is it, then?" Something was bothering her, I knew. We'd been friends too long for her to hide it from me.

"Change is coming. Can you feel it?" She rubbed her arms to warm them. "We've been on the edge of something for a while. It feels like we're finally going to jump off — or something will give us a shove. The department can't ignore all this forever, you know that."

"Aye." I knew it, all right, and I knew what the likely results would be. No more C&D licences, for a start. People like me would suddenly become one of *them*, one of the creatures lurking in the shadows with unknown powers, suspected of every little thing that went wrong, from bloody, inexplicable murders to a bottle of milk left out too long that turned before the expiry date.

"I won't let them screw you over, Henry. I can't protect everyone – even I'm not egotistical enough to think that – but I've always got *your* back."

"Are you reading my mind, you wee witch?" I chuckled. "I know, Annie. You're a good person. Devil knows you've been good to me, even when I don't deserve it, chasing after me when I can't get my shite together and making sure my reports are all nice and tidy."

"You do your best, love. I know some things are just a wee bit harder for you. It's not worth giving you grief over."

"If only you could go back in time and tell every one of my teachers that." The picture on my phone zoomed in as I approached Fife's street and I spun the wheel, cruising gently around the corner. "Look, no matter what's coming, I've got your back too. You can keep the bureaucrats and bigwigs away from me, and I'll keep the homicidal monsters away from you. Deal?"

"Aye." Fife held out a hand to shake on it. "Deal."

Chapter Fourteen

I woke to a surprise phone call from Fife.

"I can let you into the house today, Mack."

"What? Where?" I asked, still bleary from the late night. "Which house?"

"Your Granda's." Fife waited for the news to sink in. "And I've told them I'm taking a certain beat cop as my second, so you can bring Ollie if you like."

"Devil's oath, Annie, you're a saint." I rolled out of bed and stretched, smothering my yawn. "What time?"

"Be there around twelve."

I eyed my beside clock. "Twelve?" It was only eight.

"Aye. Sorry I called so early, I needed to know if you could make it so I can clear out the few people we have left on site. You've got time for a kip, though. I know you need it."

"You're right about that." I flopped back onto the bed and burrowed into the blankets. "See you then."

"Do I need to give you a wakeup call?"

"Nope." I angled the phone away from my face and hollered loudly. "Ollie! Wake me at eleven, we're going to Granda's."

"Ow, right in my ear, you prick." Fife begrudgingly accepted my apology, then said goodbye.

"Are we really?" Ollie cracked my door open and stuck her head in. "By *we*, do you mean me too?"

"You, too. Fife has it all lined up so you can be there. It will just be us, Annie and your new pet."

"He's not my pet." Ollie scrunched up her face, then added, "Though, he does remind me of an excited puppy sometimes. At least he's house trained."

"I'll fix that." I dodged her glare by diving back under my blanket.

"No you fecking don't." A blast of cold had me bolt upright a moment later. Ollie stood over me, hands on hips, blanket dangling to the floor beside her. "Get up, you lazy shite. There's research to be done."

"I hate reading." I snatched at the blanket but she yanked it away. "And you're so much better at taking notes. Besides, I outsourced my share to Quinn."

"Then you can get your arse to the kitchen and wash the bloody dishes. I might be stuck at home all day, Mack, but I'm not your bloody housemaid."

I glared at her a moment longer but couldn't summon up quite enough outrage to warm my goosebump covered flesh. "Fine."

Ollie graciously tossed me the dressing gown on the floor by her feet and I slipped it on gratefully. "Mack?"

I looked up at her, surprised by the sudden softness in her voice. "Aye?"

"What do you think we'll find? At Granda's, I mean." Ollie pressed her lips into a thin line. "Did they... you know. Clean it up?"

It was a bloody good question. "I'm not sure, love. I know the body is with the S.O.P.D., but the way Fife said it happened..." My voice trailed off. "I'll go in first, aye? So I can tell you if it's bad."

"Thanks, Mack."

She disappeared and when I finally emerged from my bedroom, I found her curled up on the couch with a fat book in her lap and a slim notebook balanced on the arm of the chair.

"Can you run over the floor when you're done, please?" She didn't look up from the book as she spoke, too engrossed to tear her attention away.

"Sure." Before attacking the pile of dirty dishes, I went to my record player and selected an album. I chose a Fleetwood Mac set, one of Ollie's favourites. She probably wouldn't notice — once the lass had her nose in a book, the rest of the world disappeared. You could run her over with a freight train and she wouldn't notice. Still, she had to surface eventually.

Minutes later I had soap bubbles to my elbows and a growing stack of dripping plates beside me. While I worked, I let my mind wander.

The spectrum of magical things that might cause havoc in the general community was wide, but for the most part, they behaved. To have someone — or something — sending redcaps and bean sith after me was unusual enough.

Ok, not that unusual. I had pissed off a few people here and there over my career as a buidseach. But for them to target me at the same time as an attack on a group of innocent kids? The S.O.P.D. had found a few illicit drugs, a stolen purse, and a warrant for one of the victims, but as far as anyone could tell, they hadn't done anything to deserve being forcibly divorced from their limbs.

There was nothing to say it was connected. The bean sith had been looking for the tapestry, and the red cap was likely set upon us by the same source, a valid assumption after being attacked right after dropping it off to Fergus. Whatever had gone after those kids, there was no obvious connection to me. I kicked myself for not interrogating the bean sith more thoroughly before burying her under the bitumen.

The bean sith pulled my mind to Claire McAdam and I added my rogue vampire to the list of shite gone wrong in the space of a few short days. Perhaps it was all coincidence? The unexpected death of a powerful practitioner, killed by something steeped in power, stronger than the strongest man I knew. A girl, killed by a vampire with no regard for the rules. Two creatures sent to find a magical trinket Granda had been after. And now, a violent attack on a bunch of teens that had no connection to this world. That was the one that threw me the most.

A shiver ran down my spine. I stared at the bubbles as they slowly merged and popped, my hands still in the cooling water.

"Ollie?"

"Mhmm?" Her mumbled response was vague but after a moment she tore her eyes from the book. "Mack, you're dripping!"

I looked down. Sure enough, the slow accumulation of terrible thoughts had obliterated anything sensible in my brain and I had walked over to talk to her without stopping to wipe my hands. Rather than go back for the dish towel, I dragged them over my shirt, much to Ollie's dismay. "Ollie… it's a demon, isn't it?"

"Well… yes. That's the most likely answer." She was interested now; the book forgotten, hands already reaching for a pen. "But what made you think it?"

For a moment, my brain skipped over too many points to land on any. I clenched my hands and forced myself to focus. "There's nothing to say those kids at Deaconsfield were connected to magic. Sure, they could have stolen something or accidentally pissed off one of the unseelie, but they wouldn't have left any proof of what they'd done. It all feels too random, like someone — or something — just ripped into them and walked off without a care."

"Right." Ollie scribbled, using my scattered thought process to augment her own methodical process. "So, we have a summoned demon… but by who? Not the kids, that's for damn sure. There would have been a ton of evidence left."

"Then someone else summoned it." I leaned against the wall, arms folded, face creased in thought. I'm not saying it hurt, but a handful of painkillers wouldn't have gone astray. "We need to find out who."

"But the only person strong enough to summon and control a demon would have god-like powers," Ollie said. "Who? Jack, maybe. Agnes, for sure. There's nobody that makes sense, though."

"Unless…" Sucking a breath through my teeth, I let the jumble of thoughts crowding my brain loose. "Ollie, you have to be old and strong and at least three-quarter seelie to *control* a demon, but you could summon one with less power than that." I waved away her shocked protest. "Aye, you'd still have to be strong. Most practitioners with that kind of power also have the sense not to dabble in stupid shite they can't control. Well, the ones that lived long enough to learn better, anyway."

Ollie fiddled with her pen, mouth pursed with worry. "You think someone called this monster up from the Otherworld and just... let it go?"

"Maybe not on purpose. But think, Ollie... Some bampot finds a spell and thinks he has the baws to pull it off. He yanks some evil bastard through to our world, but it breaks free. Probably kills the poor sod who let it out. Now it's free to wander around, killing and what have you. It comes on the kids, rips them apart, leaves. No matter if someone finds them, it's not like there's much that a demon has to be afraid of."

"As much as you might be right, Mack, it doesn't help." She shook her head, worry deepening. "We still don't know who called it up, or why, or where they got the spell. We don't even know which demon it was!"

"Maybe some idiot caught a ceasg and made a wish — they have all kinds of big magic buried in their watery gaff. Or maybe something bigger is at play and we just canna see it."

"Maybe and what if, Mack." Ollie spoke gently. "We don't know shite, yet. I'll see what I can find though, all right?"

"I feel like something bad is coming, Ollie." I hadn't told her about Jack's words from earlier. It would only make her worry. "What if something — or some*one* has just decided not to play the game anymore?"

"Game?"

"Of secrecy." I shook my head, lost in my own thoughts. "The Collective doesn't really have the power they think they do. They're what, a few buidseach with a touch of the fae, and the goodwill of all the key players from the Otherworld? What happens if the vamps and the water-ponies decide we can all go to hell?"

"Then they're found out, and the full might of a planet-load of resourceful humans come bearing down on them." Ollie shook her head. "Come on, Mack. They're tough, but they all have their vulnerabilities. You could take out an entire clan of baobhan sith with a big enough box of iron filings. How long do you think it would take the military to weaponise that?"

"Aye." Her words made sense but didn't settle my sense of doom.

"Go and wipe your hands, love." Ollie nodded at the puddle at my feet. "And mop that up before you go A over T."

"Yes, Mam." I dutifully fetched the mop and cleaned up the mess I had made before giving the rest of the floor a quick wipe. Just in time, too, as someone pounded on the door just as I finished.

Ollie looked up, startled. "Who the feck —" Her whispered panic flashed to a grin when she heard Quinn call out.

"It's me. Are you lot ready to go?"

Ollie bounded to the door and unlatched it. She stood back to let Quinn pass through and quickly closed it behind him. Anyone loitering in the hall would have seen no more than her shadow.

"Hello, Davey!"

"Hey, Ollie. Are you guys ready to go? Annie said she'd be ready for us at midday."

"Annie?" I tilted my head to one side. "When the hell did your High and Mighty Lord and Master become *Annie*?"

"Sorry. Detective Chief Inspector Fife. Better?" Quinn smirked. "If she asks, I absolutely didn't tell you we spent about three hours on the phone last night."

"Talking about what?" I looked at Ollie, wondering if she found this as ludicrous as I did. Quinn was my apprentice. If Fife wanted a lackey she could get her bloody own.

"You, mostly." Clearly enjoying the sudden power he held, Quinn turned to Ollie. "Best grab a jumper, love. It's a bit nippy out there."

"You wally. I don't get cold!" Despite Ollie's protest, she flounced off into her room and appeared a moment later with a white cardigan and a wide-brimmed hat that would hide her face if she tilted her head just so. "Come on, Mack. Don't tell me you can't find your coat again?"

I looked around, realising I could not. "It was here a minute ago..."

"It was bloody not," Ollie retorted. "You threw it on the floor of your room when you got in last night."

"Oh. Right." I quickly fetched my big trench coat and the staff propped behind my door, unwilling to leave the two scheming shites in my living room alone for more than a few seconds. "Let's get at it, then."

Ollie left via the balcony, leaving me to pester Quinn on our way downstairs. "You know, as my apprentice, it's your duty to inform me of any discussions that involve myself, my magic, or my friends."

"Is it?" Quinn's air of surprise was all too fake. "Well, then it's lucky I haven't actually signed anything yet."

"You —" I blustered to a stop when I realised he was right. "Fecking gobshite."

Quinn laughed at that, a big, cheerful belly laugh that echoed through the painted brick stairwell. "Don't stress, mate. Annie was just worried about you. She said you haven't talked about your grandad yet, at least not to her, and she wanted to know how you're getting on."

"That's all you talked about?" I asked dubiously. "For three hours?"

"She may have mentioned you're pathologically disorganised, but I'd already figured that out on my own." He chuckled again. "You're the adult poster child for ADHD, bud."

"I... am?"

He winced. "I didn't say it to be mean. You should look into it, though."

I shrugged off the idea. "I'm too bloody busy for that."

Quinn shrugged, unbothered. "I won't bring it up again."

"I'm no' saying you're wrong, lad." I pushed through the door on the ground floor. "I've just got a lot on my plate, what with Ollie and Granda and everything else going on."

"Mate, no judgement." Quinn raised his hands placatingly. "I think you should talk to Annie, though. About your grandad, I mean. It'd make her feel a lot better."

"The lass has always been a worrier."

"You know, some people might call that being a good friend."

I couldn't help a tiny smile when I saw Ollie already in the Demon, ready to go. As much as I tried to take her out, we didn't do it nearly enough. "I'll talk to her, Quinn. Promise!"

"Oh, there was one other thing." Quinn paused briefly to run a hand over the Demon's roof, admiring her fine lines and polished shine. "Hey, how the hell is your flat so messy when your car is always pristine?" He ducked down so he could see Ollie and dropped his voice to a stage whisper. "Does he take it to bed with him at night?"

Ollie thought that was hilarious. "If he could talk me into lugging it up the stairs he bloody would!"

"Feck off, you." I pointed a warning finger at my sister. "Do not disrespect my sweetheart, or I'll make you walk to Granda's."

"Ohh, sorry my wee, sweet lassie." Ollie patted the seat beside her. "I didn't mean to insult you, honest. I know you wouldn't stoop so low as to share a bedroom with Henry!"

With a groan I yanked the driver's door open. "I walked right into that one, didn't I?"

As always, the interior was as spotless as the outside. Not a speck of dust floated by in the muted sunlight that shone down. Not a fingerprint marred the leather.

"Somewhere along the line, I picked up a wee man or a boadachan sabhaill," I explained to Quinn. "They're seelie creatures that do favours for the people they've bonded to."

"Like that old fairy tale about the elves and the cobbler?" Quinn looked at the car with new appreciation.

"Aye, somewhat. They used to be found in barns, not that you'd ever lay eyes on them if they could help it. We had one at Granda's. It used to milk the cows and tend the gardens once he got too old to do it on his own." A flash of guilt reddened my cheeks. I had been a wee shite when I moved in, too wrapped up in my own grief to help the old man as much as I should have. "They usually stick to a place, at least until the whole family has moved on. Execpt this one came with the car."

"It was your Dad's?" Quinn asked.

"Not bloody likely," I chuckled. It's was Mam's. Da never let her drive it while they were together, insisted she drive something with airbags and crumple zones — he had no bloody appreciation for the Demon. Sometimes she'd sneak off to Granda's with us kids and we'd go cruising through the countryside in it."

"So your little fella moved with the car when you took it?"

"Seems like it. Mam left the Demon to me, she knew how much I loved it. I moved out, took the car, and the next morning Granda called me up, asking if I'd fecked with his helper. I was a shite, but I wouldn't have done that. And ever since, the car has been spotless every morning, even if I parked it covered in mud."

"Granda was so mad," Ollie chuckled. "He didn't talk to Mack for about a month! Not that he had any right to complain — it only took a week for Old Natty's wee barn man to start working Granda's place as well."

"It did?" I swung around to look at Ollie in surprise. "Why the bloody hell would he do that?"

Ollie snorted. "What, you didn't know? Granda and Natty were having it off, Mack."

Something caught in my throat and I choked, coughing and spluttering until my eyes watered. "Bullshit," I croaked.

Ollie sniggered. "Devil's arse, Mack, you're blind! They were making eyes at each other for years. You didn't really think Granda spent every Thursday night lookin' for Thomas, did you?"

"Thomas was old, he wasn't allowed to stay out!" Thomas, Granda's cat, was notorious for disappearing once a week. It would take Granda hours of traipsing through the fields to catch the wee prick.

Ollie howled with laughter. "Oh, Mack. You're such a wee innocent. Granda used to lock Thom in the barn, pretend he was missing, then meet Natty out there for a quick shag. How did you never notice Granda and Thom would always come back dry, even in the pissing rain?"

“I…” I had never noticed. My mind slowly turned the information over, digesting it. Then, the reality slapped me in the face. “Natty? And Granda? Shagging next to my bloody car?” The sudden need for a long shower hit me like a sack of rocks.

Wiping her eyes as she shook with giggles, Ollie could only nod.

“Your little guy did clean the seats, right?” Quinn looked as though he were about to throw himself out the window.

“Aye,” I whimpered. “I fecking hope so.”

Ollie sniffled and gulped a deep breath. “Sorry, Mack. I always thought you knew.”

“I wish I still didn’t.”

“Davey, were you going to say something before we got sidetracked?” Ollie cleared her throat, rubbed her face again, and forcibly regained her composure. “About your conversation with the Detective.”

“That’s right, I nearly forgot. She said she’s requested I be transferred to the S.O.P.D. as an interim officer. She’s not authorised to make it permanent, but she said they’re so desperate for people that it would almost guarantee me a place. Then, she’ll assign me to liaise with you, so we have more time for you to train me.”

“Oh.” I chewed on the idea. “Or, you could quit the force, tell them to feck off with all the red tape, and be my full time assistant?”

“What’s the salary?” Quinn asked pointedly. “Benefits? Holiday pay? Life insurance?”

“What the bloody hell do you need life insurance for?” Pressing my foot down as we reached the motorway, I let the rumble of the engine gently rattle my soul. “You don’t have kids, and you can’t spend it once you’re gone.”

“Very funny. I still need to pay my rent, though.”

“Sell your expensive wardrobe.” Though he was in the official Police Scotland getup today, he managed to make it look better than the other uniformed officers I had seen over the years. “That should get you by for a while, aye?”

“Piss off, Mack. You can’t ask the lad to give up his job and come work for you for free.”

“The hell I can’t.”

“You can ask, Mack, but I’m not gonna say yes.” Quinn shrugged. “The rent here ain’t cheap.”

“I suppose I can’t argue with that.” I turned my head just enough that he could see my smirk. “And anyway, it might be good to have a spy in the ice-cream van.”

“Ice-cream van?”

I gave a surprised bark. “You never noticed? S.C.O. for Scotland; Otherworld and Paranormal, that’s the O and P, Enforcement Department.” Faced with nothing but his confusion, I spelled out the acronym for him. “S.C.O.O.P.E.D.”

“Oh.” Quinn looked less than impressed.

“He thinks he’s a bloody genius for coming up with that,” Ollie told him. “Best you give him a little clap, or you might damage his ego.”

“Shut yer weesht, you insolent child.” I shook my head in disbelief. “No bloody appreciation, either of you. Well don’t you worry, I understand my intelligent humour is over your heads, so I won’t subject you to it anymore.”

“Aye, because I’m about to kick you out of the car and shove my dirty sock in your mouth.” Ollie craned her neck so she could see Granda’s house as we crested the low hill. “And anyway, we’re here.”

Chapter Fifteen

"Right on time." I cruised up the long driveway, easing carefully over the dips and loose rocks to protect the underside of the Demon. "It's only just gone twelve. Are you sure Fife got everyone out?"

Quinn tapped a quick message into his phone. I resisted the urge to see if he had Fife listed under her station, or 'Annie'. It was none of my business and besides, if he saw me looking, he'd think I cared.

Once we reached the courtyard, I pulled into one of the converted stables and waited until Quinn's phone beeped. "She said we're good."

Granda had planned to pull it down, but it came in handy on my rare visits with Ollie, allowing her to exit the car without being seen. I stepped out into the muted sunlight, pulling my collar up to protect from the icy breeze that shot between the buildings. "It's clear, lass."

Ollie streaked across the courtyard, fast enough that if anyone on a neighbouring property had been looking, they would think they had simply seen a shadow pass by. I hesitated, unsure if I should use the main entrance or go by the mudroom, as Granda had always insisted his grandchildren do.

"Feck you, old man, I'm using the front door for a change. I'm not a child anymore." I purposefully strode toward the door.

Toward the other end of the building, another door opened. "Mack! Come through here. You're kidding yourself if you think I'm going to let you traipse dirt through my bloody crime scene."

Smothering my frustration, I turned and headed toward the mudroom while Ollie chortled. "Not a child, Mack? Good to see you still do what you're told, bairn."

"You weren't supposed to hear me say that you wee witch."

"Then you shouldn't have used your out-loud voice, genius."

"Are you both twelve?" Quinn asked. "Seriously! I've seen school kids more mature than either of you."

Ollie and I stopped, looked at each other, and said in one breath, "Sounds like *someone* has his knickers in a twist."

Quinn just rolled his eyes and kept walking while we laughed.

Ollie paused at the door. Fife was waiting just inside. Without having to say a word, she assured us that the house was, for the most part, clean. "The... incident occurred in one of the outbuildings. It's still a mess, but inside the house looks untouched as far as we can tell. I wanted to bring you through in case you saw anything we didn't. Something that doesn't belong, something missing, you know?"

"Aye." I shed my coat and made to toss it on the floor but caught Fife's warning look just in time. Instead, I carefully hung it on one of the hooks along the wall. I scraped my boots even though they were mostly clean, but gladly saw there were none of those paper booties that Fife was so fond of.

"Are your forensic people coming back, Detective?" Ollie asked before stepping into the hall.

"Not unless you find something they need to look at." Fife smiled at her. "You don't have to worry, lass. No one will know you've been here."

"Thank you." Ollie slipped into the hall and inhaled deeply.

I followed her and instinctively did the same. My lungs filled with a scent that wasn't so much a smell as it was a knowing. Familiarity seeped into my bones and even with my eyes closed, there was no doubt where I was.

Blinking away the sting in my eyes, I pressed a hand on Ollie's shoulder. "Are you good?"

"Aye, Mack." She reached up to give my hand a squeeze and then set off. "We should work room by room. Separately, so we don't influence each other, aye?"

"Aye." It was a sound plan, so together we headed to the upper floor. Ollie went straight for Granda's study — not surprising, she had spent most of her time there after we moved here.

I took the master bedroom. Walking in, I was hit with a wave of nostalgia. The smell in here was more defined, despite sitting empty for several days. Old Spice mingled with cinnamon soap, thick enough to make my chest tighten and my throat hurt. I coughed, clearing my airways in case someone got the wrong idea. As much as I missed Granda, I wasn't about to start howling in his bedroom like an overtired wean.

I searched the room quickly, turning back blankets and kneeling down to peer under the bed. Granda's slippers were missing, but everything else seemed normal. He was like Ollie — obsessively tidy, chronically organised and pathologically averse to the kind of messy disorganisation a grieving twelve-year-old boy had dragged with him into the old man's home so long ago.

Rubbing my eyes and cursing the dust in the wardrobe, I fingered one of his wool coats, thinking back to my parents' funeral. Of course, it had been Ollie's funeral, too. She hadn't seen it but had listened from upstairs at the wake Granda held. He'd made me stay downstairs, mingling with sour-faced strangers until I had given him the slip, and nicked off upstairs to sit with my sister.

Together, we had pressed our ears to the vents and heard what a tragedy it was, how sad to lose such a loving family, and what a pity that Conor, Mam's brother and her only surviving relative, had simply dropped away, unable to be contacted for the arrangements.

That brought me up short and I went to look for Ollie. I found her in her bedroom, perched at the foot of her bed.

"Ollie, do you know what ever became of Uncle Conor?"

By her face, the name had brought the same sudden shock I had felt at remembering him. "No, I don't. He never contacted us again after that one letter. Ah, shite, Mack. Someone's got to tell him about Granda."

"I wouldn't even know how to get in touch." Conor — our mother's twin — had been somewhere in Denmark when our parents had died, researching the link between our old gods and theirs. He had never returned.

Conor's wanderlust had seen him away more than he was home, visiting only to see Mam and visit us kids every few years at Christmas. According to a letter he had sent, the loss of his sister had broken the last connection he had with Scotland. After her death, he had ceased all contact.

"Mack, this might sound really mean but... do you think he even cares?" Ollie frowned, looking down at the faded coverlet.

"It was his Da, Ollie. Of course he'd care."

"He didn't care enough to come back for Mam's funeral. He never visited to see how you and Granda were doing, either."

I sighed and wrapped an arm around her shoulders. "It probably hurt too much. I don't remember much of him, to be honest, but I know he and Granda fought like... well, like *me* and Granda. I can well imagine he'd stay clear after losing Mam. He adored her just as much as I adore you, you wee shite."

Ollie frowned, picking at a loose thread on the blanket. "He didn't like Da much. I think that's why he didn't visit."

"What makes you think that?" Conor was only a vague memory to me, a blurry face attached to a distant memory of warmth and Mam's glowing happiness when he came to stay. Even my recollections of his knock down arguments with Granda were hazy gaps filled in mostly by the stories Mam used to tell of them, always with a soft smile for her troublesome brother.

"I heard them fight, once." Ollie wouldn't meet my eye. "Da and Conor. He called Da a piece of shite, said Mam should never have married him, never had his kids." The corners of her lips pulled down as she struggled to hide how deeply the memory hurt.

"Maybe he never liked us, either."

"Bollocks, Oll." I sat beside her and wrapped an arm around her shoulders. "He adored Mam, as much as I adore you. Do you think I could ever hate your weans?"

"And how the bloody hell is a dead girl going to have any children, you daft shite?"

"You know what I mean." I cupped her cheek and turned her face to look at me. "Even if you'd grown up and married the ugliest beast in Scotland, one with a crooked nose and tiny, wee eyes, who drinks all day and leaves big jobbies in the loo, I'd still love you, and I'd love your kids like they were my own."

Ollie stared back, stricken. "Devil's oath, Mack, you really think my taste in men is that bad?"

"This whole conversation is going straight over your head, isn't it?" I pulled her closer as she laughed. "You know what I'm saying, lass. Uncle Conor couldn't hate us even if he and Da were on the outs. He loved Mam too much."

Ollie sniffled and rubbed her nose on the back of her hand. "I know Uncle Conor fought with Granda but that never seemed... well, *scary* like that time he went at Da. I knew he and Granda would always patch it up, but he really sounded like he hated Da. What do you think happened between them?"

I shrugged, playing down my unease. "Not a damn clue. Da was strict, and I know Mam didn't like that he spent so much time in his books and research. Maybe Conor thought he was neglecting Mam." I didn't add that there had been times I thought our sweet mother had deserved better. Our father had never been perfect, and his strict nature had often grated on my younger self.

"That's probably it." Ollie stood and smoothed down the front of her dress. "Do you think Fife would notice if I took Peggy home?"

She lifted a hand and opened it to reveal a vintage wooden clothes peg, wrapped in a scrap of cloth and with carved face so loved it had worn almost smooth. The strands of woollen hair once glued to its head had long since fallen off and the makeshift dress now looked more grey than vibrant blue. It had been Mam's, a gift from her own mother and passed down to Ollie once she was old enough to treasure it, instead of destroy it as young children are wont to do.

"I don't think she would." Come to think of it, there were a few wee trinkets in Granda's office that would not be missed, either. "Let's finish up, and head downstairs, aye?"

I left Ollie in her room and quickly scoured Granda's study. The pristine organisation worked in my favour and I quickly palmed a few stones, a dagger, a small leatherbound book and a handful of little cloth pouches. I was just dropping the last of these in my pocket as I heard footsteps on the stairs.

Quinn poked his head in, glanced at my pockets, and shook his head. "Got what you need? I hope so, because if you stuff anything else in your pants, you'll get caught."

"Is it that obvious?" I asked.

Quinn nodded, then quickly backed away as I pulled the book out and shoved it at him.

"Go on, then, down your trousers! And you call yourself a bloody apprentice, bah." Left holding the evidence of my pilfering, I debated putting it back.

"Give it to me, you overgrown peanut." Ollie took the book and promptly folded it up in her cardigan, which she then draped over her arm. She gave me the once over, then nodded. "She'll never know."

"Nothing notable to report?" I asked. Ollie shook her head and I set off downstairs. "Off we go, then."

I found Fife sorting through a stack of mail by the front door. "If there's a porno in there, I don't want to know. I heard enough about my Granda's sex life on the way here to last a lifetime."

Fife raised an eyebrow. "Nothing of note, but some of these bills are past due. You'll need to get on that, Mack."

"I know." I looked away uncomfortably. "It's been a busy couple of days."

"I know." She touched my arm gently before letting her hand fall away. "Do you need a hand with the paperwork?"

"No, it's fine." Guilt settled in my gut as her eyes darkened with worry. "Oh all right. Have you got a bit of time on Monday? You can come around and coddle me for a while and show me what the bloody hell I have to do to sort this mess out."

Fife's eyebrows slowly lifted. "Why, *thank* you for bestowing such a benevolent favour on me, Henry."

"Don't sass me, Fife. Quinn told me you've gone all soppy with worry about me. The least I can do it let you indulge your maternal instincts for a wee bit, so you can see for yourself I'm fine."

"You're *not* fine, Henry Mack." Ollie stomped over and baled me up, chest out, arms folded. For a wee shite, she managed to look quite a way down her nose at me as she spoke. "You might pretend you're all tough, but I see right through it, you big marshmallow. Ever since he died, you've been twice as forgetful with half the patience. And don't think I didn't see you blowing your nose on his coat sleeve while you were going through his stuff."

"It was the dust!" I protested.

"You keep telling yourself that, brother. Meanwhile, everyone around you will just stand here, twiddling our thumbs until you admit that yes, you miss him and yes, you bloody well need and deserve some support for all you're going through."

"I'm fine, Ollie!" If I growled the words, it was only out of frustration at her badgering. "I'm just worried about you!"

With a howl of frustration, she spun on one foot and stormed off toward the kitchen. "I need a drink."

After I watched her go, I turned to see Fife watching me. Her arms were folded too, and one finger tapped speculatively on her bicep. I jabbed a finger toward her. "Don't you start."

Fife raised her hands defensively. "Dinna say a word, Mack."

"No, but you're thinking it so loud I can hear you from over here." Blowing out a sharp hiss, I groped for a change of subject. "Should we go see the outbuilding?"

"You haven't checked the downstairs, yet." Fife hadn't moved.

"Ollie can do it. She's as familiar with the place as I am. Maybe more so, because unlike me, she actually has a working memory. Mine is worse than a goldfish on crack."

"Gee, Mack, I've known you all this time and I never noticed."

A corner of her mouth twitched up in a smile and she stepped aside. "Let's go. I get the impression Ollie doesn't want to see the mess?"

"She'll come if we need her to, but I don't want to put her through it if we can help it." Together, we headed toward the old barn that served as Granda's working space.

"I know you try to be strong for her, Mack, but you have to let yourself be vulnerable, too. For her sake, as much as your own."

"Is that what they taught you at psychology school?"

"Don't be a knob. I'm only trying to help."

I fell silent as we crossed the courtyard. Fife reached the outbuilding first. While she waited for me to fetch my staff from my car, she fished a pair of booties from her pocket. Despite what she had said about forensics not returning to the house, she still wanted the crime scene kept clean. We quickly donned them, Fife finishing first. She stood and placed her hand on the door, hesitating.

"You're right." I smiled at her surprise. "I'm being a knob. Sorry."

With that, she pushed open the door and I stepped into a living nightmare.

Chapter Sixteen

I stepped inside and blinked twice, waiting for my eyes to adjust to the sudden darkness.

The outbuilding, once a long barn used for grain and equipment storage, now served as my grandfather's altar room. It had been artfully updated with crisp, white render on the walls that left a few of the original beams exposed. Granda had installed glass panels in the ceiling to let natural light filter through and hung lamps at regular intervals for moonless nights or cloudy days. The floor had been dug up to expose bare dirt, allowing the old man a direct connection with the soil he was born on.

In all the times I had visited him here, even trained in this very room, the open space had never been properly dark, not during daylight hours. Even under the heaviest clouds, light would filter through the skylights to soften the shadows.

Now, blood and ichor sprayed across the walls and ceiling so thick it obscured the light from above and painted the walls a shade of old rust. I swallowed hard, cradling a memory of a time when the room had felt safe and inviting. As tempting as it was to cling to that, I forced myself to dispel it and let the true horror around me sink in.

I opened my second sight. Bone deep terror and a midnight darkness crept into my bones. Power pressed against my skin, a spell not long broken, a reservoir of agonising pain trapped within the psyche of the very ground below. Powerful magic had been cast here, the sort that could only be harnessed with a terrible intent.

"It looks worse than it is," Fife said quietly.

I turned to her, ready to ask how this wasn't the most awful thing it could possibly be, but behind her a dark smear caught my attention. At first glance I had assumed the thick coating on the walls was blood, but closer examination revealed that was not the case. I stuck a finger out and wiped it along an exposed beam, then sniffed it.

"Annie… have you had this analysed?"

She nodded. "Motor oil. I can get the report for you if you need it." She hesitated, as if unsure of what she was about to say. "At first, I thought it might be the same stuff we saw yesterday. You seemed pretty sure it was a different substance, though…." She left the thought hanging but didn't voice her doubt.

"You conveniently left that out when we discussed it."

Fife shook her head, resolute. "Even if I had thought it was linked, you know I like to get your opinion fresh without polluting it with my own stupid guesses."

"This isn't oil. It's an ash compound, just like we saw at that crime scene."

She opened her mouth, closed it, and opened it again. She didn't speak, though.

I rubbed the mixture between my fingers, feeling the granular texture. The cool afternoon light sapped some of the colour, but I could make out a greenish tinge to the substance. "Have yesterday's samples come back yet?"

"Yes, this morning. The predominant ingredient was burnt kelp residue. It was mixed with pig fat and some plant matter — I don't have the exact breakdown yet. It's definitely not motor oil, though."

"Doesn't matter." I nodded at the smear on the wall. "I'll bet you my car that this is the same composition."

"Our lab wouldn't make a mistake like that, Mack." Fife chewed her lip. "If you're right, someone has tampered with the results."

Guilt plucked at my nerves when I saw the doubt on her face. I knew she trusted her team and knowing one of them must be dirty would hurt. "I need you to step back, love. The doorway should be fine."

She obeyed, the pensive expression on her face quickly replaced with blank professionalism. I stifled a snort. *She's one to talk about letting yourself be vulnerable.*

Once she was out of the way, I positioned myself in roughly the centre of the room. I crouched, careful not to let my knees touch the blood-soaked dirt floor but eager to lower myself closer to what I thought might be the source of the powerful residue I felt soaking the room.

To begin, I simply let myself feel. Sensations pressed against my skin, cloying, suffocating, cloaking me in a stranger's terror. *Good, then.* The spell caster had been afraid. I hoped the bastard had pissed himself in fright.

I pressed further. Beyond the fear I sensed anger, an outrage that emanated warm familiarity. Granda. He hadn't been scared, he had been furious. Over the years I had pissed him off many a time, but only once had I seen his eyes flash with the kind of scorching heat this feeling held.

A memory surfaced, something repressed or simply discarded. Granda, staring down a police officer at his door, fingers digging into my shoulder as the officer spoke.

"Mr. MacDonald, I'm sorry. The report is quite clear. It was a terrible, tragic accident, but an accident nonetheless."

"No. You're lying. Someone killed my daughter and her family."

The officer darted an uncomfortable glance at his partner. "The results were conclusive, sir. The gas leak —"

The door slammed shut.

I jumped in both memory and present, eyes snapping open to the desecrated room. I struggled a moment to regain my centre, hearing my breath rasp in a rhythm too quick for peace, but spurred on by a deep need to know more.

My hands moved now, fingers painting pictures in the air as I drew upon my staff for power, not wanting to disturb the residues around me. The power of the spirit world suffused the sigils as I drew them, lighting them up like fat embers floating above a fire to leave a glowing trail behind. As I completed each symbol it drifted off, taking up position somewhere in the room.

Sigils done, I focused on the room again. My spell hung over the floor in a grid-like pattern, filling the room with the magic of remembrance. It emanated from each rune, weaving around the negative space left behind by the most recent spell that was cast, painting around its lines and surrounding them with an amber aura. It worked much like rubbing a pencil over a notepad, skimming over the dips and grooves to reveal the marks gouged into the world by the practitioner before me.

I exhaled slowly, eyes scanning the new pattern that had formed. A wide circle, almost touching the walls, enclosed a smaller one toward the end of the room, away from the door. Both were etched with a series of sigils and linked by a criss-cross pattern of straight lines. Despite the masterful complexity of the spell, it was messy. A couple of the grid lines were a tiny bit off, not quite parallel to the others. The larger circle wobbled and dipped, and was more of an egg shape than a true circle. Even the sigils looked hastily dashed, the lines barely touching in places that, had they been even the tiniest bit short, would have caused the spell to fail entirely.

I read the outer spell first. An entrapment circle, designed to let anyone step inside but allow no one to leave. Granda must have entered it unaware and been unable to escape whatever had been placed inside. Except… I stood, moving to a small section of the circle that wavered and shimmered more than the rest.

"What do you see?" Fife's voice was low, and I guessed she worried about interrupting my spell.

"See this?" I pointed to the anomaly before realising she didn't have the sight, and would only see air. I quickly explained the nature of the circle. "But there's a gap in this section, a weakness. The spell was rushed, messy. They closed the circle in this spot, but instead of the ends touching, they overlapped, causing it to lose potency."

"Did you grandfather do this?"

I shook my head. "I would recognise his signature." Fife didn't question that, but I saw the confusion on her face. "Magic isn't just a list of words or signs. Or, it is, but each person interprets it a little bit differently. It's like comparing handwriting, or hearing a Frenchman speak Scottish — The meaning is the same, but you can hear the accent." I closed my eyes and felt the humming energy that lay just out of reach. "This isn't Granda's work. I feel like it's almost familiar, though. Like I could recognise it, if it were stronger."

"Can you make it stronger?"

I shook my head. "It's fading quickly."

"You said it's a trap, a prison. What about the weak spot? Could someone have escaped it?"

I nodded, cogs turning. "Granda is no fool. The moment he realised he was trapped, he would have opened his sight. This weak spot is like a glaring neon sign. He would have known he could leave if he wanted to."

"Why stay, then?" Fife asked.

I eyed the smaller circle with dread. "He could have been injured. Distracted, over-confident maybe. Or... maybe he was worried something might follow him." I approached the second circle carefully. Where the aura around the entrapment spell glowed a soft, steady orange, this flickered and popped in vibrant shades of red. It was a vicious spell, dangerous, powerful. "This is a summoning spell."

"What does it summon?" Fife's voice rasped and I wondered if she was afraid as I was.

"A demon." I lifted my eyes to meet hers. "Demons are bad news, Fife. I don't recognise its name, not in this form, but the power it holds... it's something big."

Fife folded her arms tightly across her waist. "It's big. Scary. Violent, I assume?" She waited for me to nod before continuing. "So... Granda Mack comes into his spell room. The demon is waiting for him?"

This time, I shook my head in the negative. "If the demon was left here, it wouldn't have stayed. That breech in the containment circle was far too obvious. It's more likely that Granda's entrance triggered the summoning."

But how? Blood, whisky, food, death, birth. So many things could be used to activate a spell. Any source of power would do it, but this wasn't just an easy lantern-lighting. It would need to be strong, sharp, a bright flare to signal the spirit world and begin the drawing of magic into the summoning circle.

"Fife, Granda's body... were there any injuries apart from his chest?"

Fife's eyes shifted, staring into nothing for a brief moment while she searched her memory. "Yeah. There was. A cut on his right hand, across his fingers. The coroner said it didn't look defensive. It was too shallow."

"That was the catalyst." My eyes tracked the lines that skewered the circles. Nothing. Just links, all of them feeding whatever energy available in the void between them into the summoning spell. "I don't know how they did it, but whoever set this up made him bleed. One drop is all it would take — one drop to hit the floor anywhere inside this area." I outlined the larger circle with my finger.

"He could have sustained the injury outside, then?" Fife shifted so she could see the courtyard.

"Aye. Let me dispel this and I'll come have a gander." The stench of death and fear had my stomach roiling and I was eager for some fresh air. I raised my hands, palms facing the floor. Before pulling the spell energy back to dispel it, I slowed my breath, trying to ignore the tightness in my chest and the stench filling my nostrils. That stench was the spilled blood of my family. As I inhaled again, I coaxed the energy to disperse.

It didn't work. The bright marks dotting the room flared to a blinding brightness. Static hummed, forcing a painful pressure to press against my eardrums. Dazed, I stumbled back, blinking to clear the spots that obscured the room.

Instead of fading, they coalesced into shapes, shadows that

moved about the room. The vibrating buzz crackled and popped like an old radio not quite in tune. Then, the dial shifted.

Voices. I heard voices. The shadows weren't damaged retinas, they were people.

"Bloody fool, can't even handle a knife without spilling someone else's blood." Granda's low grumble hit me like an avalanche of snow, freezing my muscles and expelling what breath I had with a sharp wheeze. "No wonder Henry hates the fellow. He's about as competent as a dead ferret floating in a vat of stale beer."

Granda's insults were creative, I'll give him that. His image — more than a shadow, less than a solid picture — stepped through the door of his workroom. He clutched a cloth to his right hand. As he passed the threshold of the still-glowing circle, he paused.

One of the straight lines flared, running from his feet to the summoning circle. That flashed to life, creating a swirling vortex of black smoke that darted up into a column of darkness.

Granda turned. I watched his eyes frantically scan the room, decipher the spells. He started towards the anomaly, the weakness that could have been his saving grace.

Then, the demon stepped out.

A four-legged beast, taller than I stood, a horrifying spectre made of bone and sinew, devoid of flesh or fur, blew hot steam from a lipless mouth. One single eye glared from the centre of its head, bloodshot and unprotected. A hoof stamped angrily then pulled the monster forward, further out of the smoke, revealing the man-shape astride its back.

Unable to look away, caught in the terror and rooted in place, my mind scrambled to make sense of it. A man, all vein and muscle, organs bare, rode the horse, but didn't. He had no legs, seemed sewn on at the hips. Naked eyeballs turned toward my Grandfather.

Granda sucked in a breath. "Nuckelavee." No panicked terror, there. Just resignation. Just the face of a man who had met his death, accepted the foregone conclusion, and was even now making the decision to go down fighting.

Granda lifted his hands and twisted them into a dance, fingers scattering lines of light in the air that flew toward the monstrosity in the corner. The Nuckelavee reared, almost touched the high barn ceiling at its full height. One sinewy hand jerked forward, twisted, then crumpled into a broken bloodied mess.

Granda already had his next spell ready. The Nuckelavee lurched forward, hooves striking sparks on the wooden floorboard like flint against stone. Granda's spell launched, a string of light whipping around to tangle a foot, slowing the beast's furious charge. Another glowing rope snaked across the room, wrapping around the Nuckelavee's upper half, pinning its arms to its sides.

The Nuckelavee screamed in fury, a whinnied shriek both human and horse. It burst free of its magical restraints and pawed the ground with a hoof.

Granda turned. His eyes searched the wall behind me, never meeting mine, but somehow aware I was present... or would be one day.

"Henry? Henry, are you there?" He glanced over his shoulder frantically. "Your parents' death... It was no accident." His words came fast and low. Fife, eyes locked in horror on the demon, paid him no heed. "They were after Ollie. Get the thread, boy. Bring her back properly. But above all else, keep her safe." He gasped a breath, looked to the ceiling, and crossed his chest — an act I had never once in all my years see my heathen Granda do. More sigils, and a sword flashed to life in his hands, swirling with the glow of magic. "Give your sister my love."

He whirled back around as five quick strides brought the Nuckelavee face to face with its target. A hot cloud blew in Granda's face as the horse-head snorted. Granda swung the sword with all his might. The blade glanced off the horse's shoulder, vanishing as the power fuelling it faltered.

"Granda!" I knew what came next, knew I should look away.

The beast reached out with its one good human hand and plunged it into Granda's chest.

"No!" I watched, helpless, seeing a death that had already happened, a death that could not be stopped. Every cell in my body screamed at me to act, to stop this monster killing my Granda, to cut it down and save his life.

The Nuckelavee drew back the hand and held Granda's heart aloft, still pulsing. He raised it to his face, drew a deep breath as though inhaling through the space where his nose might have been, and crammed it in his mouth, chewing messily as Granda's body crumpled to the floor.

"No." A whisper this time, as I fell to my knees, falling with him. Heedless of the tears streaking down my face, I heaved a sob.

The Nuckelavee turned a slow circle, then galloped for the break in the barrier. When he reached it, he plunged through, then raced through the door, through Fife who stood watching.

The spell faded quickly after that. Bright lines dimmed and Granda's shadow wavered, losing what substance it had. Just as his eyes met mine, he vanished.

Fife gasped a single breath, ran outside, and retched.

It took me a few moments to regain my composure. And by that, I mean wipe my nose, scrub my tears away, swallow down a gulp of nausea that threatened to follow Fife's example, and pull myself up on trembling legs.

I staggered to the door in time to see Fife wiping her mouth. "You all right, love?"

She nodded, a jerking movement that conveyed not a shred of confidence in that assessment. Then her eyes filled and her mouth pulled into a tight, trembling line. "Mack... Mack, I'm so sorry."

Her words cracked the thin veneer of strength I had erected. When she stepped over and pulled me into a hug, she shattered the rest. I fell into her arms, sobbing like a child who had just lost his entire family.

She held me fast, silent but for an occasional sniffle of her own. We stood for hours, or maybe it was only a few minutes, while I cried.

Finally, I was spent. I lifted my head, wiped my eyes on an already damp sleeve, and took a shuddering breath. Fife drew back carefully, her own eyes red and cheeks wet. She kept a hand resting on my arm for a moment, a brief gesture of support that brought a fresh sting to my eyes.

"You're a right mess, aren't you?" I chuckled, a sound that

bordered more on hysteria than humour.

Fife understood. "Got nothin' on you, hobo."

I glanced back at the house, letting my chest tighten. I embraced the pain, let it steady me for what was to come. "We need to tell the others."

Fife huffed a shaky breath. "Aye. And while you're at it, you can tell me what the devil just happened."

"I barely know myself." At Fife's sideways glance, I explained. "I was trying to dispel the magic, not bloody supercharge it. I fecked it up. Again." I growled the final word with angry self-loathing.

"I'd say you broke the fecking case wide open, personally." Fife took my arm as we walked back to the house. "The very first thing your Granda said, did you hear it?"

I squinted, thought, then shook my head. My memory shied away from that first image of Granda, instead stupidly latching onto the life fleeing his eyes as he died.

Fife took a breath and spoke as though reciting a passage she had memorised for a school performance. "Fool boy. Can't even handle a knife without spilling someone else's blood. No wonder Henry hates him. Incompetent. Then… something about ferrets and beer?"

"Competent as a dead ferret floating in a vat of stale beer," I confirmed. I shoved the pain away just enough to summon a small grin. "He used that one on me a few times."

"He spoke like whoever it was had just left, or maybe even was still here. Mack, it's someone you know." Fife pushed the door open.

I didn't remind her about the booties. "Someone I think is as dumb as a box of bricks, by the sound of it. That certainly narrows down our suspects."

"Thinking of anyone in particular?"

"Aye. About half the population of Glasgow. I could add a few names if we're going wider than that."

Shaking her head, Fife led the way to the kitchen where Ollie and Quinn were sharing a packet of biscuits.

"Eating a dead man's food, are you?" When Ollie looked up with a startled look of guilt, I decided I didn't have the heart to sass her. "It's all right, love. I was only takin' the piss."

Ollie ignored my assurance. She came over and took my hand, looking up at my face. "You look like shite, Mack. The feck were you doing out there?"

"Watching Granda die." I coughed to clear the tightness in my voice. "It was a Nuckelavee. I didn't even know that bastard could be summoned."

"Aye, he can." Ollie's brow furrowed as she thought. "Burnt kelp is the main ingredient in the ritual." She eyes widened. "Oh, fecking hell. That's the demon that got away?"

"Seems so." Fife rubbed her face and I wondered if I should get her a bucket. "That thing was brutal."

Ollie jerked her head up. "Hang on a minute. You said you watched it?"

"Aye." I explained the misfire of my spell. "You know what my magic is like, lass. Works perfect half the time and goes baws up the rest of it."

She shook her head. "Mack, I don't even think that spell exists. Do you think you could do it again?"

I blinked. Granda's face flashed against my eyelids for the briefest moment. "No."

Ollie's face crumbled as the reality slowly sunk in. "Fecking hell, Mack. You had to watch? Oh, you poor thing."

I stepped back, dodging her attempted hug. Before she could take offence, I mustered up a grin. "It was as bad as you think, love, and I need a few to get my head back on, right?"

She nodded, eyes still big and full of concern. "Aye. We'll talk about it later."

"Not if I can help it." Despite muttering quietly, Ollie clicked her tongue and dropped a disapproving hand to her hip. "Fine! You can drag me through the wringer, but not until I'm well into a bottle of good whisky. I'd rather not have to remember it the next day."

Ollie shifted her attention to Fife. "What about you?"

Fife started. "What about me?"

"You're green as pea soup. Whatever you saw must've shook

you, but you've stopped doing the thing."

"What thing?" Fife glanced at me but I could only raise a hand in confusion. I had no idea what Ollie was on about.

"The thing." Ollie raised a hand and pointed two fingers at her face. "With your eyes, following Mack about like you think he's going to snap and start tossing fireballs into a crowded room, or throw himself into the jaws of an angry crocodile." She leaned back, arms crossed. "You two had a moment out there, didn't you?"

Fife and I shared a glance. Unfortunately, I was the only one of us who had got as red as a beetroot. "No!"

My protest was somewhat weakened by Fife's matter of fact "Yes," spoken at the same time.

"Good. I can stop worrying about you, then." Ollie dropped the subject. In her mind, that was that — if Fife thought I was alright, then I must be.

Whatever peace that brought her, I knew my next words would shatter it. "Ollie... He told me something. Before he died, I mean."

"What?" That brought Ollie up short. "When? You told me you hadn't spoken to him for months!"

"What did he say?" Fife asked. "I saw him talking to you, but I couldn't hear it."

"Hold on, hold on." Ollie grabbed my arm. "You mean to say your wee vision out there came with full surround sound?"

"Aye. Granda knew I was going to cast that spell — or screw the spell up, whatever it was I did. He said my name, said he knew I'd see this later." A fresh shudder of goosebumps prickled at my flesh as I wondered how he knew, and how long he had known. "He said Mam and Da didn't die in an accident."

"I wish I could say I was surprised." Fife sank into a chair. "This just keeps getting better and better, doesn't it?"

"What?" I snapped. "What do you know about it?"

"I told you," Fife said patiently. "Nothing. The files were sealed, Mack. Why the hell would a gas leak require top clearance to access?"

"Can you pull the files?" I asked her. "I don't care how many rules you have to break, but I need to see them."

“I don’t think so. Whoever sealed those records did a bloody good job of it.” Fife blew out a frustrated breath. “After I spoke to you about it the other day, I did some digging. Not two hours later I got a warning from the top brass about overstepping my authority.” At my raised eyebrow, she added, “But maybe I can ask around.”

“Make it happen.” I leaned over, hands flat on the table. I avoided looking at Ollie, worried she would see written on my face the words I had left out. They were after Ollie. Get the thread, bring her back, keep her safe. “I need you to do this for me, Annie.”

“I’ll do my best, Mack.” Fife held my gaze and gave me a tiny nod. That, to me, was as good as a handshake. She would keep her word. “Meanwhile, we have another problem to deal with.”

“Calling a homicidal demon running around Glasgow ripping people to bits a ‘problem’ is a wee understatement, don’t you think?” Ollie stood. “We need to find it before he finds another target.”

“Shouldn’t we be going after the idiot who created it?” Quinn asked.

“It was summoned, not created.” My brain had already skipped past that idea. “Ollie, if I get a sample of the gloop they used in the original spell, and some from the house where those young folk were pulled apart, could you help me make a tracking spell?”

“Aye, but Fergus could make a better one.”

“What about the summoner?” Fife asked. “We can’t just let them run around creating more problems. You said yourself, they must have been powerful. They’re dangerous.”

Ollie and I shared a glance. “Detective, you don’t have to worry about them making any more trouble.”

“You can’t possibly know that,” Quinn said. “Unless...”

“Aye.” I grinned, the first silver lining I had found after a storm-laden day. “The Nuckelavee got out, right? The first thing he’d have done — after killing Granda, that is — is go after the prick who cast the spell. Wouldn’t have stopped to mess round with the others until he’d succeeded.”

“Sometime soon, you’ll find a body with its heart ripped out,” Ollie said. “Then you’ll know who called that pony prick from the

Otherworld."

"Could it have been one of those kids?" Fife asked.

"Any of them missing a heart? The heart of a buidseach is the centre of their power. The demon would have devoured it on the spot."

"One of the bodies was torn open." Fife's brow furrowed and her eyes shifted to stare into space, a sure sign she was mentally flipping through her case notes. "But the internal organs were all accounted for."

I shook my head. "If I had a spare quid, I'd put it on you finding a single body with injuries close to what Granda had."

Fife sniffed, then summoned a tight grin. "I can't fecking wait."

Chapter Seventeen

I stood a short way down from the door of the Dagger Night Club, glass of milk in one hand, oat cookie in the other. I dunked the cookie and took a small bite, savouring it with gusto.

"Mhmm. Delicious. Fresh milk, right from the cow. None of this bottled rubbish, aye?" For emphasis I waved the glass under my nose, groaning with delight.

The two gille sith on either side of the door watched, eyes riveted on my beverage. I waved them over and they darted toward me. One, a blond lad with sparkling blue eyes, had wee bit of drool creeping from the corner of his mouth. His friend had the more traditional Scottish colouring with red hair, ruddy, freckled cheeks and eyes like moss. He made a small, whimpering sound.

"Oh, hello, mate. How's you morning?" I smiled widely, waving and almost slopping a bit of milk on the pavement.

Freckles eyed the ground as though he wanted to lick it. "That looks soooo tasty."

"Isn't it just?" I licked my lips. "Would you like to try some?"

They both pulled back and exchanged a look. It was the kind of look that, on the one hand, acknowledges the idea you were just proposed is a terrible one. But it's a look that suggests you're going to do it anyway.

"Fecking *oath*, yes!" Blue-eyes lurched forward but I pulled back a few steps.

"Steady on, no need to be impatient. I've only got a bit, so you'll have to share." I took a few more steps back so I was level with the corner of the building.

This time the glance they shared was one of murderous envy. "Me first," Freckles growled.

"I'm older!"

"I've been standing out here longer."

"How about," I said, raising my free hand, "a wee competition." I dunked the cookie all the way into the milk, then drew it out. I set the glass on the ground and the cookie beside it. "Whoever gets here first gets the milk and the loser gets the cookie."

I barely dived out of the way in time. The gille sith flew towards the glass, blue-eyes reaching it just a shade faster than his freckled friend. As I had planned, the rules of engagement prevented a squabble. Blue-eyes held the milk aloft, then downed it with ecstatic groans that, I'll be honest, made me a wee bit uncomfortable. His friend cupped the cookie in his hands and crammed it in his mouth with an equally inappropriate moan of delight.

It took about three seconds for the drugs to work. What can I say? Thank the devil for modern pharmaceuticals. The two collapsed in matching heaps and before any passers-by could notice, both had been snatched up and dragged behind the building.

"I could have helped with that, you know." Quinn looked put out that Ollie hadn't waited for him.

"Davey, I'm ten times as strong as you, and about that much faster, too. You don't need to feel bad about it, it's just the way it is."

"So sue me for wanting to help, kiddo."

That was the wrong thing to say. Ollie rounded on him, a finger raised and fury leaking from her pores. "I swear to Black Donald himself, David Fecking Quinn, if you call me a child again, I'll tear off your baws and hang them out for the crows to eat. And I'll make you watch them."

Quinn coughed and moved his hand across the front of his breeks, swallowing hard. "You've made your point." For some reason, his voice was a few octaves higher than it usually was.

"She bloody means it, too," I told him, grinning.

"I wasn't planning to find out either way." Quinn pushed his shoulders back in a show of bravery, but I noted that he took a casual step away from my sister. "Are we ready to do this?"

"I don't know why," Ollie said. "I mean, sure, that bit of needlework is nice and all, but it's hardly the highest thing on our list of priorities now, is it?"

I looked away. "We're hunting a Nuckelavee, Ollie. We can't afford to be fighting on two fronts. If Agnes can help us stop the attacks and distractions, all the better."

"If I didn't know better, I'd think you were up to something." Ollie's eyes narrowed, then shot open. "Oh my fecking — Mack! You're not sleeping with her again, are you?"

I threw my hands up and turned my back on her. "Oh, come on. It was one time! That's it! A quick roll between the sheets, nothing else. She wasn't even that good."

"That's a lie." Ollie primly told Quinn I had walked around in a love-addled daze for the next three weeks.

"I was anaemic, you wee gobshite." Make one mistake, tell your sister, and you'll spend the rest of your living days wishing you'd kept your mouth shut. "Can we focus, please?"

"So… you're not shaggin' Aggie?" Ollie kept her face serious but the crinkle around her eyes gave away the giggling inside.

"No!" Which wasn't to say I wouldn't, given the chance… but the Vampire Queen of Glasgow had been less than impressed with my attempt to steal a lock of her pretty hair for one of my spells, and Agnes held grudges tighter than a Scotsman holds his coin.

"You two are having me on, right?" Quinn darted a glance at me, then Ollie, then back to me. "There's no *way* you were having a cheeky root with one of those things."

"Are you judging me?" It occurred to me that Quinn had never met one of the baobhan sith face to face. Or anything else with the power of magical seduction. *This is going to be fun.*

“I think you’re a moron, but I’m not gonna judge you for it. I’ve made my fair share of regrettable decisions.” Quinn snuck a look around the corner to check the front of the club. “Are we ready?”

The lengthening shadows weren’t going to wait for us, so I nodded. “Let’s get on with it, then.”

Ollie giggled with excitement and I wondered if perhaps the sudden expansion of her social group had given her a bit of a taste for adventure.

Hefting my bag over one shoulder, I headed to the Dagger Night Club. After a quick shoulder check to make sure no one was watching — the last thing I needed was interference from Scotland’s finest because they thought I was breaking and entering, which I technically was, but that was entirely beside the point — I scrawled a quick sigil and popped the lock.

It clicked quietly open and I stifled a curse, knowing what was coming next. I swung around, back to the door, and waited for the heavy oak surrounding the handle to crack. To my surprise, it didn’t. The spell had worked. *Is it too much to ask for some fecking consistency?*

The door swung open easily and I stepped into the club’s entryway. It smelled of cleaning products and the blue carpeted floor still held dampness from a deep clean. A high counter on one side, used for checking ID, taking cover charges and hiding the occasional body stood cold and vacant. The door to the club proper was propped open, and that’s where the trouble began.

Three men, all with bulging arms and dripping hair, perched on bar stools that threatened to snap under their muscular weight. Thankfully, I didn’t recognise any of the trio. Ollie would have lost her mind if my ex-beau had happened to be in the lair of my latest squeeze.

I had to admit, kelpies had a style and they stuck to it — two wearing muscle tees, one shirtless, all wearing faded, ripped jeans. Their hair fascinated me. All three of them sported shoulder length hairstyles in varying shades of ginger to jet black. It glistened in the stark, white light of the club, wet enough that they could have come straight from flushing their own heads in the lavvy. Though the shirtless guard had droplets scattered across his very prominent nipples, the shirts on the others were dry as a bone.

"Oi! Who's that, then?" Nipples shot to his feet, leaving his friends to watch on, disinterested.

I raised two empty hands. "Am just here to talk to Aggie, boys."

"The Queen doesn't take visitors like you." Nipples stepped away from the table, grabbing his beer as he did. Clearly, he didn't think I was much of a threat.

"Do you know who I am?" Hands still up, I edged closer. "I'm the famous —"

"Aye, you're the tadger what tried to steal from our lady."

Well, shit. This wasn't going how I had expected.

"That's technically true," I admitted. "But I'm here with some very important news for Ag — Queen Agnes."

Nipples snorted. "There's nothing you could say that would interest her."

"That's for her to decide, wouldn't you think?" I approached slowly, casually lowering my hands.

Nipples slammed his drink down, slopping a bit on the table as it bubbled over the lip.

"Don't bloody waste it, Trevor," Muscle-tee number one said. "I'm not buying you another one."

"What, Aggie doesn't love her bodyguards enough to give them a bar tab?"

That hit a nerve. Nipples flexed his jaw, anger building. "What's it to you, anyway?"

"I need to see her. I'll buy you all a round or three if you just let me through."

"She'd have our arses for that." For all his bluster, Nipples couldn't resist a glance toward the bar. "No one is even supposed to know we're here."

I stopped. "Why not? Whole bloody town knows she's bangin' Achaius."

Unease crept over his face. "Really? Everyone?"

I nodded.

"Well, shite. She's gonna kill us for that."

"Aye. And she'll kill you twice when she finds out you let us in." Goading them with a wicked grin, I took a few more steps. "Especially when she sees the mess you've left out here when I'm done with you."

"Back off, buidseach." Nipples' warning held enough sharpness that the other two goons finally stood.

"About bloody time." With a downward flick of my wrist, I threw the spell I had prepared out in the street. A glowing rope of light flicked out from my hand, split into three, and hooked the ankles of the kelpies, binding them tightly enough that they all stumbled.

I jerked the rope and they fell like bowling pins. My rope faded, but my next spell was already underway. I put the finishing marks on the final sigil and pushed my hand forward, sending a ball of fire at the two rolling around under the table.

Nipples rolled to his feet and charged. I snatched a strip of leather from behind my back and pulled it tight between two hands. When he ducked his head to ram my chest, I lifted it, ready to yank the cord up and over. He twisted away at the last moment, shouldered my side instead and sent me sprawling on the floor. My elbow cracked against the foot of a table and the impact sent a shooting pain down my arm, numbing my hand and causing me to fumble the leather cord.

"Feck." I rolled, just in time for Nipples to crash his entire body weight down. Though I saved my upper half, he pinned my legs, then lifted up and drew back a fist.

With no time for a spell that involved precise calculations and intricate sigils, I simply called on the spirit world. I used the fleeting energy burst to shove him off and scrambled away.

A nearby crash distracted me for a brief moment. Ollie had tackled one of the kelpies into a table. The stink of spilled beer filled my nose. Behind her, Quinn stood frozen in shock, holding his own leather harness. Kelpie number three loomed behind him.

"Watch your —" My words cut short as something sharp struck my back. A horse whinnied behind me.

Mouth open like a fish on a hook, I gasped for air, even as I crawled under the scant protection of another table. My lungs stubbornly refused to cooperate and my colourful curse about the horse shifters and their mothers went unvoiced and unappreciated.

The blue-grey horse above me decided the table would not pose enough of an impediment to worry about and reared up. Just as I thought I might be done for, something slammed into its shoulder and the horse went flying to one side. It smashed against a stack of bar stools near the wall.

Ollie kicked it once in the face, then reached down to hook her arm around its gigantic neck. Despite the difference in size, it was no match for my sister one she got in the swing of things.

"Halter?" Ollie yelled, looking up at me. "Fecking hell, do I have to do everything myself?"

"Got it!" I wheezed. I scrambled over to where I had dropped it, then tossed it to Ollie. The flimsy bit of cowhide fluttered to the ground halfway between us.

The look of pure disappointment on Ollie's face reminded of that time I failed art class. Eager to regain even the tiniest bit of respect, I dragged myself over to give it to her properly.

"Can't breathe," I explained.

"Canna breathe, canna fight, canna throw." Ollie grinned. "You're lucky I love you anyway, you big galump." She wound the leather around the kelpie's neck, tied it off, and let it go. It rolled to its feet and stood, swinging its now-docile head up to look at her with doe-eyed adoration.

Staggering up myself, I saw she had already taken care of the other two. Twin grey horses with dripping manes calmly looked on. One dropped its head to eat a scatter of broken pretzels spilled on a nearby table.

Quinn was, unfortunately, still in one piece, casually sipping a beer as he watched.

"I'd be embarrassed to be your sibling after that, too." He raised the bottle in a toast. "Here's to phase one."

I stretched, reaching a hand across my back to check for life threatening injury. Ollie quickly came over to check. She pulled up my shirt and clicked her tongue.

"Devil's arse, Mack. I thought the bastard must have snapped your spine or something, the way you were carrying on." The fabric dropped again. "He barely tapped you!"

"Thank you for your tender care and concern, dear sister." I flipped the bird at her and stalked away, winding through the cluster of seating over to the bar and slipped behind it.

Agnes, bless the wench, knew how to stock a watering hole. I snatched up a bottle of top shelf tequila, unscrewed the lid, and put it to my lips.

Ollie growled. "Henry Bloody Mack, put that down right now."

I did as she asked — after three or four long pulls. "It's medicinal."

"She'll have your baws for stealing from her."

Fumbling in my pocket for change, I realised I hadn't brought any. "It's fine, Ollie. Quinn's got me."

"I do, do I?" Quinn sighed and pulled out a neatly folded wallet. He tossed a few quid on the bar.

"Good lad."

"It's a loan," he said. "Not a gift."

"Fair enough."

"How do we get into your girlfriend's lair, Mack?" Ollie asked with big, innocent eyes.

"She's no' my girlfriend." The door to Agnes's lair was at the end of the bar . Replacing the tequila, I headed over to press an ear against it. Silence. "Ready?"

"Aye. Lead the way, glorious tadger." Ollie sniggered, ruining her deadpan delivery.

"What's a tadger?" Quinn rolled his eyes when Ollie dissolved into giggles. "Never mind. I think I can figure it out on my own."

"Come on, children." I shoved the door open.

The lair was... well, about what you would expect from a centuries-old immortal fuelled by a lustful blood-hunger. Antique furniture dotted the open-plan apartment, as did the sleeping bodies of lingerie clad baobhan sith.

Quinn gave a strangled cough. "Where are their clothes?"

"They've got clothes on." I pointed at one particular lass, whose thick black tresses draped over her otherwise exposed breasts. "Look, she's basically wearing a top. Made of her own hair."

"Stop ogling the enemy, you two." Ollie picked her way across the room towards a wide door surrounded by a heavy, ornately carved frame. "I take it that's where the Queen Bitch lives?"

"Your hearty disapproval of the people I sleep with makes you sound overprotective." My boot tapped an ankle as I hurried to join her, and the sleepy owner raised a head, blinking slowly as her eyes focused. "Oh, shite."

Her mouth worked slowly as she squinted. Behind her, Quinn crouched down and stroked her hair. "Easy, love. Go back to sleep. That's right. Shhh."

"Don't be daft, Quinn," I hissed. "That's not going to work."

It worked. The vampire lass blinked again, eyes closed for a full second this time, before dropping her back to the thigh she was using as a pillow, finally dropping her lids with the heavy finality of a deep sleep.

"How does that work?" Quinn asked. "The sun's setting now, isn't it? I thought they'd just jump up and start killing us."

It was impossible to tell for sure in the windowless room, but I nodded. "There's a transition period between when the bottom of the sun drops below the horizon, and full dark. They start to stir then, and they're vulnerable."

"So we should be moving quickly, then?" Quinn picked his way over to us carefully.

Ollie rested her hand against the door and raised three fingers. She dropped one.

"Aye," I whispered. "Agnes is more powerful than the others. She'll already be stirring."

Ollie dropped another finger.

"Are we sure this is a good idea?" Quinn asked.

I scoffed. "It's a perfectly thought out plan. In fact —"

Ollie's final finger dropped and she shoulder barged the door. It didn't budge. "Uhh, Mack?" she whispered.

"Just use your muscles, lass."

Ollie gave it her all, leaning her tiny weight and pressed the door so hard her arms trembled.

"Well, that could be a wee problem."

I stepped back, ready to use a spell, but jumped when I felt something squish underfoot. The offending finger belonged to one of the baobhan sith, who sat up quite a bit faster than the one I kicked earlier. She got to all fours, her nightie handing low enough in the front that I had to turn my head before Ollie saw me looking.

"Intruders." Her voice rasped with sleepy fatigue but it was enough to alert the silver-haired lass beside her.

"Rise, sisters." Silver-hair hauled the two closest vampires to their feet. Their momentary squabble ended when they saw us.

"All right, then." I dropped my bag at my feet and pulled out a glass jar and a brown paper bag. "We're just here for a wee chat. No need to —"

A high-pitched screech ended my attempt to negotiate quietly.

"Mack, throw a fecking snirlie already!" Ollie dived at the three closest vampires, arm around the throat of one, feet kicking at another.

I tossed the jar and it bounced off a chaise in the middle of the room. "Ahh, Feck!" I shoved the paper bag at Quinn. "Here."

He peeked inside and pulled out a handful of small fishing weights. "What the hell do I do with these?"

"Throw them!" I bellowed as I plunged into a slowly writhing pile of waking vampires. I kicked one in the face and narrowly dodged the black claw of another as I hurled myself at the jar.

A hand plucked it up. "Och, what's this, then?" A plump, red-haired lass looked down on me with a smirk. "I don't think so, wizard." She stomped on my hand, piercing it with the heel of her stiletto.

"Oww!" I clutched the injury to my chest. "Who wears heels to fecking bed?"

The vampire hissed as something hit her cheek, sizzling like a hot brand pressed to a cow's flank. She dropped into an offensive crouch. Another ball of pure iron smacked her square between the eyes.

The distraction was all I needed. With my good hand I drew a small sigil. Nothing fancy. I uttered the words to go with it and used a hint of energy to push it towards the jar. When sigil met glass, it wobbled like a horizon smudged by a heat mirage. The glass slipped to the ground.

I could have caught it, but that wasn't the point. It hit the ground, bounced once on the floorboards, and rolled to a stop. "Ahh, feck me." I struck out with a foot and kicked it sharply. The jar shot into a chair leg and finally cracked.

At first, nothing happened. It hadn't entirely broken, but the crack went right through and the magic slowly seeped out. When it split into two, spilling the fine grey powder onto the floor, I knew I had been successful.

It began as a soft breeze, a swirl of air that gently shifted the metal filings, scooping them into a pile. It gained speed, twirling and twisting, lifting just a few scattered bits of powder, then more as the funnel of wind spun faster. It stretched up into a tube that reached from floor to ceiling, whipping the silver and iron filings around in a deadly spiral. Waving my hand, I directed its movements like an orchestra conductor. It dipped and swayed before cutting a path from one side of the room to the other.

The four baobhan sith that lay in its way screamed in agony, clutching eyes and faces, one holding an arm to her chest that had been burned by the metallic tornado.

Quinn tossed a handful of iron weights at Heels, and she collapsed into a howling heap. Her arms were spotted with angry blisters where she had tried to knock away the barrage. I swept my hand to one side and the snirlie raced past and finished her off. She collapsed face first onto the floor.

Ollie lifted a waif-like girl with a pixie cut into the air by the throat. "Look, Mack, I finally found one as short as me!"

"Love, she's got a few inches on you at least." I gave her a thumbs up anyway as she tossed the writhing vamp into a wall.

"Quinn!" Pointing at the bag, I told him to toss out another snirlie.

"A what, now?"

"The jar!" I shook my head. "I really need to prepare you better if we do this again."

Quinn grabbed at the bag at his feet and drew the second jar out. He slammed it against the door frame, shattering it instantly.

"Why didn't I bloody think of that?" I muttered. Careful not to step in the glass, I went to Quinn, Ollie joining us soon after to watch the carnage.

The second snirlie quickly joined the first, making short work of the remaining vampires. Those still alive withdrew, huddled under blankets or hidden under furniture as I called my two spells to me, then directed them to linger close by.

"What is the meaning of this?"

The ice-cold voice behind us sent a chill down my spine. Definitely not a thrill. Nope.

"Aggie!" I spun, taking the opportunity to weave my weapons around so they stood slightly between the Queen of the Vampires, and my small team of amateur vampire hunters.

Agnes Ban-Righe, Vampire Queen and one of the more esteemed members of the Collective, stood in the now-open doorway. Her lavender hair flowed in smooth tresses over one shoulder, complementing the black silk wrap she wore over bare feet. The glass shards she stepped on showed no sign of hurting her.

"You." Agnes seemed less than pleased to see me. In fact, if I didn't have such a high opinion of my bedroom expertise, I might have said she was downright pissed.

"The one and only." I gave a flourishing bow, though I wasn't stupid enough to duck my head and take my eyes off her. "Love what you've done with your hair."

She had been platinum blonde last I had seen her. "It took me eight months to grow out the bald patch you inflicted upon my scalp."

Oh. "Sorry about that, love. I admit, I probably should have taken it from the back, aye?"

Ollie groaned. "You're determined to get us all killed, aren't you?"

"Who are you?" Agnes slipped past one of my snirlies, coming to stand before Ollie. "You smell of death."

"And you could use a toothbrush, blood-breath." Ollie glared up at her and I silently cheered. Having both of them offside would be a bloody nightmare.

"Apologies, ban-bhuidseach." Agnes inclined her head respectfully, which was not a good sign for my health. "I simply meant that you are not entirely of the living."

"I am not." Ollie lifted her chin regally. "I accept your apology, Ban-Righe, and offer my own in return. Even if your maw did stink, I have no olfactory senses to judge."

A tiny smile touched Agnes's lips and I shuddered. It was not an expression of happiness so much as a quiet victory of some sort. Ollie had, for the most part, stayed hidden from the Otherworld. It suddenly occurred to me that letting one of the most powerful factions know Ollie was, in a manner of speaking, alive, may not be the smartest idea I had ever had.

Not that there would have been any way to talk the lass out of coming to finally meet my ex-lover, however brief our torrid relationship had been.

"Olivia MacDonald, I presume." Agnes glanced at me. "Henry, I can't believe you never mentioned that young Olivia was still... around."

"It's complicated, Aggie."

A slender eyebrow lifted. "I take it you aren't here to ask me out to dinner. Not even you would be that stupid." Then, she paused with a quizzical tilt to her head. "Would you?"

"I just came to have a wee chat, love. After all, we're still friends, aye?"

"Friends do not steal from friends, Henry." She had a point, there.

"I have something you need," I said firmly. "In return, I need information."

Agnes gave a delicate snort. "What could you possibly have that I might need, human?"

"Oh, Ollie gets the fancy title and I'm just a stupid human, am I?" Clenching my teeth, I reminded myself we weren't actually here to fight, regardless of the unfortunate mess in Agnes's apartment. "I have video footage of a baobhan sith killing a human woman — a protected human woman — openly and without provocation. Unless you have made a significant deviation in your plans for the unseelie court, I assume it was not at your bidding."

That caught her attention. Agnes's eyes flashed and her face went dangerously still. "Show me."

I smiled and took a step back. "Not until I get what I want."

"And that is?"

"The name of the arsehole who is wheeling and dealing with the unseelie to harm, damage, eliminate, assassinate or otherwise harass my delicate constitution."

Agnes frowned. "Someone is hunting you?"

"Don't be daft, Agnes. You know every move of every player in the Otherworld. Who has a hit out on me?"

Agnes resumed her blank expression. "I do not know who wishes you dead, Henry MacDonald. On this, I swear."

That was unfortunate. Agnes couldn't lie under oath like that, so I was no closer to finding out who could be after me. Still, she might still be able to help.

"Then I will make you a new offer. The vampire I have on film is likely linked to my query. I'll show you footage, but only if you swear that, once you find her, I can have her first. For questioning."

"I shall ensure you have the opportunity to speak to her." Agnes reached a slender hand out, but I didn't take it.

"No. I will have her answer my questions, Aggie. No bloody point promising I can speak with her if she's already dead, because she'll no' answer, will she?"

A sparkle of delight bubbled up in the ancient vampire queen. "Oh, Henry. You are a clever boy, aren't you? Very well. I shall keep her alive and you may do as you wish with her until you get what answers you may. After that, however, I make no promises."

"Deal." I stuck my hand out and Agnes shook it before wiping it on her gown. "That was a bit rude, love."

"Can you blame her, Mack?" Ollie shrugged apologetically. "You smell like wet horse."

Agnes's eyes flickered briefly. "I must insist we wrap this up. I have meetings to attend."

"Meetings, shaggings, same thing, aye?" I grumbled. "What the bloody hell do you see in that stupid, wet-eared pony anyway?"

Agnes smirked again, and I wondered what she thought she had on me this time. "Achaius brings with him certain benefits a mere human could not comprehend."

Ollie coughed and muttered something about stallions under her breath.

Resisting the urge to spit a nasty taste out of my mouth, I picked up my bag. After digging around a moment to find my phone, I showed her the video Fife had sent me. "That's your lass. Do you know her?"

"We've not met." Concern settled over the queen like shadow. "But I believe I know how to find her. I will be in touch, buidseach."

"Finally." I straightened at the use of my proper title. "Oh, and Aggie? One more quick question, if you don't mind."

Agnes sighed heavily. "What is it?"

"You haven't by chance seen a stray Nuckelavee running about, have you?"

"If I had, I would be safely cloistered in my Prague estate, far away from the kind of havoc a creature like that would cause in our city." Agnes paused a beat before adding, "Anything else?"

I considered if it was worth pushing my luck. "No. I'd ask you to dinner, of course, but your new squeeze might get a wee bit jealous, what with my reputation. Farewell, Aggie!"

Chapter Eighteen

I sent Ollie home with Quinn, handing over the keys to my car with great reluctance. I had one more stop to make and I didn't want my sister with me when I made it.

Fergus was, as I expected, awake and at his shop despite the late hour. When I knocked at the door and peered through the clouded glass, I saw him jerk his head up with a scowl. Seeing that I was no ordinary customer, he quickly shifted to a grin and hurried over to unlock the door.

"Henry! I was just about to call you."

"Call me?" I waited until he had re-locked the door behind me. "It's past midnight."

"You would have taken this one, guarantee it." Fergus didn't stop to chinwag but hurried back to his workbench, where the tapestry sat under several ring lights and a wide magnifying sheet. "But unless you've developed the sight and not told me, you're not here for this, are ye?"

"Actually, I have a few things to chat with you about." I pulled two small vials from my pocket. "To begin, I need a tracker. I was going to use a basic geolocator spell, but I have reason to believe my target is on the move, which makes that a bloody useless idea, doesn't it?"

"Aye, there's that." Fergus disappeared out back. I didn't follow him — you only stepped foot out there if you were explicitly invited. He clattered around searching for something in what sounded like a box of cooking pots, finally returning with a small stopwatch. "All out of compasses, I'm afraid," he explained.

"That'll do. As long as there's a pointy bit to tell me which way to go, aye?"

"Aye." Fergus went to set the stopwatch down, then realised the workbench was taken. "Over here, then." He moved to the table of treasures in the middle of the shop and dragged out a big wooden box from beneath it. With his good arm he swept a corner free, letting the small pile of cogs and gears fall into the box haphazardly.

Now that he had a free place to work, he set about creating my demon tracker. First, a circle of salt to contain any loose energies. He bustled about searching for the rest of the tools — a small pile of grass, two jars of seawater, another jar labelled 'Orkney snow', and some pristine white sand. He placed the grass, still fresh enough to tickle my nose with the scent, to the bottom of the circle, just inside the boundary. The snow — which looked an awful lot like water — he poured into a thimble at the top. The seawater was trickier as he couldn't find a vessel to hold it. Eventually he dug through his rubbish and found a bottle and its cap.

Fergus dipped the bottle cap into the jar labelled 'Atlantic', filling it with water before he gently placed it to the left of the circle. He then spilled a few drops from the second jar, this one noted as 'North Sea', into the empty beer bottle and set it down opposite.

"Between the northern isles and the English, the eastern sea and the west, if your beastie is in the land of the Irn Bru, we'll find him." Fergus dropped the pocket watch into the centre of the circle and thumbed open the first of the two vials I had supplied. He sniffed it, pulling a face at the acrid odour. "The feck is this shite, Mack?"

"Nuckelavee." I leaned against the table casually.

Fergus was having none of it. "No! No, no, no! Am no' helpin' ye kill yourself, laddie. Besides, I said our bonnie Scotland; This pish won't work in the Otherworld!" He screwed his face up tighter and glared up at me. "And another question, how the bloody hell you ye think you're getting' there?"

"Ease up, Fergus. I don't have a way to get to the Otherworld. As much as it pains me to say, your trinket will find the Nuckelavee just fine."

Fergus crumpled in on himself. "Oh, no-no-no. No, tha's bad, Henry. Very bad."

He sucked in air through his nose and blew it through his mouth, repeating the exercise three times. "Nope, dinna help. Old Fergus is in a panic." He shook his head, panting. "Nuckelavee, Mack? Are ye sure?"

"Aye." I gripped his shoulder. "Fergus, that's what took Granda. Some fool set a trap for him, and it killed him. Now it's loose and it's already killed a house full of young 'uns."

"You're tellin' me the bastard killed Auggie... and it killed *babbies*?" Fergus's voice rose higher with each word, ending in a strangled screech.

To be fair, teenagers were practically babies compared to Fergus. I felt no guilt for not correcting his assumption it had taken out a dozen wee bairns. I needed his help, and he needed to focus.

Harnessing his wrath, Fergus breathed again, this time snorting air out like an angry dragon. "You find that son of a sea mither and you show him what we Scotsmen do to wicked beasts that come for our babbies, MacDonald." He flicked the vial over, finger as a stopper. Poking the pocket watch angrily, he wiped the drop of ichor on its face, then did the same with the second vial. He wriggled his finger in the blackened substance, smearing it into the shape of a sigil.

I had come to Fergus because there was no buidseach better at creating technologically supported magic, even if that technology all happened to be as old as Fergus himself. Though he usually stayed out of altercations between seelie and human, he could be relied upon to protect those he deemed under his protection; namely, every child under the age of five on the entire continent.

The old man would even cross the border into England — which he deemed enemy territory — if he had to.

Fergus hovered his palm over the pocket watch and closed his eyes. He opened one again, the other still closed in a wrinkled squint. "Lad? A few steps back, if ye don't mind. I know ye canna help it, but I don't want your magic upsettin' mine."

Obliging, I stepped back until my back bumped the shelf behind me. His theory that my unpredictable grasp on the spirit world might affect him had no basis, but I needed the old man on my side and arguing would only hurt my cause.

Fergus mumbled a few words too quietly for me to make them out. His hands waved and his fingers twitched, but I kept my sight closed. Fergus trusted me, but it was just plain rude to spy on another's magic.

He continued chanting and I wriggled, stifling my impatience. Just as I was ready to ask how much bloody longer it would take, Fergus looked up.

"The big hand is the one ye want, lad. It'll point ye true." He handed me the newly-enchanted Nuckelavee GPS.

"Thanks, Fergus."

"If ye want to thank me, rip the bastard's hooves off and shove 'em fair up his arse." Fergus huffed, then packed up the ingredients he had used for the spells. He tossed the water on the floor; the essence would be used up now and would only dilute the potency of future spells if he added it back to the jars.

"Aye, I'll do that. I owe the prick for what he did to Granda, anyway."

Fergus nodded but didn't speak. I knew Granda's death had hit him hard.

"You said you were going to call me," I reminded him. "Is it about the tapestry?"

"Not the tapestry, lad," Fergus said. "It's the thread they used to stitch the cauldron." He gestured for me to come over and pointed through the plastic sheet.

I leaned over to look. The thread that had glowed with magic before now pulsed with vibrant energy. "It's bright."

"You've no idea," Fergus cackled. "Mack, there were about six layers of powerful cloaking spells over that magic, and it still shone through. Do you have any idea how much power it takes?"

"Quite a lot, going by your excitement." Granda's words echoed in my head and I clenched down hard on the flutter in my stomach. "Fergus... what kind of magic is it."

Buidseach magic harnessed the powers of the underworld. A gift first bestowed by the devil himself, it had a bloody awful reputation, one that is entirely undeserved. Well, maybe not entirely. Witches drew from the same source, but any practitioner worth their summoning salt knew it wasn't the only source. Old magic came in many forms — some of it sith, some of it unseelie, some even older than that. Earth magic, death magic, sacrificial magic; if there was ever a deity or mythology that existed, you could find scraps of power aligned to it in the form of talismans, stones, spells, or other relics discarded by the ancient people who worshipped them.

Fergus stared down at the fluorescent glow for a moment. When he looked back up, tears shone in his eyes.

"Fergus... You're not saying..." Only one thing could move the crotchety old man that deeply. Fergus loved Ollie almost as much as Granda did, and though he never held my actions against me, it cut him to the core as it did me, knowing how much she would miss out on. Over the years, he had worked as hard as I had to find a way to bring my sister back from the space between life and death.

"It's Cailleach Bheur magic, Mack. Real, proper, eternal cauldron kind of shite." His lip trembled. "Paired with the right ritual, this could be what you've searched for all these years. This could be what gives your sister her life back."

I tried to answer but a lump tightened in my throat. I coughed to clear it. "Don't tell Ollie yet, aye? Not until we have all the pieces. I don't want to get her hopes up."

Fergus nodded. "It'll be wonderful to see it done, aye?"

I nodded, not trusting myself to speak. "Should I leave it with you for now?"

Fergus sucked his teeth. "I'm not sure I can do much more with it, lad. It's big magic, though. If you take it with you, can you keep it safe from those what are lookin' for it?"

"Maybe," I said. "But I'd be happier leaving it here, to be honest. Your shop is like a bloody fortress."

"Aye, it is that." Fergus rolled the tapestry up and looked around. "I told you it was cloaked five times over? I didn't destroy the wards, I transferred them to an old calfskin I had hangin' about. They had faded a bit, but I recharged them. No bastard will find it once it's all wrapped up... if only I could remember where I put the bloody thing."

"Fergus, you're a good man." I clapped him on the shoulder, allowing a tiny spark of hope to flare in my chest. "If anyone can keep it safe, it's you."

"Now, where's that skin..." He looked around the worktable, frowning. "Ah. I guess I packed it up. Hold here, Mack, I'll see if I put it out back. Once she's all safe and sound we'll have a wee dram for your sister, aye?"

He ducked out to his back room, closing the door behind him. He returned a moment later, empty handed.

"No luck, then?" Though Fergus's shop looked like a pile of clutter to me, it was unusual for him to lose anything.

"No. I swear I put the bloody thing —" A music box started up in a corner and Fergus stuttered to a stop. "I've had a thought, Mack. Maybe we'll take a raincheck on that dram. It's awful late and my old bones need their bed."

"What? You don't *ever* sleep, you stubborn old git. And you promised me a drink!" The music box gained speed and I recognised the tune. It was rock a bye babby, but somehow the metal tings gave the song an ominous sound.

"No!" Fergus ushered me toward the door. "I mean to say, it's late, Mack. I'm goin' to take meself off for a lie down, and you're going to go home. Aye?"

"Huh." It finally occurred to me that something might be wrong. "I suppose you're right. I'll leave it with you, then." *Whatever it is, he doesn't want to tell me. Or maybe... he can't?* I paused with my hand on the door and rummaged around my brain for some way to ask if there was a problem, without asking there was a problem. "Fergus, have you seen Rosie of late? I've been meaning to call on her."

Fergus gave a wavering smile. "Not of late, Mack, but I've a feeling I'll be seeing her soon."

Rose was my mother's name. There wasn't another that Fergus knew, I was sure. He had just told me he expected to die, probably right after I stepped foot outside. So, I did what I had to. I tugged my coat on, waved goodbye, and opened the door.

Then, I shut it again. By this time, I already had my last snirlie jar in the palm of my hand and when Fergus's back door crashed open, I hurled it as hard as I could.

Thankfully, my aim was better than it had been at Aggie's. Less fortuitously, the wee beastie that slipped out was no baobhan sith, or anything else that an iron whirlwind might cause a bit of damage to. The red cap bared its teeth in a gleeful grin and hopped over the table between us.

Now, I'll admit, I'm not the most organised buidseach in Glasgow. You would think that could be a problem... except it wasn't me who had packed the bag.

I dug in my bag, groping around until I found something cold and cross shaped. "Ollie, you bloody champion!" I brandished it and the red cap, already sailing through empty air towards my pretty face, screeched. It smacked into the cross with a hissing stench and quickly dissolved into a gelatinous lump. Its agony faded beneath the clatter of a stack of spoons, knocked off a shelf by my unattended snirlie that had gotten itself wedged in a corner.

"Mack, watch out!" Fergus's voice came from somewhere under his workbench.

Solid choice or hiding place, I thought, *though some bloody assistance would be nice.*

The warning in question was, I assumed, regarding the grey-skinned glaistig weaving past the snirlie. I flicked a hand and it slammed into her. She screamed but pulled free, face pock-marked and bubbling. It had been Ollie's idea to mix steel with the iron, so I silently thanked her for that, too — only iron was needed to take down a baobhan sith, but Ollie had always liked to err on the side of caution.

Out of the corner of my eye, I saw Fergus tumble out from beneath the workbench. A wet, greasy substance coated his shoulder and a redcap dangled by the ankles from his grip, ramrod straight and seemingly frozen solid.

"I thought you were hiding from the fun under there, Fergus!"

"Hiding? Ye big shite, I was dealing with the other three reddies ye didn't see!"

"Three?" Whoever wanted this tapestry wanted it bad. Hands outstretched, I scratched a couple of sigils that blossomed into a blade of light in my left hand. Bringing it between us, I beckoned the glaistig with my right. "Come on, lassie. Dance with me."

Her eyes narrowed and she bared pointed teeth in a wicked grin. "I like dancing."

To prove it, she spun into a pirouette. As she whirled back to face me, her leg flicked out in a sharp kick. I slashed at it as I ducked, wishing I had stuck with the karate lessons Granda had enrolled me in as a child.

At first I thought I had missed her but a yelp and a quick, hobbled retreat suggested not. The glaistig hissed, anger dulling whatever pain she might feel, and she darted forward again.

This time I was ready. I clutched my ephemeral weapon, slicing it down only when she was in range. It slashed her chest open and she fell to her knees, eyes wide.

"Ah, there's the vampire!" Fergus cackled gleefully. "I thought ye were going to set up camp out there, ye big heckit jobbie!"

I tore my eyes from the dying fairy, expecting to see a pretty lass in need of a decent manicure. To my horror, it was a different sort of vampire standing in the doorway. Nine feet tall, pale-faced and very much created in the image of a man, it lurched forward in the convulsive manner of a zombie.

It was no true vampire, closer in nature to a reanimated corpse, but the name given to it back in the fifties had stuck. A Gorbal's Vampire was a summoned being, like a demon, but less powerful and with a healthy appetite for small children. In the absence of a tasty bairn, they would happily eat a middle-age buidseach, though.

The Gorbal's Vampire pulled its lips back in a hideous grin to bare a set of glistening iron teeth.

"Fergus!" I didn't even bother to look in my bag. A Gorbal's only weakness was a good, old-fashioned beheading. "I'm going to need some help here."

"What do you fecking think I'm doin', whippersnapper?" A ring of light surrounded Fergus, spinning so wildly it had begun to wobble. He whipped a hand over his head, guiding it like a cowboys lasso. "Don't just gawk, distract the bastard!"

The lumbering beast had already adjusted his course, heading for Fergus. *Well, there's only one thing for it.*

I leaped, sword aloft, the sort of heroic act only seen in a blockbuster movie.

The reality fell short. And so did I. I tumbled to the ground two arms-lengths form the vampire, landing on my foot funny. I went down like a sack of wet jobbies.

The vampire glanced my way, saw I was no threat, and focused his beady eyes back on my friend.

"Take this, you ugly brute!" I flung the light-sword and pushed at the spell, shoving my power through its sharp point and into the bicep of the vampire.

That got its attention. Unfortunately, it didn't seem to do any real damage. The vampire took three lumbering steps to turn, and I backed up a little, then laughed. "You're slower than old soup, lad. How are you supposed to catch anyone, let alone a child? Those bastards run like the wind."

Normally, prodding a Gorbal's Vampire into action was a terrible idea, but I had faith in Fergus. The beast lowered his big head, bunched its muscles, and sprang. It cleared half the room, and slammed into me at full speed, sending me crashing through the glass shop door.

For the second time that day — or perhaps the second day in a row, seeing as it was gone midnight — my lungs decided to collapse into a whimpering heap. The weight that pressed down on me crushed my limbs and threatened to squeeze my guts out of my mouth, but it was a dead weight. It was when I realised that, that I also noticed the warm gush of liquid dribbling through my hair.

"Oh... yuck." I tried to hold my breath, but, unable to suck a bit of air in first, my body protested. Mouth wide, I finally gasped in a thin sliver of precious air.

Of course, that's when the body exploded.

Hot gobbets of flesh stuck to my skin. One fell in my mouth and I gagged, spitting out the wee bit of air I had just breathed. With one eye open, the other stuck shut by the devil-knew-what, I rolled to my side and emptied my guts.

"Hey, Mack. What's that thing you said to me?" Quinn's shiny boots stepped in front of my face. I could only assume the rest of him was above them. "That's right. You're looking a bit polly wally, mate."

Fergus laughed so hard it should have killed him. In fact, I wished it had. "Oh, a fine apprenctice you'll be, lad. A fine one indeed!"

"It's peely-wally, you cheeky sack of shite."

Quinn reached down and offered a hand. I took it, making sure to smear what was left of the clear goop over his fingers as he hefted me up. To his credit, he didn't say a word of complaint.

"What in the hell was that?" Quinn asked.

"Gorbal's Vampire, boy. Otherworld beastie, taste for human flesh, bloody line backers if ye can tame 'em." Fergus passed Quinn a sodden hanky.

Quinn took the cloth but let it dangle between two fingers. He used the cleanest corner to dab at his hands. "At least they clean themselves up when they pop."

"Aye." I dusted off my now-dry clothes and ran a hand through my hair. It caught a knot and I winced.

"As for you, Henry Mack." Fergus balled his hands on his hips and stared up at me. "What the bloody hell were ye thinking, lad? I told ye to go! I had it sorted, now look at the bloody mess you've made!"

"Sorted?" I barked a laugh. "You admitted to my face you were facing down your death. Do you really think I'd step away from a fight when the life of a friend is handing in the balance?"

Fergus screwed up his face. "Death? What are ye on about, ye silly lad? Old Fergus can squash a few reddies, a pished fairy and a big, ugly prick like him." He gestured vaguely at the spot the vampire had fallen. "Could do it without smashin' up me shop, too."

"Fergus, you said you'd be seeing Mam soon. In the Otherworld. Remember?"

Fergus sucked his teeth, then chuckled. "Ye bampot. I was talkin' about Rosie." At my blank look, he laughed harder. "Rosie? The masseuse? I was tellin' ye that after I put down this rabble I might be a wee bit sore, not deid!" He rolled a shoulder. "And it were a bloody good idea. I think I threw my back climbin' out from under that table with a reddie hangin' off me snout."

"I don't blame you for being out of sorts, Fergus." Quinn stuck his head inside and grimaced. "Mack, you've trashed the whole damn shop."

"Me? I don't give a shite about the shop; I was trying to keep my life intact." Speaking of keeping things intact, I headed over to check the tapestry. "Fergus? Where'd you stick our wee cloth?"

"It's on the bench." Fergus waved irritably at his workbench, too busy stacking up a pile of tin cups on his table.

"No it isn't." I crouched down but the floor was clear except for a couple of blood-soaked caps, a scatter of teeth, and the skeletal remains of a dead mouse. "Fergus?"

The growl in my voice finally pulled his attention. Fergus hurried over, searched the bench, bent down to look under it. "It was here, right here! I swear to ye, Mack."

"I already looked there, you old bampot!" I slammed a fist into it. "They must have it, Fergus."

He didn't hear me, still too busy running his hands through piles of paper, panic pulling his wrinkled face into a dismal gloom. Finding nothing, he ran to the back room, then howled.

"Ye fecking pricks! I'll find ye, ye rotten bastards! See if I don't!" Fergus shook his fist at the back door to his workshop, wide open and slowly swinging in the breeze. Finally spent, he sagged against the door. "I'm sorry, Mack" he sobbed. "There must have been another one with them. They took it. They took the thread."

I patted his shoulder, but the hurt I felt was too deep to offer any more consolation than that. A noise behind me gave a welcome distraction and I looked back at Quinn, who shuffled his feet awkwardly.

"We found an item that might have given Ollie back her life." I coughed to clear the lump from my throat. "And they took it."

"Who's they?"

I threw my hands up. "How the feck would I know?"

"Ok, suspect unknown. *Why* did they take it?"

His question rankled me more, but his sombre face and intent stare pushed the anger down. "It's powerful rebirth magic. Not a lot of things you can do with that sort — it's not destructive in itself, and it doesn't heal the living."

"If the applications are narrow, so are the motivations for stealing it." He nodded as though having made a decision. "That means we can figure it out."

"We?" I snapped. "Quinn, I've got a fecking demon on my arse, half the bloody unseelie court is hunting me, and I just lost the only thing that has mattered to me since Ollie died." I shoved him in the chest, pushing him back and out of my way. "I don't have time to babysit."

"I'm not asking you to." Quinn let me storm past but followed on my heels. "I want to help, Mack. I know I can't do squat when it comes to magic — not yet. But I can still help. I'll read books, research, talk to people. I can access the database of the Scotland PD, maybe there's something there."

I stopped so suddenly he ploughed into my back. "Are you stupid? They log every key stroke in that bloody program — Fife has told me that enough times."

Quinn laughed. "So? The worst they'll do is fire me. Are you saying my job is worth more than Ollie's life?"

"Of course I'm not bloody saying that!" *Was I?* "Pah, stop twisting my words. There's no reason you would willingly sacrifice your livelihood for my sister."

Quinn's answer was so quiet I almost missed it. "Yeah, there is."

I stopped again. "What are you talking about, lad?" If his goal was to distract me from an impotent rage... it was working. He's probably not that clever, though.

Quinn grabbed his wallet and flipped it open. He pulled a small photo from one of the card slots. "That's my family. It was taken a few months before Mum died. We knew about the cancer, but not how bad it was. Looking back, I think Mum must've known she didn't have long."

Indeed, the woman in the photo was beautiful, but thin and frail with pale skin and dark smudged beneath her eyes. The man beside her, skin as dark as Quinn's, had glanced at her the moment the photo was taken, the tenderness on his face clear as the eye could see. Oblivious to his attention, the woman smiled down at the two children at her feet. A boy – that would be Quinn – arms crossed with a shy smile. Beside him a girl, a full head taller but with features unmistakably similar to his, one hand poking two fingers up behind her brother's head with a jaunty grin.

I jabbed my finger at them. "You didn't tell me you had a sister!"

"Didn't I? I thought I'd at least mentioned her..." He sighed. "It's complicated. I mean, we're not fighting or estranged or anything, we're just..."

"Different?" I asked quietly. That was a feeling I knew well.

Quinn nodded. "I was a bit of a mummy's boy growing up. I did well at school, kept out of trouble, did everything I was supposed to do. Cassie wasn't a troublemaker, but she just never stopped. Swam like a fish, loved to be out on the boat with Dad, constantly up a tree or in a hole digging up spiders." He slid the photo away, closed the wallet and tapped it against his hand. "She stayed in Australia when Mum died. We took turns flying out to see each other a couple of times a year, but you know how it is. We drifted apart."

"You miss her like fire, though, don't you?"

Quinn nodded. "Our lives are too different to ever be like you and Ollie. But I'd take a bullet for her. Any day, without even blinking. Because she's family. And if I *couldn't* be there, or even if I could but it wasn't enough, and someone else stepped in to offer a hand..."

"That's why you want to help Ollie." It wasn't a question.

I knew that if ever asked me to fly across the world and rescue his sister, a lass I'd never met, from a nest of stroppy kelpies I would be hard pressed to say no. All because I knew. I knew what it was like to have a sister who looked at you like you were her world, like you would keep her safe from anything, like she'd love you to the moon and back no matter how much you'd fought just moments before.

"Fine." I started walking again.

"Mack?" Quinn had stopped a few steps back. "The car's this way. Unless you want to walk home."

Chapter Nineteen

"Mack? Mack!" A cold hand tapped my face. When I groaned and rolled away, it stripped my bloody blanket off. "Come on, I know you're tired, but the Detective needs you."

"What detective?" I asked into my pillow.

"Annie? Annie Fife. Annie from the Ice Cream Van." The pillow vanished, leaving my head to thump on the mattress. "Devil's arse, Mack, stop being such a lazy shite!"

"Lazy?" I finally lifted my head to give Ollie a half-hearted glare. "I got in at half three! After getting my arse kicked by a red cap, a glaistig and a giant bloody vampire. The Gorbal's sort, not the pretty ones."

"And I want to thank you, Ollie, so much, for sending wee Davey over to save my arse and drive me home." Ollie's words dripping with saccharine sweetness.

"He didn't save anyone's arse, he got there too damn late for that. Have to give you points for sending him, though. Walking home after a day like that would have done me in, love." With a shove, I rolled myself off the bed to land on my feet.

Ollie neatly sidestepped, then handed me my phone. "You'd

best give her a ring. I wouldn't have answered it, except she kept calling and you kept bloody sleeping through it. She said the Nuckelavee has attacked again. I've already filled her in on what we know."

"Aw, shite." I looked around for the tracker Fergus had made for me, only for Ollie to dangle it inches from my face.

"Don't fret, brother. I've kept a watch on it while you slept, it hasn't picked up a thing."

"It doesn't work?" I scowled. "That's not like Fergus. His pretties are usually up to scratch."

"We don't know that yet," Ollie chided. "Wait until you see the detective before slandering the good man's name."

"Fine." I dragged out a fresh set of clothes, shooed Ollie out, and changed.

Not long later, I pulled the Demon to a stop at the address on my GPS. Fife didn't wait until I was out before heading over, so I handed her my staff to hold while I donned my cloak.

"Mack, you better be able to do something about this thing."

"I thought I had a way to find it." I showed her the compass. The big hand still spun gently, but the smaller one was now locked at the nine. "It's a tracker. It's supposed to point to the bastard when he's around."

"Ollie mentioned that. When did you get it?" Fife asked. "And why didn't it tell us about this attack?"

"Last night." I ducked her accusatory glare. "This morning? I don't know, about two or three."

She backed down. "Coroner says this happened before midnight."

"Oh." I tucked the tracker back into my pocket and took my staff. "I take back everything I said about Fergus on the way here."

"Why isn't it showing anything now?" Heedless of my personal space, Fife plucked the tracker out of my pocket to examine it again. She twisted it back and forth, watching the larger clock hands lazily swing in directionless motion. The smaller hand, however, moved in a rigid manner, fixed in a particular direction. "The little hand — it's pointing at the house."

"Aye." I frowned. It was probably a coincidence. Fergus had never made a mistake before.

Fife looked up, eyes wide, face pale. "Tell me it's not —"

"Not a chance." Of that, I was certain. "Annie, the thing is huge, and fed by violence. If it was still in the house, you'd know about it." I twisted the watch again. "It must be locked onto the demon's most recent location."

"Why isn't it showing a current location, then? Is it too far away?"

"In a manner of speaking." I snatched the item back and this time, shoved it in the wee pocket inside my pants for safe keeping. Fife might be grabby, but she wouldn't go there. "Our nefarious summoner called this bastard from the Otherworld. It doesn't have to stay here, though. The summoning drags it over, breaking the hold of whatever keeps the beastie in check — in this case, a goddess called the Sea Mither — and normally traps it here, bound by obedience until it can be sent back safely. If the spell fails, like in this case, skeletor-horse can do whatever the feck he pleases, jumping from this world back to his whenever he damn well likes."

Fife looked less than pleased at that. "So, our hands are tied until he comes back to wreak more havoc?"

"Don't worry, lass. The moment he steps back across the veil between worlds, I'll be on his arse like a blind pimple."

"We, Mack. You're not going up against this alone." Fife darted a look at the house behind her. "Promise me."

"Fife, this is bigger than you can handle. I won't go alone, but that's as much as I'm going to promise. I'm not letting you anywhere near that thing."

"Who will you take?" It wasn't like Fife to delay going into a crime scene, but I didn't point that out.

"Old Jack, maybe. Fergus is two parts of fecking useless outside his shop." I shrugged. "Ollie will be there, of course. She's tiny, but she's incredibly tough."

"I've called Rattray about forty times." She reflexively glanced at her phone screen. "He won't call me back."

"You don't want him on this, either." When she tried to brush me off, I pressed a hand on her shoulder. "No, Annie. This is beyond what I think of him as a person. He's not competent, not by a bloody long shot. He'll get himself killed, and maybe put others at risk too."

Fife took that on board, finally nodding agreement. "You're not looking so good yourself, Mack. Are you up to this?"

What semblance I had of alertness crumpled at her words and I yawned widely. "Not really. My magic muscles are exhausted, I'm desperate for a nap, and I haven't had any breakfast." My stomach growled to punctuate my point. "Once I get a bit of sleep, I'll be fine."

She frowned. "Maybe you should go home. I can handle this on my own."

"Don't be daft, Annie." I flexed my bicep. "Plenty of strength left in this old bastard. And you wouldn't have called me here for nothing, so let's get to it."

"Mack, I need you on this case more than I need you here right now." She glanced over her shoulder to the squat, single floor abode behind her, teeth worrying at her bottom lip. "If you burn out, there's no one else."

Her hesitance worried me as much as her insistence I should go. "I'll be fine, lass. The Nuckelavee has gone back to its home in the Otherworld for now. It probably won't be back until after dark. We'll do what we need to here, I'll pop home for some shut-eye, and we'll be ready for a tussle come nightfall."

"Probably isn't definitely, Mack."

She may have had a point, but I wasn't going to let her know it. "Annie, trust me. I'm *fine*. Now, are we going to go inside or stand out here jabbering all bloody day?"

Fife bit down on whatever argument had been on the tip of her tongue and turned on one heel. I followed her up to the house with an eerie sense of familiarity. It was a middle-class family home, a little run down but in a good neighbourhood. Police tape surrounded the property and a sheet of opaque plastic hung over the front door.

And of course, a box of standard issue paper booties sat squarely in the middle of the porch. I grabbed doubles before Fife could suggest it and quickly pulled them on over my boots.

Fife pulled the curtain open to reveal a room just as bad as I expected. Blood, grease, limbs, organs. Whatever illusion I was under to think I was prepared to face it quickly faded.

"Seven victims, just like the last scene." Fife took a large step to avoid a path of streaked blood past the doorway.

"I thought there was six at the last one?" I tried to place my feet where Fife had but missed by a few inches. The next step I took left a wee splodge of blood behind to show where I had been.

Fife twitched a shoulder. "When we added up all the pieces, it came to seven. Minus a hand and three toes. Not from the same foot, either."

"Tell me about this lot."

Fife quickly rattled off a list of names. Three were women, two men, and two I wasn't sure. I didn't ask though. My feeling was that the Nuckelavee was attacking in a random pattern, that if there was a particular draw amongst the two crime scenes, it would be random. For example, the number seven.

"What were they doing?" Not that I had to ask.

A plastic tablecloth still clung to a corner of the kitchen table. Fife gestured to it, then to the scattered deck of cards and strewn snack foods that soaked in the blood-covered floor. "Bridge game. Nothing like the last victims. We've not found any drugs or even alcohol, except two bottles of red tucked away and unopened."

"How old?"

Fife's eyes restlessly scanned the room, avoiding mine. "In their sixties."

"Bloody hell."

Knowing from experience that it wouldn't get any easier, I set about doing what I had to. I took some scrapings off the walls, poked around for anything that didn't fit, and only stuck my head out the window for some fresh air once. When I finally finished, I hurried for the front door, pulled off the stupid paper boot covers and breathed in the cold, damp air. It had rained earlier in the morning and would rain again soon, I guessed.

Fife soon joined me. "Anything useful?"

I shook my head. "Not yet. Ollie is hitting the books again today, looking for a way to take the bastard down."

"What about your recruit?"

"Probably helping her." Truth be told, I had rushed off without asking Ollie if she needed Quinn's assistance today. In fact, I had barely looked at her, too soaked in guilt with the knowledge I might have just lost the one thing that could bring her back to life. I rubbed my face, trying to dislodge a squeezing headache.

Fife touched my arm. "You know you can talk to me, right, Mack?"

"Aye." I bit down on the urge to unleash my ills onto her. She might be a friend, but she had her own troubles.

"Fine." Fife crossed her arms. "If you're going to make me drag it out of you, I will. What's wrong, Henry?"

"You mean apart from losing my Granda, watching him die, knowing there's a terrifying flesh-beast on the loose killing people, and having the fate of the city in my shoulders? Not a damn thing!"

"Bullshit. If you don't want to tell me, just say it. But don't lie to me, Mack. I can tell when you're hiding something."

Fife turned to go back into the house.

"Annie?"

"Aye?"

"Meet with me tonight." The words slipped out before my brain caught up.

Fife raised an eyebrow. She didn't answer, but she didn't walk off, either.

"At the Stag. We'll have a drink, and a chat. I'll need something to keep me awake while I keep an eye on my new toy." I raised the pocket watch and let it dangle.

"What time?"

"Around eight? There's no way to know for sure when this beastie will pop through to our world, but most nasty things prefer the wee hours."

"Alright. I can't pull an all-nighter, I'm already burning the candle at both ends and about four places in the middle. But I'll come for a drink, and I'll stay for an hour." Fife turned on her heel and left me standing outside.

That's when the skies chose to open, dumping an icy cold sheet of rain over my bare skin and running down my spine.

"Eight it is, then," I muttered.

Though I had told Fife the Nuckelavee wouldn't be back until nightfall, I checked the compass anyway. This wasn't the kind of thing to be wrong about. I glanced at it quickly, reassured by the wavering indecision of the longer hand, and dropped it back into my pocket. I took three steps toward my car, then froze. I pulled the watch out again.

The big hand lazily drifted to and fro, but the small hand was, like before, locked in place. Except, when I had looked at it earlier, the small hand pointed right at the house full of bodies. Now it pointed north-east. I slowly turned. The hand turned with me, locked on a point somewhere in the distance, steadier than any compass.

"Feck me. Annie?" I called the name over my shoulder before spinning back to look for her. An officer loitered at the front door, so I called to him. "Get Fife for me, lad. It's urgent."

He leaned over to pull the plastic curtain aside and I heard the muffled yell for DCI Fife. She appeared quickly, shoving past the plastic with an irritated huff.

"What is it, Henry?"

"You need to come with me." I didn't wait for her to follow. "*Now*, Annie."

I slid behind the wheel of the Demon and waited. Fife stood in the yard, frowning and looking about. "Terry? Cover me, will you? I've just got to go and check something out."

She opened the car door with a jerk and threw herself in. "It's back already?"

"I don't think so." I was hedging my bets, unwilling to pay too much attention to the small theory blossoming lest I jinx it.

"Good. What, then?"

"I don't think good is the word I'd use to describe what I think we might find, love."

Fife pressed her lips together, clearly frustrated at my vague reply. Still, she knew the benefit of going in clean. "Is it pertinent to the case we're working?"

"Aye. It is that." I handed her the pocket watch. "You're navigating."

Fife directed while I drove. "Next left. Yup. Keep going. We need to angle right a bit, so head past the uni and then go left at the main road." She fell quiet for a moment. "Mack, what are you expecting to find at the end of this goose chase?"

"The wee pointer you're following you're following was locked on that house, Annie. Right up until I came out."

"You think — straight ahead for now — you think there was another attack, one we missed?"

"I'm betting on it, love."

Fife let out a slow breath, closing her eyes for just a moment. "I've seen festivals torn apart by zombies, twelve car pile ups, I've seen accidents with mass casualties... but the last couple of days have been harder than any of it, Mack."

"I know, lass." It wasn't the number of deaths, but the brutality of them, and the knowledge that the creature causing it was just that — A creature. Something inhuman, unfeeling, completely lacking in any remorse. Not an animal killing for food or defence, but a monster who sought violence, pure and bloody.

"Should I call a team in?"

"We're working on a hunch, for now." I glanced down at the watch, pointed just a shade to the right of the midnight mark. "Fergus insisted only the big hand tracks the beast. I trust him with my life, and I trust his magic, too. If I'm right about what it is, it won't make a lick of difference if your people turn up now, or in twenty minutes."

It was a kinder way of saying that whoever was at the location we were moving towards was probably long dead and beyond any help we could give.

"Go right at the junction. Wait, no take the second exit. Left, now." Fife's attention was riveted on the tracker, which swung wildly as we moved closer to our destination. "Right ahead, stop just up there. I think we're — Oh. Oh, no. Mack..."

"What is it?" I parked on the side of the street, killed the engine, and waited.

Fife lifted her eyes to the row of terrace houses beside us. "Mack... you know who lives here, don't you?"

I shook my head, heart plummeting to my boots. It's someone she knows. I reached a hand out to squeeze hers. "Whoever it is, I'm sure they're ok. We might not even be at the right place."

Fife clenched her fists on her knees. "Look. I know you don't like him, but if you say a word about him deserving it —"

"Who?" My brain tripped over a dozen suggestions and when it settled on the most obvious one, I choked. "Rattray? This is *Rattray's* house?"

"Shut up."

"Devil's arse, Annie, give me some credit. Alan might be a prick but I'm not going to jump for glee if we find him dead." *At least, not until I'm alone.*

Fife jerked her head down in a single, sharp nod. "Let's go."

We approached the door and Fife knocked sharply before calling Rattray's name. The house was closed up tight, the curtains drawn. Fife knocked again, then rested her hand on the doorknob.

"Wait. Let me check it first." A few moments with my second sight engaged, I confirmed there was no sign of life coming from the dwelling. There was, however, the same undertone of anguish that had lurked at the previous crime scenes. "No one is here. But... brace yourself."

"Should I call the paramedics?" Fife spoke quietly, and without hope.

"If there's a call to be made it'll be the coroner we need, not the paramedics." I tried the door, but it was locked.

"I could justify breaking it down," Fife admitted. "But I'd rather not, if we can help it. Can you open it?"

"Only if you promise you won't arrest me for breaking and entering."

Fife's legendary patience was beginning to run out. "Henry MacDonald, if you —"

"Sorry, love. Sorry." I held my hands up to the door and took a slow breath, sending a silent cry to the spirits to ask their assistance in opening the door without blowing it up. I didn't want to embarrass myself in front of Fife. "You know my juvenile humour is just a coping mechanism, aye?"

"That's awfully introspective." Fife raised an appreciative eyebrow when the locked clicked open.

I held her back from entering, waiting. When nothing exploded, I grinned. "It's safe to —"

Pop. The lock bulged with splintered wood.

"As I was saying, it's safe to go in now." I snarled at the twisted, glowing door handle. "Best not touch the knob, though."

"Aye, I figured that one out all on my own." Fife nudged the door slowly open with her foot. When she stepped inside, her face fell. "Oh, Alan. What have you done?"

Alan Rattray, amateur buidseach and licensed catch and dispatch officer, dangled from a metal spike shoved through his open chest and into the wall behind him. Below, a few cold, melted candles pooled on a stone altar pinning down an unrolled scroll.

The scene was less gruesome than the other attacks we had examined, yet it somehow chilled me in a way that they didn't. Rattray's face, teeth bared between lips pulled back in a frozen grimace, seemed to mock me. His eyes stared ahead with a glassy fixation and every inch of him, from the thin combover to cheap leather boots and even the soft fabric of his worn shirt stood stiff and frozen.

Fife cautiously reached out a hand. "There's something odd about —"

When she softly brushed the edge of his coat, the stasis spell disintegrated. Rattray's skin sagged, the blood soaking his shirt turned black and his face swelled with the effects of decomposition. Fife gagged and staggered back, the sudden stench hitting her like a wall.

"What the feck?" She coughed and clamped her coat over her nose and mouth.

"Annie, I don't think he's just a victim." I pointed at the scroll while pulling my own shirt up to filter the reek of death. "That bit of paper there? Covered in notes for a summoning spell. I'll give you one guess what it's meant to dredge up."

"It came for him first. That explains why he smells so bloody bad." Blinking away tears, she scurried for the door.

I followed, gulping in the fresh air once we were out. "I'm sorry, Annie. I know you thought better of him than I did." It wasn't exactly a compliment, but it was the nicest thing I could think of to say about the dead man.

"I did bloody not." Fife snatched up her phone and tapped madly, sending messages to whoever she thought needed to know the bad news. "I thought he was a snivelling weasel with barely enough brain cells to mark his own territory. My gut always said he was corrupt, but I couldn't prove it, and my supervisors wouldn't let me cut his bloody hours. Feckin' bastards. I can't wait to tell them I was right."

"Oh." It didn't surprise me that she had kept that from me — my own feelings about the ratfaced man were more than obvious to anyone and if I had known Fife agreed, I would never have let the issue go.

If nothing else, I know my own flaws.

"There's just one problem." I pointed through the front door. "That spell isn't the sort of thing Rattray could get his hands on without help. There's no way that wee ferret did this on his own — though I'm not a bit surprised he cocked it up and got himself killed."

"Who, then?" Fife eyed the front door. "We've got to go back in before my lot trample all over it. Are you up for it, Mack?"

I slapped my cheeks, jogged on the spot, and shook my hands out. "Aye, Captain."

"That's DCI, thank you." Fife sighed. "Though I wouldn't say no to a daring escape via pirate ship right now."

"Hold on." I dashed back to the car and returned with a wool scarf. I passed it to Fife. "That might keep the smell off you a bit."

She held it up to admire the burgundy fabric. "Pretty. The colour suits you, love."

"It's my sister's. I keep it in the Demon in case she ever has to make a run for it in daylight."

Fife clutched her chest. "Henry Mack, taking precautions and being organised?"

"I didn't say I was the one who put it in there." I shrugged. "I just never took it out after Ollie stashed it."

Fife pulled some plastic disposable gloves from a pocket and flicked me a pair. "Just don't traipse anything in. I didn't bring any shoe protectors with me." She wrapped the scarf around her face, but I could see her wrinkling her nose.

"I suppose a bit of smell is to be expected, aye? Ollie does try to keep the odour down..."

"No, it's fine." Fife kept the scarf in place. Apparently, the faint reek of zombie was preferable to the overpowering decomp that lurked inside Rattray's flat. She led the way back in and, after hoisting my shirt back up to cover my nose, I followed.

"Are you descended from Black Donald or a woolly mammoth?" Fife pointed at my exposed belly, her voice muffled by the scarf. "I've never seen a man so hairy."

"You've never seen a man so manly, you mean?" I jerked my head at the wall art. "I bet he hasn't got a single hair on his skinny chest."

Fife winced at that. "I'd rather not know, either way. Now, you take the altar and I'll have a gander over here."

I set to work, carefully lifting the edges of the spell scroll free of the spilled wax. A scatter of white granules jumped and bounced as I tugged at it, and a quick taste — behind Fife's back, because I didn't want to face a lecture about the safety of eating strange substances — proved it to be salt. I guessed the candles had been lit inside a salt circle as an attempt to form a protective spell, but only a fool would have believed it would work. The dangling corpse above me was the sort to rely on half-baked theories like that, though, so it wasn't a stretch.

The edges of the parchment sprang up once it was free and it curled into a double-barrelled tube. I smoothed it out again and quickly checked it over, but there was no sign of where it might have originated. I flattened it, folded it a few times, and jammed it in my pocket.

"Oi!" Fife's eyes were on my arse, but I didn't think she was admiring it. "You can't take that."

"I bloody well can, and I bloody well will. Do you know what kind of damage this could — oh, right, I suppose you do know what happens when spells like this are left lying about." I thrust a finger towards Rattray. "*That's* what happens. And the kids at that party happens, and the mess at that geriatrics bridge club or whatever the feck they were doing. I'm not giving it up."

"Shite. You're saying, even if we banish this bastard back to where he comes from, someone could use that to bring him back?"

I nodded. "The rest of that rubbish —" I waved a hand at the candle wax and salt " — was his attempt to rein it in. But this? You don't want this lying about where any old fool can get a hold of it."

Fife blew out a slow breath, then relented. "I don't get paid enough for this shite."

"Find anything on your side?" As I spoke, I knelt under the altar — which was a covered card table with the legs cut short — to look underneath. I pulled out a small box of partially-burnt candles, a leather bound notebook, and an unlabelled jar of salty water (which I tasted in case it was vodka. For research, of course.) I checked to see if Annie was watching and then tucked the notebook in my pocket, hiding it under the scroll.

Fife had already rifled through the bookshelf pressed against the wall, opened the few books it contained in case one held a hidden secret, and carefully examined the sparse décor that filled the gaps between.

"I don't even know what this is supposed to be." She waved a statue at me, then held it still so I could see the twisted man-figure from Munch's The Scream — except, it sort of resembled a certain left-wing political leader. "I hope he's not been hexing the establishment."

"I'm pretty sure they were selling those online for a quid in the lead up to the last election." I took the statue and held it up, opening my second sight to examine it properly. Amongst the scattered mess of magical residue in the room, the statue itself was dull and lifeless. "No magic on it. Just bad taste and dubious political affiliations."

"Huh. Maybe that's it." Fife carefully felt along the top of the bookshelf, finding only a handful of thick dust.

"What's it?"

"Maybe he's affiliated himself with some kind of group." She sneezed and wiped her hand, leaving a dusty print on her navy trousers. "You know, like a cult or a terrorist organisation."

"It's not a bad theory. He seems like the kind of weak-willed numpty that would be sucked into those kinds of things."

"Do you know of any?" Fife's eyes shuttered, making me wonder if it was a double-edged question.

I took the safe route, feigning ignorance. "Numpties? Plenty."

"Organisations, Mack." Fife's expression allowed me no wiggle room. "Ones out to bring down the status quo."

"Well, there's The Collective. They're above my status, apparently, so I don't have a lot to do with them. I do know The Collective are very invested in the status quo. Their whole reason for existing is to keep this sort of thing from happening, so it's not them." I paused to think. "There are a couple of factions in the vampire and kelpie population that are vying for power, but none of them have succeeded yet. And even if they did... this? Enlisting a barely competent human to summon a Nuckelavee, taking down the best buidseach in the city, letting it run wild on a killing spree?" I shook my head, resolute. "Annie, there's not a being in the Otherworld that would have approved of this."

"Then you think humans are behind it." Fife's mood dropped further. "Even after that vampire attack?"

"There is a world of difference between an exhibitionist dinner party for one and a rampaging demon, love. The Unseelie might be up to something, but even they wouldn't drag his nibs into it. The demon is dangerous to us, and to the other sith, to an extent. But there's an even stronger power that normally keeps him at bay. The Sea Mither would wipe the floor with any of her own kind that messed around with her prisoner."

However, Fife was right to be concerned about the baobhan

sith, and I made a mental note to call Aggie as soon as the sun was down. Even if she hadn't found her dine and dasher, she might have heard a rumour about the theft at Fergus's shop. It was the sort of place people in power kept an eye on, if you know what I mean.

"But that power is just fine with a human doing the same thing?" Frustration bubbled behind Fife's flat words, held in check by a willpower far greater than my own.

"Annie, I don't know what to tell you." That, at least, was the truth. I stumbled on, despite the twisting in my gut. "The Otherworld is full of cold-hearted animals, but they still have a sort of code they follow. And they rarely act on the kind of motivation people do. Anger, lust, jealousy. For the sith, it's all just a giant game of chess, with strict rules and clever plans, but no real sorrow over knocking a wee pawn off it's square." I pointed at the dangling corpse. "Does *that* look like a man who plays chess?"

"No, but it doesn't mean he isn't being manipulated by someone who does," Fife pointed out. "You're right that Rattray was likely in this for some kind of twisted revenge — against you, or maybe even your Grandad. He was always pissy about the buidseach, thought they all looked down on the 'self-starters' as he liked to call himself."

I snorted at his description. "He started something, alright."

Fife ignored my comment. "How hard would it be for anyone, with any motivation, to convince him that he's special? That only he could carry out a job like this?" Fife turned back to Rattray with a pensive stare. "Anyone could be behind this."

The notebook in my back pocket weighed on me uncomfortably and I felt a little guilty for keeping it from Fife. Not enough to come clean, of course. I at least owed her a drink.

"It could be any*one*, but I don't believe it's any*thing*." The last thing I needed was for one of the most competent officers of the Otherworld and Paranormal department gunning for the entire non-human population of Glasgow. "Can you trust me on that, at least?"

Fife held my gaze, frowning. "I've always trusted you, Mack. And you were right the other day. If the general public knew about people like Agnes, there'd be an absolute genocide. You know I wouldn't stand for that. Right?"

The squeeze in my chest eased off just a little, but again tightened when she thumped my arm.

"You bastard. Have some bloody trust, you big knob!"

"It's not that I didn't —" I stopped, knowing there was no way to dig myself out of the hole I was in without ending up beside a prehistoric skeleton or two.

"You didn't." She softened, though. "But there's more at stake than my pride. I know that."

A car pulled up out front and Fife nudged the curtain back. "That's my team," she said. "Do you need to do anything else?"

I could have checked the room for recently cast spells, but the memory of Granda's death was still too fresh. I didn't want to see Rattray's, much less face down the skinless pony and his half-a-rider again. "I'm done with the spooky stuff, but will they mind if I keep poking about?"

"Go ahead. Just make sure you follow the rules, Mack." Her eyes dropped to my pocket, sharp with a warning.

"Won't touch a thing, I promise." She didn't see the fingers crossed behind my back, but I did intend to keep my pledge. It didn't take me long to complete a quick search of the studio flat and take a few snaps on my phone. I made sure to catalogue his books, his pantry ingredients, and his bathroom products. I mentioned to Fife that she may want her people to check the shaving oil and the spice rack, just in case anything didn't match the label — oils and plants were common spell ingredients, and if I gave a shite about keeping my doings a secret, it would make sense to hide those things in the most obvious places. Of course, if I were keeping it a secret I wouldn't have a wax-covered altar in the front room and a corpse hanging from the wall, either.

Before I left, I made sure Fife still intended to meet me later. As much as I wanted to avoid any touchy-feely conversations, it meant something to her. She was a good friend, so I owed it to her. To a point. There would be no teary wailing into a jug of beer, just a brief confirmation that life sucked, but I was dealing with it.

At least, that's what I told myself.

Chapter Twenty

To my surprise, it wasn't just Fife waiting at the Stag for me when I arrived twenty-five minutes late. I had already texted to let her know I had overslept, and that Ollie still insisted I shower and eat before I left. Fife, apparently full of the same pragmatism as my wee sister, had responded that she would rather wait until I was clean and fed anyway, and insisted I take whatever time I needed to make that happen.

That said, I did not expect to find her in the arms of a shirtless kelpie when I finally arrived, her face turned up to him with wide eyes and pink cheeks as they swayed to the music. It wasn't just any shirtless kelpie, either. It was *my* shirtless kelpie, or at least it had been for one night after a very drunken set playing at the wake of a local hedge witch. Even as I watched them, the kelpie lifted his head from behind Fife's ear to wink at me. My irritation prickled deeper.

Not that I was jealous or anything. That was Fife, my colleague and friend, being seduced by a homicidal, unseelie, pond-dwelling horse-man. She traced a finger over his skin, catching the droplets from his hair and coaxing them across his collarbone.

"The feck? Jack, what are doing letting one of those bloody

equines put their hands on my friend?"

"She's a grown woman," Jack said. Then, he nodded toward the end of the bar. "You've got someone asking for you."

When I saw the blonde-haired man-treat look up with his soft blue eyes and pouty mouth, I stifled a groan. "Achaius. What brings you to this side of town?"

The kelpie king brightened when he saw me. "Henry MacDonald! It has been a long time, my delicious friend."

"Aye." I went to stand near him, but not too near. I threw back my drink and set the empty glass down on the bar, making sure I was just out of arms reach of Achaius. "I can't imagine why that might be."

"'Tis a sad thing, is it not? If not for the strident demands on our individual time, we could become such close friends." To make his point, he sidled a little closer, leaning forward to conspiratorially whisper in my ear. "I heard you speaking with my dear Agnes last night."

"You were there?" A spark of fear pulled my attention from Fife, who was allowing the kelpie — damned if I could remember his name — to gently nuzzle her neck.

"Of course! We had planned to spend the evening in the throes of passion, feasting both upon each other and the very best cuisine available in your fine city. Alas, it was not to be."

For someone who spoke like he still lived in the fifteen-hundreds, Achaius had certainly embraced the more recent values of sex-positivity. "Speaking of snacks," I said, eyes drifting back to Fife. "Is your man over there aware that using glamour on an unprotected human who happens to be a very good friend of mine is likely to get his legs cut off?"

I had already drawn the sigils to do so. I let them hang in the air, but Achaius simply laughed. "I doubt he realises. Young Nathan is usually well behaved — it surprises me that he would feel the need to compel the affections of a human, I will admit. As you would know, yourself." He whistled, a quick, three-toned command. The kelpie dancing with Fife didn't show he heard, but casually disengaged himself from her neck and stepped back to leave a space between their bodies.

Fife looked up, shook her head, then tipped her head quizzically to one side. Nathan gestured at Achaius and Fife looked over, saw me, and waved. She didn't leave her dance partner, though.

"Last warning, Achaius." My fingers twitched, eager to let the spell fly.

Achaius looked surprised. "He has obeyed. There is no magic keeping your friend in his arms."

I looked again, this time paying attention. The room came to life, swirls of glowing light looping and pulsing around almost every person in the bar. Even Fife had her own faint orange spark, twinkling in her eyes and highlighting the contours of her face and body.

Nathan, though brilliant with green and aqua energy, lacked the deep purples of a glamour. Achaius was right. Fife simply wanted to dance with him, even now that she was free of the snare of his magical compulsion.

I dropped the spell with an irritated flick of my hand. "What do you want, Achaius."

The kelpie king seemed positively thrilled I had asked. He looked up and clicked his fingers, drawing a dour glance from Clarissa. "Bartender, another drink for my friend."

I thanked the lass for the whisky she poured me, before prodding Achaius to answer my question.

"After you spoke with Agnes and made your request, she abandoned me to my own devices as she looked for her miscreant baobhan sith. So, I did a little investigating of my own." The smile touched a corner of his mouth again, curling his perfect lips into a sultry smirk. "And I soon came across news of an incident on Buchanan."

Fergus's shop was on Buchanan. "And?"

"And... I may be able to help you."

"Your price?" The unseelie beasts rarely granted favours without a contract.

Achaius, though, had come full of surprises. "No price. I do this as a gift for you and yours." He leaned close again. "Though if you should ever wish to repay my glorious generosity, Agnes has a bed so large it could fit six. Perhaps a few more, if all were to lie in such a way that —"

"Ahem. Right. Message received, Achaius. No need to elaborate." I gulped down my second whisky, somehow without choking on it.

"If my information is correct, I will be able to apprehend the baobhan sith you want by dawn. I will secure her in a safe place and send a messenger to you with the address. Please do leave the girl alive. I wish to present her as a gift to my sweet Agnes, and I am sure my Queen will have her own questions to ask." Achaius stood and flicked a few gold coins on the bar. They were old coins, warped and dented from the hammer that made them, and fell with a clink that hinted at their weight. "We shall meet again soon, I expect."

He stalked off with a regal air, whistling once. Fife's new friend immediately bowed his head to her and followed his master, quickly joined by two other kelpies that lurked about nearby.

I hurried over to Fife. "That bloody swamp-horse."

"What? You mean Nathan?" Fife laughed. "He was perfectly lovely."

"The hell he was. You couldn't tell because he had you all softened up with his magic. It sucks you in, makes you all malleable and open to suggestion." I coaxed her over to a seat, worried how she would feel about being taken advantage of in such a manner.

She laughed. "Mack, I know. I asked him to!"

"You *what*?"

"I got here early — devil knows why because you're never on time. I struck up a conversation with Nathan and he was telling me all about his kind. I wanted to see what it felt like to be enthralled by kelpie glamour, so I asked him to use it on me. It was just a little magic, and Jack promised he'd watch out for me in case Nathan tried to take advantage." She touched my arm. "You said I could trust Jack with my life, didn't you?"

"Aye," I grumbled. "I might not offer that promise again, though."

She let my arm go but not before giving it a gentle shove. "Come on, Mack. Don't act like a jealous boyfriend, you're better than that."

"Am not jealous." I winced, realising my voice had been a little too loud to corroborate my words. Jealous of who, I was less sure of. I'd never considered Fife as more than a friend, and I certainly hadn't thought of Nathan since our tumble between the sheets several months back. "I was just worried about you, Annie. These Otherworlders operate on a whole different wavelength to us."

"I could say the same about you, love." Fife beckoned Jack over and asked for a whisky and soda with lime. "Any movement on the tracker yet?"

I clicked it open and set it on the bar between us. Both hands circled the face slowly, seeking an anchor. "Nothing so far. Fancy a nibble?"

Fife eyed the wall of liquor behind Jack. "I don't see a kitchen."

"It's upstairs. Don't bother looking for a menu, it's just a plate of whatever is going. It's always good, though."

Fife agreed and I waved Clarissa down as Jack deftly tossed margarita ingredients into the air for a ceasg at the bar. "Two plates, love. And a couple of drinks, aye?"

Clarissa eyed Fife. "Alright." She walked over to a blank panel on the wall and knocked twice. A moment later she slid it open to reveal a dumbwaiter. Inside were two bowls of steaming food. "Herb chicken with mashed totties, Don't ask me what's in the sauce, Jack's told me twice and I've forgotten both times." She slid them across the bar, then added two spoons. "It's good though." She set about pouring two drinks but when she offered one to Fife, the detective shook her head.

"Two for me, then." I grinned and tucked into the food. As promised and as expected, the meals were finely crafted delicacies fit for a fancy restaurant with a few of those Michelin stars.

Fife's eyes widened in surprise as she tasted her chicken. "My God, this is *amazing*!"

"Aren't you glad you trusted me?"

Fife laughed. "My waistline might not be so appreciative."

"Oh now, don't be one of those, lass. You've got a fine figure."

"I don't recall asking, but thank you." Fife took another bite and made a point to savour it. "And if you *ever* comment on my body again, you'll suddenly realise this Nuckelavee isn't so bad after all."

"I deserved that." I soothed my guilt with another mouthful of potato and washed it down with whisky. Just as I was winding up for a repeat, Fife grabbed my arm.

"Mack. The watch."

I looked down to see the larger of the two hands locked on the quarter-past one mark. "That's terrible timing. I'm no' done with my dinner!"

Fife gripped her bowl like she wanted to empty if over my head, then shoved it towards Clarissa. "Thanks, but we have to run. Don't we, Mack?"

I couldn't answer, having stuffed the last of my meal into my mouth. Raising my glass to Clarissa, I tried to mime my intent to return it at a later date. She either didn't understand me or didn't believe me, but I was gone before she could stop me.

Fife snatched away the keys I plucked out of my pocket. "Not a bloody chance. You've had two whisky's and you're halfway through a third."

She was right so I didn't argue, even when she settled herself behind the wheel of my beloved Demon. I didn't even complain when she adjusted the seat and mirror. When she reached for the vintage radio, though, she crossed the line.

"Touch it and I'll cut your bloody fingers off."

Fife snorted. "Bit precious about your car, are we? Don't worry, I'll take care of her."

True to her word, Fife started the Demon and pulled out of the parking spot smoothly. She drove carefully, following my garbled directions in between barking orders into her phone to some dimwit at S.O.P.D.

"Fecking oath, Sandra. Just tell the team to hold back until I get there. We don't know what we're up against."

"Left, left!" The tracking hand swung wildly. "We've overshot."

Fife ended her call and tossed the phone in my lap. She braked and yelled at a young man standing in the road, fiddling with his keys as he tried to lock his beat up honda. "In your car, now!" She flashed her credentials at him. "I need that spot."

"What? It took me a bloody hour to —"

"Do you want a fecking ticket, or a night in a cell?" Fife barked.

The man paled, nodded, and dove back into his car. Moments later Fife was safely in his spot as his tail-lights disappeared around a corner, probably stalking the same small area for another free space. Good luck to him — Sauchiehall Street was one of the busier districts of Glasgow for this time of night.

I hopped out, holding the tracker in one hand while fishing around the back seat for my staff and bag.

"I guess we're going with conspicuous." Fife tossed her coat off and I saw she had her police tunic on underneath, complete with epaulettes bearing the three white diamonds that indicated her rank. The badge on her belt reflected the strobing neons of a nearby nightclub, and she walked with an air of authority that, in my most unbiased opinion, outranked any fancy shoulder patches or shiny badges. "What's the plan?"

I side-eyed her. "That's your job."

Fife started jogging towards the nightclub indicated by the tracker. "You're the expert on this one, Mack. I'm just here for crowd control until backup arrives."

The club door flew open. Screaming terror washed over the street as people poured outside. Women stumbled on heels while men shoved past them, sequined dresses and pressed suits spattered with blood.

"Keep your lot as far away as possible." Our hurried pace and the scenes of horror up ahead churned my stomach. I regretted that last drink. "They're not equipped for this."

"Are you?" Fife stopped at the nightclub door and held it back, to aid the flow of evacuees. "You said you'd call in backup, but we ran out of there without bringing your bartender mate."

I leaned down so that I could level with her eyes. "Annie, if this goes badly, go back to the Stag. Tell Jack. He'll know what to do next." In reality, he probably wouldn't have any better idea than I did. He would keep Fife safe, though, and that was all that really mattered.

Fife's face went slack. "Mack? You *can* handle this, can't you?"

"Most likely." I shot her a wicked grin. "But if I go down screaming, don't tell my sister, aye?" I snagged a fleeing bloke who tried to struggle out of my grip. He looked back with wide-eyed terror that only abated a little when Fife flashed her badge.

"What's going on in there?" she snapped.

He shook his head, shock turning his words to gibberish. I did catch the words 'dead' and 'run', though.

"Did you get that?" I asked Fife.

"Just enough to know that we need to get in there." Fife shoved aside a woman who had stalled in the doorway, her face streaked with mascara and speckled with red. "Come on!"

We bypassed the downstairs bar, where diners looked around with eager curiosity at the people fleeing past them. None looked nearly as worried as they should have been, except perhaps a security guard with the uncomfortable expression of a man who knows he should be doing something, but can't quite bring up the nerve to do anything. Fife flashed her badge and yelled at him to start clearing people out. He looked almost relieved that we weren't sending him into the flood of fleeing patrons and immediately started barking orders to anyone in hearing range.

Leaving him behind, we took a narrow staircase, ducking and weaving past the rapidly thinning stampede, towards the thumping bass and muffled shrieks. A body lay across the second-to-last stair, hidden by deep shadows that mingled his dark suit with the black carpet. My foot caught on his leg and I went sprawling next to Fife, who was crouched beside me checking a pulse.

She shook her head, expression grim. "Sorry, thought you saw him." Fife hauled me up, then pushed my back to the wall beside the double doors leading into the upstairs nightclub. "I see more people inside."

"That's my cue." My headlong charge was cut short by Fife, who threw herself in front of me with a hissed whisper.

"Don't just run in there, you idiot! What's your plan?"

"Go in, throw a few spells at him, and probably die." I threw my hands up. "Annie, I have no fecking idea what will even work on him!"

"So why bother trying?" Despite her small stature, she could be quite intimidating when she wanted to be.

"I want to give the people inside a chance to get out."

"Then you *do* have a plan." Fife nodded as if I'd just handed her a six-page document detailing my strategy. "Right. You go in first. Make a scene, whatever you've got to do to distract him. I'll clear out as many civilians as I can. My team won't stay out once they're here — but their priority will be getting those downstairs to a safe distance before charging up, so it'll just be us for a while." She drew her gun, something I had never seen her do in all our time working together.

"If you try to shoot it, you're as good as dead," I told her. "I might not know what will take the bastard down, but that's not it. You could shoot it right in the face and it'll be nothing more than a red flag to an ugly bull."

She shrugged. "If it saves lives, it's a risk I'm willing to take."

She slipped back to her spot beside the door. I kicked the swinging door open with my foot and stormed inside to the beat of a Billie Eilish song like it was my personal battle soundtrack. That's the trick with unseelie beings. The moment they sense weakness, they won't hesitate to make you their next victim. An angry buidseach with a give-no-fecks glower, though, they can sometimes be persuaded to reason with.

"Oi! Put the wench down, you bag of weepin' bones!" I used a wee bit of magic to project my voice over the thumping bass that saturated the room and amplify the thump of my staff on the wooden floor. "You're no' wanted here, Nuckelavee."

Chapter Twenty-One

The Nuckelavee looked up, dropping the arm of the woman in his grip. She hung, limp, already missing one of her legs from the knee. A chunk of her scalp had been torn away and dangled from a small flap, blood streaming down the length of her hair and pooling on the floor. He stamped one hoof and the music stopped, the sudden silence made louder by the occasional hiccupping sob from one of the remaining hostages.

"You think you hold power over me, mortal?" The Nuckelavee spoke from both mouths, his words clear despite the lack of lips and tongue. "Watch, descendant of the dark one. Watch as your precious world bleeds."

In a single motion he tore the woman's arm off, sending a limp spray of blood into the air. I guessed the body he held had already died, bled out enough that there was nothing left for her heart to pump.

At least, that's what I told myself as I clenched my teeth tightly against the fury that built inside.

The demon tossed his victim aside like a broken doll. He took a step, raised an arm, and gestured. I raised a shield of spirit energy just in time to divert the spell, but its power slammed against me anyway, tugging at my insides, sapping me of strength.

It ebbed. I attacked. A sharp blade, not unlike the sword I had used in Fergus's shop, but this time designed to throw. I shoved both hands forward, sending a pulse of energy with the slender disc. The Nuckelavee laughed and waved a hand, dispelling the glowing weapon. He didn't, however, see the magical blow that followed it.

He staggered as the force impacted his flank, but quickly righted himself. He reared onto his back legs, the horsehead screeching loudly in a terrifying rendition of a horse in pain. I ducked, cupping my hands protectively over my ears.

It was an effort to pull them away, but I made short work of a quick sound-dampening sigil. I let this one float in the air, sacrificing a tighter, more effective spell that would only protect myself in order to offer a lower-level effect to the people behind me.

The Nuckelavee dropped back down to the ground and shook its horse-head while the glowing red eye in the centre of its head pinned me with a murderous stare. The human half — or the half-a-human, however you'd like to put it — angled a little to one side.

I risked a glance in the direction it faced. Fife stood at the door, ushering the last stragglers outside before yanking the swinging doors closed and cuffing them together. It was a solid plan, except for one thing... Fife was on the inside.

"Get out, Annie." I turned my attention back to the Nuckelavee, stepped forward, and lifted my staff, hoping to draw the whole beast's attention to me and away from Fife.

"I'm not leaving you here, stupid. Hurry up and kill the bloody thing so we can go, aye?"

A rumble echoed in the closed room, the ambience strangely muted under the effect of my spell. It took me more than a moment to recognise it as laughter. I took a chance and banished the sound-dampening sigil.

"Dance with me, mortal." The beast's human arms spread wide, and he chanted old words in a language I didn't recognise. The tiny flecks of sparkling magic that drifted through the room swayed and swirled. His arms dropped. In a glimmering wave, the surrounding magic rushed towards him, flooding him and leaving the room bare.

"That's one for the books," I muttered. The bastard hadn't left me a drop of magic to spare. Luckily for me, I had come prepared.

I lifted my staff and slammed the butt on the floor with a thud, drawing on the magic stored inside — magic only I could use. The amber stone at the staff's tip flared bright enough to light the room, though a regular human wouldn't see it. A manic grin touched my lips. "Let's see what you've got, you overgrown show pony."

The Nuckelavee charged and I threw myself to one side, saving myself from probable death but not quite avoiding harm.

The beast brought a fist down to meet my wrist and I felt the bones snap. Shock dulled the pain, but my staff dropped to the floor as my fingers hung useless from the damaged hand. He laughed as I skittered around to face him, madly drawing sigils in the air with my one good hand. Even discarded, the power in the staff was mine to draw on... but it was a finite resource.

I threw a series of weak spells, some sharp, some blunt, some hot and some cold. He shook most off and dodged the others, but I used the momentary distraction to dig in my bag. My next attack was a snirlie, this one made of silver, iron, steel, copper and salt. My hope that at least one of the five would damage the demon was soon squashed as he stood in the centre of the whirlwind and laughed.

He dived forward again. This time, his shoulder slammed into my chest and trapped me against the wall. I coughed and spluttered, glad he'd hit me high enough to avoid my still-tender diaphragm but somewhat concerned my heart might be crushed. I quickly decided that would be preferable to enduring the stench of raw blood and rotted fish for much longer.

A quick burst of magic in the shape of a slender dagger thrust though his neck and he reared again. My sudden freedom stole my balance and I stumbled to the ground. I raised my good arm to protect my head and rolled, crying out as I squashed my broken wrist, but avoiding the deadly hooves aimed for my skull. My bag cracked under me and warm wetness flooded my shirt. A quick check revealed it wasn't blood — a water jar, then. That gave me an idea. I snatched up my staff and scurried back before unleashing a new spell, one Ollie had led me through a few times. I had never relied on it in a fight, though, preferring short, instinctive spells of force rather than the complex concoctions my sister was prone to creating. Still, desperate times and all.

The Nuckelavee stopped, turning to me in confusion. He opened his human mouth and water spilled out, splashing over the fleshless horse neck and dribbling to the floor. The horse head choked and spluttered before vomiting pink fluid onto the floor.

I gripped the staff tighter, sucking more magic through it to fuel the spell. *Come on, you bastard. Drown*. A manic flush of hope flared as the Nuckelavee took a step, then paused as another gush of fetid water erupted from both mouths.

The human mouth sucked in a gargling breath. Then, it laughed. "I am of the sea, fool." The words bubbled out between dribbling streams. He brought his hands together in a thunderous clap. "Enough!"

My spell slipped away and the water steamed, drying in moments. Fury stabbed my guts, this time directed at myself. Ollie had mentioned the Nuckelavee spent most of the year under the domain of the Sea Mither, an ancient goddess that flitted about the waters surrounding the northern isles. Though fresh water might prove a barrier to the Nuckelavee, its body would be soaked in the salty brine of its home, immune to the water I had drawn into its lungs and stomach.

"Silly fool I am," I muttered. Then, to the Nuckelavee, I added, "I don't suppose a nice, hot flame will kill you?"

The Nuckelavee snorted. "I expected more from a descendant of your line."

"Aye, so did my Da." Of all the insults he could have thrown at me, he chose the least offensive. "How about you? Does your mam know you're up here causin' havoc?"

"She sleeps." The Nuckelavee spoke matter-of-factly, but the simple statement held an ominous undertone thanks to the sinewy spectre's lipless mouth.

"I dare say she won't be pleased when she wakes up." I circled him as I spoke and he lazily followed my path. "Fancy tellin' your mam you dipped to Glasgow, upset the Collective, and got on the piss while she was napping?"

Despite a concerning lack of eyebrows, or anything else that conveyed expression, the Nuckelavee managed to look confused for a brief moment. The flicker of interest gave me time to unleash my next spell. An entire shelf of liquor, now positioned directly behind him, rocketed forward and exploded, showering him with spirits.

With a quick prayer to the devil himself that the offering might be deemed worthy, I lit him up. The Nuckelavee screeched and spun, trying to escape the flames that licked at his flayed body, unabated by the sudden spray of water from the ceiling sprinklers. As he slapped away one fiery tongue, another would spring up, racing along the oozing ropes of muscles and tendons.

I launched another cluster of bottles and heat battered my face as the Nuckelavee exploded in a whoosh of fresh flames. The Nuckelavee stomped and reared. When his feet struck the ground, the flames vanished.

I was running out of ideas. Heaving a breath, I squeezed my eyes shut. *Come on, Mack. Dig deep.* The fight had drained me physically, and my staff was fast running out of magical residue for me to draw on.

"Come on, would you throw me a fecking bone?" I groaned, frustration seeping past my fear. "Do us all a favour and just die? Beat me up, steal my lunch money and bugger off back home?"

He stopped and glowered, steam snorting from his nostrils as he pawed the ground. The human face remained impassive. "No."

Instead of the violent charge I expected, the Nuckelavee shifted its gaze. It walked over to Fife with slow, deliberate steps, ignoring the rapid-fire gunshots directed at its massive equine chest.

"Don't you fecking touch her," I yelled, preparing a fresh barrage of force-spells to take him down. The first one fizzled and I cursed, panic welling up and scattering my attempt at the second. Even if my staff had held the magic for a third try, it was too late.

The Nuckelavee snatched Fife up with a human hand, grabbing her throat and lifting her into the air. She struggled, punching at his arm with the butt of her gun in futile anger. Her eyes rolled toward me, filled with desperate panic.

The lethargy that had settled into my bones fled, replaced with something new, some roiling combination of anger, fear, and love for a friend who had stood beside me always, accepted my faults, given me her trust and now, followed on my heels into an unwinnable fight.

My soul cracked open. I canna tell you what that means, just that it did. The world split, a seismic shift that affected nothing, but everything.

The magic that lurked beyond the veil between worlds, intangible and ephemeral, flared into existence in the physical realm. It soaked my bones, filled me with raw, uncensored power. Every cell in my body buzzed with life and my chest ached to release this new strength. All around, the once-dull air sparkled with potential.

Careful, Mack. Careful does it. Despite every instinct in me screaming to lay the demon to waste, to lay the whole damn city to waste, there was no ignoring Fife, still dangling from his decrepit fingers. She no longer struggled, instead hung limp with rolled back eyes and pale cheeks. I would not let her become collateral damage, no matter what it cost.

The demon stared at me, suddenly curious. He dropped Fife, and she crumpled to the floor, unconscious. "All that power — yes, I see it. It drapes over you like a funeral shroud. So proud, you are, so confident. And yet, I could still squash you like the wean of the tiniest fly, like a tiny babe struggling on its back, unable to defend itself."

His words brushed past me in my power-drunk daze, but something snagged in my thought processes. Forcing my brain to concentrate, I redirected the instinct to draw harder on the magic soaking the room.

Instead of seeking the spirits, my senses sought life. Tiny, mindless lives, wriggling and thrashing as hunger drove them mad. I pulled, summoning the wee creatures with a gentle twist of my hand.

A tiny plop landed on my wrist. I drew it close to my face, eyes still locked on the snorting Nuckelavee. "Hurry, my wee soldier," I whispered. "Hurry, for there isn't much time. Feed yourself and your little friends." I flicked it toward the Nuckelavee.

The demon stared at me, ignoring the maggot rolling across the floor. He took a step and crushed it. "Perhaps I will let you live, buidseach, just to see the havoc you loose upon your world." Another maggot fell, this one landing on its snout. The Nuckelavee looked up, disturbed by the interruption. Three more dropped down, two smacking its over sized eye, the other vacuumed up in an unfortunately timed snort.

The Nuckelavee sneezed, then reared back as another handful of the tiny, worm-like creatures fell onto its head. "What is this? What —" The beast's flank twitched, and a human hand swatted away a few maggots stuck to its equine neck.

A slow smile spread over my face as it began to rain. Not water, but maggots. A shower of the tiny beasts fell like a downpour, landing on sticky arms and exposed organs, piling in mounds on head and back, frantically delving into the dead demonflesh to sate their tiny, rumbling bellies.

The Nuckelavee twitched, then flinched. I called more, this time using an improvised version of the spell I had used to flood its lungs with water. The Nuckelavee choked, then coughed. A handful of maggots flew out of its mouth, shooting across the room.

"Do not think you have won, Henry MacDonald." The beast coughed again, retching until a piling of bile-soaked, wriggling worms landed on the floor. Lifting only the horse head, one baleful red eye stared me down.

I did not back away. "We'll see about that." My tingling senses brushed against the pulsing of his veins, the deep heaving of his breath. I wrapped my magic around it, prepared to pull the very life from the demon even as the maggots ate his rotting body.

The Nuckelavee vanished. Thousands of tiny maggots fell to the floor, some still sticky with the blood and fluids they had soaked in while inside the Nuckelavee's stomach and lungs. With a roar of frustration, I sought any trace of the demon's rancid life force. Instead, I touched something closer, warmer, more familiar. And it was slipping away.

I rushed over to Fife. Cradling her head in one arm, I checked for her pulse. It was weak and thready. Bruises lit by the shimmer of the Otherworld already blossomed across her throat and her shallow breath sucked in the dip above her sternum.

"Come on, lass. Don't let the bastard beat you." I sucked in a ragged breath of my own before laying her back down. "Come on, Annie. Open your damn eyes. You don't want me to do this — I'm shite at finicky spells, you know I always cock them up."

Fife remained still.

Stifling a stab of doubt, I placed one hand over her chest, vaguely noting it was the wrist I had snapped earlier. It moved freely and without pain, my skin unmarred by injury. *That better be a good sign.* I rested the other hand on her forehead.

I worked gently, carefully, channelling the finest thread of magic I could focus into Fife's body. I kept my breath slow, ignoring the suffocating panic that tightened my chest and begged me to suck in air faster than my heart could beat.

Fife's bruises withdrew, leaving pale, unmarred flesh as they folded in like a billowing smoke on a video played in reverse. Fife took a deep, nourishing breath and opened her eyes. Her lips turned up in a small smile. "Hey."

"Hey, yourself." I flicked a maggot off her shoulder.

Fife blinked, her eyes focusing on the room behind me. "Oh, shite!" She scrambled back to press against the wall. When she realised the danger had passed, her eyes narrowed suspiciously. "Mack? Tell me we're not standing in a room full of maggots."

"We're not standing in a room full of maggots," I said in a cheerful voice. "I'm kneeling, and you're sitting in them." To be fair, only a few had started their frantic journey across the room. The rest had discovered the poor lass that the Nuckelavee had dismembered and were happily munching on her corpse.

"Ugh!" Fife pressed one hand to her stomach and clapped the other over her mouth. She took a few steadying breaths before speaking again. "What happened?"

"He tried to kill you, so I shot some hungry flesh eaters at him."

I shrugged like it was no big deal. "He didn't like that."

"Did you kill him?"

With a dejected shake of my head, I explained he had fled back to the Otherworld. "He'll be back, though. And we'll be ready for him."

"We were supposed to be ready for him this time." Fife made a fist and hit the floor gently. "Christ, Mack. So many people have died already. Tell me you know how to beat the bastard."

Instead of answering, I collected my things. The silver cross had fallen out of my bag so I stuffed it back in, then pulled it out, emptied my bag, turned it upside down and shook out the broken glass and pooled water. Damp shards clung to the lining and I realised my efforts were futile, much like my attempt to kill the Nuckelavee. With defeated exhaustion, I tossed it in the corner. I would have to buy a new one. Grabbing my staff, I walked over to Fife. "Go home, Annie. Rest up. You've been through the wringer, even if you don't feel it yet."

The healing I had done would come with a price. In a few hours her body would catch up, and Fife would be ravenous and exhausted. Besides, I needed her out of my hair so that I could grill my sister for information. We needed to kill the Nuckelavee, and I would much prefer to do it without having to put a friend in danger in order to access some latent magical ability I knew nothing about, other than the fact that I sure as the Devil's arse shouldn't have access to it.

Pushing away the questions that brought to mind, I offered Fife a hand. She grabbed it and I pulled her to her feet, steadying her when she wobbled. Moments later, the doors jiggled.

"This is the S.O.P.D.! Open up!"

"Hold on." Fife dug in her pocket for the key to the handcuffs holding the doors closed. When the pounding resumed, she snapped, "Steady on, McArthur! Feck's sake, it's under control."

"I thought you lot used plastic cuffs now." I leaned my back against the wall and folded my arms, watching as the cuffs popped open one at a time.

Fife pocketed them and pulled the door open. A dozen black-clad officers flooded the room, ready for battle. "They're special issue."

"Ahh." I wondered if they were a special blend of metals designed to target the various weaknesses of the unseelie court — typically, iron, silver and steel. Fife's higher-ups still weren't ready to officially admit that shite existed, but they had so far been willing to fulfill her unusual requests without asking too many questions.

One of Fife's officers approached her and she walked off, debriefing her team in a near indecipherable language. She talked of 'suspects of unidentified origin' and 'events of undetermined cause', throwing in the occasional 'multi-disciplinary attack methods'. She snapped orders, endured questions, and eventually convinced her team that, despite her frantic call and the convoluted stories of the people she had evacuated, there was nothing for her team to do here but bag and tag the evidence.

As soon as she found a moment, she slipped back to speak with me. "Mack, you should go. I don't want you caught up in this if you can help it. My superiors are going to shit bricks when they get this report, and they'll see anyone involved as a political scapegoat."

I nodded, more than ready to flee the crowded room. "Annie? I'm sorry I failed."

"What?" She slapped my arm. "Mack, we saved lives today. *You* saved lives." Her eyes darkened as they rested on the body bag unrolled beside the victim. "Don't get so hung up on the ones you didn't, that you forget the ones you did. They're the ones who matter now."

Somehow, I doubted she would take her own advice.

Chapter Twenty-Two

Ollie listened to me recount the tale of what happened with studious attention. She made me repeat everything after the attack on Fife several times, peppering me with questions each time.

"You're sure you didn't say anything to trigger the magic? Gaelic, Celt, old Scots, new Scots? Tell me what it felt like again. Oh, and have you had any other visual or auditory hallucinations lately?"

"Feck me, Ollie, I didn't imagine it." I shook my head, battling a wave of fatigue. "I just got mad when the bastard went for Fife. Like when a mam is in a wreck and she suddenly has the baws to lift a car off her weans."

"That's not the same." Ollie frowned at the stack of books in her lap. "Mack, our connection to the Otherworld is tenuous at best. It's our mortality that modulates the quantity of power we can draw at any one time. We simply don't have the physical capacity to act as a conduit for more. It would be like trying to run high speed internet through a single copper wire — you just can't."

I raised an eyebrow. "And when did you become a telecommunications expert?"

"It's not like I've got anything else to do, sitting around here most days." She jumped off the couch and set the books on the floor. "And there's only so many resources on ancient Scottish magic available online. At some point, a girl has to expand her interests."

"Wait. Is that why our wifi bill doubled a few months ago?" I vaguely remembered getting a bill that was twice the usual rate and from a different provider, but I had forgotten to ask Ollie about it.

"Come on, you didn't notice your silly cat videos load twice as fast now?"

"I don't watch silly cat videos," I protested. "The wee goats are much funnier."

"Sometimes I'm not sure if I should admit we're related." Ollie grinned. "But you didn't answer my question. Did you see anything when the magic hit you?"

I shook my head. "Sort of? Maybe. For a moment it was as if everything split in half and was doused in glitter, like using the sight but brighter. Except, not like that at all." There really weren't words for what I had experienced. "I don't know, Ollie. It happened so quickly and the power itself... it was incredible. I felt like I could do anything."

"Did you get the impression the Nuckelavee knew what had happened?"

I shrugged. "He definitely noticed my improved internet reception. It didn't worry him, at least not enough to knock him off his high horse."

Ollie ran a finger over one of her bookshelves and pulled out a slim volume. "I still haven't found anything to help with banishing the Nuckelavee, Mack. You can't go chasing him down again. If you can't harness that extra power on command, he'll squash you like one of those maggots you threw at him." She cocked her head. "Which, I might add, was a bloody fantastic idea. What made you think of it?"

"I was staring at the most revolting thing I've ever seen, trying to think of a way to out-revolt it." I shrugged. "Water didn't work, and he put out the flames right quick. He doesn't have the same weaknesses as the rest of the unseelie, I was running out of things to try."

"But how did you know you *could*?" Ollie asked for about the fourth time now. "You can't just take a thing and teleport it to where you are. Do you have any idea how crazy that is? Actual, real, live teleporting. And they survived! And how did you even find the wee buggers?"

That, I could answer. "I felt them." I had intended to leave it at that, but when Ollie baled me up with a withering glare, I explained. "Like when we feel for scattered magic, I guess. Sort of expanding the senses out. I could feel lives, humans and rodents and all kinds of wee beasties, but then I felt a mass of life that was looking for death. They only eat dead flesh, aye? I could feel that, in my bones."

"Makes no bloody sense." Ollie slumped back into her chair. "We'll figure it out, though. For now, all I have on the Nuckelavee is that he's fair afraid of the Sea Mither — but she's not strong enough to secure him at this time of year — and he doesn't like crossing fresh water. You'd need an awful lot of it for that to work, though. Short of finding an actual deity to help, I can't see a way to banish it."

"I swear on the Devil's arse, if Rattray wasn't dead, we'd be having words right now," I grumbled. "And by words, I mean fists. In fact, I'm tempted to dig him up and give him a piece of my mind anyway."

Whatever other threats I had planned against the corpse of my old nemesis were interrupted by my phone pinging. It was a message from Achaius.

Greetings, friend. My contacts have secured our target, as discussed. I shall deposit her safely and communicate the location to you at sunrise. As per your agreement with my indomitable lover, she shall be in excellent shape for questioning. I do hope you will reconsider my offer. Agnes said she was most pleased by your ability to —

I shoved the device back in my pocket before reading the rest.

"Mack, what was that message?" Ollie asked, curiosity piqued.

"Achaius. He's got the vamp that had Claire McAdams as a midnight snack."

"So why is your face even redder than your hair?" Ollie made a grab for the phone. Her supernatural speed gave her the advantage and she flicked the message back open.

"Oi! You ripped my pocket you wee demon. You owe me a new pair of breeks!"

Ollie gagged and handed it back. "That is so much more information than I ever needed to know about my brother. Devil's arse, Mack, you could have warned me!"

"You were too quick. Serves you right anyway." I held out my hand and when she returned my phone, I tossed it on the coffee table. "Am going to bed for a quick kip. Don't wake me unless it's life or death. And even then, make sure it's someone I really care about, aye? If I don't catch up on sleep soon, I'm going to fall asleep in the middle of fighting the Nuckelavee."

"I'll make sure you're not interrupted." Ollie waved me off. "Go on. You've only got a few hours until sunup."

***

I was woken by a sharp tap on my cheek. I brushed it away and was rewarded with a hard peck to the hand.

Opening my eyes, I scrambled out of bed, sheet clutched to my belly to maintain my dignity, and cursed at the black crow on my pillow.

"Get off with you!" I snapped. "Don't you know better than to sneak up on a man while he's sleeping? And how the bloody hell did you get in?"

The bird stretched lazily, a wingtip pointed at the open bedroom door.

"That bloody sister of mine needs to learn how to knock before letting guests in."

"Caw." The crow coughed, then vomited up a tiny, tightly-wrapped scroll. "Caw?"

"No, I'm not fecking tipping you, you wee prick." I scowled at the crow.

It responded by lifting its tailfeathers.

"Wait!" I growled, then reached for a bowl on my dresser. "Fine, I'll pay. But if you leave a fat bird jobby on my pillow, I'll pluck you and cook you for breakfast."

"Caw." The tailfeathers dropped and the crow hopped to the end of my bed. It waited patiently while I sorted through the collection of shite I was too lazy to put away properly, until I found the shiny metal button from a pair of jeans I had destroyed while arguing with a spectre. I had intended to fix them, but had never gotten round to it. Now, I guessed, I never would. "Here." I flicked the button at the waiting bird.

The crow caught the token in its beak and fluttered its wings happily.

"Is that all?" I asked. "Because unless you want to see a buidseach's staff, I suggest you piss off and let me dress."

The crow settled in to watch.

"Aww, feck off." I yanked my window open and shooed the bloody bird out, shivering as a blast of wind chilled the room. I quickly dressed, then unrolled the message it had brought. The paper clung to my fingers, still damp from its journey inside the bird's stomach. "Bloody sith." Why Achaius couldn't have sent the address by text message I didn't know. Then again, he was a kelpie. He probably just did it to piss me off.

The street wasn't familiar. When I showed Ollie, she said it was deep in one of the industrial areas where Agnes owned a bunch of real estate. That made sense — the baobhan sith not only had expensive tastes, they had been around long enough to acknowledge the usefulness of big, empty buildings in areas mostly abandoned after dark.

"Are you coming with, love?" I asked.

Ollie shook her head. "I want to see if I can find anything more to help you take out your legless horseman. Davey will be here in a few, though, so you could always take him?"

"What? Why the bloody hell is he coming here?"

"You haven't done the paperwork yet, Mack. If the Collective discovers you have an unregistered apprentice, they'll audit you. Neither of us want that."

She had a point. Audits were ruthless, I would never be able to hide her existence if the powers that be decided to look through my life with their seemingly limitless resources.

"It'll take me hours to fill all that shite out." I groaned inwardly, knowing I would have to face it sooner or later.

"Not if it's already done for you." Ollie beamed at me. "I'm getting awfully good at forging your handwriting. It's not easy, mind — you write like a one-legged chicken scratching for its feed — but I did it. Davey gave me all the information I needed for his side, so all you have to do is sign it together, say the oaths over it, and put the bloody thing in the post."

"I thought we had to return it by way of fire?" The Collective were sticklers for tradition, and for as long as I had been alive, the procedure for submitting forms had always involved burning them over a blessed candle, in the presence of a witch and a member of the seelie court, while chanting an incantation that would convey the message to an ever-burning bonfire in the courtyard of Collective's office building.

"They had to put it out." Ollie giggled at my surprise. "Oh, devil's oath, Mack, how'd you miss that? It was the talk of the town for weeks — one of the neighbouring offices lodged so many complaints about the smoke, the bloody council made them put it out!"

That did make me laugh. "You're shitting me! One of the sacrosanct traditions of the Collective, undone by the bloody bylaws?"

"Aye. They were right crabbit about it, too." Ollie's eyes widened and she jumped back up with a grin. "He's here."

She ran to the door, waited until heavy boots stopped outside, and checked through the peephole before opening it.

"Morning, Olls."

"Morning, Davey." She stepped aside to let him through and quickly closed the door behind him again. "You're off on an adventure, today. Mack has a homicidal killer to interrogate."

“Sounds like fun.” Quinn dropped his coat over the back of one of my chairs. “Hey, where’s that stuff you said I have to sign?”

Ollie retrieved a stack of paper from the kitchen and plopped it on the coffee table with two pens, a candle and a small knife. The knife was part of the set Fergus had given me a few days ago at his shop. “Here it is. I’ve marked all the places you need to sign or initial.”

I eyed the pile dubiously. “Shouldn’t we at least read it first?”

“I already did.” Quinn made himself comfortable and settled the pile of forms on his knee, pen out and ready. “Ollie sent me the digital copies yesterday. It all seems pretty reasonable — except the bit about your firstborn kid, but that won’t be a problem for me.”

“Sensible,” Ollie said. “Children are cretins.”

“You won’t hear me argue with that,” I said, side-eyeing my sister. “Right up until they hit about the metre-forty mark.”

She stuck her tongue out at me. Ollie was only one-thirty-eight.

Quinn passed me the pages he had initialled. “Here, I’m done with these.”

“Gee, thanks.” I didn’t bother to read them. It would take too long and I wouldn’t remember any of it anyway. “Ollie, what’s the short version?”

“If he screws up, you’re responsible and owe the aggrieved restitution. If he dies, you’re responsible and you owe his family restitution. If he goes rogue, you’re responsible and you owe the Collective restitution. If you slack off and don’t teach him anything, you’re responsible, and you owe Davey restitution.”

“That sounds like an awful lot of restituting...”

Ollie ignored my grumbled complaint. “He’ll need a registered member to sponsor him in his third year, and the Collective have the right to tell him to bugger off at any time.” She pursed her lips, thinking. “Umm... his firstborn will have to be inducted too, they added that a few years ago because numbers are dropping so fast. Oh, and you’ll need to pay tithe every twelve months on top of your registration fee and insurances.”

I dropped the papers. “Fee? Insurance? Ollie, how bloody

much is this going to cost me?"

"Twelve-hundred quid in the first year, and about eight after that. You'll get the four hundred bond back in seven years, assuming he doesn't die or blow anything up before then. Don't worry, they offer payment plans."

Quinn paused his paper shuffling and awkwardly cleared his throat. "Look, I don't want to put you out. If you want me to cover the costs —"

"Don't be silly." Ollie waved him down. "Mack can probably claim it back from the ice cream van anyway. I'm sure the detective can sort it out for you, right Mack?"

I nodded reluctantly. There was no way I would let Quinn front the bill after I had allowed Ollie to drag him into this, despite having nothing to do with the process myself. "Aye. Still, they're bloody crooks." I set to signing the papers, while grumbling about the greedy hands of The Collective and the little good they did for the magical community of Scotland. "After all," I finished up with a flourish. "If the bastards cared, they'd be hunting Granda's killer right now instead of hiding in their bloody offices whining about the lack of ceremonial bonfires."

Once Ollie had flicked through the paperwork to verify everything was correct, I lit the candle.

"Last bit, my boy. Don't worry. It'll sting a wee bit, but you won't care in the end."

So far, Quinn had given me help only in the usual sense of the word — assembling ingredients for the snirlie jars, packing my tools, and accompanying me places. Once his apprenticeship was official, though, the real work would begin.

I stood across the table from him, the forms neatly stacked between us under the candle in its glass holder. It wasn't a fancy candle, just some smelly thing I had picked up from Asda to make the bathroom smell pretty for Ollie. It served its purpose, though.

I held the knife over the flame until I was sure it was hot and, hopefully, sterilised. If Fergus had once owned it there was no telling what might lurk on the blade. A quick flick against my thumb drew a thin line of blood and I pressed it against a sigil on the bottom of the last page — one that promised to protect my new ward, while teaching him the ways of the ancients. That was the implication, anyway. Ollie said the symbol was just an old way of signing off a document. A pre-historic 'the end', if you will.

"Give me your hand, David." I pricked his forefinger and he left a matching bloodied print on the forms. "It's official. Now, for the fun part."

"We... get drunk?" Quinn looked nervous for the first time since we had begun the process.

"Better." I lifted my hands and cupped his head. "Close your eyes, lad, before they fall out of your head. That's right. Now, stay still or you'll lose an eyeball."

The next part of the ritual was simple, but for the initiate, an experience he would never forget. I opened my sight and took a slow breath to calm my nerves. Exploding Quinn's head would not make for an auspicious start to my first mentorship. I sucked in just enough magic to make my nose tingle, then dragged my thumb in a pattern to represent *an da shealladh*, the second sight.

Quinn gasped. His eyes snapped open and a look of gentle wonder crept over his face. His shoulders softened, his breath steadied, and he tipped his head up, basking in a warmth I couldn't feel.

"It's... beautiful." His words whispered like a soft breeze, a current of power passing beneath them.

"Aye." An unexpected tenderness had entered my own heart as I remembered my own initiation. My Granda had been the one to open my sight to the Otherworld with this same ritual. I was nine at the time — Ollie had undergone her ritual a year earlier, ever the overachiever.

The pressure of my Granda's warm thumb had left an impression on my psyche I would never forget. "Feel that, Henry?" he had asked.

There was no need to answer. The impossible lightness, intangible warmth and the soft buzz of excitement that touched every cell in my body filled me with an indescribable joy as, for the first time, I saw.

All around me, trails of glittering, golden light. Like scatters of dust kicked up by recent movement, they swirled and mingled along paths cut by those who came before. Old spells, new deaths, or even the fleeting presence of an Otherworlder or one who could touch their magic would leave a faint imprint, a residual memory of magic that could be drawn in, accessed, harnessed. In my Granda's house, where the old man had traipsed every hall a thousand times, leaving his imprint behind with each passing, the world twinkled like a shaken snow globe.

As my Granda had when my sight had been opened, I channelled a bit of magic so that Quinn could see me draw on the remnants of Otherworld energy. His eyes widened as I pulled the power in, like hoovering a cloud of smoke, knowing my body would glow with it. I only took a little — I only needed a little for what I planned.

I drew circles with my forefinger, swirling patterns in the golden dust. I lifted it, crafting the flickering lights into a shape with nought but a mental image and a few motions with my hand. When I finished, a sparkling pony sat upon the palm of my hand. I gently blew on it and the wee horse reared, then galloped away into the air before crumbling back into floating dust.

Ollie sniffled. Tears ran down her face as she watched me, unable to see the magic. I dropped what power I held and scooped her into a hug.

"I'm sorry, lass. I wasn't thinking."

"No, it's fine." She drew a shaky breath. "Really. I'm glad you showed him, Mack. It was Granda's favourite trick. He'd be so proud of you." She might not have seen the wee pony, but the gestures I used mimicked Granda's right down to the final puff of breath.

"Proud of a little finger twirling?" I asked.

She shook the head buried in my chest. "For taking an apprentice, you numpty."

"I think he'd be more concerned that I'll screw it up, love." I patted Ollie's head until she lifted it and wiped away the tears. "You okay?"

She nodded. "It wasn't the magic. It made me remember..." She swallowed hard and rubbed her eyes again. "I just miss him. I really, really miss him, Mack."

"Do you want me to stay?" As much as I wanted to ignore the first rays of sunlight creeping through the window, I knew that Achaius's prisoner was unlikely to be kept for long. If I missed my chance, I would not get another. I would give it up in a heartbeat if Ollie asked me to.

"I'm not a bloody invalid, you big shite." Ollie shoved me away. "Go on, out with you both. Go find Granda's magic hanky."

Without checking again — I didn't want a broken nose, after all — I grabbed my bag and staff and headed for the door. "Come on, Quinny-boy. You heard the lass."

Quinn followed, his eyes still saucer-like as he watched the magic swirl around me as I moved. He followed me downstairs, almost tripping once he was so distracted. When he almost walked right into the open door of the Demon, I sighed.

"Right, lesson one: How to turn the pretty sparkles off."

"Turn it off?" Quinn asked. "Why would I want to do that?"

"So you don't end up flattened by a bus, or fall down a hole, or some other ridiculous accident caused by a lack of focusing on your surroundings."

"Wait up. Is that why you're always so distracted? It makes so much sense..." Quinn shook his head as if having discovered something monumental.

"Nope." I started the car and pulled out onto the main road. "I've always been like this. Now, I need you to close your eyes."

Chapter Twenty-Three

By the time my phone announced we had reached our destination, Quinn had a fairly good handle on focusing his Sight and turning it back off again.

"Ollie said your Granda mostly used Gaelic symbology, but your spells are more eclectic," Quinn said. "She tried to explain it, but..."

"Let me guess: she went off on a rambling tangent about the history of Scotland, the Picts, the Gaels, the bloody Vikings and that loon David?"

"That's pretty much the sum of it." Quinn's forehead scrunched up as he tried to remember the details.

"Don't worry, lad. Plenty of time to get your head around it. The easy version — and all you really need to know — is that the magic of bonnie Scotland is a hodge-podge of stuff from a couple of different groups that lived here through history. You might see a buidseach using gaelic or old norse, they might dabble with the old viking gods, they might even have the poor taste to follow the kirk. And don't even get me started on the more recent migrants. They might all come from different rivers, but they end up in the same ocean."

"Right." He didn't look any more enlightened than before we began. "I'm sure I'll catch up in no time. For now, do I want sparkle-vision on or off?"

"Off, until you're used to it enough that you're not walking into the furniture. Even then, keep it off for the most part, unless you're actively casting a spell. Or if you think something is hiding around a corner wanting to eat you."

"An Otherworld resident will light up like a Christmas tree, then?"

Stopping outside the building, I quickly engaged my own Sight to check for dark spots. Nothing stood out, but I held it for a moment, taking note of the imposing, red-bricked building we stood before. "No, lad. The opposite. What, you think a bean sith is just going to leak all their magic out for anyone to use?"

"Right." The pained look had returned and I wondered if I had looked so stupified trying to learn the ins and outs of magic.

Of course, I had grown up with it. And as much as it tickled me to have one over my new apprentice, I decided it wouldn't be charitable to lord it over him. "Look, we're only human. We can harness the scattered magic that's left lying around for a wee bit, make use of it in the moment. But we can't hold it for long, it's like scooping water in a sieve. The Otherworld is made of magic, though. Those that come from there are made of it, they can use it, manipulate it, store it, and probably shite it out when they've had a big enough meal. They don't just hoard their own magic, they absorb the loose bits around them." Satisfied we weren't about to be jumped by said bean sith or anything else, I tested the door. Thankfully, it was unlocked. "And as I discovered quite recently, some of them can suck an area dry of it if they want to, which means I need to start you on crafting your staff a bit quicker than I thought I would."

"I get it." Quinn clearly didn't, but he followed me through the door anyway. Once inside, he gave a low whistle.

Despite the shabby exterior, the inside was painted crisp white and offset by plush charcoal carpets. Tall pillars held up an expansive glass roof, giving the spacious room a light and airy feel despite the clouded sky above. The property in the centre of Glasgow's business district was a worthy addition to Agnes's portfolio, purchased for a mind-boggling price just three months earlier — a tiny fact we had discovered while checking the deeds to the place earlier.

The vast room was empty but for one thing: a single black coffin, set in the giant square of muted sunlight streaming down from the windowed ceiling.

"That's our girl." I started toward the coffin, but Quinn grabbed my arm.

"Do you have a plan?"

I shook him off. "Bah. What is it with you lot and your bloody plans? Plans are for people with no creativity, no ability to improvise. Turn your eyes on, though. If the lass gets her claws into you, you'll have no choice but to do as she says. A bit of magic will keep you safe until you learn to deal with her type." Walking over to the coffin, I knocked on the lid. "Are you awake, lass?"

A muffled cry was my only response, so I took it as a yes. I hefted the lid open. It was a two-parter, the sort used for open casket funerals for dead people with too much money.

The lass inside screamed. She buried under the remaining lid, squashing herself down to stay out of the sunlight. I caught a quick glimpse of blistered skin as she tucked her arm around her.

"Please! Please, don't torture me."

"Don't fret, lassie. We're not sadists. Tell us what we need to know and we'll off you quickly and with dignity." I hadn't *technically* promised to leave her alive for Agnes, though Achaius would be mighty displeased if I ruined his lover's 'gift'.

"Why would I tell you anything if you're just going to kill me?" Her sudden change in attitude made me chuckle.

"If you don't, we'll leave you here for Aggie. Unless she's already had a wee chat to you?"

Silence.

"Mack, maybe this is a bust. We can just call your kelpie prince to come get her, right?" Quinn somehow managed to talk quietly, while projecting his voice enough for the captive baobhan sith to hear.

"Achaius? I dare you." Her smug words drawled out with a confidence that worried me.

I snorted. "Wake up, lass. Who do you think handed you over to us?"

A low growl echoed from the casket. Then, in a sniffling tone, she said, "Just put me out of my damned misery, then."

"Okay." I reached into my bag and drew out an iron stake. Stakes weren't specifically linked to Scottish vampires, but iron was, and we've learned a thing or two from the Romanians over the last few hundred years. "Heart or eye socket?"

"What?"

"The stake." I tapped it on the coffin handles so she could hear the metallic clink. "I can shove through your heart, or through the eye socket and into your brain. It's pure iron, so it won't take long to kill you. Only if you've given us what we want, though. Otherwise I'll start at your feet and work my way up."

"I —"

"Eye socket it is." I grabbed the lower half of the lid and jiggled it, but it didn't move. "Come on, lass, open up. No point delaying the inevitable. If you don't open it, I'll just poke holes in the top until I can use your corpse to drain my pasta."

"Wait! I don't want to die," she snapped. "That isn't how this is supposed to go."

"What, you think I'm going to chat you up, then smuggle you out of Aggie's lair?" I barked a laugh. "She'll have the whole place under surveillance. My life wouldn't be worth living if she even thinks I'm double crossing her."

Silence. Then, a subdued, "Leave me here, then. I'll find my own way out from Agnes's claws."

"Good luck with that," Quinn said dryly.

"An optimist, are we? Maybe you'll get lucky." I lazily tapped the coffin again. "First, though, you need to answer some questions. If you don't, you won't live until Agnes drags her pretty arse out of bed."

"What questions?" The miserable voice beneath the wooden lid did nothing to pull at my heart strings.

Quinn was similarly unmoved, though I could see his eyes trace the trails of magic that criss-crossed the room. He saw me watching him and pulled his attention back to our task. "Why'd you eat that nice lady over in Coatsbridge?" he asked, his rounded Aussie accent making the question seem almost casual.

"What lady?" Inside the closed half of the coffin, something snapped rhythmically. Either the vampire had a nervous tic, or she was completely and utterly bored. Her coy tone suggested the latter. "Look, I'm a hungry girl. You'll have to be specific if you want details about my snacking habits."

"Her name was Claire." I punched the top of the coffin, hard. "Claire McAdams. You drained her blood right in front of her security camera."

Snap. Snap. Snap. "She had something I wanted."

"Right. That wouldn't happen to be a wee stitching of the Cailleach Bheur, would it?"

The silence that followed suggested our little vampire hadn't expected me to have that scrap of information.

"Listen, lass, you have exactly two choices here. You either tell me every bit of information you have, or I walk out of here and leave you to Agnes."

"He'll kill me if I betray him." Fear threaded through her words. "Or worse." Tick. Tick.

"Lass, you're dead no matter what. I might be persuaded to petition Agnes on your behalf, for a quick death." I waited, but no answer came. "Look. I'm not in the best of moods, all right? My Granda's dead, I've trod through two massacres, narrowly averted a third through methods I don't even understand myself, and I haven't slept properly in days. That's not even touching on multiple attacks from rogue members of the unseelie court, like yourself. If you don't tell me why the hell you want a bit of magical string, I'm walking out of here, going home, and going to bed. And you can rot in this coffin until the vampire queen herself decides just how badly you're going to suffer for exposing her kind to the S.O.P.D. and the

Glasgow Police Department as a whole. Because they all saw that footage, you know."

"It went public?" The lass's voice trembled. "My Queen will be so angry."

"Public? It practically went viral. They're formulating an official statement as we speak." That wasn't quite true — as far as I knew, only Fife and a few select members of her team knew of the existence of the video, and none of them wanted to deal with the repercussions they would face if they pushed to make it known to the superintendent. "You really should have thought of that before breaking every rule in the book and committing cold blooded murder. On camera, no less." Uncertainty prickled between my shoulder blades. She had looked right into that camera, known it was there. And yet now she was surprised she had been seen?

"Devil's arse. She'll want me dead, won't she? My Queen is no stranger to vengeance." She blew her nose, on what I don't know and don't want to know. "I'll tell you. There's no point hiding it now. The thread is a piece of the Cailleach's shroud. It holds her magic, or near as you can get."

"Tell me something I haven't already discovered."

Snap. Snap. The sound tickled at my brain with a familiarity I couldn't quite place. "We're going to use it to summon spirits." She waited for our reaction.

"And?" I pressed, stifling the urge to rip whatever she was fidgeting with out of her hands. "A few stinking spectres pop up, and then... what? Surely there's more to it?"

She sobbed again. Or that's what I thought. It took me a few moments to realise the sound was actually laughter. Slightly hysterical, aye, but laughter nonetheless. "You idiot. You have no idea how much power it has, do you? With that kind of magic, we can raise an army."

"A ghost army? Lass, I've been fighting those moaning morons since I could draw sigils. There's a whole bloody police department trained to deal with them!" Trained badly, but that wasn't pertinent to our discussion.

"You really are an idiot. How do you think Glasgow will fare against thousands of them? Tens of thousands? Ravenous, mindless beasts, intent on killing as many living people as they can find, no one to stop them except a few poorly trained humans, most of them with no magic at all."

This time, it was me who laughed. It didn't sound as psychotic as my prisoner's, but it did sound a wee bit less confident. "Tens of thousands? No one can call that many spirits. And even if they could, who would want to?"

"The threads hold the magic of the cailleach bheur, and the magic of the eternal cauldron itself." She spoke as if reciting something she had been told. "The cauldron is the vessel for the souls who have crossed. How many do you think it can hold, buidseach?"

"Why?" I growled.

"My people have been living in the shadows for too long." The passion of a true believer stripped away any fear she had about her fate. "The unseelie court tires of Agnes and her insipid rule. We will walk the earth, live openly, cleanse the city of its vermin and govern it with absolute rule. The humans who oppose us shall die — those who wish to live may do so, as long as they submit to us."

"And how does the Nuckelavee fit into this?" It was a shot in the dark, but Fife's comments about cults and manipulation weren't too far off what our zealous friend described. When she didn't answer, I thumped the coffin again.

"The Sea Mither's son has joined our cause? I didn't know that," she admitted. "Our plan was to use the spirits. With the cailleach's magic we can control them, and even if we cannot, they pose little risk to us."

"Who is 'we', lass?"

No answer.

"You killed my Granda so he wouldn't be around to protect the city?"

Silence again.

I cracked the coffin lid. "I'll burn it out of you if I have to."

Snap. Snap, Snap. "That wasn't us!" She grunted and twisted around until her pale face peered out from the shadowed depths of her prison. "We spent years looking for this magic. When our spies told us Fergus had found it, we knew our time was close. Why would we risk discovery by killing Augustus? One man canna stop an army the likes of the one we're raising. No, whoever did that had their own agenda."

"So you didn't know Fergus had sourced the thread for my granda?"

"No." Her face fell, then brightened with false optimism. "I don't suppose you'll let me make one last phone call before my unfortunate demise?"

"Mack?" Quinn gestured me over, away from prying ears. He lowered his voice and leaned close. "Her mood keeps shifting. She's not scared... She's stalling."

Even as he spoke, the coffin hummed, a low vibration like a phone set to silent. *She has a flip phone.* That was the irritating snap. I had a new appreciation for Ollie's rage seven years ago when she had tossed mine out the window, thoroughly sick of the snap, snap as I flipped it open and shut.

I shook off the memory, hefted the stake and approached the coffin.

"Looks like we're out of time, lass. I'm late for my appointment to stop an apocalypse."

"Stop it?" She smirked. "Not a chance. But the other bit was right... You're late, Henry MacDonald. You're far too late."

That made me hesitate. "What are you on about?"

She twisted and a vintage phone flew out of the coffin, towards my head. I dodged, but Quinn caught it.

"Mack..."

He held it up, open to show the text message on the screen.

We have the girl. You will be remembered for your sacrifice, dear one.

"You won't stop the apocalypse, MacDonald, because it's your wee sister that's going to cause it." She giggled, a cold echo of joy that didn't reach her eyes. "While you were pissing about here, Achaius was off grabbing his sweet little lamb."

The vampire watched me raise the iron stake with benign interest. Before I could plunge it through the flimsy wooden lid and her fleshy body beneath, she managed to say one more thing.

"After all, every good uprising needs a worthy slaughter."

Chapter Twenty-Four

Quinn had the Demon running by the time I got to it. Without argument I threw myself into the passenger seat. "Drive!"

The tyres were already screeching when I spoke. Quinn drove like a man possessed, but I urged him to go faster even though I knew in my heart we were too late. Achaius had betrayed me, betrayed Agnes, betrayed all of the unseelie court. And he would have done it the moment I left the flat.

The gaping hole where I had left my balcony doors suggested my assumption had been correct. I raced upstairs, Quinn hot on my heels. My front door hung from a single hinge and inside was a mess of broken furniture and the occasional puddle.

"Ollie!" I yelled her name, shoving aside a busted dining chair. "Ollie!" I ran to her room, but it was empty. The bathroom, too. My own room was untouched.

"Mack, come and look at this." Quinn squatted on the floor behind the upturned couch, behind a pile of gelatinous sludge. "Is it just red caps that turn into jelly when they die? Because this might offer us a clue if not." He dug in the slop with two fingers and plucked out a long, stringy bit of seaweed.

"That's dead kelpie alright. There would have been a dozen of them at least. Achaius wouldn't be dumb enough to go after Ollie alone, he doesn't take risks." I cursed, running a hand through my hair. "Devil's oath, Quinn. The feck are we going to do?"

"You're gonna hate my answer." He stood, flicking the goop from his fingers.

My fury threatened to spill over onto Quinn, despite his help so far. "If you even *dare* tell me not to go after —"

"Woah, mate. I'm not gonna stop you hunting these bastards down. I just think we need a plan first — a real one. And I have an idea of where we can start."

I clenched my fists and breathed. "Where?"

"With allies. Jack, Fergus, maybe those folks at the Collective you keep moaning about?"

I gave my head a quick shake. "They're just bureaucracy. They won't get involved in this."

"Still, Achaius didn't just screw us over. Think about it — who else is he screwing over with his little coup, and who also happened to be shagging him just the other day?"

"Agnes."

"Exactly. I'm sure she'll be happy to help us tear him a new one." Quinn tapped frantically at his phone while he spoke. He pressed the screen one more time and I heard the tiny *ting* of a message successfully sent. "I've let Annie know what happened. I told her to meet us here."

I had my own phone to my ear. If Achaius wanted a war, he was damn well going to get it. "Fergus? Achaius took Ollie. He double-crossed us. Bastard horse= took the tapestry, too. Aye. Aye, and I expect Aggie will jump in too. Here, as soon as you can." I ended the call and made another. My short conversation with Jack was almost exactly the same, right up until I went to end it.

"Mack?"

"What?" Despite my need for his help I couldn't keep the impatience out of my voice.

"Do you remember what I said to you that night when I took you home?"

A chill ran over my skin and I gritted my teeth, determined to ignore it. "She canna do magic, Jack. She's no' a risk."

"Am not sayin' she is, Mack. We'll find her, don't you worry." Jack ended the call and I looked at the darkened screen of my phone, fighting the urge to crush it in my hand out of pure frustration.

"That's Fergus and Jack." I dialled Agnes. "Aggie's not answering."

"It's mid-morning," Quinn pointed out.

Tossing my phone on the couch, I spat a curse.

"What now?" Quinn asked.

"We prepare for war."

Chapter Twenty-Five

Fife arrived a little after Fergus. Jack had already declined my invitation in favour of assembling some backup, promising he would be there when it mattered. Quinn had cleared the mess and the floor of my flat was scattered with jugs of water, glass jars, bags of various metal filings, and shotgun shells. And bags upon bags of salt.

"Oh, Mack." Fife went straight for a hug, which was the last thing I needed at that moment.

"No." I pushed her away gently. "Don't you bloody dare. I have too much to do to be fecking around with that shite."

"What shite?" Hands on hips, Fife stared me down. "Feelings? Emotions?"

"Exactly." Focusing on my task helped keep the sting in my eyes from devolving into anything messier. The scroll I hunched over was only half-complete and I let my concentration pull back to it as I dipped a thin paintbrush in a pot of black ink and started on the next sigil. "Trust me, Annie. I'm mad as a cut snake, and that's how you want me. I'm no bloody use in battle if I'm too busy greetin' over my sister."

She considered it a moment before sighing in defeat. "Fair enough. Honestly, I'm surprised you're here and not out blindly combing the streets for her."

I shot Quinn a dark look. That had, in fact, been my plan. "As my new apprentice pointed out, Achaius owns north of forty-two properties in the Glasgow region. He also has access to some or all of Agnes's buildings. It would take days to search them all, and they'd see me coming from a mile away."

"Do you know what they're planning to do with her?"

I sat back and dropped the brush into the pot. "The magic I used to raise Ollie was... different. It wasn't a summoning or reanimation spell, it was a healing." I realised that for her to understand, she would need a crash course in magic itself. "Magic is a form of energy. Well, not really, but close enough, aye? The Otherworld is like a giant power plant, pumpin' it out like nobody's business, but it doesn't just fling itself into our world. It leaks through, a wee bit at a time, and it clings to people when they pass through the worlds."

"You said people can't go to the Otherworld," Fife pointed out.

Clearly my teaching skills needed work. "It's where we come from, when we're born. And we go back when we die. Our souls do, anyway. And when we die, a bit of the magic we brought in with us leaks out. And it leaks through the gaps when a fairies or spirits jump between. Over the years it builds up, and people — buidseach — figured out a way to harvest it and turn it into something we can use."

"So where does your sister come into all this?" Fife asked.

"The scattered bits of energy left lying around this world are finite. Collecting it is like trying to fill a bag with the dust off a mantelpiece. Even if it's sat undisturbed for a hundred years, you'll only get so much, aye?" I waited for Fife to nod. "To fill the bag would take years and years of painstaking work. The spell that rose Ollie hoovered up every speck of magic in a six mile radius. She can't use it, but it's what keeps her alive. And, far as I can tell, it's still inside her."

"She's the bag of dust," Fife said slowly. "A rich source of energy for powering spells."

"Aye." The idea of the self-proclaimed kelpie king cracking her open like an egg to use in a recipe send a shudder through me. "But… I think there's something else, too."

"Life magic." Quinn spoke the words quietly, but they scared the daylights out of me anyway.

"Who told you that?" I demanded. It wasn't a theory I had shared with anyone.

He shrugged. "Ollie told me that the magic you used to bring her back wasn't the sparkly orange stuff you're teaching me to use. She said you didn't know what it was, but she guessed it was some kind of life magic inherited from your mum. And when you told me about the tapestry — that it was a kind of magic linked to life and death — I wondered if it was related."

"You weren't the only one wondering," I admitted. "And now, I'm wondering if that horse's arse figured it out, too."

"I don't really understand any of that," Fife said. "But I don't have time for lessons. What do I need to know?"

"We'll give you a run down on what you can expect to face. Is your team ready?" I asked.

"Aye." Fife glance around the flat. "At least, as ready as they know how to be."

"You'll need salt." I paced back and forth, shaking my hands out as I thought aloud. "Loads and loads of salt. And make sure all your men have silver bullets on hand, crosses, iron and steel."

"And what are my men and women to be doing with all of those?" She tapped a lengthy message as she spoke, probably relaying my instructions. "I know iron and steel are good for Agnes's lot, and salt will help against the spectres. What else?"

"The salt is worst-case-scenario business." I frowned, trying to assemble my ideas into some kind of chronological order. "Hopefully, we'll stop the ritual to raise the dead before it happens. You'll need to be ready to face any number of unseelie, then prepare for a spectral apocalypse if we fail to stop them."

Quinn took point. "If it's knee-height and smells bad, hit it with a cross, right on the flesh. If it looks like a man or a horse, shoot it. The pretty girls get a shot of iron or steel. Salt circles will offer protection from most things, but not all." He thought for a moment before adding, "Mack, are we expecting to need threads?"

"Aye." I hadn't thought of it myself, but there was no guarantee Achaius hadn't enlisted a few witches or even a few stray buidseach to his cause.

"Tell everyone on your team to tie a red string around their wrist." Quinn's knowledge was bloody good for a beginner, I had to admit. "It will help to disrupt any spell effects on them. It's not perfect, but hurt is better than dead, right?"

"I suppose that's one way of looking at it." Fife looked up from her phone briefly. "When and where are we expecting this to go down?"

"They'll want all their people in place," I said. "Which means it won't be a daylight job. I expect they'll move in right after sundown. The blood sucker said they plan to summon tens of thousands of ghosts, that counts out a few of the smaller graveyards in the city."

"It leaves an awful lot, though." Fife chewed her lip a moment, then fired off another round of messages. "I'll get my people on it. Research, surveillance."

"As soon as they move, we'll know." I nodded toward Fergus. "They're cloaking her location now, but they won't be able to keep it up in transit. Your people can't enter the graveyard, though."

"Why?" Fife finally dropped her phone away from her face. "Mack, we can deal with spectres. We're trained."

"Aye. If it were just a few kelpies or a couple of sith, I could believe it." I lifted my head for a moment, pinning her with a glare she had used on me many times before. "But Annie, you heard what I said. Achaius will be bringing half the unseelie court, if I'm right. Fairies, vamps, kelpies and glaistigs, sith of all types. You may have met Agnes and her clan, but you've not fought them. Stronger than any man, faster, too. They can supernaturally seduce a man in seconds, and rip him to bits before the officer next to him even knows it's happening."

"Who's going in, then?" Fife asked.

"Me." I paused just long enough for a hint of outrage to

percolate before grinning. "And some friends. Don't worry, Annie. We have a plan!"

She snorted. "And what's that? Go in, wave your dick about and hope for the best?"

"He's not joking, Annie." Quinn was, perhaps, the only one who might convince her. "He has a real, actual plan. It's a terrible plan, but he put a lot of thought into it, came up with contingencies, and even wrote it down."

"Bullshite." Fife looked me up and down, then shook her head. "I'll believe it when I see it. Written where?"

"Right... here." I finished the next sigil and, before dipping the paintbrush back in the ink, I gestured at the scroll.

She examined it, cocking her head to one side to line it up with some vague memory in her mind. Then, her eyes widened. "No. Henry Mack, you wouldn't."

"It's a plan, innit?"

She couldn't argue with that. It was, indeed, a plan... even if it was the worst plan in the history of mankind.

Chapter Twenty-Six

The southern necropolis lay quiet, the already bland colours washed out even further by the fading light. The streetlights along the A730 flickered on coldly but didn't penetrate the looming shadows that crept across the graveyard. It did, however, make the angry Scotsman with his heavy leather cloak look like a dirty crim, according to Fife.

"I don't see why a nice, respectable coat wouldn't be just as good." She tugged the hood. "This looks like something a medieval re-enactor, or a thirty year old man who still lives in his Mam's annex would wear."

"It has a lot of pockets," I said. "You have no idea how many pockets. And I need every single one of them."

"You don't have to preach to me about pockets," Fife muttered. Before I could ask her what that meant, she patted my shoulder. "Keep in touch, aye?"

"I've got your radio. It's in one of my pockets, in fact." I hopped the brick fence with minimal difficulty and turned to help Fergus over, only to see him dart over like a seventeen year old parkour enthusiast.

“You know I’m going to have to start a file on him,” Fife said quietly.

I raised an eyebrow. “Go ahead. When you do, tell me what you find out. I’ve known the old bastard since I was knee high to a grasshopper and I still know barely a thing about him.”

“You’re sure you can trust him, though?”

“Like my own Granda.” I patted her shoulder. “Fergus might not be an open book, but few of us are. Doesn’t mean he’s not like family to me.”

“What about your bartender friend?” Fife asked. She kept glancing over her shoulder toward the office building behind her, where the rest of the S.O.P.D. had camped out — partly to be ready in case things went pear shaped, and partly because more than one wanted the opportunity to watch their favourite catch and dispatch officer in action. “I don’t see him anywhere. Are you sure he’s coming?”

“He’ll be here.” I believed my words, but I also knew that if Jack didn’t show, there wasn’t a damn thing I could do about it. He had always been my friend, but rarely spoke of his place in Otherworld politics. All I could do was trust that he would have my back tonight, for Ollie’s sake if nothing else.

“And you’re sure you don’t need David to help you?”

I rolled my eyes at that one. “Annie, come on. The whippersnapper got his magic licence yesterday. He doesn’t even know how to form magic, let alone make it do anything useful. He’d be dead the minute they lay eyes on the lad.”

“Fair enough.” Any police officer with a few ranks under their belt knew the dangers of taking an untrained rookie into a dangerous operation. Fife sighed, then leaned over to grab my shoulder. She hugged me tight, ignoring the cold brick fence that dug into my stomach as she did. “Promise me you’ll be careful, Henry.”

“I’ll be fine.”

“That’s not what I asked.” Fife glared at me. “I don’t give a toss if you’re fine. I’m worried about the mass destruction of public property, the potential deaths of at least two civilians and a report to file that will take me well past my retirement to complete."

Her mock outrage was the reassurance I needed. A tight knot in my gut loosened enough for me to chuckle. "Alright, lass. I promise to be careful. Now, just keep your lot out of sight — I don't want to have to go running after some wet-behind-the-ears ice cream vendor who catches the eye of a bored kelpie, or worse."

It was the 'worse' that worried me, but I put that thought out of my mind for now.

Fife backed away and I set off through the darkness. I used a torch rather than a spell to light our way, not wanting to exhaust my resources just yet, or to draw attention to my presence. We followed the small road that cut the cemetery into tidy squares, following a tiny tooth strung up by a hair that pulled in Ollie's direction.

She would be right pissed when she found out I had let Fergus drill through the baby tooth Mam had kept tucked away all these years, but I would face her wrath happily if it meant we both survived the night. Unless, of course, there was a way to have both...

"I'm blaming the tooth on you," I said to Fergus.

"Ollie loves me," he said. "She'd never lose her temper at old Fergus."

"Exactly." A cluster of trees ahead cut hard lines through a soft glow blossoming behind them.

The sky had finally reached full dark. I paused, cupped my phone in my hand to hide the glow, and checked the screen. Nothing. I hadn't been able to contact Agnes, though I had sent her approximately seventy-two thousand messages elaborating on Achaius's betrayal, my desperate need for her help, my extremely dangerous plan for thwarting him, and three requests to catch up for drinks when all this was done.

So far, she hadn't replied. I wondered if it was the suggestion of a date that kept her silent, or perhaps she had forgotten to charge her phone. I deliberately ignored the stray thought that suggested the possibility that Agnes might, in fact, see validity in Achaius's master plan.

"Henry!" The whisper came from above and I swung the torch, looking for the source. It landed on Carissa, perched on top of an oversized urn on a tall gravestone.

"What the bloody hell are you doing here?" I hissed. "Feck's sake. Where the hell is Jack?"

"Over in the trees." She pointed in the direction Fergus and I were headed. "Jack said you needed help, but if you're going to be a prick about it..."

"I do, but not to pour bloody drinks." I jumped back as Carissa flipped off the tombstone and landed in a crouch.

"Carissa, my dear." Fergus swept a low bow and Carissa made a show of tittering with delight in return. The old man's ears turned pink at the attention. "Don't mind Henry. He doesn't mean to be rude, he's all abother over his wee sister."

She straightened, and her face cut by light and shadow from my upturned torch grinned. Sharp pointed teeth glistened between lips redder than any cosmetic could paint them and golden light shone from her eyes. Above her shoulder, the glittering hilt of a weapon protruded. "I'm not just a bartender, Mack. I have other hobbies, too."

"Oh. Thanks for coming, then?" I sidled back, wondering how in the hell Carissa had kept her fae nature from me.

"Don't be like that, Henry. I'm at least three quarters human." A pointed tongue flicked out and disappeared. "How's Annie? It was so lovely to meet her last night. I do hope she becomes a regular at the Stag."

"You keep your unseelie hands off of her," I grunted. "Or so help me, I'll —"

"You'll what, forbid her from talking to me?" Carissa snorted, then sprang ahead a few metres. When I caught up to her, she added, "Annie Fife is her own woman, and she doesn't seem averse to the occasional pair of fae hands — seelie or otherwise. I'd like to see you tell her to her face that I'm no' allowed to talk to her."

Gritting my teeth, I wondered if Jack had sent her to help me, or to destroy any chance I had of making it out of here with my temper intact. "Fine. Keep your wicked hands off her, unless you have her full, consenting, informed permission."

"Sounds fair." She jutted her chin toward the trees. "Achaius brought at least four dozen with him. And a coffin, bound by chains. Clyde thinks that's where they're keeping Olivia."

"You didn't check?" Clearly Carissa had been scouting for Jack since they arrived. "And who the bloody hell is Clyde?"

Carissa grinned, her eyes giving off a mischievous glint. Then, she tipped back her head and gave a low whistle.

I waited, listening to the silence, and almost squealed like a ninny when something with a hot, wet breath snorted in my ear. I stumbled back when I realised the thing towered over me like a furious demon, and for a brief second wondered if the Nuckelavee had come to finish me off ahead of schedule.

"This is Clyde. Clyde, meet Mack. He's not much, but he'll do, aye?"

I had the very uncomfortable feeling that it wasn't the impeccably groomed Clydesdale Carissa was referring to as 'not much'.

"What is he?" I asked, after clearing the hoarseness from my throat.

"He is a horse." Fergus spoke the words slowly, then raised his hands as if holding a pair of reins and trotted on the spot. "You know... clip-clop, clip-clop?"

"You know what I mean." He wasn't wet, so not a kelpie, but I refused to believe a horse of that size could sneak up on me without some sort of magical ancestry.

Carissa vaulted gracefully onto Clyde's back and landed with impossible ease. Before she could answer, a scream split the air, high-pitched and rasping, but child-like and filled with terror.

"Ollie!" Throwing all caution to the wind I started running for the sound, only to trip over something heavy and soft. I fell, smashing my face on the old brick path.

The torch rolled away but Fergus scooped it up and highlighted the fresh corpse of an ageing security guard. "He's seen better days."

Carissa leaned down from Clyde's back to help me up, but gripped my arm tightly when I tried to pull away. "Mack, you canna fight off four dozen unseelie. Not even with me and Jack in your corner." She spared a glance at Fergus. "Not even with the old barn man himself."

"I have weapons," I spat. "And I know their weaknesses."

"There are kelpies and baobhan sith, red caps and ceasg, boadach glas, fuath, and sluagh. Can you fight all of them at once?"

I snatched my arm back, but my feet remained frozen to the ground. "Sluagh haven't been seen in our world for centuries. The boadach glas left decades ago."

"And yet, they're here." Carissa stepped closer, tipping her face up to mine. "Ye canna fight them, Mack. But *he* can." She flicked a finger on the roll of paper slung across my back.

"That is a last resort. Even if I bring him here, I can't control him."

Carissa stared at me a moment longer, then stepped aside, bowing and gesturing for me to continue on my way. "Go, then. Go and punch the old kelpie king in his nose, and as he kills you, know that your sister will be next, and that your failure will be the doom of your kind and mine."

I pushed past and took five steps before halting abruptly. I glared at Fergus. "Any input, barn man?" I threw the title at him like a weapon, irrational rage filling me at finding it out through a bartender, of all people, instead of from him directly.

Of course, if I had ever asked, he probably would have told me.

Fergus shrugged. "I'm here, Mack. I'll fight for you. I canna tell you which path to take, though. Only you can decide that."

My fists clenched so tight my arms shook. I threw my bag on the ground, then hurled the scroll at Fergus.

"Hold it down and point the light at it." I watched him unfurl the paper impatiently.

Ollie screamed again and Clyde shuffled on the spot, snorting and fidgeting. On his back, Carissa scanned the darkness, a shining sword held in the casual manner of someone who knew how to use it. Fergus dug a lump of clay from who bloody knows where to pin one side of the scroll down, while he secured two corners with his hands, torch clutched between his teeth.

I sucked a deep breath and murmured a quiet plea to Ollie. "Hold on, lass. Just hold on. Henry's coming."

I began the spell. Golden sigils floated above their inked counterparts on the paper, steadily glowing with the power of the other. As I sketched over the summoning spell with one hand, I used the other to draw wards of protection on myself, Fergus and Carissa — and by extension, Clyde. I thrust my staff towards Carissa. "Any chance you could fill her up for me?"

That was not a question one should ask the sith, who hoarded their magic like a squirrel's winter nuts, but times were desperate.

"Do you think I'm the bloody electrical company?" Despite her words, the girl and her horse shifted, their figures blurring ever so slightly. When she handed it back to me, I could feel the buzzing energy leaking from it. "If you *ever* tell anyone I did that, I'll feed you to Clyde."

Clyde stamped a hoof in agreement.

"Fair enough."

Another scream, this one louder, longer, and filled with pain. I worked faster, two-handed now, hurriedly tracing shapes that glittered with energy. "Done," I muttered, bringing my two forefingers together, then parting them to draw a circle around my work. Right before they met again at the bottom, Ollie screamed one more time. This time, her cry for help was cut short.

"Ollie!" Abandoning any attempt to hide, I struck a hand through the intricate glowing design, slashing a careless line of light through it. I sprinted away, not bothering to look back at the spell as it crumbled and faded. I would simply have to trust it had worked.

Beside me, Clyde ran with silent, loping strides. Carissa leaned down to offer her hand and I took it, pushing off the ground as she pulled with supernatural strength. Whether it was the magic of the beast or his rider, I landed smoothly behind her.

We ran for the light, now bright and flickering as the bonfire reached into the branches above, swaying and twirling, making the shadows dance on the ground.

A gust of wind sent the fire shooting into the sky, lighting my path. If it hadn't, I would not have seen it collapse ahead of us. The old stones crumbled into a hole and Clyde lurched to a stop, whinnying as a withered hand thrust out of the exposed soil. The corpse crawled out, growling.

"Zombies? Achaius isn't summoning ghosts; He's raising an army of fecking zombies!"

A shot rang out, the zombie exploded, and Fergus's cackle echoed in the darkness. I heard the shotgun click as he readied for the next one.

"Mack?" Carissa pointed and I spun to see the entire cemetery tremble and warp as mounds exploded and tombs cracked open. Skeletal creatures with tight leathery skin climbed over each other, looking for escape from their dark prisons. "Off you get."

"But Ollie —"

"Your ugly arse monster is on his way, I can feel him." Carissa dismounted after me and drew the sword from her back, nodding towards the path we had taken. "Go to your sister. We'll take care of this lot and buy you some time for old horse-guts to arrive." Clyde snorted and nudged my shoulder with his head, pushing me in the direction of the extinguished fire.

"Fine. But don't slow down Nuckles. I've got plans for that ugly bastard."

Fergus sprinted toward us, shotgun in hand. He gave an excited holler. "This is how to spend a Saturday night, m'boy!" He spun and let off another shot, just as the zombie behind raised an arm in preparation to grab him.

"It's Thursday," I said dryly. "You got this, old man?"

"Me?" He tossed the spent gun on the ground and pulled out an iron bar. "Dinna fash yerself about old Fergus, lad."

A rotting corpse darted for us. "Mine!" Fergus called, so I stepped aside, only to see the beast fly back moments later. When I glanced over my shoulder, Fergus raised his iron rod with a wild grin. "Home run!"

I nodded approval and, when another zombie sprinted for us, I ran straight for it. The sigil I had placed on myself lent me speed and power, and when I slammed my shoulder into my target, it crumpled to the ground. A precautionary handful of salt sizzled when it touched the zombie's flesh — unlike Ollie, these rotters seemed susceptible to it, meaning they were closer to spectres in nature than to my sister.

The ground shuddered behind me and I began running again. "Come on, you big ugly donkey! Come and get me!" I hollered as loud as I could, running straight for the copse of trees.

I burst into a clearing and immediately realised I was surrounded. Achaius, naked and dripping, laughed at my breathless surprise.

"You are too late, my friend. We have completed the ritual. Glasgow — and Scotland, and perhaps even the world — is about to realise who holds the real power."

"Aye," I panted. "But it's no' you."

Achaius angled his head in momentary confusion. "What —" His eyes widened, unable to deny the pull of putrid energy emanating from my equine friend. "What have you done, MacDonald?"

"You were having a party, so I brought a mate." A manic grin overtook me.

Achaius eyed his followers, who had fallen silent. Every one of them would be able to feel the power that approached. They began to shuffle, and a few faded back into the trees around them. "Stay!" Achaius screamed. "Stay and fight, you worthless cowards! This is our moment of victory, the night we rise!"

A Baobhan sith looked at the kelpie, face drawn, eyes wide. She sank to her knees.

Achaius straightened, victory giving his smirk a vicious twist. It fell away a moment later. His mouth opened, silent, before a glut of blood gushed over his shirt. He lived just long enough to roll his eyes back and met the cold, furious glare of Agnes Ban Righe.

The Nuckelavee shoved past a tree, snapping its trunk as he forced past it. Agnes paid it no heed, simply staring at the crumpled corpse at her feet.

The rest of the unseelie tried to scatter, but the Nuckelavee grabbed two kelpies and tore a limb from each before snatching a red cap that foolishly tried to climb a tree to escape the demon's murderous appetite. The red cap squealed right up until its head was removed from its shoulders.

Intoxicated by the magic residue soaking his victims from the ritual they had just completed, the Nuckelavee roared, the thick, gurgling sound that would surely spread across Glasgow like a low rumble of distant thunder. The fae in the clearing scrambled, some trying to fight the beast, most running. Meanwhile, the graveyard filled with the sound of fighting as the army of risen zombies came against those trying to confine them to the area.

Jack swung from a tree by a shining silver rope, beheaded a bodach glas with a sword that matched Carissa's, and dismounted to land on a sluagh, whose twisted, gray features quickly erupted into a gelatinous mess when Jack's blade plunged through an eye.

None of it mattered to me. Not the carnage, the fighting, or the dead kelpie king lying at my feet. Agnes crouched over him, stroking his hair. She glanced my way, a brief tenderness showing as she pointed to a nearby crypt. "She is there. For what it is worth, I am sorry, Henry MacDonald."

No.

I stared at the doorway, a deep, black shadow with edges that wavered in the light of the unsteady fire. One step, then another. Part of me wanted to run to it, to get to Ollie as soon as I could. Another wanted me to wait, to put it off, to avoid the knowledge that lay within.

Step after step. Suddenly the crypt tipped sideways and was snatched away. Wait, no, I was knocked sideways and dragged away. I kicked at the zombie as it tried to take a bite out of my calf, and it took a few shattered teeth for its efforts. A lack of both pain sensors and general intelligence meant it didn't let go, so I twisted and prepared a sigil. Before I could finish, the zombie's head split in two.

There's not much that can survive their brains being splattered on their feet and reanimated corpses, dumb as they are, are no exception. I gave Jack a quick nod of acknowledgment and scrambled back to my feet, hesitation gone. Carissa and Clyde joined me in my sprint across the clearing. Clyde reared into a majestic stretch at the doorway, then kicked his strong legs backward. The zombie behind him went flying into the trees. Carissa dismounted and pressed her back against the crypt, waving me past.

"We've got your back, Mack." She nodded, then brought a crossbow up and loosed a half dozen bolts that zinged over my left shoulder.

I didn't look back, trusting her aim was true. The darkness enveloped me, blinding me for a brief moment while my eyes adjusted to the transition away from the roaring fire to the flickering shadow of the tomb. A stone coffin jutted from the floor in the centre, draped in a shroud that covered the unmistakable shape of a small body.

Ollie lay quiet, frozen in time. Her hands had been carefully folded atop her stomach, just beneath the leather-bound hilt of a knife. I yanked it free and tossed it aside. The tight quarters between the bricked-in sides of the crypt and the central dais left me just enough room to crouch beside Ollie so I could lift her head and cradle it against my chest.

Her skin chilled mine. I pressed her face to my throat but I felt no movement, no gentle puff of air or slight tilt of her head to settle against me. Feeling for a pulse was useless. She had none, hadn't since she died the first time.

"The only bloody time, you idiot." Startled by my own voice, I pulled back to look at my sister.

When I had first pulled her back from death all those years ago, I thought I had failed. Her pale, bloodless skin, uncanny stillness, and clouded pupils all convinced me she was dead, no matter how fast she talked or how tight she hugged me. It was only now I saw how wrong I had been.

Even in sleep, there had been a life to her. An energy, a vibrant sense of her that still lurked at the corners of her eyes and the twitch of her lips when she stifled a smile.

Now, there was nothing. Ollie was empty, a shell, a void in space that held flesh, but no soul.

"No." A sob tore free of my chest and I clutched her tighter. "No. Ollie, come back. Come back, lass. I won't lose you again."

I had brought her back once. A child, new to the unwieldy power he held, clumsy in its application but filled with an anguish that lent strength to the spell I had chosen.

Laying Ollie back down, I ran my hands along her arms to her hands. A thin cotton thread looped around her wrists and reflex brought my fingers to it, ready to snap it and free her.

I stopped just in time. *The thread.* I quickly searched her body but apart from her thin cotton shift, I found no other sign of the magical thread stolen from Fergus's shop. Opening my sight, I saw the crypt as a dark void, empty of magic. Empty, except for a faint glow around Ollie's wrists and the pulsing beacon of my staff.

It had to be enough. It had to. I forced my frantic mind to a state of calm, knowing that I would only have one chance at this. The residue of the Cailleach's power, supplemented by Carissa's gift, was all I had to bring my sister back. It would not be enough. And yet, it had to be.

I clutched Ollie's stiff and frozen hands, pressed a thumb against the knotted thread, and drew a breath. The magic seeped into my skin, prickling and humming. It passed through me like a current, gently swelling as I added in the magic drawn from my staff. I held this new, unfamiliar power with tender control for the briefest of moments, learning its feel, getting to know it. Then I coaxed it out, through my other hand, into the spot where my thumb pressed against Ollie's wrist.

For a brief, glorious moment, we connected. The magic flowed like warm honey, in one hand and out the other, suffusing my entire body with the ephemeral sense of life, of potential, of humanity itself.

And then the stream slowed to a trickle before stopping entirely. I forced back anger and sorrow and tried again. *Nothing.* I grabbed the knot, clutching it so tight it snapped free. Tears streamed down my face and I heaved, all sense of calm and control gone as I felt my sister's last hope fade away even as my chest filled with agonising pain.

No!

I screamed. The world shifted.

I saw the tomb, empty, sapped of magical energy. At the same time, I saw a second world overlayed like a blurry double-vision. This world was like ours, but not. It moved and swayed, and echoed with a millennia of history, memory and magic. And it was full of magic.

When I looked down at the bit of cotton dangling from my hand it was both empty and full, soaked in a blinding magic that dripped from the broken ends into shimmering pools on Ollie's dress.

A sensible buidseach would question a source of apparently limitless power. He would use caution, question thoroughly, tread softly.

A buidseach cradling his dead sister is not a sensible buidseach.

I called on the magic, felt it rush through me, and shoved it out as fast as I drew it. I watched it fill Ollie, blossoming across her chest and running in slender trails down her arms, inching up her neck like frost creeping up a windowpane.

The flow of magic increased, scorching my veins as I channelled it, scouring my soul clean, popping and sparkling across my eyes until I only saw light.

Ollie gasped. Her back arched and she sucked in a breath. I heard a thump, a pounding echo as my heartbeat rang in my ears.

Except it wasn't mine.

I felt two beats, one against my ribcage as my own heart painfully crashed against it. The second fluttered under my fingers as blood pulsed through Ollie's veins.

A hand covered mine, pulling it free. "Feck's sake, Mack, you're going to snap my wrist if you don't let go."

This time it was my face pressed on my sister's chest as I sobbed like a baby. She rested her cheek on my head and rubbed my back, while gently telling me I was the biggest bloody sook she had ever met.

"Is that fighting I can hear outside?" she asked.

"Aye." I sniffled. "There's a few thousand zombies and a Nuckelavee out there — that's assuming all the unseelie have been taken care of."

"Then what are we waiting for, Mack? Let's go kick some demon-butt."

Chapter Twenty-Seven

We stumbled outside to a scene of pure chaos. Seelie, unseelie, dead and undead cluttered the spaces between the trees, occasionally scattering with supernatural speed to avoid a swipe from the Nuckelavee, who seemed to be having his own private party as he launched a decapitated head into the back leg of a Kelpie, who went down with a sharp whinny. I was fairly certain the head's owner had been dead before he lost it, but that didn't make the idea of receiving a fleshy football any more appealing.

"You had fun while I was gone, didn't you?"

Ollie's murmur caught the attention of a nearby baobhan sith, who launched herself at us with a screech. "MacDonald! You'll pay for what you've done."

Before my fingers had traced even the first sigil of a defensive spell, a whirling blade of magic sliced her in half. I turned to look at Ollie in shock.

She shrugged. "Did I forget to mention I got my magic back?"

"Your ma —" I ducked to avoid a pair of hooves aimed at my head. "We can talk about that later."

"Henry MacDonald! I see you, buidseach." The Nuckelavee's

growl boomed over the cacophony.

"Later sounds good." Ollie surveyed the battleground. The tight packed fighting was the only thing creating a small safety buffer between us and the angry demon, who had already started wading past undead and unseelie fighters, his glowing eyes drilling into my soul. "All those bloody people. Wish they'd get out of our way."

"You're crazy." I grabbed her wrist and pulled her away, into the trees. "Run!"

She didn't resist, instead running with me. She did pull her wrist from my grasp, replacing it with a firm grip on my arm as she guided me under branches and over bodies. We headed away from the noise and the light, only for Ollie to slide to a halt, almost ripping my arm out of its socket in the process. "Shh."

I ducked in the shadows, waiting. A twig cracked nearby. Then, a thud.

"Bloody corpses!"

The distinctly Australian mutter was as much a balm to my soul as it was a slap of concern. "Quinn?"

"Yeah, it's me. Ollie!" The two quickly embraced.

"What the feck are you doing here?" I snapped. "You're going to get yourself killed, you bloody fool."

"DCI Fife said —"

"Fife is not your direct superior," I reminded him. "Your orders regarding anything magical or supernatural come from me. She doesn't outrank me on those matters."

"Agreed." Quinn shrugged unapologetically. "But she said she'd string me up by my balls if I didn't come check on you, and honestly? She's a lot scarier than you are."

He did have a point there. When Fife got an idea in her head, anyone standing in her way would be shown the meaning of true fear. "Well, you've checked. I'm alive, now get back to safety."

"Um, about that..." He shifted, sucked in a breath, and let his words out in a frantic gush. "One of Achaius's people broke the salt line and a few of the corpses got out. And by a few, I mean a few hundred." He winced. "It's not good, Mack. We've got a dozen men down already."

"Feck." I couldn't leave innocent people to the undead, and the idea of Fife getting hurt... behind me, the ear-splitting crack of a ruptured tree trunk reminded me that abandoning my post here wouldn't exactly help the stability of the current population of Glasgow, either.

I glanced at Ollie, whose wide-eyed, pale face offered no solace or answers. Quinn waited patiently, the stance of a man ready to do whatever I asked even if it meant running straight towards his inevitable death — and almost every scenario I could imagine ended in exactly that.

"Feck." I put my fingers to my mouth and whistled sharply, doing my best to imitate Carissa's earlier call. More crashing through the bushes, but no thud of hoofbeats. "Come on, Clyde! You're no bloody use to us if you don't come when you're — eep!"

I scurried away from the warm flutter on my neck, then gave the animal a baleful glare. "We'll talk about that later, you prick. Now, Quinn here is going to jump on your back, and you're going to take him to Carissa, aye?"

Clyde pawed the ground, then awkwardly lowered himself in front of Quinn.

"I'll take that as a yes." Quinn patted Clyde's neck and the horse clambered back up. "Carissa, the girl from the bar?"

"*Girl* is putting it loosely," I said. "But she'll know where Jack and Fergus are, and make sure those on our side are where they need to be. Which, right now, is anywhere but here."

Quinn hesitated. "I can't leave you —"

"I've got it handled," I assured him. "But it'll get messy. I don't want anyone caught in the crossfire."

Quinn nodded, then clutched Clyde's mane as the horse took off.

Ollie shook her head. "You've not got this handled one bit, Henry Mack."

"Aye. But I had to get him somewhere safe."

She cocked an eyebrow. "You sent him off to fight a few hundred undead to keep him safe?"

"You cannot hide from me, MacDonald." The Nuckelavee burst from the trees, wet tendons glistening in the flickering firelight, eyes hot embers in the shadows.

"Safer than here," I murmured.

Ollie nodded slowly. "You got me there, brother."

Chapter Twenty-Eight

Ollie dropped into a defensive crouch, her fingers flying as she traced sigil after sigil. "Tell me you have a plan, Mack." Her first spell flew at the demon, plunging a glowing spear in his chest. He snarled, sucked in a breath, and absorbed it.

"Plan? Don't be daft." I lifted my hands, spreading them wide as I cast my own spell. Ropes whipped out, encircling the Nuckelavee's arms and pinning them to his sides. With a grunt, he snapped them, the magic dispersing into nothing as he sucked in the residue.

The Nuckelavee started toward us again, his gargling breaths puffing hot steam into the cold night air. "Children of the devil, born of prophecy. What sweet triumph to call your deaths my own." He snorted and lifted a hand, beckoning. "Do not run, children. You are braver than that."

I exchanged a glance with Ollie. When I looked back at him, her hand slipped into mine, small and blissfully warm. The thread still dangling from her wrist brushed against mine, tickling. I gripped her tighter. "You'll not have us."

"But I will." The Nuckelavee stopped just a few feet away, unconcerned at the shimmering protective shield that burst up from the ground between us. "I have tasted your magic, MacDonald. I know its flavour, deep within my bones."

"Aye," I spat. "Tastes like apples, right?"

"It tastes like that which brought me here." The Nuckelavee paused, letting me digest that. "How does it feel to know your death will come from one of your own line?"

"Feck off." I barked a laugh. "That moron —"

"Not him." The Nuckelavee took two steps forward, his breath panting, hands clenched with distant passion, as he recalled the summoning spell that woke him. "That pustulant weakling tasted of naught but fear and greed and piss and blood. He used the work of another to call on me, too foolish to see he could not control me. No, not him, but the one that called before, who bonded me with perfect lines to do his heinous bidding." His teeth widened in a horrific approximation of a smile.

"Why?" Ollie's voice trembled, choked. "Why were you summoned the first time?"

The Nuckelavee laughed. Quiet, at first, but quickly growing into a boom that sliced at the night air.

Ollie's hand thrust out and the laughter cut abruptly. Her fingertips glowed as the Nuckelavee's human throat choked, an invisible grip lifting his front hooves from the ground.

"WHY!" Ollie screamed the word as magic sparked and crackled around her.

A chill ran down my spine and washed over my skin. *No. No, it couldn't be...*

"I remember that night." Despite the crushing grip on his throat, the Nuckelavee struggled not. "I remember your eyes as the life drained from them."

With a howl of pure, unbridled fury, Ollie flung her hands asunder. The Nuckelavee's neck snapped, head dropping to his chest at an awkward angle. And yet, he did not fall. With all the pizzazz of a b-grade horror movie, he lurched toward us.

Ollie flung herself at him, abandoning magic for fists.

"Ollie!" I ran for her, throwing myself past the softly shimmering wall. "No!"

She fended off the Nuckelavee's feet as he reared, punched through his equine belly, and yanked a handful of ropey intestines. She tossed them aside and raised her arm again, but he caught her tiny fist. With a rough yank he lifted her into the air and she spat and flailed, trying her best to wriggle free.

"Get your hands off my sister!" I roared. I reached out, pushed past the deadened zone of vacant energy created by the Nuckelavee's presence until I found what I needed. *Magic.* It infused my body down to my bones, hardening my skin, giving me the strength I would need for what was to come. I ran.

My new strength allowed me to cover the distance in a few leaps. I reached for the beast's arm, pulled myself up with ease, and reached for my sister.

He swatted me away with ease, but I persisted. Ollie's legs kicked and I grabbed them, climbing her like a rope as she struggled, her hands gripping the monster's wrist.

Finally, I could reach. I slapped a hand on her wrist, locking my fingers around the tiny bit of thread that encircled it. Ollie stilled as she felt me draw on the magic, draw on her. The Nuckelavee screeched a piercing whinny but her grip on him was as strong as his own.

The Cailleach's magic filled me to bursting. As it flowed through me, it flowed through Ollie, mingling our powers until I could no longer tell where I ended and my sister began. My sight opened to the Otherworld, painting mine in the vibrant, swirling light of limitless magic, allowing me to see life itself — the remnants of the unseelie still battling beyond the trees, the trees themselves... and the Nuckelavee.

We needed no words.

As one, we each wrapped a tendril around one half of the Nuckelavee's soul, the life force that sustained him in our world and in his.

As one, we cleaved those two halves apart.

The Nuckelavee burst open, showering us with rotting blood and clumps of flesh coated in burning ichor. I fell to my knees and heaved, the foul taste permeating my mouth and nose as I vomited onto the ground.

A hand patted my back as my stomach emptied itself. Tentative, reassuring, questioning.

"Jesus, Mack. What the hell did you eat today?"

Chapter Twenty-Nine

We found Quinn by following the trail of shredded clothes, disintegrated shoes and the occasional limb that had been lopped off. And, of course, the bodies. Zombie after Zombie littered the ground in a trail that led us to the ongoing battle between the risen dead and the protectors of Glasgow.

After fighting our way to the front of the queue, I was pleasantly surprised to see my young apprentice was not only alive, but shirtless. Though that second observation was quickly quashed by an elbow to my ribs.

"Focus, you drooling idiot." Ollie thrust a foot out to one side, kicking straight through the knee of a woman in a tattered wedding gown.

With a quick motion, I drew a few sigils that would keep the dead lass where she belonged. "I'm allowed to look."

"Christ, Mack, can you not focus on the situation for five minutes?" Ollie dropped down to plant both hands on the trampled grass.

The ground trembled and I threw my hands out for balance as a chasm opened to swallow half a dozen of the enemy surrounding us. Quinn's head, bobbing over the horde between us, turned in our direction. "Mack? Where the hell have you been?"

"Phhrrrm." The gentleman that lurched toward me still wore a flat cap, despite lacking half his skull. Even as I grabbed a handful of salt from my cloak pocket, I wondered if the cap had been supposed to hide the injury that assumedly caused his death. If so, it hadn't worked. There's only so much you can do to hide half a missing face.

That's where I threw the salt, followed by a sigil to keep the bastard down.

"This is getting ridiculous." Ollie's frustration boiled over and she planted her feet with a furious glare. She worked her fingers in a complicated fashion, sucking up glittering sparks of magic from her surroundings, breathing it into her being, holding it until I thought she might burst. Then, with a triumphant roar, she released it. Not as a blade or a club, not an earthquake or void, but a net, made of shining webs as fine as a spider's. It drifted down to settle on the faces of those we fought, wrapping them, tangling tighter as the undead tried to shake it off.

"Come, children." Ollie's eyes glowed with the same eerie light that formed halos around each of her decomposed disciples. As one, the undead stilled, then turned to face her. "Rest, my wee darlings. You shouldn't be here. Return to your graves and go back to where you came from." Her voice, flat and toneless, sent a shiver down my spine, and yet they obeyed.

Like a horde of ants, they swarmed past, passing barely a finger width away but never jostling or bumping into us. Unable to contain my curiosity, I reached an arm out. The undead ducked, swerved, and rolled to pass just out of reach.

"How are you doing this?" I whispered.

"Magic, Mack." The life and joy had returned and my sister tipped her head up. A cheeky grin reached from cheek to cheek. "What, did you think I had a bag of puppy dog treats in my pocket or something?"

"Or something is right," I muttered. There was no time to ask her about it, though — ahead, Quinn had backed away from the rest of the ice-cream van, his hands raised defensively. He faced a dozen officers, every one of them armed with a weapon trained at my sister's head.

"She's on our side, boys," he called, voice tight but steady. "She's one of the good ones — if you want to shoot her, you'll have to take me down first."

I stepped forward to join him. "Come on, you bloody numpties. You all saw what Ollie did; she's the reason you're not still waist-deep in dead people."

"She's stringing the dead along like puppets. How can we trust her?" one man called, causing the others to shift nervously.

"You know me!" I said. "Come on Pork. It's me, Mack. Would I lie to you?"

"You lied about the fiver you 'borrowed' to buy lunch last month, you prick."

"Ok, fine." Bastard was kidding himself if he thought he was getting it back now. "But would I lie about something like this?" I quickly lowered a hand and fished my credentials out of my cloak pocket. "You kill me, and you lose the last competent catch and dispatch officer you have." I tossed the plastic card on the ground.

Another officer — Pike, who had often partnered with Pork, whose real name I had forgotten long ago — disengaged his weapon and lowered it. "Look, fellas, I know Mack's a right prick —"

"Oi!" My hands went to my hips, but a sharp glare from Quinn silenced my protest.

"And I know he's fecking useless at doing his paperwork," Pike continued, "But every damn one of us has worked with him. And he's a whiny gobshite, and sometimes smells like a garbage can, and god only knows how he remembers his own name, but it's Mack. He's never let us down on the job. I say we trust him."

"We trusted Rattray," Pork retorted. "And look how that turned out."

He was met with jeers and the rest of the team immediately lowered their weapons in disgust. "If you were a big enough idiot to trust that wanker, I'll shoot you myself," Pike said.

Pork grumbled, but finally stepped down. "Fine. You're right, the weaselly shite was always a bit off."

"Gentleman," I said as I dropped a bow. "Meet my sister, Olivia Mack."

Ollie dropped a curtsy to the dead silence of the watching officers.

Eventually, Pike cleared his throat and spoke. "Anyone else need a drink right now?"

Chapter Thirty

The tiny church ceremony held to honour the life and unexpected death of Claire McAdam was almost as bland as her decor, despite the bit of dust that stung my eye toward the end.

Quinn had accompanied me, probably to make sure I was on my best behaviour. Fife stood on my other side, the formality of her dress uniform somehow unmarred by the arm tucked inside her jacket, secured by a sling. She had broken it in the battle with the undead, trying to save a civilian who had gotten caught up in the mess. Trying and succeeding, mind you. Fife lost three members of her team that night, but damned if she'd let a civilian get hurt on her watch. The bloke in question escaped with nothing more than a black eye, and a story he'd be telling at the local pub for the rest of his life.

"You getting a bit teary there, love?" Fife murmured as the minister wrapped up his surprisingly moving speech.

"Don't be daft." I cleared my throat and rubbed the offending eye. "It's the pollen."

"In the middle of winter?" Quinn didn't look at me as he spoke, he didn't hide his cheeky grin, either.

"Aye, in the middle of bloody winter," I said. "And you, son, are at a funeral. Show some respect."

"But it's finished." Quinn gestured at the retreating figure near the pulpit. "Fife and I are headed to the pub. You coming?"

Fife was already on her way. I chased after her, not wanting to be caught in the press of bodies leaving the church. Emerging into the surprisingly bright sunlight, I stretched. The ceremony, pretty as it was, had been long enough to cramp my muscles from sitting still — or behaving, as Quinn called it.

"I have to get back home." Ollie was waiting, and we had things to discuss.

"How is Ollie?" Quinn asked. "She's not... you know?"

I had told him about the brief flutter of Ollie's heart as I'd healed her, and the gutting disappointment upon realising it hadn't stuck. "Just as dead as she always was. Still got her magic, though, even if it's a bit shaky." And that wasn't even touching the fact that she had controlled the movements of the dead, something folk had been trying without success for as long as people have been dying.

Quinn patted my shoulder, but thankfully didn't talk about the hour I'd spent weeping like a bloody wean. Ollie didn't — and never would — know how close I had come to bringing her back to life, but Quinn had made it his mission to make sure it wasn't a burden I had to carry alone.

I cleared my throat, blinking the stupid pollen out of my eyes again. "Why don't you both pop round for some scran later on? Won't take me long to whip something up."

"Aw, Mack." Fife turned back with a pained expression. "I know inviting people around is a new thing for you and Ollie. That's lovely, really, but... you can't cook for shite. If we come, we're getting Chinese."

I shrugged. "Suits me. Then I don't have to wash up after."

"You know she's bringing paperwork with her, right?" Quinn laughed at my crestfallen face. "You're lucky she's even talking to you."

"Forty-two pages," Fife grumbled. "Not counting a bloody dissertation on who the baobhan sith and the kelpies are, or why we weren't prepared for them to riot — without pointing out the fault for that lies with the very people I'm submitting the paperwork to."

"Hard to prepare for something you're not allowed to admit exists." I heaved a sigh. "Fine. I suppose I'll help you with it. And by me, I mean I'll butter Ollie up and she'll do it. Her handwriting's better anyway."

"You're lucky you've got her." For an off the cuff comment, Fife's words held a surprising tenderness.

I smiled. "Yeah. I am."

* * *

THE END

Amy Hopkins

Amy Hopkins is an Australian author committed to inclusivity and neurodiversity. She has written sixteen books across the fantasy genre that feature big themes and plenty of heart. As an autistic and ADHD adult, she is passionate about creating positive and realistic representations of neurodiverse people. When she is not writing, Amy enjoys spending time with her husband, two children, and her beloved dog, Peanut. She is an avid reader and loves learning new things.

The Talented Series

A Boggart's Journey
A Drop of Dream
A Dash of Fiend
A Splash of Truth
A Promise Due
A Festive Day
When Magic Fades

Penny and Boots- An Unveiled Academy Series

Snakes and Shadows
Werewolves and Wendigo
Pixels and Poltergeists
Bunyips and Billabongs

A New Dawn - An Age of Magic

Dawn of Destiny
Dawn of Darkness
Dawn of Deliverance
Dawn of Days
Broken Skies
Broken Bones

CPSIA information can be obtained
at www.ICGtesting.com
Printed in the USA
BVHW042016300323
661468BV00003B/15

9 780648 976158